THE
LONGEST
ROAD

THE
LONGEST
ROAD

Jeanne Williams

ST. MARTIN'S PRESS   NEW YORK

DESIGN BY JUDITH A. STAGNITTO

Library of Congress Cataloging-in-Publication Data

Williams, Jeanne.
    The longest road / Jeanne Williams.
      p.   cm.
    ISBN 0-312-08838-8
    1. Depressions—1929—United States—Fiction. I. Title.
PS3573.I44933L66 1993
813'.54—dc20   92-37730
                                               CIP

First Edition: February 1993

10 9 8 7 6 5 4 3 2 1

*For my mother, Louella, who died young but lives in my heart;
for my father, Guy Kreie, who had a generous spirit
and liked to laugh.*

*For my brother, Lewis, my sister, Naomi, my Aunt Dorothy
and Aunt Thelma and Uncle Lou, who remember the blowing
dust and whose memories helped bring reality to this book.*

Author's Note

This book truly began on the western Kansas-Oklahoma border where my first memories were of drifted dust and tumbleweeds and dreams of the end of the world. The catalyst was listening, half a century later, to Woody Guthrie singing "So Long, It's Been Good to Know You," and discovering that it was not only a Dust Bowl song but an end-of-the-world song, too. On those marvelous Library of Congress tapes, recorded by Alan Lomax in 1940 (Rounder Records, Cambridge, MA), Woody not only sings of those days when so many people were forced on the road, but he tells of his own experiences. His songs fused with my memories and half-memories and I knew I had to write this story of my homeland and my people.

As well as recording her own recollections, my sister, Naomi Zebrowski, did valuable research and gave many helpful suggestions. I cannot thank her enough for her interest and encouragement during the long months it took to write the story. My brother, Lewis Kreie, told me details he remembered, as did my aunt, Dorothy Thompson, and my "kissin' cousin," Alice Shook. My cousin, Jack Salmon, videotaped my aunt and uncle, Lou and Thelma Salmon, as they reminisced about their many years in Kansas. Also useful were written and taped interviews made thirty years ago with my father, Guy E. Kreie, and my grandmother, Susanna Salmon. John Wylie was my mentor on Model Ts and the oil fields.

Gaydell Collier lent me a wonderful book from Oak Publications (New York, 1967) titled *Hard-Hitting Songs for Hard-Hit*

People, compiled by Alan Lomax, music transcribed and edited by Pete Seeger, and with notes of the songs (many of them his) by Woody Guthrie. Woody's autobiography of his earlier years, *Bound for Glory,* Dutton, New York, 1968, gives the flavor of the thirties as he rambled to California and composed some of the most "American" songs ever sung, "Pastures of Plenty," "This Land Is Your Land," and many others.

Mary Magoffin lent her vintage collection of the *Saturday Evening Post.* Sally Spofford gave me her copy of *Helen's Babies,* a book I remembered with fond nostalgia from my childhood and which is one of Laurie's treasures.

Works useful for oil-field background were *Voices from the Oil Fields* by Paul F. Lambert and Kenny Franks, University of Oklahoma Press, Norman, 1984; *This Fascinating Oil Business* by Max W. Ball, Bobbs-Merril, New York, 1940; *Folklore of the Oil Industry* by Mody C. Boatright, Southern Methodist University Press, Dallas, 1963.

Help on the road came from *The Harvest Gypsies* by John Steinbeck, a collection of articles run in the *San Francisco News* in 1936 published by Heyday Books, Berkeley, CA, 1988; *The WPA Guide to 1930s Oklahoma,* compiled by Writers Project of WPA, University Press of Kansas, Lawrence, 1986; *The WPA Guide to 1930s Arizona,* compiled by Writers Project of the WPA, University of Arizona Press, Tucson, 1989; *Texas,* compiled by the Writers Project of the WPA, Hastings House, New York, 1940, and *Route 66,* a photographic essay by Quinta Scott with text by Susan Croce Kelly, University of Oklahoma Press, Norman, 1988.

The Dust Bowl by R. Douglas Hurt, Nelson-Hall, Chicago, 1981, gives a stark picture of those days. More emphasis on the environment is given in *Dust Bowl* by Don Worster, Oxford University Press, New York, 1979. Also helpful were several volumes of *This Fabulous Century* by Time-Life Books, New York, 1969. "The Okies—Beyond the Dust Bowl" by Williams Howarth with photos by Chris Johns, *National Geographic,* September, 1984, Vol. 166, No. 3, has eloquent photos and useful maps.

Many people told me their stories of the thirties. I hope that everyone who remembers those days will find echoes here to touch their hearts and memories.

—Jeanne Williams
Cave Creek Canyon
The Chiricahua Mountains
May 1991

1

April warmth had opened the buds of the little cherry tree to lovely pink blossoms and its smooth bark was a deep wine color. The sapling had looked dead when Daddy brought the tree home in February from one of his trucking hauls out of eastern Kansas, but Laurie watered it faithfully and hopefully with water saved from rinsing dishes. Now, Laurie thought, its glory drew the eye from the weathered privy at the back of the lot and the boxlike little house with its blistering yellow paint.

Maybe this spring would be different. Maybe the winds and dust wouldn't blow and the tree would flourish, grow big and strong as the black locust in the front yard, the only other tree in this straggle of houses near the edge of town.

Suddenly, as she stroked the red bark and tried to imagine that the blossoms smelled as sweet as they looked, the light changed. She turned. Her heart stopped, then plunged and began to pound.

Black, towering in the sky, a shadow thickened in front of the sun before obscuring it completely. The sky wasn't really black but brown like a black horse left out in the weather—a darkness not shadowy and soft like night but thick and weighted, roiling in billows churned up from the soil as if the earth had spewed up its center, as if its navel cord had been ripped, and the insides were erupting.

The gleaming galvanized top of the grain elevator vanished first, the second story of the bank, the emblem at the top of the Masonic hall, then the tall steeple of the Methodist church lording it over the white cross of the tabernacle across from the Fields' house.

Jackrabbits streaked by, trying to outrun the stinging blast. Birds flew ahead of it, hawks and great horned owls as frantic to escape as the larks, sparrows, buntings, and curlews that were usually their prey. The poor prairie chickens! Any of them surviving in bits of unplowed grassland would hunker down and suffocate like the flying birds would when their wings could no longer carry them.

Darkness at noonday. Rivers of blood. *One shall be taken and the other left.* . . . Terror froze Laurie. It was the end of the world, the way Brother Crawford was always preaching. Mama and Daddy would be swept away in the rapture and she'd be left with the wicked to pray for the mountains to fall on them while the angels poured out the vials of wrath. Only there weren't any mountains here.

But there was a tree, a blooming cherry tree. Laurie ran inside the screened porch and grabbed a sheet out of the laundry basket. Biting grit slashed at Laurie's face and fingers as she struggled to knot the ends of the sheet so the tree wore a lopsided hood. Her eyes watered from fear and grief as much as from the stinging dust.

Covering her head with her skirt, she ran inside and took the wet towel Mama gave her to hold over her face while she helped stuff rags under the door and along the crack where it opened. They didn't need to talk; they had done this all too often. The windows were already sealed with tape and Daddy had puttied every crack he could find. Last year, after the blowing season, the family had stayed at Floyd and Margie's while Daddy cleaned dust out of the attic, half a ton of it, and then carefully sealed the walls and roof. Not everyone had bothered, and ceilings had caved in all over the west parts of Kansas, Oklahoma, and Texas.

Dust storms weren't like the tornado that touched down last year, whirled up Slim Ellis's barn and wagon, and dropped them in shattered boards over in the next county. That great twisting funnel roared down like a freight train, swooped, and was gone in a few minutes. Laurie was used to spring dust storms just as she was to winter blizzards, but this day's storm was different, and worse, partly because of the cherry tree.

Daddy came in and shut the door as fast as he could. Laurie couldn't see his face but she knew it was him from his height. He was the tallest man in town—six feet two in his stocking feet—the best-looking man, too, with waving brown hair and sunny blue eyes. He had a dimpled groove in his chin and liked to joke a lot and talk to folks. Mama said he'd gotten his easy way of visiting with even total strangers from his father, Harry Field, who was such a horse trader that he'd been able to persuade seasoned buyers that Indian ponies brought down from Montana's Wind River Range were fine horses that just needed a little handling.

Even before Daddy reached her, Mama cried, "Ed! Isn't Buddy with you?"

Daddy stopped, looming in the murk as if he'd been turned to stone. "He's not here?"

"No. He took his .22 and started for Point of Rocks."

That jutting butte from which Indians had watched travelers along the Cimarron and sometimes preyed on them was a favorite picnic spot for townfolks. Grandpa Field, who was sixty-two, remembered—or claimed he did—when Custer was killed at the Little Bighorn in 1876 and he vowed he'd seen Geronimo when the train carrying the Chiricahua Apaches to prison in Florida stopped in St. Louis in 1886. That was a long time ago, even before World War I.

Daddy gasped. "Buddy's out in this?"

"Maybe he's at Tom Harris's," Mama said. Tom was Buddy's best friend. "Or when the storm came up, maybe he went in the nearest house."

"And maybe he's out by Point of Rocks," Daddy cut in. "I've got to find him!"

"Ed! You'll just get lost yourself! More than likely, he's fine. And if—if this is the end of the world, Jesus will take him."

"Well, I'm his daddy. If the world's ending I don't want the poor little guy to be by himself."

"Jesus will—"

"Rachel, that boy don't know Jesus like he knows me."

"Wait! Let me get you a wet towel to put over your face." Mama vanished into the dust.

The light bulb hanging from the middle of the ceiling glimmered like a smoky lantern. Mama's shadow merged for an instant with Daddy's. Then he was swallowed in the darkness that rushed in thicker as he opened the door. As it slammed shut, Laurie started after him.

"You come back here!" Mama caught her, drew her so close it hurt. "No use you running out there like a chicken with its head cut off!"

Laurie buried her face against Mama's warm, soft neck where the two small brown moles were. They held each other. It terrified Laurie that her mother sobbed, too. "I—I put an old sheet around the cherry tree, Mama. Maybe it'll be all right."

It wouldn't. She knew it wouldn't. Ever since Laurie could remember, the winds blew ferociously from February till May, the month's crops were planted and started to grow. That happened every year. What was different these last years was that there was little or no rain to bring up plants that would bind the soil with their roots. Sprouts that managed to get a few inches above the soil were blasted right out of the furrows. Any that lived were buried by powdery dust driven from whatever fields it came from to wherever it could settle till the wind swept it up again into the skies.

The scarred old black locust could stand the winds but the cherry was only a little taller than Laurie. The storm must have already snapped off the blossoms, razored the bark, smothered the limbs.

It was wicked to grieve about a tree when her brother might be lost or when the world might be ending, but Laurie couldn't believe Buddy would come to much harm. He hadn't broken his neck when he'd jumped off the neighbor's garage, or drowned when he'd fallen in the river when it was flooding, or got but one scar from the chicken pox he'd given her. She still had a dozen tiny indentations on her forehead and chin.

As for the world ending—the sky would roll up like a scroll, the moon would turn as red as blood—she had dreamed of it ever since she could remember. Now that it might be really happening she wasn't as scared as she'd been at first, or even as she had often been before. Many nights, when that awful moon fell toward her, growing larger and larger, she woke up screaming her throat raw. Mama always hurried in, never too tired or sick to comfort Laurie and pray with her. "If you were saved, honey," she'd say, "you'd be glad the Lord was coming—be glad this wicked old world was ending."

Laurie didn't argue about that but she didn't believe it. She loved the world, the fresh bright leaves of spring, the white and yellow breasts of meadowlarks soaring upward, the mocking-bird's song, snapdragons and pansies and sweet-smelling four-o'clocks that Mama cherished till wind and dust got them. People might be sinful but it didn't seem fair that along with them, and because of them, God would destroy all the other creatures, turn rivers to blood, make oceans boil so the great whales died, destroy the forests and mountains Laurie had never seen but which must be so beautiful.

"The heavens declare the glory of God, the firmament sheweth His handiwork." If people were the problem, why didn't He just get rid of them and leave the earth to the birds and animals?

Nothing made sense, though, when the ground that was supposed to stay under your feet and nourish flowers and trees and crops churned up in a wild, suffocating force that scoured the soil down to hardpan and when at last the wind died, what had been soil once settled in shifting, pulverized drifts where nothing could grow. It was a chaos of destruction, not creation.

What scared Laurie most was that Daddy and Bud were out there someplace in the howling dark and Mama was coughing so bad. She'd nearly died two years ago from dust pneumonia and that was when she'd lost the baby sister Laurie had wanted so much.

Bud had been fun to take care of when he was a baby but

since he started school, he was always off with the Harris boy, Tom, or out hunting, or hiding out in that pitiful little hole he called his room. He kept the door shut with a rusty old padlock—as if anyone would want to go in there! Laurie could peek through a crack in the wall and see that all he had of any possible interest were some Big Little Books, thick cardboard-bound volumes about three by five inches printed on cheap paper, and the G-Man badge, decoder, and ring he'd sent off for with some cereal boxtops. These, along with arrowheads garnered from Point of Rocks and a huddle of snake rattles and shed skins, occupied a shelf above the cot spread with an old Navajo blanket. A coyote skull was nailed over the shelf, its moth-eaten tawny hide made a rug, and a few nails held Buddy's clothes except for socks and underwear. These Mama neatly arranged in an apple crate when she entered once a week to change the sheets while Bud stood guard to make sure Laurie didn't intrude.

Yes, a sister would have been nice, especially since Mama wouldn't let Laurie play with children whose families were worldly and that included just about all the Prairieville girls Laurie's age except Mary Harkness, who wasn't any fun, and Beulah Martin, who lived out on a farm and rarely got to town. Mary knew all manner of interesting things and when they were beyond earshot of adults, playing in the houses they built of tumbleweeds, she used words that Laurie knew were dirty and forbidden, though she didn't understand what they meant and wouldn't ask for fear of being laughed at. *Shit* must mean the same as *fuck,* and that had something to do with what men did to women, though Laurie couldn't imagine how the little nubbin she'd seen on Bud when she changed his diapers could possibly turn into anything that would do the scary and fascinating things Mary said it could. Once when the girls had seen two dogs hooked together, Mary said that was what grown-ups did to make babies. Laurie wouldn't, couldn't, think Mama and Daddy had done that.

If the world ended now, she'd go to hell because she'd listened to Mary talk nasty, hadn't repented for throwing hot oatmeal on Bud when he wouldn't dry the dishes, and wasn't saved, let alone sanctified. She prayed nights with Mama when she was scared but she'd never "prayed through." That was why she'd never gone to the altar during revivals even when she was sure she'd die that night for committing the unpardonable sin, which, like the age of accountability, was hard to figure out exactly, though it had to do with hardening your heart against God. Mama had been sanctified years ago—that meant she couldn't sin or backslide—but Daddy was only saved. He backslid so often that he never kept saved long enough to reach that next state of permanent righteousness.

"Oh, God," prayed Mama through racking coughs that shook Laurie, too, since they still had their arms around each other. "If you're coming to judge us, have mercy on Ed! Forgive anything he's done wrong since the last time he got saved. He's a good man, Lord, though he's had to battle his temper, but when you think how his dad put him out to work for neighbors when he was eight years old, and how hard he's had it, maybe you'll give him credit for tithing ten percent even when there's holes in his shoes."

Laurie's thoughts veered after Grandpa, Harry Field, who farmed on the shares down in southwestern Oklahoma. He was a tough, stocky, bald-headed, hook-nosed man who had lost one eye in a saloon brawl when he was a soldier in the Spanish-American War. His tight slit of a mouth was profane with tobacco, whiskey, and foul language. He and Mama couldn't stand each other so it was lucky he lived three hundred miles away. Just to aggravate Mama, he rattled up in an old truck every few years with his invariably pregnant young third wife, Rosalie, and stair-step kids who took possession of Laurie's small room and Buddy's tiny nook partitioned off the back porch. These *aunts* and *uncles*—yes, that's what they were— jumped on the beds and sofa with dirty feet, always had snot running down their faces, and, worst of all, wet the beds so that the mattresses were streaked and had a faint stink for weeks no matter how hard and soapily they were scrubbed or how long they were left out in the sun.

Mama, tight-lipped, adjured Laurie to be polite and show respect to her grandfather but Laurie detested him till her insides twisted. He made her ashamed, ashamed that he was her kin. In spite of his wife's slovenliness, Laurie couldn't help liking Rosalie, who was pretty, good-natured, smelled good, and shared the gum and pop she bought for her kids. She could also tell spine-tingling ghost stories. Enduring these visits was like living through a small war, and when the truck rumbled off, Mama always said under her breath, "Thank you, Lord, for my good husband, who doesn't take after his father except for never meeting a stranger and liking to tell jokes and being too friendly with women brassy enough to roll down their stockings."

Now, in the terrible storm, Mama was still praying for her husband. "You know, Lord, he gave his good sheepskin coat to a tramp last winter, and he's always ready to help anyone who needs it." Mama paused as coughs doubled her over and went on breathlessly, hugging Laurie close. "Nevertheless, Lord, if you can't spare Ed, let me stay with him. I don't want to go to heaven if he can't."

There was a pounding on the door. "Sister Rachel!" That was the preacher, Brother Arlo. Laurie had heard him bellow often enough to recognize his voice even in the shrieking wind. "Let us in, sister! The roof's blown off the tabernacle!"

Mama let go of Laurie and groped toward the door. Laurie hurried to pull away the rag wadding. She couldn't make out people's faces as they poured in, driven by the wind, but she recognized the bulk of Mr. Echols who ran the feed store, the mousy odor of scrawny Annabel Howard, the square stockiness of Brother Arlo. There was a whiff of the lavender scent worn by Sylvia Palgraves, who played the piano and had a job at the bank that paid ten dollars a week, an unheard-of wage. Margie, Mama's closest friend, had suggested to Mama, only to be firmly squelched, that Sylvia might be friendlier than she ought to be with her boss, Henry Tate, the banker.

Smelling cigarettes and oil on the skinny man behind Sylvia, Laurie guessed he was Jack Dakin, the town mechanic, who must have dashed into the tabernacle because it was the nearest shelter, since he didn't go to any church. The last person in was Barney Smith, the dairyman, whose broad shoulders narrowed to a slim waist and hips. He didn't go to church, either. When he shut the door, Laurie stuffed the cracks again.

"The roof plain lifted off," gasped Annabel. "I looked up, expectin' to see the Lord in the sky, but there was just this awful dust. He's a-comin' though. Never saw anything like this in all my life."

The hazy light from the bulb weakly lit Brother Arlo's ruddy, heavy-jowled face so that it and the other faces looked like masks peering out of the dark. "Brothers and sisters, anyone who's not right with God better get that way."

Laurie fumbled for Mama's hand, expecting to see a gray-green statue descend, like the one of Moses she'd seen in a book, the one with his hair twisted into horns who was reaching under his throne for thunderbolts. But there was only thick darkness and the blurred glow from the bulb.

"World's got too wicked," Brother Arlo went on. "God made it and now he's wroth. Goin' to end it."

"Yeah." Barney Smith nodded. "There's all the wars—Japan fightin' with China and Italy takin' over Abyssinia and purges in Russia and that Adolf Hitler over in Germany—can't keep up with all the troubles. And here in the United States there's folks robbin' each other with the banks the biggest thieves of at all. I'm glad I'm not Henry Tate to have to answer for fore-closin' on my neighbors and drivin' orphans and widows out in the cold." He hesitated a minute. "Hey, Jack, maybe when I sold you that truck I should've said there was a little problem with the engine."

Dakin chuckled. "That's okay, Barney. When I told you that cow I sold you had been tested for Bang's disease, I didn't mean she didn't have it."

"Sylvia," called Annabel Howard, her big nose and small chin emphasized by the shadows. "It was the sin of envy made me tell the ladies at sewing circle that your hair's not natural auburn. I hope you'll forgive me."

"I suppose I have to," grudged Sylvia. The spit curls over her ears had been blown out of place like the crimped waves of her hair. "I always knew you for a jealous cat, Annabel. Ever since I got to be pianist instead of you, you've run me down something scandalous. Don't think I haven't heard about it. I'm just too much of a Christian to take notice."

"Or maybe you're too busy meeting the choir director when no one else is practicing," Annabel jabbed.

"Ladies!" That was Brother Arlo. "You better give each other a kiss of peace and set your minds on eternity. Nothin' else matters."

Like arch-backed cats, the women approached each other, muttered apologies beneath their breath, and kissed each other's cheeks without getting closer than they had to.

"If the Lord tarries," ventured Barney Smith, "could be folks better start listing the fields and planting cover crops the way they did for a while before World War I. Remember how they talked the railroads into putting up some money—after all the railroads make their money haulin' crops and machinery and supplies—and they got soil conservation going? I listed for my dad—acres and acres with the furrows turned opposite so the earth wouldn't blow." His head lowered. "We saved the farm that time but then along comes the war and the government wanted us to plant more wheat."

"And we did," said Jack Dakin. "I remember planting all night and running a combine all night. We bought tractors and combines on credit and then prices fell after the war and we had to plant more to pay our debts."

"Yeah." Barney nodded. "Wheat that brought sixty cents a bushel in nineteen-twelve was only worth thirty cents in nineteen-twenty."

"We broke a lot of virgin sod in Ford County," remembered Dakin. "Tore up old knotted grass roots meshed so deep they tied down the topsoil just like a net of anchored ropes. Once I plowed through a prairie-dog village that must have covered eighty acres. Couldn't keep from hitting some of the little critters, slicin' 'em apart. Kind of a shame."

"Might of been better if more grass had been left for grazing cattle," said Dakin.

Mr. Echols shrugged. "One good wheat crop pays more than ten years of raising cattle on the same acreage."

"You've got to sell your machinery, Mr. Echols," Dakin

allowed. "But what cattle are left are crowded onto land that won't carry 'em. That's just as hard on the soil as wearin' it out with plowing. There's been years as dry as this spell but the land wasn't ground to powder then. One of them farm-extension fellas says this kind of earth gets so pulverized in about five years that unless something's done to root it down and bring it back to life, it's ruined, plumb and absolutely."

"Blows away down to hardpan," Barney grunted dolefully. "But some don't care, like them suitcase farmers, if they get a few good crops first."

"Sure." Dakin scowled. "They don't live here. They got another business. They can hire broke farmers to plant and harvest for 'em on the shares or get a few hands and come do it themselves now that machinery speeds everything up so much. If there's a poor crop, they don't even bother to harvest. Why, instead of plowin' a bad crop back into the ground for fertilizer, they just burn it off—don't add nothin' to the soil. Don't care about it except for what they can get fast."

"They're like men who don't pay any attention to their wives except when they want a quick—"

"Mr. Smith!" objected Brother Arlo.

"Beg pardon, ladies, preacher," mumbled Barney.

"Turn your thoughts from worldly things," Brother Arlo advised severely. "If there's anything you need to say to each other, do it. Bare your hearts and make your peace."

Barney's big ruddy head turned as he looked around. "So long," he said with a grin. "It's been good to know you. And now, good neighbors, storm or no storm, I got to have a cigarette. I'll go out the back door, Miz Field, so you won't get a lot of dust in here."

"Don't go out in this," Mama pled. "Smoke on the porch."

"Thank you kindly," said Barney, but a second after the back door shut, they heard the one to the porch close, too.

"A dog to his vomit," Brother Arlo said. "God have mercy!" He lifted his arms. "Oh Lord, we know Thou art a God of wrath as well as a God of love. We implore—"

Laurie wished they'd sing instead of pray. Singing made her feel better when she was blue or scared. Sometimes a tune got

---

11

in her head and she hummed it for days. Softly, so no one could hear above the storm and Brother Arlo, she started humming "Onward, Christian Soldiers" because it had a brave, marching swing to it.

Brother Arlo was still praying when she worked through all the verses so she began "The Battle Hymn of the Republic." All the time, she was praying, too, that the world wouldn't end, that Daddy and Bud would come home safe—and that the cherry tree would live.

2

Bud slit the soft gray-brown hide from neck to bottom, peeled it off, and gutted the rabbit. That made three of them—three nickels he'd get from Mr. Haynes. It would've been four but one skinny old rabbit had boils and Mr. Haynes wouldn't take the ones that did. The rabbits weighed three to seven pounds before they were dressed out. Bud left the guts and skin for the coyotes, bundled the rabbits in a gunnysack, and started for the river to wash.

At first he'd got sick at his stomach when he cleaned a rabbit but it didn't bother him now except when he didn't kill one with a shot and had to finish it. Daddy had given him the old .22 last Christmas and taught him to use it. Since then, he'd had his own money and didn't have to ask for a penny or nickel like Laurie did if she wanted an ice-cream cone or candy. After he saved up enough for a pump for the .22 so it could shoot more than once without being reloaded, he was going to buy Laurie that book of poems she wanted so bad, maybe in time for her birthday that October. Even if she had thrown that hot oatmeal on him, most of the time she was a lot better than his friends' big sisters. Let's see—there were fifty shots in a box that cost six cents and when he was real careful, he almost never missed unless the jackrabbit heard him and ran. They covered the ground, too. Daddy said they could go thirty miles an hour, at least for a while. Supposing he hit forty out of fifty, that was—he frowned, struggling with the sums.

Two whole dollars! After he paid for the box of shorts, that left $1.94 profit. Till now, he'd never thought about it that way, just spent his nickels as he got them, choosing Big Little Books that Mama wouldn't forbid the way she did comic books, reveling in whole Baby Ruth candy bars, or getting a dip of strawberry as well as one of chocolate, sometimes treating his friends. It felt good to do that but he was going to have to cut out his free spending so he could buy the pump and Laurie's book and some cowboy boots to wear to school that fall.

As he wiped his hands on his overalls, the cottonwoods bent at the top, making a sound like rushing water. Boy howdy! Why hadn't he seen that big black cloud before? It was boiling over the plain, heading right for him. Oh, if only he hadn't come on out here when he couldn't find Daddy!

He wouldn't leave the rabbits behind, though, or his .22. Guessing that Mama would be too glad to see him to spank him and forgetting the blood on his clothes, he struggled to get the bag over his shoulder so it would balance more easily, grabbed the rifle, and trotted toward town.

Within a few minutes, his side ached and he panted for breath. The wind gusted harder now that he was out of the shelter of the trees and the lower land near the river. Dust blinded him. He burrowed his head against the arm holding the rifle and stumbled on, coughing.

So dark. Couldn't see the sun, see anything. The storm wailed like ghosts. He went to his knees, dropping the rifle, groped for it, and went forward, doubled over. At least he thought it was forward. He didn't know where he was.

Was it the end of the world? It sure was dark, like Brother Arlo said it would be. Would he go to hell? Would Mama and Daddy ever know what had happened to him? He told lies to get out of whippings and sometimes, in his room, he and Tom MacKay showed each other their things and played with them, seeing whose got biggest. Once a rabbit had just one little boil and he'd cut it away and sold it to Mr. Haynes. He'd stolen and smoked one of Floyd's cigarettes and—and—

The list of sins grew. Bud was sure that he'd reached that awful age of accountability, all right, or he wouldn't know what he'd done wrong. Moaning as a trickle ran down his leg, he began to yell, not that he expected anyone to hear, but he was just too scared not to holler.

"Mama! Daddy! Mama!"

The wind snatched away his cries. The rifle was loaded. If he fired it, maybe someone would hear. Dumping the rabbits at his feet, he held the .22 as straight up as he could and pulled the trigger.

"Son!" Buddy's heart leaped. The call was far away but it sounded like Daddy. He managed to reload and fired again. "Dad! Dad!"

If he just comes, I'll never be bad again! I'll put a nickel in the collection plate every Sunday! I won't cuss and—

"Buddy!" The voice was nearer.

"Dad!" Bud lunged forward with the bag and rifle. "You came!"

Shielded inside his father's jacket, a wet cloth held over his nose, he felt safe even though they were still out in the storm. He didn't want to die, didn't want the world to end, but if one or the other had to happen, it was sure a sight better to be with your father or mother.

"Bud, we're going to wait till the storm dies down." Daddy ripped the towel in half. "Hold that over your nose and sit down so I can hold my jacket around us both."

Through the cloth, Bud croaked, "Daddy—is the world comin' to an end?"

"I don't know, son. But you're young enough you don't have to worry, and your mama's praying for us. I'm with you. Whatever happens, I'm going to hang on to you."

The jacket smelled like Daddy. The wind tried to tug it away but Daddy held on tight and knotted the arms. He fumbled and thrust something into Bud's hand. "Here's a stick of gum, Bud. Your favorite. Juicy Fruit."

It didn't seem like you could chew gum if the world was ending. Maybe it was just an extra-bad storm. Bud hadn't sat

14

in his father's lap for years but now he snuggled close and chewed real slow to make the sweet flavor last.

When he really knew what was happening again, Daddy was untying the jacket sleeves. Dust fine as Mama's lilac talcum powder poured in on them as the sleeves unfolded. Dust that was packed solid against their legs and up to their waists slid away reluctantly. More sifted from Daddy's shoulders as he straightened. Bud sneezed and gazed through eyes watering with grit at what must be the sun.

It looked like a spoiled brown orange in a brown sky. The bag of rabbits was a mound in smoother drifts, like a small grave. Bud began to shake, though he wasn't cold.

If Daddy hadn't come, he'd be like that. Dead as the rabbits. It made him feel a stab of pity for them. Thinking of the nickels they'd bring and what the nickels would buy, he'd got so he really didn't think about them dying, guts or brains smashed by a shot, but seeing them like that as if they were buried—the way he would have been—never to see the light or breathe or move—

Bud hadn't cried in two years. He tried not to now. His throat ached with the effort but tears crawled down his nose anyway.

"It's all right, son." Daddy helped him up, steadied him since his feet had gone to sleep. "Let's get home. Your mother'll be worried." He fished the .22 out of the dust that covered it though the barrel had been tucked between them and with his foot cleared away the mound. "Get your rabbits and let's go."

Bud didn't want to pick them up, but Daddy would think he was a baby if he said so. And there were the nickels.

It was a scary, brown, dead world they moved through. Not even a grasshopper chirred up from the Johnson grass and young Russian thistles that had choked the ditches when Bud had come this way. Everything was buried. The lacy new fronds had been scoured off the few black locust trees. The sandhill plum thicket was stripped of leaves and tender buds, only a few bare twigs thrusting from a mound of dust.

Maybe the world had ended. Shaking again, Bud tightened his grip on Daddy's hand. Maybe Mama had been raptured up to heaven and managed to take Laurie with her. Maybe he and

Daddy were the only people left! But Daddy was saved. He'd have gone to heaven, too. Unless—unless his coming after Bud, trying to keep him from dying, was some kind of a sin.

Through the veil of dust, the elevator's dull sheen towered above the rest of the town, higher than the Methodist steeple, which Bud had to squint to make out, higher than the square, dark hulk of the red-brick bank building. Then there was a sound of engines and headlights flickered on the road out of town.

Two shapes took form, one smaller than the other. One was coughing. "Rachel!" Daddy let go of Bud and hurried through the drifts as fast as he could.

Bud plunged after him. Mama, wrapped in a damp sheet, left Daddy's arms to hold Bud tight. Laurie hugged Daddy and he gathered them all close. They were still like that when the first of a line of trucks and cars pulled up and Barney Smith shouted to the vehicles behind, "They're here! Both of them! They're all right!"

The world hadn't come to an end.

But it did. Mama kept coughing. She came down with dust pneumonia again, coughed up mud, clots of it that were filling her lungs. This time she died.

The body in the coffin looked like a life-size china-faced doll in Mama's only good dress and the white summer shoes she had admired in the store window. Bud had bought them with his hoarded nickels because Daddy had been so ashamed that her only pair of shoes had worn-out soles.

Dust rippled like a bleached tan ocean over the grass in the cemetery, covering the headstones. At least Mama's grave was under a honey locust. The storm had buried all the irises and daffodils but the tabernacle ladies sent a big spray of white carnations. Mama's only living close relative, a half-brother who'd gone out to Oregon to rive timber, wired American Beauty roses. Laurie had broken off the only branch of the cherry tree that still had a few buds left when the sheet was untied. The tabernacle women had been bringing in food since Mama got sick. After the funeral, they put the extension leaf in the round table and spread a big dinner. Laurie couldn't eat though there were things that had seldom been on the table before: ham and fried chicken, all kinds of salads, pickles, and relishes, besides mashed potatoes and canned green beans and peas, canned peaches and pears, and a dozen kinds of pies and cakes.

People said what a good woman Mama had been and how she was bound to be in heaven and the dust had broken her health and who knew what lay ahead so maybe God had been merciful to take her home.

Laurie wanted to scream at them, yank the tablecloth off and crash the food to the floor. She ran to her room and cried, though she still thought she'd surely wake up and find out it wasn't real, that Mama was alive.

The next week passed in a haze, though Laurie made sure Buddy's face was clean and his eyes clear of duck-butter before they went to school. Every night, she dreamed the world was ending and woke up half out of bed, wanting to run to her mother. Then she remembered. Strange how she forgot, how it would seem for a few minutes that everything was all right, and then it flooded over her and she knew that nothing would ever be the same again.

One morning while they were eating the oatmeal Laurie had scorched only a little bit, Daddy said, "Kiddies, I'm in debt to the undertaker and the doctor and for the cemetery lot. I've got to find something that pays better than drivin' another fellow's truck."

They stared at him. His eyes were red and swollen and he hadn't shaved. There were little black bristles on his jaws and some white strands in the brown hair that curled over his forehead, since he hadn't slicked it down and combed it. "This dust took your Mama," he went on with a gulp. "I promised her it wouldn't take you. I'm going out to California and find a good job, one that'll pay off these bills and let me take care of you right, the way I promised Rachel."

"California!" Bud's eyes sparkled. "Why, we can eat oranges every day and sleep outside all winter and—"

Daddy shook his head. Not looking at them, he stirred the

Postum Mama had fussed him into drinking because coffee made him nervous. "I hear tell it's not always easy to get work out there. Thousands of folks have gone out there from here and Texas and Oklahoma, even Tennessee and suchlike places. I'm a hard worker. Given time, I'll find a good job, but I don't want to have to worry about you kiddies goin' hungry or not havin' a roof over your heads while I'm getting settled."

Laurie put down her spoon. She felt sicker than she had at the funeral dinner, like she was bleeding inside, thick and muddy as if dust had worked through her skin and stuck in her arteries. "I'm going to leave you with your grandpa," Daddy said.

Bud's eyes went round and he put down his spoon.

"No!" Laurie choked. "You can't leave us there, Daddy! The kids wet the bed and I don't like the way Grandpa cusses and yells, and his wife's lazy and—"

Daddy slapped her across the face. Laurie gasped, knocked nearly out of her chair. He never had hit her before. He had spanked Bud and Mama had spanked her, though that hadn't happened for a couple of years.

"Shut up!" Daddy's face was red now as his eyes. "I'm doin' the best I can for you! You'd ought to help, not bellyache! Soon as we're packed up, I'm takin' you to your grandpa's and that's all there is to it."

Bud clamped his hand over his mouth and ran out the back door. They could hear him throwing up. Laurie's stomach heaved, too, but she swallowed the bile and got out of her father's reach.

"Please, Daddy! Take us with you! We can sleep in the car! I'll work—we can do anything, anything in the world, just so we stay together!"

"You'll do what I say!"

"I can cook and do the washing and ironing and take care of Buddy," she begged. "Oh, Daddy, don't—"

"One more word and I'll take my belt to you, girl. Start gettin' our things together. I want to pull out of here day after tomorrow before sunup."

"But our furniture—"

"I've talked to Gus Rounds." Rounds had a room of used furniture behind his main showroom. "He'll pay enough so I can put a few dollars down on all the bills and still buy gas to get to your grandpa's and out to California."

The broken-springed sofa had come from the dump, like two of the straight chairs, but the proudly burnished carved rocker and round oak table with clawed legs spreading out from the central pedestal had belonged to Mama's mother and been brought out from Iowa by her parents, who had homesteaded here while Indians still roamed the plains. Bud and Laurie had been rocked in that chair; so had Mama and her mother, Grandma Phares, whom Laurie faintly remembered as a small, silver-haired woman who smelled of lilacs and once gave the children a whole package of gum each, not a stick snapped in half.

"Can't we fasten the rocker on top of the car?" Laurie begged.

"It'll bring a couple of dollars. Your mother would want me to pay our honest debts. Don't go blubberin' and makin' it worse."

Honest debts. Laurie had always wondered what other kinds there were and how you could tell the difference. More gently, Daddy said, "I want your mother's Bible and you can keep anything you want out of her trunk. We'll have to leave it. Pile all the bedding in the back of the flivver to make a bed so you kiddies can sleep on the road. If you want to keep that ruby-glass sugar bowl and pitcher and such, wrap 'em in sheets or blankets. I'll tie the suitcase on top of the car along with a tarp to hold anything that won't fit inside." He pondered. "I'll need the frying pan and dutch oven and a few dishes. And we'll take all the canned stuff we can manage—eat it on the way and give the rest to Rosalie to help out a little with feedin' you till I can send some money."

Living in Grandpa and Rosalie's house, eating their food, with Mama dead and Daddy far away? Unless the kids were housebroken now, the beds would stink. Defeated, Laurie hoped she and Buddy could have pallets on the floor, maybe sleep outside through the summer.

"Daddy, you'll send for us quick as you can?" she mumbled through stiff lips.

"Sure I will, honey," he said more kindly. "But I got to find a steady job first so you won't have to live in the car like lots of folks are doin' out there. Bud, you help your sister, and remember, we can't carry a lot of junk. You go to school this afternoon and tell your teachers you'll need your report cards and notes to your new school."

Go in the classroom and have all the kids watch her with pity or curiosity? And Mrs. Morse would be angry that they were leaving before school was out. Laurie dreaded it but she dreaded even more making Daddy mad enough to hit her again. Unable to finish her breakfast, she got up and started sorting out things in the kitchen. As soon as her father was gone, she ran back to her parents' bedroom, fell beside the bed, and buried her face in her mother's pillow, which still had a faint, sweet, sad smell of Mama's lilacs. The tabernacle ladies had given Mama's few clothes to a needy, godly, and deserving woman. There wasn't much in the wood-reinforced metal trunk—Buddy and Laurie's schoolwork and report cards; scraps saved from the good parts of worn-out clothes for quilting and patching, a beaded belt and watch fob Daddy had bought from the Sioux Indians when he worked on a ranch up in South Dakota; Grandmother Phares's tortoiseshell combs; some embroidered pillowcases and tea towels and several dozen fancy handkerchiefs, embroidered or appliquéd, that had been presents.

Not sure of what they'd need to enter another school, Laurie put the report cards in Mama's little cedar chest where she kept her New Testament and the amethyst lavaliere that she couldn't wear because it was jewelry, added the belt, fob, Grandma's combs, and the nicest handkerchiefs. This she wrapped in the best pillowcases with Mama's red-letter Bible—it had all of Christ's words in red and some beautiful pictures and interesting maps of the Holy Land—and rolled the bundle up in the bird quilt Mama had made her. The quilt had blue backing and strips between the squares that were each embroidered with a different bird—familiar ones like the meadowlark, chickadee, barn swallow, oriole, mockingbird, and bluebird and others never glimpsed here, like the cardinal and blue jay.

What had happened, Laurie wondered, to the mockingbird who had been singing so melodiously the morning of the storm? Covering the floorboard with a rag rug, Laurie stuffed the quilt bundle behind the front seat of the car and began to pack the bedding around jars of watermelon pickles, chow-chow, sand-hill plums, tomatoes, and peaches and peach preserves made from those bruised by the trucking haul from Grand Junction.

Mother would have wanted them to start clean on their journey. Laurie pumped a tub of water and scrubbed out Buddy's other overalls and shirt, her other dress, and Daddy's shirt and socks. She started to wash her darned stockings, hesi-tated, and then crammed them to the bottom of the sack of discarded school papers. Of all the girls at school, she was the only who had to wear those ugly brown long cotton things, who didn't get to wear anklets. Mama thought it was sinful to show your naked legs. Would she know?

Seized by guilt, Laurie started to retrieve the hated stockings but then she stopped. If Mama knew how they were having to move and get rid of the rocker and table and how Laurie and Buddy would have to stay at Grandpa's till Daddy got work—well, alongside all that, the stockings couldn't matter much.

At afternoon recess time when the kids would be on the playground in back, Laurie and Buddy went in through the front of the school and got their report cards. To Laurie's relief, neither teacher argued or scolded. They just said they were sorry Mama had died and how it was up to Laurie to make sure she and Buddy both finished school so they could amount to something.

"Laurie," said Mrs. Morse solemnly, "there's two weeks of school left, but I'll make your final grades what you've earned so far—*As* in everything except a *B* in Deportment, if you promise to finish the work in all your books, and if you'll see that Buddy does the same, I'll ask Miss Reed to give him marks for the full year, too."

Laurie promised. She was finishing sixth grade this year and Buddy was in second. Mama had hoped they could go to high school but Laurie, with a wrenching of her insides, was afraid she'd never go to school again. Grandpa Field kept his kids out to work in the crops so they only got to go about four months in the winter. He didn't think girls needed to go past sixth grade, in fact he didn't think girls needed to know more than how to read and write and cipher a little.

Daddy would send for them, though, she told herself, blinking at tears as she cleared out her desk. Everybody liked him and he was such a good worker that maybe it wouldn't be very long till he had a place for them—maybe that summer.

The tabernacle ladies had a farewell supper for them that night in the tabernacle basement where Sunday-school classes met and where the monthly socials were held. Laurie didn't want to go but her father insisted that she show appreciation. She ate a little potato salad and slipped home to pump water for the cherry tree. If she gave it a good, deep watering, nine or ten buckets, it ought to live till someone rented the house. Almost anyone would water a fruit tree.

That night, she didn't care if the world ended. Fitting her body to the familiar lumps of the mattress, which would be left to pay on their debts, she heard her father making peculiar sounds in the next room. It came to her in a lightning flash that he was crying. Daddy! Before he'd hit her, before he'd changed into this swollen-eyed stranger of uncertain temper, she'd have jumped out of bed and run to comfort him. Now she was afraid to try, and in a way she hated him for changing, for being lost, for making her and Buddy stay with his dirty, blaspheming, wicked old father. In this queer mix of feelings, she had some understanding of how awful it must be for Ed Field to sleep in the bed he'd shared with his wife, to come in the house and not find her.

No, probably he couldn't stand to stay here even if it hadn't been for their debts, but why, why wouldn't he take Laurie and Buddy with him? Maybe, like the house and bed, they reminded him too much of Mama. Though she had to believe he'd send for them, Laurie had a sick, miserable feeling that they'd never see him again, that he was leaving them as irrevocably as their mother had. I'll have to take care of Buddy, Laurie thought. All we've got now is each other.

Somehow the night passed. She must have dozed, for she jerked awake to Margie's voice in the kitchen. Dressing hastily, without the hated stockings, Laurie went to the privy, waking Buddy on her way. In the kitchen, she washed her hands and face in the washbasin, with soap, the way Mama had taught them—she'd have to remember real well how Mama did things so she could teach Buddy.

Laurie sat down to the bowl of oatmeal Daddy had ready. "I brought some fried rabbit and cole slaw for your trip," Margie said. "And a dried apple pie."

"Thank you, Margie. That's nice of you."

"Wish I could do more. Hate to see you leave this way."

"Hate to leave friends," said Daddy. "But Margie, I've got to see if I can't do better for the kiddies. Hurry up, Bud. We need to get as far as we can before it heats up. That's a long old dusty road to your Grandpa's."

Margie stood up. "I'll keep weeds off Rachel's grave like I promised," she said. "And make sure the stone's lettered right and is pink marble like you paid for. Is there anything else I can do?"

"You could water the cherry tree," Laurie said. "Mama was so proud of the way it bloomed this spring."

Margie hugged her and Buddy, kissed them good-bye. Wash the dishes, stuff them in the back of the car with the sheets off the beds. Close the door of her bedroom for the last time, touch the rocker, the round table. Laurie ran out to the cherry tree, pressed her face to its storm-scarred bark and the few remaining withered blossoms.

Good-bye. Good-bye. Stay alive, little tree. Bloom for a lot of springtimes, bear your sweet fruit. Then she was in the long front seat with Buddy, feet poked in among bags and water jars. Daddy moved the left-hand lever coming off the steering column in order to retard the spark so he wouldn't get kicked by the crank. Then he set the throttle, a lever on the right-hand side of the column, for a fast idle and made sure the neutral lever was upright. Only then was he able to crank the car. It started

---

23

the first time. He climbed in—there was no seat on the driver's side—advanced the spark to operating position, released the neutral lever, and at the same time, pushed on the low gear pedal. Once the Model T was moving, Daddy released the low gear pedal and set the throttle. It was all so complicated that Laurie didn't think she would ever learn to drive, but Buddy couldn't wait.

She gazed back at the tree, not the sad little house with its flaked paint and naked windows. Anyone could look in now. It wasn't their home anymore. She shut her eyes to hold the sight of the tree and didn't open them till they were a long way from town.

3

Even if the storm, and others before it, hadn't left all western Kansas and the Oklahoma Panhandle drifted in dust, this would have seemed like the longest road in the world, through what used to be called No Man's Land and looked like it was close to being that again. It was mostly ranches where skeleton cattle hunted for mouthfuls of grass among the sagebrush and soapweed thrusting from the rippled dust.

Lots of rabbits were smashed on the road, smears of fur and blood. The dust had blinded many of them, and caused boils, too. The animals would have less chance than usual in the drives, when people made a huge circle and moved inward, chasing the rabbits toward the center, where they were clubbed with baseball bats. The meat that wasn't eaten was shipped east in big barrels.

The Model T rattled along for miles without passing other vehicles or even a farmhouse. Towns were few. At Buffalo, they stopped for gas, Laurie and Bud piling out so Daddy could lift up the front-seat cushion to get to the gas tank beneath. The next wide spot in the road was Supply. It had been Fort Supply during the wars with the Plains Indians, Daddy said, but now made its living off an institution for the feeble-minded. There was a shorter route that ran closer to Texas's eastern border, but it was gravel and dirt, could be badly drifted, would surely be dusty, and Daddy thought the highway, mostly paved with either concrete or asphalt, would be a lot better.

The Model T made about thirty miles an hour. Daddy had hoped to drive the three hundred miles to Grandpa's before night, but they had two flats before noon. The second happened close to a dry wash, where there were some cottonwoods that must have leafed out fresh green and hopeful after the storm.

"Sister, you take the food and water over to the shade," Daddy said as he got the jack. "We'll eat and rest a little bit."

Laurie's skin was gritty and she'd licked her dry lips till they were raw and chapped. There wasn't enough water to really wash, but after she and Buddy had gone behind some willows, she poured a little water on a washrag and wiped Buddy's face. He was flushed and his eyes looked sunken and dull. To keep from suffocating, they had to ride with the windows down but the wind had heated fast after early morning. When Buddy didn't protest at being washed, Laurie scrubbed his hands, which had somehow gotten grubby, and demanded, "Buddy, are you all right?"

"I'm hot."

"Drink some water and lie down on the sheet under that big tree. You'll feel better after you eat."

He almost whined, which was not like Buddy. "I—I'm sick at my stomach."

"You can't get sick," she snapped. Her own insides twisted with fear. He looked the way he had when he'd caught scarlet fever, except that he was pale around the eyes. She held the jar for him to drink and spread the sheet where it was shadiest. "Stretch out, Buddy. Maybe you just hurt from being all cramped up. Or you maybe got carsick."

She washed as best she could with the clean part of the rag and then folded it across Buddy's forehead. Sand got in her shoes and hurt her feet so she untied them and left them in the car, hurrying across the hot dust with lard pails of rabbit and slaw, returning for the pie. She didn't feel good herself. Her head ached, her eyes and nose smarted from dust, and the greasy smell of the rabbit made her stomach lurch.

After urging more water down Buddy, she sipped from the mason jar. The tepid water had a flat, dead taste but you could get sunstroke from heat or if you didn't get enough water so she drank slowly. When she could trust her legs, she took the jar to Daddy, who was pumping up the inner tube after adding one more patch to a surface that was more patches than tube. The shirt she'd washed yesterday was smudged now and wet under the arms. He wasn't as feverish-looking as Buddy but his cheeks were red.

"That's Daddy's girl," he said, trying to grin as he handed back the jar.

She didn't know yet how she felt about him, not after the way he'd slapped her, and most of all because he was leaving them. It was as if he wasn't her same Daddy anymore but someone she didn't know and couldn't depend on, someone she was afraid of, like Floyd when he was drinking.

Getting a tea towel to spread on the dust for a tablecloth, she decided it was pretty simple after all. If Daddy sent for them, she'd love him again. If he didn't—well then, she'd never forgive him, either. But she wet another washrag and handed it to him so he could clean up.

"Think I'll catch a couple of winks," he said. "No use tryin' to drive when I might go to sleep and run off the road."

He lay down by Buddy. Somehow, flies had found them. You'd think the pesky things would die for good and all in a storm like the one that had buried houses and barns and crops and grass over this whole country. There weren't any flowers under the trees, or any grass save some of last year's dead clumps jutting up from the sand, but here came the flies though the lids were still on the pails. Laurie tied a washrag to a fallen branch and waved it over Daddy and Buddy when the flies settled on them.

Already, Daddy was gently snoring. He must not have slept much last night. She heard the crunch of a twig and whirled as a soft voice behind her said, "Howdy, sis. Could I share your tree a while?"

He wasn't as tall as Daddy, but leaner and somehow solider, as if his muscles and bones were knit together snug and smooth. He was a whole lot younger, though he was a grown man. He had a long nose, long mouth, and long jaw that rounded to a broad chin with a cleft so deep that it almost looked like a scar. A scruffy felt hat, so greasy and stained that there was no guessing its original color, tilted back from a high, wide forehead and unruly black hair. All his skin that showed was burned brown as an Indian's. What Laurie noticed most was the merry curve of his lips, and the dancing light in eyes she thought were gray till he moved into the sun and they sparkled green.

He carried a sack over his shoulder and some kind of big, funny-shaped case patched with black insulation tape. His faded khaki work pants and shirt were almost as stained as his hat and a blue bandanna hung partway out of one pocket.

"The tree's for everyone." Laurie whispered so as not to wake her father and brother. "Sit down and you can eat with us."

"Mightily obliged." He kept his voice down, too, but it had a deep male ring to it that pleased Laurie's ears. "I sure could use a drink if you can spare it."

Laurie nodded at the jar. "Drink all you want. There's more in the flivver. I'm sorry it's not cold."

"It's wet."

Tilting back his head, he took a couple of swallows. She admired the way the muscles of his throat stood out firm and strong as he drank. He grinned at her. "When you're thirsty, water beats the best corn likker ever made."

Liquor? *Wine is a mocker, strong drink is raging.* Laurie thought that anyone who took a drink of beer or whiskey turned into a wife-beating, reeling, scary drunkard who didn't know what they were doing and didn't care. Like Floyd who beat up Margie and who'd once pulled a butcher knife on Daddy when he intervened. This man certainly didn't act like Floyd but Laurie's alarm must have shown because the stranger looked kind of embarrassed.

"Don't worry, sis. I don't have any booze in my stuff and

haven't had a drink in a month. Right now this suits me better'n any Kentucky bourbon." He drank what was left in the half-gallon jar, sitting cross-legged in the dust. "You folks moving?"

Laurie nodded, ducking her head. She was ashamed to say Daddy was leaving them at Grandpa's. "Well," said the brown-skinned, gray-green-eyed man, "I'm glad to see you're not headed for California."

The name roused Daddy. His eyes opened. He kind of jumped when he saw the stranger and sat up in a hurry. The younger man thrust out his hand. "I'm John Morrigan, sir. Hope you don't mind my restin' off with you."

Daddy evidently liked what he felt in the other's handshake. "You're sure welcome to what we have. If we're travelin' your direction, you can squeeze in and ride with us."

"Wouldn't want to crowd you."

Daddy grinned. It was the first time Laurie had seen him really grin big since Mama died. "You can help me fix flats."

"I'm good at that." John Morrigan had a deep, soft chuckle, kind of surprised, like he'd just learned something nice.

"I'm Ed Field," Daddy said. "This is my daughter, Laurie, and Buddy's havin' a nap."

Daddy's eyes filled and a tear oozed through the dust on his cheek. *Don't tell him about us!* Laurie begged silently, making as much noise as she could in taking lids off the lard cans, sticking a spoon in the slaw, and setting forks in the pie pans they were using on the road, pushing hers toward Morrigan. *Don't tell him Mama's dead and you're dumping us like kittens you don't have the heart to drown.*

Daddy had loved Mama an awful lot but he enjoyed sympathy. Laurie hated it, at least the kind you bought by showing your sores and deformities like the beggars she'd heard about in big cities. She felt poor and ashamed because Mama was dead. Daddy's leaving made it worse. So she shrank and suffered while Daddy told Morrigan about Mama and his plans.

"Did I hear you mention California?" Daddy asked.

Morrigan nodded. "I just got to Amarillo in time for that storm. Goin' out to see my mother for the first time in a couple of years. She lives north of McAlester."

"And then you'll go back to California?" Daddy asked.

Morrigan's chuckle wasn't pleasant this time. "If I'm goin' to starve, I'd rather do it closer to home."

"But there's all that fruit to pick—all that cotton."

"Yeah, and there's a hundred men for every job of work, Mr. Field. I've worked in the oil patch since I was fourteen, got to be a tool dresser." At Laurie's puzzled look, he grinned. "That means I dressed the tools, honey—heated the bits when they got dull from drillin' and hammered 'em out. A toolie's second to the driller, and I drilled a little, too. But oil prices went way down a few years back and the way Alfalfa Bill Murray—he was governor of Oklahoma in thirty-one—the bright idea he had to fix that was to close down the wells complete."

"Doesn't seem to make much sense." Daddy's tone was sympathetic, though he'd always said he'd never work in the oil fields. On top of a rig was a good place to get killed, and oil-field people drank, gambled, and cussed a lot worse than the cowboys who came to Prairieville once a month after payday.

"When I couldn't get work in Texas," Morrigan went on, "I'd heard about jobs in Arizona and headed that way. The ads and promises those big Arizona growers had spread all over this part of the world sucked in so many folks the farmers took their choice just like a slave market—and let me tell you, people are slaves to their bellies, they got to eat. Arizona's got real tough laws about drawin' relief—can't get a dime unless you've lived there a couple of years." He laughed grimly. "In the last few years, I've walked the tracks and rode the rails and slept under most of the important bridges in this land of the free and I can tell you in lots of places it's a jailhouse crime not to have a job unless your daddy had a pile of money and left it to you. Well, when the cotton was picked and the main work done, Arizona shoved us over into California, and it was the same thing all over again. I'd heard they was payin' five dollars a day but instead I wound up glad to get a dollar."

"Maybe you weren't in the right place." Daddy looked pale and kind of sick. In spite of herself, Laurie felt sorry for him, though she was glad that now he'd surely change his mind.

"Mr. Field," said John Morrigan, "I'm afraid there isn't any right place in California. After I visit my mother, I'm tryin' the oil patch again, maybe go down to Texas. And this time, I'm not blowin' what I make as fast as I get it like I always done before. Goin' to save up and buy a spudder, talk some of them old Panhandle farmers whose topsoil's roostin' over in New Mexico into lettin' me drill to see what's under the hardpan."

"That's likely the best idea for you seein' as how you've been in the oil fields all your life," Daddy said. "No offense to you, John, but I've heard so much about California that I guess I've just got to try it. There's no work here of the kind I'm used to."

He gave Buddy a little shake. "Wake up, son. Time to eat before we hit the road."

Buddy was still flushed. His eyes were glassy when he opened them. "I'm thirsty."

Laurie took a water jar around to him, propped him against her, and helped him drink. He didn't push her away. That proved he didn't feel good. His eyes closed again.

"Buddy—" He liked the fried, crusty part of rabbit, and she broke off a little and tried to get him to taste it. "You better eat."

"Don't want to."

"He looks kind of feverish," Morrigan said. "You got any aspirin?"

They didn't have anything in the way of medical supplies except a bottle of Mercurochrome and a thermometer. "Don't matter," Morrigan said cheerfully. His voice calmed the fear-induced nausea churning in Laurie's stomach. "There's some willow along the wash. It's mighty good for lots of ailments. Get a pot of water boilin', honey, and I'll fetch some bark."

Daddy broke up some dead limbs and had a fire going by the time Laurie unearthed a cup and the teakettle and tipped water into it. "We sure don't need Buddy gettin' sick on us," Daddy said heavily.

"Maybe he's just hot and tired," Laurie consoled. "It's lucky we're close to some willows and Mr. Morrigan can make fever medicine."

"That's how your mother would talk." Daddy's voice was gratified and sad at the same time. "Wouldn't surprise me if

---

Morrigan's part Indian. They know a lot about plants and curing."

Laurie was washing Buddy's face and arms to cool him when John Morrigan came up in an easy swinging stride. He dumped a handful of white inner bark shavings into the boiling water, let it come back to a full boil, and set the kettle on the ground. His neat, quick, way of doing things didn't waste a motion.

"It's none of my business, Mr. Field, but the kids might hold up better if you wait a couple hours and travel after it cools down. Looks like you got your bedding. You could sleep out tonight and get to your father's place before it gets real hot tomorrow."

Daddy looked like he was going to argue. Then he looked at Buddy. "Reckon that's good advice, John, but I sure hate to sit around when the old Ford could be makin' miles."

"And flats. They'll be easier to change when it's cooler."

"Guess you'll want to hitch a ride with somebody else," Daddy said regretfully.

Morrigan shrugged. "Liefer visit with you folks, play a few songs to pass the afternoon. I got some canned peaches and salmon we can have for supper and a sack of oatmeal cookies a lady gave me along with dinner yesterday for fixin' her screen doors."

Laurie's mouth watered for a cookie but Daddy said, "We can feed our company. Is that a guitar you got?"

"That's what it is." Morrigan poured willow brew into a cup and handed it to Laurie. "Maybe your brother will take it better from you."

Laurie doubted that. Buddy had to be spanked sometimes before he'd take his medicine. Mama always made sure he'd swallowed it because otherwise he'd hold a pill in his mouth till he could get away and spit it out. As Laurie gingerly raised the cup to Buddy's lips, Morrigan smiled at the boy.

"That's what Choctaw Indians use for upsets like yours, son. It's broke me out of a bad fever many a time."

Buddy took a sip, struggled not to make a face, and gazed at Morrigan with wide, glittering eyes. "Are you a Choctaw, mister?"

"Grandma was a full-blood married to a quarter-Scots MacIntosh so that made my mother seven-eighths Choctaw. Grandpa Morrigan came over from Ireland and married a girl who was half Chickasaw. That made Dad a quarter Chickasaw. So—let's see now, Bud: I'm one-eighth Chickasaw on my father's side and one-sixteenth white on my mother's side, so what do you figure that makes me?"

Spellbound by Morrigan's teasing, lilting words, Buddy drank without protest, but shook his head at the question. "What does it make you, mister?"

For a moment, Laurie was afraid Morrigan would say "half-breed" but instead he laughed and gave Buddy's hair a gentle ruffling. "One mean Irish Injun! Shall I sing you a song about a man who was even more mixed up?"

Buddy nodded. By the time Morrigan got out his guitar, wiped it lovingly with a soft rag, tuned it, and rollicked through "I'm My Own Grandpa," Buddy had finished another cup of tea and was sweating. His eyes had lost some of their mirrorlike blankness and he didn't squirm when Laurie, sparing of water since they might not be able to fill their jars that day, moistened the rag again and bathed his face, neck, and arms.

When she started to fold the cloth across Buddy's forehead, Morrigan said, "It'll do more good across his throat where it'll cool those big arteries on either side of his windpipe. Like some special song, Buddy?"

"Do you know 'I Love Bananas Because They Have No Bones'?"

Morrigan did. And he played "Amazing Grace" for Daddy and "Pretty Redwing" for Laurie. "Now here's one about that dust storm," he said. "I was visitin' this friend out by Pampa, Texas, when it came up and he wrote this song. Mighty good songmaker Woody Guthrie is. This was just how it was, folks thinkin' the end had come and just sayin' good-bye to their neighbors."

A dust storm hit and it hit like thunder,
It dusted us over, it covered us under,

Blocked out the traffic, blocked out the sun,
Straight for home all the people did run singing:

So long, it's been good to know you,
So long, it's been good to know you,
So long, it's been good to know you,
This dusty old dust is a gettin' my home,
I've got to be drifting along.

There were a lot of verses. They told exactly how it had been, and how it was, but this wasn't a sad song or a sad tune. Morrigan's deep sweet voice lilted soft or swelled high, rollicked along till your foot tapped, and made you believe that even if the dusty wind was blowing you and other folks away from home, there'd be a place to stop, a place to live again, in your own house with your own family. . . .

No, that couldn't ever be. Mama was gone. Without her the finest mansion wouldn't be home, but there could've been a kind of a one, even under a tarp, if Daddy would take them with him.

But he won't, thought Laurie, struggling with tears. He still wants to go to California even after Mr. Morrigan told him there aren't any good jobs. Daddy wants to get away from us. I guess we remind him too much of Mama and how it was. I guess he can't stand it. But how are *we* going to stand living at Grandpa Field's? It's not fair. Daddy can leave us wherever he wants and it doesn't matter a bit what we want.

Still, she was heartened by Morrigan's singing, and cheered that Buddy was looking better. She smoothed back her brother's hair and closed her eyes, drawing the melody into her blood and breathing, filling the emptiness Mama's dying had left in her with John Morrigan's voice. *"It's me, it's me, it's me, Oh Lord, standin' in the need of a home. . . ."*

Wasn't it funny how a sad song could make you feel better? More as if you weren't alone, that other people had gone through as bad or worse and managed to make music out of it? She tried to remember the words of the songs Morrigan sang that she didn't know so she'd have them later, when he was gone.

> You got to walk that lonesome valley,
> You got to walk it by yourself.
> Nobody else can walk it for you.
> You got to walk it by yourself. . . .

He played and sang till the sun slanted low in the west. A little breeze made the shiny new cottonwood leaves whisper though, thank goodness, it didn't stir up dust or ashes. Laurie wished they could stay here, that they didn't have to travel on and lose Morrigan.

Daddy, eager as he was to get shut of them, must have felt a little the same. He sighed as he got to his feet and stared south. "Guess we'd better chug along. How far can you ride with us, John?"

"Why, if you can put up with me that long, I'd like to get off in Clinton—catch a ride there on the Chicago, Rock Island and Pacific. If the railroad bulls don't throw me off, I can go all the way to MacAlester on that line. Or I can hitchhike east on good old Route Sixty-six."

"What're railroad bulls?" asked Buddy.

"Oh, you might say they're police the railroads hire to make sure nobody rides in their empty boxcars that're shuttlin' back and forth over land the government gave the railroads in order to get 'em to build as a public service. Yessiree, it's a public service 'long as you can pay your fare."

Speaking in a hurry, because of course riding a train without paying for it was pretty close to stealing, Daddy said, "We can drop you right in Clinton, John. Glad of the company."

Somehow they got Morrigan's guitar and sack tied on top with the suitcase. Buddy settled into a nest of bedding in the backseat, and Laurie sat between Daddy and Morrigan, turning her knees in order to give Morrigan's long legs more room. She savored his closeness and his odor. It was woodsmoke and salt and man scent that had no sourness or discouragement to

---

34

it like Daddy's. She smelled tobacco, too, and ruefully concluded that Morrigan must be a sinner—but she didn't care.

Talk flowed back and forth between him and Daddy. They had to raise their voices above the sound of the engine and whine of the wind. When they neared a man shambling along in the other direction with a battered old cardboard suitcase, Daddy stopped and gave him what was left of the fried rabbit and a jar half-full of water.

"My landlord got money for tractors from the NBA," said the shrunken, stoop-shouldered man whose face was wrinkled as a prune. "So he tells me and two other guys who were farmin' for him to clear out. Don't need us. Goddam gover'ment. Goddam machinery!"

"Brother, it don't help to take the Lord's name in vain," said Daddy.

"Don't seem to have helped you not to. But I shouldn't have cussed in front of the kiddies." The wizened face split to show good teeth and Laurie realized with shock that he must be no older than Daddy. "You just forget that, sissy, and remember how I sure am obliged. Good luck to you folks."

"Good luck to you," said Daddy, and Laurie echoed that.

"Want me to drive, Ed?" asked Morrigan, for Daddy had asked him to drop the "Mr. Field."

"Glad for you to." Daddy took up more of the seat than had Morrigan and Laurie had to brace herself to keep from jouncing to the floorboards. She forgot her discomfort, though, in the glory of the sunset that crimsoned the whole western sky, scarlet streaked with fiery gold. The brilliance deepened to glowing purple red, then slowly faded to hazy violet.

"They say dust makes these pretty sunsets." Morrigan grinned. "Reckon that's the only good thing about it. Glad you gave that old boy back there some food. I've been mighty hollow myself and you know what I found out?"

"What?" asked Laurie, Buddy, and Daddy all at once.

"No use goin' to the churches. I've been run off from every brand of church under the sun. I knew better'n to go to the rich houses, but the middlin' ones won't feed you, either. What you do is go to the poor folks. They've been hungry. Whatever they've got, they'll share it. Funny thing is that these holy folks wouldn't let Jesus in their churches or homes if He came back today. They'd call him a hobo and jail him for not havin' a job. But you know, Ed, I have an idea that if He was here, he'd be with the Okies in those stinkin' California camps."

Daddy looked startled but then he nodded. "The Lord said the foxes had holes and the birds had nests but He didn't have anyplace to rest His head."

"There's another song Woody taught me," Morrigan said. "Goes to the tune of 'Jesse James.' " Softly, he began a song about Jesus and how he was killed. From that, he moved on to songs Laurie had heard all her life, "Chisholm Trail," "Strawberry Roan," "She'll Be Comin' Around the Mountain," and "Swing Low, Sweet Chariot."

Laurie and her father joined in the choruses. It made her feel better, lightened the sick heaviness of her heart. Maybe as long as you could sing or make up songs about how you felt, it kept you from feeling quite so hopeless and poor and lonesome. Singing made you think about whoever made the song and all the people who'd sung it since, and everybody who was in the same fix, made you know you belonged to the human race even if your home was gone and your family busted up and you didn't know what was going to happen.

I'll try to keep Morrigan's songs, Laurie vowed. If I can remember them after he's gone maybe it'll seem a little like he's still with us. Uncomfortable as her perch was, she didn't want this time with him to end.

Close to the road, they passed a blistered farmhouse where a family was piling furniture and belongings into an old Ford truck. In spite of this melancholy occupation, they waved, so Daddy stopped to ask if they could fill their water jars.

"Help yourself, mister," said the graying man, weathered and gnarled as a cottonwood root clinging to an eroded bank. "At least the well ain't dried up yet."

His wife, except for her ruffled sunbonnet and faded dress, looked remarkably like him, too old to be the mother of the towheaded little girl peering from behind her. The oldest boy was taller than Laurie. Three other youngsters stairstepped between him and the toddler, all fair-haired, blue-eyed, and clad in patched overalls that obviously descended through the children according to size till they fell off the thin, sunburned bodies.

The Fields and Morrigan climbed out, each taking a jar, and headed for the well at the side of the house. The door of a sagging barn creaked and swung in the wind. There wasn't a tree in sight, nor any flowers or bushes. It didn't seem to Laurie that any place could be more forlorn but as they paused to visit a few minutes, she saw tears in the woman's eyes.

"Owned two sections of land free and clear in twenty-nine," the farmer said. "But the bank closed with all our savin's and me owin' for this truck—it was new then—a combine, tractor, and seed. Never got out of debt again because I never made another good crop. If wind didn't blow it out in spring, or hail pound it into the ground, the grasshoppers gnawed it to the roots in summer. Just kept a-plowin' money under. Mortgaged the land. The bank's foreclosed on us so we've got to go."

"My first baby's buried here," said the woman, picking up the ragged little girl and burying her face against the soft neck. "He'd be sixteen this June. Onliest one of the young'uns that had brown eyes and hair like my daddy. There was a yellow rosebush on his grave and a honey locust shadin' it. I kept 'em watered, but hoppers killed them."

"Headin' for Californy," said the farmer. "With all of us but the two least 'uns workin' hard for a year or two, we ought to get together enough cash for a start. They say that earth's so rich that anything you plant just plain jumps out of the ground."

Morrigan frowned. It was clear he hated to discourage these hard-hit folks but hated worse for them to be too disappointed. "Well, mister, you got a good work crew for certain, but I'm just back from California and I hope you'll let me give you a word of advice. If you find work on your way out, a place where you can live decent, better stop right there."

"But I've heard a man can get five dollars a day pickin' fruit or cotton!"

37

"Not with thousands of folks like us comin' every month, dead broke, and havin' to work for whatever pay they can get," Morrigan said. "You see, since the Gold Rush, California's had cheap labor. First Chinese, then Japanese and Filipinos and Mexicans. Now they don't need 'em to work, they're forcing lots of Mexicans to go back to Mexico whether they want to or not. Now the growers have Okies—boy howdy! have they got Okies! That's what they call us whether we're from Kansas or Texas, Arkansas, Tennessee, Colorado, or New Mexico. Californians treat us just like they do folks with dark skins. Signs in some movie houses say 'Negroes and Okies in the balcony.' " He shook his head. "That California water Jimmie Rodgers sings about tastes more like vinegar than cherry wine, friends. Sure, you can sleep out every night because there's no roof you can afford unless you're pickin' on a farm where they make a whole family live in one of their one-room shacks and pay a dollar a day for it."

"Maybe you was just in the wrong place," said the farmer.

"I sure was." Morrigan shook hands all the way down to the tiny blond girl who finally, shyly, answered his smile. "Good luck. But I'm sure hopin' for you that you find a good place short of California."

"I won't be far behind you folks," Daddy said, also shaking hands. "Whatever's out there can't be worse'n this."

As they drove off, Laurie didn't look back. It was too sad, watching the family pack up their lives and years and hopes into an old truck. But for one thing she envied them. They were together, and they'd stay together.

Morrigan was driving. They'd all drunk their fill of cold, sweet water from the well. Now they stashed the jars where they'd stay coolest and settled down for the drive to Clinton. Morrigan started humming. It turned into words mocked by the curl of his lip and the bitter edge of his voice.

> "California water tastes like cherry wine.
> California water tastes like cherry wine.
> Oklahoma water tastes like turpentine . . ."

They drove through Woodward in the twilight. It had a courthouse, Carnegie library, American Legion Hall, brick business buildings, and several parks. A pretty little town, Laurie thought wistfully, a good place to live and feel you belonged. Would their family ever settle in a place like this again, have a real home?

"We're gettin' east of where the storm was worst," Daddy said, as the headlights flickered wanly on the road. "Fences aren't drifted over and there's grass amongst them Roosian thistles that sure are lookin' healthy. When they dry up, tumbleweeds'll be scootin' across the land like they was people. Farther we can get tonight the less drivin' we'll have in the heat of the day. How's about we travel till nine o'clock or a flat tire, whichever comes first?"

"Fine by me," said Morrigan.

The flat tire came at eight-thirty, according to the kitchen clock Daddy had wired to the dashboard. Luckily, they were near another dry wash where enough limbs had dropped from cottonwoods to build a fire. By its light, the men jacked up the car and fixed the flat while Laurie and her drowsy brother got out the bedding and plates and utensils. Laurie put on the coffeepot and, at Morrigan's insistence, got the cans of salmon and peaches out of his old canvas sack, opened them, and set the cans on a tea towel with bread and what was left of the slaw.

Buddy was hungry now. He must have been sick from heat and the motion of the car—and from leaving home. As they ate by the cheerful dance of the fire, Laurie couldn't help but think how different that day and the night to come would've been without Morrigan. *Did you send him, Mama? Do you know what's happening to us? Do you still love us or is it like the preacher says, that folks in heaven don't grieve anymore? Is being with God so wonderful that you've forgotten us? I don't believe that! I don't believe it at all!* Even worse than Mama's dying was thinking that maybe she didn't care about them now, that she couldn't love anyone but God.

No matter how Laurie tried to deny that shattering fear, it took away her appetite. She nibbled at some bread and ate a little salmon because Morrigan put it on her plate. When he offered peaches, she shook her head.

"No, thank you very much," she said the way Mama had taught them. Manners don't cost anything, Mama used to say. Laurie had to remember, remember everything, so she could teach Buddy.

Morrigan's right eyebrow climbed to his dark hair. "My singin' turn your stomach, honey?"

"Oh, no! I just—" Daddy had gone to the car for something. It was parked just off the road and he was out of earshot. Laurie blurted, "Do you think dead people know what's going on with people they used to love? Do you think they care?"

Buddy quit chewing. His eyes fixed on Morrigan. Had he been wondering the same thing? She'd have to get better at guessing what went on inside her little brother. He wasn't going to tell her, and she was all he'd have. If Morrigan laughed or said she was silly—

He considered for a moment, brow furrowing. "Why, Laurie, if there's anything left of us at all, it has to be love. That's one thing I agree with in the Bible—love is stronger than death."

The way he said it made her believe it. She'd believe anything he said. She brushed at tears. "I don't want Mama to feel bad, Mr. Morrigan. But it—it'd be so lonesome if she didn't care about us anymore—"

Setting down his plate, he put one arm around her and one around Buddy. "She cares. She loves you. But where she is, she can see past what's going on now. She knows you'll do fine, both of you, and that when you've lived out your good lives, you'll be with her again."

"Do—do you really believe that?" Buddy asked.

"I believe it more than anything I've ever said." Morrigan gave Laurie a blue bandanna handkerchief that had his smell on it. "That coffee sure smells good and I've got a can of evaporated milk." He glanced up at Daddy who had returned with a clean shirt for tomorrow. Daddy was particular about how he looked and kept his shoes shined even when the soles were mostly cardboard patches. "Is it okay for the youngsters to have coffee this late if we put in plenty of Borden's?"

"If they want some, I guess it's fine." Daddy chuckled at Buddy's delight.

The golden peaches tempted Laurie now. She had some with a cup of creamy rich coffee and felt content and lazy, as if her bones had dissolved. She was by no means sorry that there wasn't enough water to heat for dishes.

"I'll take care of these." Morrigan collected the plates, forks, and spoons. From fallen bark, he tore off the fibrous lining and wiped the things clean before discarding the fuzzy scourers a good way from camp.

When he returned almost soundlessly, first a shadow, then with the firelight on him, Buddy said, "Could you play your guitar again, sir?"

"Son," rebuked Daddy, "Mr. Morrigan's tired."

"My strummin' fingers are a mite sore," said Morrigan. "But I can sure play you some tunes on the harmonica."

He got it out of his bundle, which was astonishing in the way it seemed to hold just what was needed. The french harp was about six inches long, plated with scrolled silver that flashed in the firelight. Sitting cross-legged, Morrigan made music you couldn't believe come from such a little contrivance: trains thundering down the tracks, whistles blowing, coyotes laughing like the ones in the distance, hooty owls, and the mournful wailing of the wind.

The man's body moved to the music, sort of a pulsing, and his long brown fingers could flicker across the front of the harp, causing a poignant vibration like a sob. He used his tongue to make trills and tremolos. It was magic. The only thing Laurie didn't like, because she loved his voice, was that he couldn't play and sing at the same time.

"Want to try it?" he asked, wiping the harmonica off on his shirt. Buddy had fallen asleep and Daddy was yawning but Laurie carefully took the instrument, admiring the curlicues around the name, Hohner, and blew into it. She only got a rustle.

"You'll have to puff harder than that, honey. Don't worry, you're not goin' to wake the neighbors."

She blew with more assurance. The sounds were pretty even

if she didn't know how to put them into a tune. Oh, lovely! If she had one of these, she'd practice till Morrigan would be proud and surprised. Well, someday she would. When she grew up—

"Better tuck in," said Daddy. "We need to roll out early so we can get to Pa's before the worst heat."

Reluctantly, Laurie handed back the harmonica. "Can you play the dust song on this?" she asked. "The one about 'It's been good to know you'?"

"Sure." He did, winding up with a spirited flourish. That might be an end-of-the-world song and a dust song, but it was mainly about folks gaining comfort from each other in the stifling darkness of the storm—able to say that it had been good—good to know each other, good to have shared their lives.

Just as it had been a saving grace to meet John Morrigan when they had even though the winds were soon going to blow them different ways. She'd never forget him, or his songs, and so she wouldn't lose him. "Thanks, Mr. Morrigan," she said. "Good night."

"Good night, Laurie." He smoothed her hair, smiling, and the smoldering firelight made his green-gray eyes almost golden. "Sleep tight now."

He went off into the night. She thought he was answering a call of nature but as she began to drowse, she heard him playing, muted by distance, as if he had things to say to the night and the wind. It was with his music gentle in her ears that she fell asleep. For the first time since her mother died, she didn't dream of the end of the world.

4

They were on the road before sunrise. Morrigan said laughingly that he was just like a rooster, dawn made him sing, and he sang merrily—about the boll weevil who was looking for a home and took the farmer's, "The Yellow Rose of Texas," "Cotton-Eyed Joe," "Hobo Bill," and "Orange Blossom Special." As a town that had to be Clinton came into view, he led off in "Will the Circle Be Unbroken?" and they all joined in.

"Clinton's a pretty prosperous little town," Morrigan said. "It's at the junction with Highway 66 that runs all the way from Chicago to California, tucked in here at the bend of the Washita River and it's got the big state tuberculosis hospital. Hear tell colored folks are in the regular wards since there's no other place for them."

"Didn't this used to be part of the Cheyenne-Arapaho Reservation?" Daddy asked.

"Till it was opened up to homesteaders in eighteen ninety-two." Morrigan shrugged. "That's how it was in Oklahoma, you know. First it was roamed by the real wild tribes like Comanches and Kiowas. Then what they call the Five Civilized Tribes, includin' my Choctaw and Chickasaw kin, got driven off their homes in Georgia and Florida and states like that and got dumped in the eastern part of what by then was bein' called Indian Territory." He pulled a wry grin. "Uncle Sam promised them this country as long as grass grows and water runs. Well, Uncle kept sending more tag-ends of tribes to the Territory, and then used the fact that some Indians fought for the South in the War Between the States—hell, plenty of 'em were so plumb civilized they had colored slaves—well, the government used that excuse to grab most of the western part of the territory."

"Did Indians have slaves?" Laurie was both intrigued and scandalized.

"Sure. My Indian great-grandparents on both sides owned colored folks. Just because a race of people get shoved around don't mean they're softer-hearted than anybody else, honey. Anyhow, starting in eighty-nine, there was one land openin' after another and all kinds of skullduggery, especially after oil was found. Whether the Cherokee Nation or the Choctaw Nation or the Seminole Nation or the Chickasaw Nation or the Creek Nation—and they were nations, with their own laws and courts and constitutions—well, whether they liked it or not, and most didn't, their Indian Territory was lumped with Oklahoma Territory and made into a state in nineteen-o-seven."

"I remember that," frowned Daddy. "Guess I thought the Indians would be tickled to be part of a state."

"Not hardly! I reckon you can see in Oklahoma better than you can anywhere else in the whole United States how the Indians got swindled from start to finish—how their governments were run into the ground and the land they'd owned in common was broken up into little allotments."

"Didn't a lot of them get rich off oil?" Daddy asked.

"Some did, but a sight more got cheated."

"Did you have an oil well on your place?" asked Buddy, eyes big. Most of this was news to Laurie, too. It certainly wasn't in her history books.

"Nope, but my grandmother did." Morrigan's laughter was bitter and proud at the same time. "She never would cash the oil checks on account of she was so mad that the government gave her an allotment when she'd wanted the land to all stay owned by the Choctaw Nation. Her white second husband cashed the checks, though, and the minute she died, he sold her allotment and went off and married an Osage woman for her headrights. The Osages held on to their oil rights as a tribe and shared the royalties out according to inheritance. Step-grandpop got him a woman with three headrights. Far as I know the old devil's still buyin' a Cadillac every year and drinkin' the best bourbon his bootlegger can rustle."

None of the Fields could think of anything to say to that. A little way on the other side of town, Morrigan pulled over and sat with his lean brown fingers loose on the wheel. "Well, folks, guess this is where we part company. I hope everything works out fine and it won't be long till you can get back together."

"Good luck to you, John." Daddy offered his hand. "We sure have appreciated your help and your singin'. You're always welcome to share whatever we've got."

"Who knows?" Morrigan smiled and his eyes rested on Laurie. "I'm just like a tumbleweed, blowin' all over the country. Could be we'll meet again."

Laurie's throat ached. He'd only been with them less than a

day, yet it seemed she'd known him forever, that he was intended to be part of her life. How could he just disappear? Vanish down the road or swing onto a train?

But if he hadn't come—if he hadn't known what to do for Buddy, helped Daddy with the flats and convinced him not to drive in the heat of the day—if he hadn't made music and sung, how awful the trip would have been. And she had learned most of the words of his songs she'd liked best. She was glad he'd come, thankful, even if it hurt so bad to think she'd probably never see him again. It was almost as if Mama had begged God into sending them an angel, and angels, of course, never stay long.

He started to climb out of the car. "Mr. Morrigan," she ventured. "Could you sing that song about 'So Long, It's Been Good to Know You'?"

"Why, sure I can." He got down his guitar. The Fields got out to stretch while they listened. Standing there, Morrigan played and sang, grinning at the passersby who stopped to hear. He wound up with a rousing sweep of the strings, put his guitar in its case, and reached into his bundle. "You keep this harmonica, Laurie," he said, giving it to her. "It's a good friend. You can always tell it exactly how you feel."

Her fingers caressed the silver whorls even as she protested. "But you'll need it!"

"Got my guitar. And I can buy another harmonica. Rather you had this one." He touched her cheek before he shook hands with Buddy and again with Daddy. "So long." He picked up his bundle and guitar. "It really has been good to know you."

They waved till, with a last salute, he passed out of sight behind some warehouses. Slowly, the Fields got into the Model T. Daddy tried to make a joke. "Hope we don't have any more flats."

Too choked to answer, Laurie nodded.

"Let me see that harmonica," Buddy wheedled.

Laurie started to refuse—it was all she had of Morrigan now—but you can't be selfish with what's been given you, especially by a sort of angel.

* * *

45

Rutted wheel tracks turned in at the tarpaper-covered shack with its windmill and rickety outbuildings, while other ruts ran on toward endless fields of young green plants that Laurie knew must be cotton and corn because that was mostly what Grandpa Field grew for his landlord. This was far enough east to have missed the worst of the storm and besides, the rolling hills and valleys to the west made farming difficult so that land had been left for grazing and was held down by matted, inter-locking grass roots.

It was the plowed prairie, long broken to wheat, that had swirled into the sky all the way from the Texas Panhandle to southern Nebraska, from eastern New Mexico and Colorado to the edge of the Oklahoma Panhandle. Morrigan had drawn a map in the dust for them, traced the Dust Bowl in the shape of what looked like an animal's skull, cranium in Nebraska, jaw gaping open just above Lubbock, Texas. It was as if the spirit of the ruined prairie was in turn devouring its destroyers and all their works.

A pack of skinny greyhounds ran out barking, and sur-rounded the car. There were really only four of them but though Laurie loved dogs and it was one of the sorrows of her life that her parents said they couldn't afford to feed one, these sharp-muzzled, prominent-ribbed, narrow-flanked creatures frightened her. It wasn't just their din or their color of sullen gray twilight. They looked like starvation made flesh, death's hounds in some of the Irish legends, that could never sate their hunger.

Grandpa came out, cursing and kicking the dogs. Daddy's lips tightened at the profanity. Maybe Grandpa would cuss so bad that Daddy would decide he couldn't leave Laurie and Buddy. This hope died as Daddy opened the car door and said, "Well, Pa, like I wrote you, I've brought the kids till I can get set in California."

A stream of tobacco juice hit a tire. Bald head gleaming in the sun, Grandpa folded his arms and appraised the children, his good eye, a piercing blue, probing to make up for the sightless one that was sort of a bleary white. "Reckon they're big enough to earn their keep," he grunted. "Rosalie's always whinin' that she don't have enough help what with Belle only six. But these kids better not take after that woman of yourn. She was always sickly."

Daddy went dull red. "Rachel couldn't help that."

Children peeked from the door and windows. Several trailed Rosalie as she hurried out, brown legs flashing beneath a dress that didn't much more than cover her knees and had several buttons missing in front. Rosalie was slim in the waist but her bosom swelled out of the faded, short-sleeved garment. She wore gold hoop earrings and her lips were redder than could be natural but in spite of all these sins, her arms were outstretched and Laurie went into them.

"There, there, sweetie," Rosalie soothed.

Her warm body smelled good, like vanilla and cinnamon and roses and she was soft with firm muscle and bone beneath. You couldn't imagine her being sick; couldn't imagine her dying. . . . The comparison made Laurie feel disloyal.

Reluctantly, Laurie straightened, took her own weight back, though it would have been a relief to let go and sob in those comforting arms. Laurie didn't want to break down in front of Grandpa, not now, not ever, or let him know she was scared of him. With his hooked nose and bald head, he reminded her of a chicken hawk—and he made her feel mighty like a pullet addled at looking up to discover swooping talons.

That was silly! He was her grandfather, after all, Daddy's own father! But Daddy had hit her, Daddy was deserting her and Buddy. So maybe the father she'd loved, the one she'd known—maybe he'd been that way because of Mama and now she was gone, he was different.

"Come along in!" Rosalie hustled Laurie and Buddy toward the house. It didn't have a proper foundation but sat on concrete blocks with sand blown away from them. The greyhounds must have lived under the house, for there were bones and the remains of a rabbit with long, delicate ears and an eye lolling out of the chewed head.

A spindly rambling rosebush with a few tight buds clung to a strip of old hogwire stretched from the single step to the roof, a brave try for beauty against ragged lengths of black tarpaper nailed over the board walls to seal cracks and help turn rain. Grandpa strode in ahead of them, not holding the screen door open. He wasn't a big man but there was a kind of explosiveness to his movements and he shook the floor when he walked.

"You can unload after dinner," Rosalie said, "but right now you pull up to the table while the biscuits and gravy are hot. Ed, you look like you could use some coffee. Belle, fetch the pie plates and some forks and knives. Ev'rett, get some milk out of the cellar. Ernie, Billy, get a couple of crates for your—" She burst into laughter that began deep in her belly. "Almost said cousins! Well, Laurie and Bud, I think that's what we'll call you anyway. Plumb ridiculous for you to call kids younger'n you are 'aunt' and 'uncle'!"

Swept through a rickety screen door fringed with oilcloth to scare off flies, a device that didn't seem to affect the population, Laurie didn't dare say she and Buddy should wash their hands first. She didn't want to hurt Rosalie's feelings or provoke her grandfather's wrath with what he'd call her mother's persnickety qualms. He was likely to point out that washing her hands and brushing her teeth hadn't kept his daughter-in-law from dying young.

Sitting on an apple crate, Laurie, beneath the table, wiped her hands as carefully as she could on her underskirt, which was cleaner than her dress. Would Daddy say grace?

He didn't. Just like a heathen, he took a big helping of pinto beans, a hunk of fat side meat with the hog's skin cooked soft enough to chew, thanked Rosalie for the coffee she poured him, and took three golden-brown biscuits.

Everett, who must be about ten, came in with a jar of milk. Hair and eyebrows bleached white as cotton, he had deep blue eyes that looked strange with his sun-browned skin. Like all the children, he was barefoot. Two-year-old Babe, angelically blond and earthily dirty—the one Rosalie had been pregnant with last time Grandpa visited, was kilted in a low-slung diaper over which her belly button protruded. The other children wore ragged bib overalls without shirts, including Belle.

There uniformity ended, except for skins tanned wherever the overalls didn't cover. Pug-nosed Ernie, eight, had straight brown hair and hazel eyes. Billy, a year older, had sandy curls and gray eyes. Skinny little Belle, who darted around like a hummingbird, was dark of hair and eye like her mother. Laurie hoped she'd stopped wetting beds because most likely they'd share one. Babe's odiferous, stained diaper testified that she was a long way from housebroken.

When Rosalie was so nice, it was a shame she wasn't more particular. Mama used to excuse her by saying she'd grown up the sixth of nine children in a cabin over in the Kiamichi Mountains, with a part-Choctaw father who didn't do much but drink and hunt and a mother who died birthing the last baby when Rosalie was five so that the brood more or less raised themselves. Grandpa liked to joke that he'd had to chase Rosalie down and put shoes on her before they could get married.

She was a mighty good cook, though. After plates and pie pans were cleaned with morsels of biscuit, she took a big pan from the warming oven and wedged it among the emptied bowls and kettles. Melted sugar left caramelly streaks where juice had oozed through artistic slits on the good-smelling crust of the plum cobbler.

Spooning out big helpings, Rosalie said, "This is the last of the plums I put up last year. Ever picked plums, Laurie?"

When Laurie shook her head, Belle bounced on her crate. "It's fun! We go to the river and have a picnic and eat all the plums we want!"

"Yeah, and you get a bellyache and throw up!" jeered Ernie, who was closest in age to her. "Bellyache Belle! Bellyache Belle!

He was sitting next to Belle. She grabbed as much of his brown hair as she could and gave it a wrench. He yelped and dragged her fingers loose, giving them a yank backwards that made her shriek and duck her head to bite him.

"No bitin'," Rosalie said, giving each child an absentminded cuff. "You're not wild critters. Anyhow, human bites swell up and get infected worse'n a dog's. You're not goin' to do one another like that."

The two subsided and worked on their cobbler and milk. The milk tasted rich, though it had surely been skimmed. Laurie remembered Rosalie telling Mama that Grandpa let her use the butter and egg money for dressing the family and "extras" which, according to his lights, included sugar, cocoa, oilcloth for the table, dishes, cookware, and kerosene for the lamp.

"When it's too dark to see, it's time to be in bed," he'd always said, during his visits, and had taken himself off to Mama and Daddy's room. They slept on the couch during these invasions but they couldn't get to bed till late because Rosalie liked to talk or read magazines after her children had fallen asleep wherever they wore out and she'd settled the boys on a pallet and put Belle in bed with a reluctant Laurie.

If I have to sleep with Belle, I'll make sure she goes to the toilet last thing before bed, Laurie thought, and wondered where everybody slept. This good-sized room that served as kitchen, dining room, and living room had a bed in one corner and the door was open to a smaller room with another bed and a dresser. As far as she could tell, there wasn't any other room, not even a porch.

All of a sudden, the cobbler didn't taste so delicious, though Laurie told herself she and Buddy had their own bedding and Rosalie might let them make down pallets. After dinner, while Daddy and the boys unloaded from the car what would be left here, Grandpa stretched out on the blanket-covered couch and was snoring long before Laurie, Rosalie, and Belle had cleared the table. Rosalie swabbed most of the scraps into the slop bucket for the hogs but she sent Ernie out with a pan for the chickens.

"Kind of encourages them," she laughed and half-filled the dishpan with hot water dipped out of the reservoir of the cast-iron range.

The box beside it held "slack" coal, mostly dust, the kind that sold cheap at the railroad yard. Sudsing the water by rubbing a bar of yellowish homemade soap with a sour-smelling dish-rag, Rosalie washed faster than Laurie could rinse the dishes in a big kettle, dry some, and hand the others to Belle, who stood on a box.

The tea towels were smudged and full of holes. There were a few shelves for cups and pans and cooking supplies and a box to hold utensils but the dishes were just put back on the table.

There were a lot. From the traces of dried egg and oatmeal on some of them, it was clear that Rosalie did breakfast dishes along with dinner ones. Laurie was beginning to understand why Rosalie didn't keep her children and house very clean. When every bucket of water had to be pumped and carried, a person would be tired before ever starting a wash. And what was the use of mopping a linoleum that was worn through to the black underside except around the edges and beneath the stove?

Rosalie tossed the greasy dishwater out the back door. "If the rinse water's cooled down, you can pour it on the rosebush," she told Laurie. "Then we'll figure out where to put your things and rest a little while before we chop weeds out of the cotton." She rubbed her back. "Sure wish cotton and corn grew as fast as crabgrass and careless weed."

Daddy was repacking the suitcase and car now that he and the boys had carried in Buddy and Laurie's things, including their bedding, and most of the pickles and plums and peaches Mama had canned last year. "Buddy and the boys took the twenty-two and went to see if they can get some rabbits for supper," Daddy said. "You put up his clothes and stuff, Laurie, so they don't get scattered around."

Belle tagged them curiously as Rosalie, after a little thought, located two apple crates. "They can go right under the bed next to my kids' boxes," she explained. "Be handy since Buddy'll be sleepin' with the boys in the bed. You'll be on the sofa with Belle, honey. Plenty of room if you each sleep with your head at a different end and don't kick much."

"I kick like a Missoury mule, Pa says." Belle sounded proud of it. She picked up the little cedar box with the brass plate engraved with Mama's first name. "What's in here?"

"Handkerchiefs." The child's hands, miraculously dirty again after having come clean from the rinsed dishes, left fingerprints on the metal and polished rosy wood. Laurie flinched, restraining an impulse to grab for the chest.

This wasn't her home. Rosalie wasn't even her grandmother, but was taking her and Buddy in out of kindness. Even though Laurie would much rather have gone with Daddy, even though she cringed from the thought of having to sleep on the sofa with Belle's feet in her face, Laurie had to remember that and behave the way Mama would expect.

The handkerchiefs, mostly gifts to Mama from women friends, were lawn and voile and linen, fancy with embroidery, cutwork, or lace, much too nice to use, Mama said, and anyway, they'd scratch your nose. Mama's only jewelry besides her wedding ring, with which she'd been buried, was a little lavaliere, an amethyst pendant on a fine silver chain that Daddy had given her while they were courting. Wedding rings and watches were the only jewelry the tabernacle allowed so after she got sanctified, Mama had put the lavaliere in the box along with locks of her mother's and children's hair—Laurie's had been yellow though it was now a dreary dishwater blond—and other small treasures.

Rosalie swept the chest out of Belle's hands. "Now listen, Belle, you leave Laurie's things alone, hear? Don't you touch her stuff unless she says you can." Rosalie handed the box to Laurie, who felt selfish and ashamed enough to lift the catch and select a pink lawn handkerchief embroidered in silk with deeper pink roses for Belle and a lace-edged white linen one for Rosalie.

"Please take them," Laurie urged over Rosalie's protest. "Mama would have liked you to have a remembrance."

"She was a real lady." Tears glinted in Rosalie's dark eyes and her voice trembled. "I know Rachel didn't approve of Harry but she was always nice to me. I'd have given the moon to talk educated like she did, have good manners, and—well, be like she was, exceptin' for quite so much religion." Rosalie laughed sheepishly. "No offense, honey, but your mama was so good it plumb discouraged me. Only time I ever saw her rile up was when Harry made some kind of slightin' remark about Ed." Rosalie gave Laurie's shoulder a pat. "I'm going to change the baby and lay down with her and a magazine for a little bit. You just make yourself at home. We're glad to have you. Here, let me put away your winter coats and mittens and caps. You won't need 'em till October, maybe later."

Oh Mama, Laurie pleaded. *Help us be gone by then! Help*

Daddy get a job quick so he can send for us! Shooing Babe into the bedroom, Rosalie closed the door most of the way. Laurie put the chest in the bottom of the box along with the ruby-glass pitcher and sugar bowl and then looked helplessly at the bird quilt and piles of belongings, hers and Buddy's, that had been dumped on the bed.

It gave her a funny, sick feeling to realize this was all they had left in the world, that they truly didn't have a home but were just stuffed into the corners of another family's life. Laurie chewed her lip, blinked at tears, and conjured up Morrigan's smile, his deep, warm voice saying, "If any part of us lasts, it has to be love."

Steadied, Laurie went at her task. Daddy was taking Mama's red-letter Bible, but Laurie had the treasured books she'd gotten for Christmas and her birthdays: Hawthorne's *A Wonder Book; The Little Lame Prince* by Dinah Craik Mulock; Anna Sewell's *Black Beauty,* so sad Laurie had only read it once; and Robert Louis Stevenson's *A Child's Garden of Verses,* which was a mighty disappointment to Laurie. Why, when she only got a book or two a year and wanted so many, didn't her parents ask which one she wanted? When it came to poetry, she much preferred Alfred Noyes, Rudyard Kipling, Vachel Lindsay, and some of Longfellow, like "The Skeleton in Armor," which she'd learned by heart from library books while she was doing the ironing or the dishes. She had enough poems in her head to recite for hours. That was almost as good as having the books. She loved the gallant colonel's son in "The Ballad of East and West" and thrilled as she declaimed haughtily:

"Lightly then answered the Colonel's son: 'Do good to bird
     and beast,
   But count who comes for the broken bones before thou
     makest a feast. . . .' "

And while reciting "The Highwayman," her heart swelled with pity for the landlord's red-lipped daughter who "watched for her love in the moonlight and died in the darkness there," and for the bold outlaw.

The last of the books, which she placed standing up in the box so she could get to them without messing up her clothes, was *Helen's Babies*. Mr. John Habberton had written it in 1876 and the title went on and on: *Some Account of Their Ways, Innocent, Crafty, Angelic, Impish, Witching and Repulsive. Also a Partial Record of Their Actions During Ten Days of Their Existence, by Their Latest Victim.* The bachelor uncle's verdict on his small nephews—"Born to be hung, both of them!"—always sent Buddy into laughing fits. Maybe Belle and the other children would enjoy it.

Touching the beloved books, all of them written in by Mama, even the little Faultless Starch booklets, made Laurie feel a little better. Rosalie was nice and would certainly be glad of her help. There wasn't any question of being more than able to earn her and Buddy's keep. They wouldn't be taking charity. So far, Grandpa hadn't said a word to either of them. That suited Laurie fine.

At least it seemed likely that Rosalie wouldn't make her wear long stockings and suspenders, especially since she'd gotten rid of her old ones. The clean dress was wrinkled. Laurie shook it out as best she could and placed it on top of the muslin under-skirts, bloomers, and nightgowns Mama had sewn for her, two of each besides the underwear she had on.

That was all, except for her comb and toothbrush. . . . No, there was still the best thing of all except for Mama's lavaliere and the books! Morrigan's harmonica. She tucked it into a nightgown, just in case one of her "cousins" snooped.

Buddy had more keepsakes than she did: a rattlesnake's whispery transparent shed skin, the coyote's skull and coarse pelt, a bag of flints and arrowheads picked up around Point of Rocks. There was his trove of Big Little Books and a tobacco pouch of small treasures like his G-Man ring secret decoder and two boxes of .22 shorts. Buddy, so protective of his tiny lair, was going to miss it, but maybe he'd have enough fun with the boys to partly make up for the loss of his private kingdom.

Laurie didn't know what to do with the snakeskin but she stacked the thick, chunky little books from bottom to top on one side of the box and then put her brother's keepsakes on the other, placing on top his socks, underwear, other pair of over-alls, and two shirts. She folded the bird quilt neatly and put it at the bottom of the bed. Rosalie had taken charge of their other bedding except for the pillow and sheet Laurie would use that night. Sleeping with Belle wouldn't be so awful if Laurie could roll up in the quilt stitched by Mama's hands but she'd have to be careful not to get it dirty.

Now to find something to hold their toothbrushes, a jar or can. Rosalie's children never brushed their teeth but Mama had always been particular about that.

Going outside, Laurie was grateful that the hounds had gone with the boys and averted her eyes from the savaged rabbit. Thank goodness, there was a toilet. It buzzed with flies and spiders and had webs in several corners but Laurie was grateful for it. Holding her breath while she relieved herself, she got out of range of its smell and squinted in the hard, bright glare as she surveyed the surroundings.

Down by the rickety barn, the turning blades of the windmill caught the sun and creaked dolefully as it pumped water into a big, round metal watering tank. Would Grandpa let them get in there this summer to cool off? The corral with the tank opened to a pasture where five black-and-white Holstein cows rested under the only two trees in sight, drowsily watching three calves play king of the hill on a little slope, charging each other, heads down, their tails seeming almost as thick as their rangy legs.

A tractor and other machinery ranged outside the corral along with a truck so rusty there was no guessing its original color. Using the corral for its back fence was a good-sized garden with rows and hills of young plants. A sag-wired pen enclosed a chicken house and barren sand pecked over by a score of Rhode Island Red hens and a floppy-combed rooster. In the nearby pigpen, a big spotted hog slept beneath a tin roof extending from a rough shelter and a sow suckled squirming little piglets that showed pink through coarse white hair.

On all sides of this farmhouse center stretched planted fields that Laurie vaguely knew required a lot of work even before the cotton was picked or corn harvested. High above, a chicken hawk circled, hunting for a meal. Laurie hugged her arms close to her, a little cold in spite of the heat.

She wished her own grandfather didn't remind her of the bird of prey, especially since she was going to have to live with him a while. Oh, if Daddy could just find a place for them soon! Right now, with Mama dead and Daddy leaving, it was as if their family was blown like the dust, swept up from where it belonged and scattered by the winds. She'd hold tight to Buddy, though. As long as they stayed together, they were a still a *little* bit of a family.

There was a trash pile, mostly rusting tin cans and broken dishes, between the chicken pen and pigpen. Laurie hunted till she found a small cracked jar for the toothbrushes and went to the pump to wash it. She had to really throw her weight on the handle to bring it down, but after a few downward pushes, water gushed out, and she scrubbed the jar clean enough to use.

She was rinsing it when the crunch of steps made her turn. Daddy took off his hat and rubbed sweat from his forehead. "Laurie doll, I think I'm goin' to take off soon as Buddy gets back."

She gasped as if he'd hit her in the stomach and knocked the breath out of her. "Daddy—"

"I can get a hundred miles or so down the road before dark," he said hastily, looking away out over her head. He swallowed and put his hand on her shoulder. "Honey, the sooner I get to California, the sooner I can get work and send for you and Buddy."

Through the thin sleeve of her dress, his fingers didn't feel alive, or maybe it was her shoulder that was numb. The baked earth moved under her feet and her head went swimmy. Why did it matter, whether he left now or tomorrow? But it did. Tears squeezed from her eyes though she struggled not to make a sound.

"Bawlin' won't help." Daddy's tone roughened. "You're old enough to understand. I'll send for you kiddies as quick as I can. That's what you want, isn't it?"

She nodded, gulping, tasting the salt of the tears that had trickled to the edge of her mouth. "Rosalie's a nice woman,"

Daddy went on, "but she was brought up by worldly folks and Pa never set foot in a church in his life. It's up to you, Laurie, to make sure Buddy says his prayers every night, and on Sundays you can read a chapter out of your mother's New Testament." He did look at her then. His light blue eyes were wet. "You try to remember all the things your mother taught you, try to behave like she'd want you to, and teach Buddy."

"I—I'll try."

"That's Daddy's girl."

He hugged her and kissed her cheek but Laurie still felt as if she or he or both of them were made of wood or rock and their blood was drained away. She carried the jar inside and set it under the bed between her box and Buddy's. Somehow, when she put their toothbrushes in it, it made her feel more than anything else had that they didn't have a home. She reached blindly for the harmonica, gripped it tight, and ran out to the barn.

5

The barn was always cooler than the house and soothingly dusky. Besides two doors it only had one small window up in the hayloft through which a square of light gilded the fragrant cured hay. It was often Laurie's refuge as days ran into weeks and weeks into the months of that long summer.

The real refuge, of course, was John Morrigan's music, and the memory of that brief time, less than a day, when he'd made a difference to all of them but especially to her. She'd never forget the way his eyes changed or how he laughed or the things he'd said, but mostly she remembered him singing, made him as real as she could whether it was while she slapped at gnats and chopped weeds or when she woke, heart pounding, as the sun fell toward the earth, or when she missed Mama so bad that her insides weighed heavy as stone.

Practicing in the barn, sometimes tagged by Belle, she experimented with brushing her fingers over the reeds and the effects she could get with her tongue. She learned to play most of Morrigan's tunes well enough to be recognized and made up a few of her own, about how she felt every morning when she woke up and realized she wasn't in her own room, in her own home—that she'd never sleep there again. She hoped whoever rented the place was watering the cherry tree.

Several postcards had come from Daddy. Moving from one job to the next, he lived in the car and under a tarp stretched from its door to wherever he could fasten it. "Saving every dime I can," he scrawled. "If there's any five-dollar-a-day jobs, I ain't found them. Have met up with a nice family here, the Halsells, and I get my meals with them. Mind Rosalie, kiddies, and Laurie, you remember to read the New Testament to Buddy on Sundays. Not any use trying to write to me, we have to keep moving from one job to another."

A father you couldn't even write to or know where he was! It gave Laurie a queer, empty feeling. She did read the New Testament to Buddy, though he fidgeted impatiently except when she read about how John the Baptist was beheaded, or Herod had all the boy babies killed, or Jesus cast devils out of people and sent them into swine. She herself liked where Jesus comforted his friends by telling them that in his Father's house were many mansions and that he was going to prepare a place for them. Mama was in that place, really, not in the dust-blown grave on the plains.

As for taking refuge, there hadn't been much time for that, right from that afternoon in mid-May when Buddy and the boys came up to the house with four half-grown rabbits, and Daddy had kissed both his children, rubbed at his eyes, and driven off.

Before the dust cloud raised by the Model T had faded from sight, Grandpa said to his grandchildren, "Find a hoe that fits you and choose your row. Ev'rett, you show 'em how to cut the weeds under the ground good and get out all the roots."

They had learned. Learned to dig down to uncover the roots of the Johnson grass and pull every single little rootling out with the edge of the hoe so it wouldn't start another clump; learned to chop out the crabgrass without hitting a good plant, cotton or watermelon, peas, pumpkin, and corn; learned to chop down deep at the tender part of the careless weed roots, which could grow thick as her ankle, so tough a blade couldn't dent them. All the time the sun beat down, and if it wasn't gnats or blister bugs or great big horseflies making you miserable, it was grasshoppers whirring up from the leaves they'd been chewing full of holes, landing on your clothes or skin with their raspy feet, or tangling in your hair.

Sometimes they got inside the overalls Rosalie had bought Laurie for field work. She knew they couldn't bite or sting or do any real harm, but the scratch of their brittle bodies against her skin sent Laurie almost into fits. This delighted the boys, who added entertainment to their labor by sticking hoppers down her back till Rosalie put a stop to it.

Laurie was grateful for Rosalie, whose nature, like her body, was soft and comfortable till you pushed against the underlying bone and sinew. Rosalie seldom scolded or instructed her children, or interfered in their fusses, but when she did, they paid attention. From what Laurie could see, Rosalie had much the same attitude toward Grandpa and what she expected. Apparently she didn't grudge his spending money on tractors and such while she scrubbed out clothes on a washboard and lived in a tarpaper shack, but she insisted on keeping cows and chickens so there'd be milk and eggs for the children, and on the well-built cement storm cellar, which was stocked with water, canned food, and a lantern.

"I saw a tornado pick up a house and smash it down on some folks once," she said. "When one of them big black funnels comes twistin' out of the sky, I want a good place to run."

Rosalie was so different from Mama or anyone else Laurie had known that she spent considerable time puzzling over her. It was the first time Laurie had tried to understand a grown-up, what they did, what they felt, and most of all *why*. It seemed a little indecent and underhanded to be examining someone without their knowing, like peeking at them while they undressed, but it was like unraveling a mystery, looking for clues the way Nancy Drew did.

Rosalie didn't have nice furniture or curtains at the windows but she had a radio—with a loudspeaker so you didn't have to plug in earphones—on which she listened to "Stella Dallas" and "Our Gal Sunday." The whole family enjoyed "Fibber McGee and Mollie," the Carter Family's gospel singing, "Saturday Night Barn Dance," "Gangbusters," "Death Valley Days," and listening to Bing Crosby on the "Kraft Music Hall." After Grandpa was in bed, Rosalie loved to listen to Duke Ellington, Benny Goodman, Tommy Dorsey, or Wayne King. She especially loved Will Rogers.

"That's a good man," she told Laurie. "Hasn't got stuck up over gettin' rich and famous. He's raised scads of money for Dust Bowl folks and when there was an earthquake in Nicaragua, he flew down there and raised money for the ones that'd lost their homes. If he was president, this country would be in a lot better shape." That spurred her into saying that Pretty Boy Floyd, who'd come from her part of the state and been shot by lawmen the year before, wasn't as much a robber as the banks he'd held up. "At least Pretty Boy helped out a lot of poor families and he was better thought of and liked by folks who knew him than any governor Oklahoma had ever had, or any president of the U.S., either!"

Most of the time, though, Rosalie didn't fret about politics. She bought movie magazines and *True Story* and *True Confessions.* She had an ornate bottle of Evening in Paris perfume, which she was glad to share with Laurie and Belle, a spilled-over cake pan of Tangee lipsticks, powder, rouge, mascara, face creams, and Cutex nail polish, and she had earrings and necklaces and bracelets, shiny patent leather shoes with high heels and two good dresses, one of swingy, flowered, navy rayon, the other of yellow chiffon.

When she put on the low-cut chiffon for the Fourth of July, Grandpa caressed her bare arm and called her his sunflower. She laughed and kissed him full on the mouth.

The kiss wasn't a bit like the way Daddy and Mama kissed when he went to work or even when he came back from a haul to Colorado. It made Laurie blush and look away. She could hear the bedsprings creaking almost every night and knew Grandpa and Rosalie were doing what got babies. Because he was so much older—Rosalie was twenty-seven—it seemed wrong even if they were married. As pretty and young as Rosalie was, it looked like she'd hate to have the old man touch her, but there was no mistaking that she loved him, or that he cared for her, though he ignored his children except to give orders. The times Rosalie didn't go along when he took cream or eggs to town, he always handed her all the egg money and anything left from selling the cream after buying chicken feed and the few groceries they needed, and he never fussed over how she spent it.

About once a month, the whole family went to town. Laurie was stunned the first time at being given a whole shiny nickel to spend just like her cousins. Except when Rosalie had visited, Laurie had never gotten more than a penny at a time, and that not often, which was especially galling since Buddy had his rabbit money. He'd lost that income since Grandpa ruled that any rabbits shot belonged on the table. It was the only fresh meat they had except on the Fourth when Rosalie killed two old hens to fry up for their picnic. Side meat and a few jars of sausage were still left from the hog butchered last fall. It made Laurie feel a little queasy to know that the friendly spotted hog she fed every day would, on some cold November day, stop his eager hunting for morsels and become food himself. She tried not to think about it but she was sure she couldn't eat him.

Those wonderful nickels, though, would buy a double-dip ice-cream cone, a fizzy limeade or cherry Coke from the drugstore fountain, a Big Little Book, a package of chewing gum or pieces of Dubble Bubble, Life Savers, or you could pick from an array of candy bars—Baby Ruth, named for President Cleveland's daughter; Milky Way; Charleston Chew, named after the dance; Tootsie Rolls; and Hershey's. On Laurie's first trip to town, she stretched her nickel by getting a 3 Musketeers with three sections, vanilla, strawberry, and chocolate. She swapped Buddy the chocolate section and half the strawberry for the top dip of his ice-cream cone.

The nickel was only the start of the orgy. They got hamburgers with lots of sliced onions and dill pickles at a café, and then went to the Saturday afternoon movie. Laurie had a wrestle with her conscience over this. Movies were denounced by the tabernacle for being every bit as sinful as dancing, bobbing your hair, or smoking.

Buddy had no qualms. He marched right along with the boys and Belle. "Come on, honey," called Rosalie, hoisting Babe to her shoulder as she paused in the dark entrance.

"I-I—" Tempted but afraid—it was so dark in there, just like the mouth of hell—"Mama never let us."

Rosalie came back and got Laurie seated beside her on a bench out of the way of people going in. Her dark eyebrows puckered as she thought for a moment. "Listen, dear," she said at last. "I sure don't want to undermine what your Mama taught you, but you can't very well do everything she said all your life unless it grows out of your own heart and makes sense to you. For one thing, you're going to come up against things she won't have told you about. Now you know there are all kinds of churches and over the ocean, there's plumb different kinds of religion, but there has to be just one God. What do you suppose he thinks about all these rules folks make up for worshiping him, especially when they hate and kill each over the rules? My guess is it makes him pretty sad and disgusted."

"But people do bad things in the movies. They smoke and drink and lust and—"

"Laurie, do you know what lust is?"

Laurie flushed. "Not—not *exactly*. But it's when men and women want to do things with each other that they shouldn't till they're married."

"Mmm." Rosalie smothered a chuckle. "I reckon we'd better have a talk about all of that one of these days. But look, honey, there are books that have bad things in them, too. Your Mama never told you not to read, did she?"

"No, but—"

"To my way of thinkin', movies are the same way. Of course there are some you shouldn't see now and some you shouldn't see ever, prob'ly. But this afternoon—gracious, Laurie, besides the previews and newsreel, there's Donald Duck and Porky Pig cartoons, the main feature's *In Old Santa Fe* with that new singing cowboy star, Gene Autry, and the second feature is an Andy Hardy show with Mickey Rooney. Not a thing your Mama could worry about if she'd seen some movies for herself instead of taking her church's word that they're wicked." Rosalie paused. "Now I'm not tryin' to talk you into this. You can go to the library if you want, or over to the park. If you do come in, and they start showin' something you think is wrong, just get up and go and meet us outside when the show's over."

It was scary, doing something she'd been taught was sinful, but it was true that Mama had never seen a movie—and equally true that she'd have been scandalized had she known what was in some of the books Laurie had checked out of the library, especially those about Greek and Roman and Norse gods. But to use her own judgment instead of her mother's—oh, that made Laurie feel guilty and nervous and at the same time exhilarated as if she'd been breathing fresh, clean air real fast after having been shut up in a stale, musty closet.

I'll leave if they show anything bad, she assured herself, and followed Rosalie down the aisle just as light hit the screen. On her two other trips to town, apart from the Fourth of July, she'd seen *King Kong* and a dancing couple named Fred Astaire and Ginger Rogers in *Flying Down to Rio*. Mama wouldn't have approved of the dancing but it was beautiful to watch and again Laurie couldn't see what was wrong about it.

She had never been able to even get saved and now she fatalistically concluded that since she couldn't go to heaven anyway, she might as well enjoy what was lovely and fun in this world—though of course she wouldn't do anything against her conscience. This line of thought was probably what Mama would have called "hardening the heart" and maybe Laurie's would wind up tough as a football, but losing herself in the world on the screen made her forget for a little while that Mama was dead and Daddy had left them.

Among the differences between Mama and Rosalie was how they used money. In the Field household, one-tenth, the tithe, would go to the tabernacle first thing of all, because it was God's. Then came food, the rent, light bill, doctor, and the most necessary clothing. If there was anything left after that, and in

Laurie's memory there'd never been a time when at least one of the family wasn't in desperate need of shoes, the children got a penny to spend and Mama might slip a few coins in her "home" box.

This was a syrup tin with a slit in the top that set on top of the little tablet Mama used to write letters. She used it for another purpose, too, as Laurie found out when she was packing. Daddy must have added the coins to his money because the tin was empty but when Laurie glanced through the tablet, she found the back pages filled with plans of the home Rachel had silently longed for.

There was a sketch of the whole house, with both vegetable and flower gardens and trees, and drawings of each room with furniture marked in. A room each for Laurie and Buddy; a big kitchen with a Frigidaire and real sink; a screened-in porch with a washing machine and closet for cleaning supplies and the ironing board; a small dining room with a china cabinet and the round table; and a living room with big overstuffed armchairs, a radio, Victrola, library table with a globe; and a spare room. It was unthinkable to have a room that went unused except when there was company so this one had a daybed and dresser and housed a sewing machine and dress form. One door opened to the bathroom, which of course served everyone. A real bathroom with toilets like those at school, a sink, and tub.

"White linoleum," Mama's girlish handwriting detailed. "Blue curtains. White and blue striped wallpaper and blue towels and bath mat."

This glimpse of Rachel, wistful for nice things like any woman though she had never complained, stabbed Laurie then and still did. It gave her a quick flash of Mama as something other than dauntingly good with her heart and mind completely bent on heaven. It made Mama a real person who had wanted a nice home with indoor plumbing and a Frigidaire and washing machine.

Now she could never have them. No matter what Laurie did, even if she somehow won a million dollars, she couldn't give Mama anything, never in this world. Wrestling with this final part of death was what hurt worst, realizing that Mama would never smile again or see the cherry tree bloom or sit with Laurie in the night to vanquish nightmares.

Laurie burned the tablet out by the cherry tree and buried the ashes there, deep, so they wouldn't blow away. It was a private grave for the woman who'd had secret, human dreams and longings, who had lived inside the wife, mother, and Christian in the cemetery. When grief about this overwhelmed Laurie, she slipped to the barn at her first chance and played Morrigan's harmonica.

He had given her songs for every need, and his voice resonated within her as she played the Negro spirituals that seemed to hold all the sorrow in the world along with the will to endure.

No more weepin', no more weepin',
No more weepin' after while,
And before I'll be a slave,
I'll be buried in my grave,
And go home to my Lord and be free.

She sang, too, when she was doing dishes or ironing, any work that didn't need concentration, and soon Belle was singing along with her. *"Goin' to lay down my sword and shield, down by the riverside, down by the riverside . . ."*

"Honey, why don't you ever play your harmonica in the house?" Rosalie asked one day. "I heard you when I was feeding the chickens. It sure sounds pretty."

Laurie colored. "I-I'm just learning the best I can," she stammered. "And you've got the radio and Victrola with lots better music than I can make."

"It's not the same." Rosalie gave a decided shake of her head. "Sure, I'm glad to have the radio and hear Will Rogers and the good singers and have records with Louie Armstrong and Cow Cow Davenport and Jeanette MacDonald and Nelson Eddy. But it's not the same as having someone real playing."

"Grandpa—"

"He won't pay you any more mind than he does the radio except when one of his favorite programs is on. Of course if you really don't want to—"

Rosalie sounded so disappointed that Laurie said quickly, "All right, I'll play the tunes I know the best, but remember, you asked for it!"

Rosalie laughed and hugged her, making Laurie ashamed that she'd instinctively wanted to keep Morrigan's songs to herself, a special bond between them. He shared his music. He'd want her to, even though her playing wasn't anything as good as his. So now, in the hottest part of the day after dinner and dishes, she often played for a little while, before they went out to battle weeds.

They could hack out the roots of crabgrass, careless weed, and Johnson grass, but they couldn't make it rain. It was so dry that the plants began to look wilted even in the mornings. Rosalie said that happened when the roots sucked moisture from the plant because there wasn't any left in the soil. All anyone could do was get out the weeds with their roots that went deeper than those of the cotton and bank up earth against the plants to protect any tiny bit of dampness from wind and sun.

The blisters on Laurie's hands had long ago hardened to calluses and the soles of her feet were baked so tough by the scorching sand that she didn't, as she had at first, try to cool them in the shade of plants. Her back and shoulders and wrists still ached, though. She didn't think she'd ever attain the steady methodical way that Rosalie, wearing an old straw hat and one of Grandpa's shirts to cover her arms, swung the hoe and edged up the roots from right beside those of a crop plant.

Still, what tasted better than roasting ears fresh from the stalk, juicy gold kernels dripping with butter? Or the crisp red flesh of a watermelon cooled in the big trough in the well house? Or, starting the season of bounty from field and garden, marble-sized new potatoes and tender peas blending flavors in rich, white cream sauce? Luscious tomatoes, string beans, crunchy radishes, carrots, cucumbers, crook-necked summer squash, and blue-green collards continued to come from the garden long after green onions and lettuce succumbed to the blasting heat, but how tasty that lettuce had been wilted with hot grease and vinegar and served with scrambled eggs!

66

Laurie had never eaten so well nor been so hungry by meal-
times. When more vegetables were ripe than could be eaten,
Laurie helped Rosalie can jar after mason jar to carry to the
cellar and store on shelves that ran around all sides, floor to
ceiling. The sight of rows of sparkling jars filled Laurie with
pride and made the hours of steamy work seem worth it.

Not that she wanted to eat this food. She still prayed silently
each night when she knelt with Buddy that Daddy would send
for them right away—at least before school started. Lots of kids
spent summers with aunts and uncles and grandparents but
when school started you should be with your real family in your
real home.

One afternoon when Laurie was snapping stems off beans
and pulling off the tough strings that ran from end to end before
breaking them into several pieces, Rosalie stared at the front of
her overalls. It had hung loose nearly three months ago, but
from little pinkish-tan nubs on a flat chest, Laurie's breasts had
started to round, and the seat of the overalls fit so tight that it
pinched when she bent over. She had let out the straps as much
as she could but she was just plain outgrowing the garment. At
least it wouldn't go to waste. Everett could wear it next summer,
if not before.

"Gracious, child!" said Rosalie. "You're bustin' right out of
those overalls! Better try on your dresses tonight to see if we can
make them do for school. Now, honey, did your Mama tell you
about how you'll bleed once a month when you're able to make
babies?"

At Laurie's stare of horror, Rosalie somehow managed to
give her a comforting hug without touching her with hands and
fingers stained from scalding and peeling tomatoes. "Don't
look so scared, dear. You can't make babies without a man."
She sobered and seemed to be speaking almost to herself. "Depending on the man and how it happens, that can be the loveli-
est, sweetest thing in the world, or it can be the ugliest."

Simply, encouraging Laurie to ask about anything that puzzled or troubled her, Rosalie said the monthly flow of blood
carried off the egg that didn't have a baby starting in it. "When
a man wants a woman, his thing gets hard so it can push up

inside her and leave his sperm—kind of seeds—where it can find her egg. This don't always mean a baby'll grow, but there's a chance. A man can put on a rubber—sort of a close-fitting bag—to hold his sperm, but rubbers can leak or break so it's not as safe as some boys will try to tell you. Nothing really is, so don't let a boy do anything to you, no matter how he begs and promises, till you're sure he's the one you're going to marry. Best thing's to wait till you're married. Otherwise, he might change his mind—decide you're not fit for him to marry, even when he's the one who made you not fit."

"That's not fair!"

" 'Course it's not," said Rosalie practically. "No more than what's just fun for the man may start a baby in a woman. But since that's the way it is, a girl needs to be mighty careful. And don't think that because a man's old enough to be your daddy that he don't mean anything by pettin' and huggin' you."

Grandpa's old enough to be your father, Laurie thought. As if she guessed what Laurie was thinking, Rosalie blushed to the edges of her dark hair. She slipped the skin off another tomato and straightened her shoulders.

"I know you've wondered why I married your grandpa and why I think so much of him." She continued her work with her back to Laurie. "This isn't nice, honey, but I reckon you need to know the kind of stuff that can happen. My real daddy died before I can remember. The man I called daddy was my stepfather, no blood relation. By the time I was Belle's age, he—he was doin' things. He said he'd kill me if I told Mama. When I was fourteen, I told him I'd kill him if he didn't stop." She gave a harsh little laugh. "I guess he believed me. I was so ashamed and felt so dirty inside, so different from the other girls. I quit school when I finished eighth grade and got out of that house, but I couldn't get what happened out of me. I tried, though. I sure tried, but what I tried and the ones I tried with made it worse. I wasn't fifteen years old but I was spendin' every cent I earned waitin' tables on rotgut whiskey so I could forget what a mess I'd made of my life."

She turned to look at Laurie. "Harry came in one day—just sat and watched me while he ate and drank three or four cups of coffee. When the noon rush thinned out, he asked me if I wouldn't like to go home with him. That's what he said—*home."* She drew a quivering breath and her smile was blinding as she glanced toward Laurie. "It was like he was my real daddy mixed in with a man who could make me feel clean and new and pretty again, get rid of all the ugliness. I don't know how he saw what I needed but it was the luckiest thing ever happened to me that he did and that somehow I knew I should go with him. Hadn't been for him, I'd be dead by now or a worn-out whore."

Rosalie set another jar in the big kettle and started to fill another. "So don't you feel sorry for some guy who tells you how bad he hurts when he can't finish his lovemakin' or says you don't love him if you won't go all the way. If he loved *you,* seein' how much you've got to lose, he wouldn't try to talk you into it."

Struck by the wisdom of this, Laurie nodded. Rosalie reached for another tomato. "In three-four years when Ev'rett starts gettin' ideas, I'm goin' to set him down and give him a good talking to. I'm tellin' him not to go with any girl he doesn't care enough about to marry, because if he ever gets one in the family way, he's goin' to do just that, no matter what kind of reputation she's got. That's what I'm tellin' all my boys." She grinned. "Of course, Harry'll explain to 'em about rubbers and all those bad diseases they can catch, so with any luck, they won't get a girl in trouble."

About a week later, while the family was picking plums along the North Fork of the Red River, twinges began in Laurie's stomach that increased to real pains. She'd been eating the ripest, juiciest red fruit. Maybe she'd been such a hog that she'd gorged herself into a stomachache.

It was steamy hot among the sandy dunes of the river bottom, with cottonwoods and reeds and willows cutting off any stray breeze. She kept picking into the milk bucket she shared with Belle and Rosalie, but her head throbbed and the pains got so bad that she was afraid she might have appendicitis. Appendixes were sneaky, mysterious things that could swell up and burst and kill you, the way Mama's Aunt Ida's had done.

Frightened as she was, Laurie didn't want to complain or ask if they could go home. That would call Grandpa's attention to her, something she preferred not to do because he'd probably say she was sickly like her mother. Grandpa must have been nice to the scared, despairing Rosalie of twelve years ago, and still was in his gruff way, but it seemed like he'd used up all his kindness on her.

At last four buckets were filled. Under the shade of a big cottonwood, where a plum-stained Babe napped on a tattered quilt, they spread an old tarp and poured out a mountain of fruit.

"Ripest go in these two buckets." Rosalie set one at either end of the tarp. "Fairly ripe in this one, and greenish in the other. Wormy ones—" She chuckled. "Eat 'em or throw 'em away, whichever you've a mind to." Her gaze swept over the children, then fixed on Laurie. "What's the matter, dear? You're lookin' puny."

"I—" Grandpa's green eyes swung to Laurie and she blurted, "I must have eaten too many plums."

Rosalie touched her forehead. "You're clammy-cool, honey. Could be on your way to sunstroke. Drink some water, not too much, and lay down there on the quilt."

Laurie sipped lukewarm water from a jar. She felt so dizzy and weak that she would have shared the quilt with Babe even though the little girl's diaper needed changing, except that Grandpa said, "Rachel was like that. Wilted in heat like a chopped-off weed. That's one reason, on top of the dust, that Ed had to quit farmin'. Rachel couldn't stand up to the work."

"Ed!" chided Rosalie. "You go along, honey, and rest. Anybody can get too much heat on a day like this."

"I'm all right." Laurie gritted her teeth and began sorting plums. She worked till the last fruit was in a bucket and then ran off to vomit in the cover of some willows. During the dusty, bumpy ride to the farm in the back of the truck, she struggled not to get sick again.

Rosalie marched her inside, made her lie down on the sofa, washed her face and arms and neck, and had Buddy fetch her a drink. "Better now?"

"I think so," Laurie whispered. "But—it—it feels like great big thumbs are digging at my insides—kind of twisting. Rosalie, do you think my appendix is getting ready to bust?"

A sudden gleam brightened Rosalie's eyes. Glancing around to make sure no one was in earshot, she said, "I'll bet you're about to have your period, honey. Has there been any blood on your bloomers today?"

Laurie felt herself going crimson. "I don't know."

"Well, you look next time you go to the toilet. Lots of times it starts with a lot of cramping and precious little blood but it usually doesn't hurt much after the first day or so. I never had any trouble at all after Ev'rett came though I cramped something fierce till I left home and what was happenin' there." Smoothing Laurie's hair, she smiled. "I know you feel plenty warm but a hot-water bottle's what you need right now, and some ginger tea."

Whether it was the bottle, tea, or hope that the pains were natural, Laurie soon felt well enough to help fix supper. That evening her bloomers were streaked with blood. When she got Rosalie aside and told her, Rosalie looked both relieved and sorry. After she showed Laurie where she kept her blue box of Kotex and gave her an elastic belt with hooks, Rosalie kissed her and held her close.

"You can make a baby now, honey, and that's about the most important thing in the world, but don't you get in a hurry. Let your heart and mind catch up with your body."

Another world had ended.

6

Why didn't Daddy send for them? For weeks there hadn't been a card. They didn't even know where he was. Laurie's anxiety was heightened when Will Rogers and Wiley Post crashed their plane in Alaska on August 15. If an important, famous, good man like Will could die so suddenly, so senselessly, anybody could.

When school started and Daddy hadn't written, Laurie despaired of joining him before next summer—and by then she was afraid they could never be a family again. Buddy ran wild with his cousins when they weren't chopping weeds. He wouldn't say his night prayers anymore or listen to her read from the New Testament on Sunday because the other boys teased him, and he wouldn't brush his teeth, even when Laurie reminded him how important Mama said that was. If they stayed another year—well, Buddy would belong more to Grandpa than to Daddy, to Grandpa who hadn't liked Mama and who never missed a chance, in spite of Rosalie's shushing, to make some slighting remark about her poor health, what he called her "per'nicketiness," or her religion.

The week before school started, Rosalie had Laurie try on her two dresses. She could scarcely wriggle into them but Rosalie, after some study, thought wide gussets under the arms would solve the problem for a few months and if the hems were let out all the way, they'd *almost* cover her knees.

"Rickrack'll hide the old hemlines," Rosalie said. "But you're goin' to have a new dress for the first day of school, honey, and so's Belle. You can pick out the material when we go to town Saturday to get shoes and schoolbooks."

Before that expedition, there was a great sorting of last year's books. Only Everett and Laurie would need "new" secondhand ones since Ernie's second-grade texts went to Buddy and his first-grade books, much worn after having been handed down by Everett and Billy, had been saved for Belle, who was somewhat consoled for the tattered condition of her primer and speller by the promise of the biggest box of crayons in the store.

Rosalie judged, after pinching to see if the prospective owner's toes had room, that new heels, half-soles, and some stitching would allow handing down of all the boys' shoes except for Ernie's, which had already been worn by Billy. That meant that Everett, Laurie, and Belle got shoes—and also that there were no movies or hamburgers that Saturday. Rosalie had emptied all her egg and cream money into her purse but she didn't buy any magazines and the children got a penny each instead of a nickel.

"Please, I don't need a dress," Laurie told Rosalie when urged to pick from the array of many-colored bolts in the dry-goods store. She bit her lip, lowering her eyes. "Daddy hasn't sent any money. You shouldn't have to dress us on top of everything else."

"Don't talk silly," Rosalie adjured. "You've worked like a full-grown woman all summer. By rights, we'd be payin' you on top of board, and some board it is, sleepin' with Belle's feet in your face! You pick something out or I will. This blue-green sateen print would just match your eyes."

Touching the lustrous cloth with its peacock-feather pattern, Laurie gave in. It was the prettiest dress she'd ever had, with puffed sleeves, a ruffled neck, and a flounced skirt to which another flounce could be added as she grew, and Rosalie had bought her two pairs of the long-desired anklets for school. No more ugly mustard-colored long cotton stockings!

In spite of the new dress and shoes and anklets, though, Laurie's stomach was a tight knot as they set off on the two-mile trudge to school with their books and lunches in lard cans. Laurie had packed their lunches, a boiled egg apiece, bread and jelly, and molasses cookies. The boys all ran ahead so Laurie arrived with Belle, who started crying when they came in sight of the building.

"I wanta go home!"

"Well, you can't," Laurie said roughly, to herself as much as to the whimpering little girl.

"I-I'm goin' to wet my pants!"

"You run to the toilet," Laurie ordered. "It's the closest one. I'll take your books."

Belle streaked for the privy that had GIRLS painted on the door. There weren't any trees or cover between it and the BOYS twenty feet away, and the playground, with a couple of swings and a teeter-totter, was between the two-room frame schoolhouse and the toilets.

How awful, to have to go to the building with the boys watching! Worse, at recess, there'd probably be a line. Laurie resolved to try to only go once a day, during lunch hour, when the boys might be too busy playing to notice. Belle emerged nervously from the toilet and stood there as if the boys playing crack-the-whip were cannibals.

"Belle!" Laurie called in exasperation. She had to go take the child by the hand. "Don't be a baby! You won't be the only one in first grade. Just remember to go to the toilet at recess and lunch. Look, there's the teacher! Doesn't she look nice?"

"I—I like Mama better!"

"Of course you do, silly, but you have to go to school so you won't be an ignorant heathen or go in the wrong toilet because you can't read the sign." As she urged Belle toward the school, Laurie wished she could run away herself.

Three girls who looked close to her age were chattering and laughing. The blond one in a pretty pink dress with matching hair ribbon and anklets pointed to her and said loud enough for Laurie to hear, "That one's an orphant who's living at her grandpa's. He's one of Pa's croppers."

"Hope she won't sit next to me," said a pig-tailed redhead. "Mother says croppers lots of times give you head lice and the itch."

Burning with mortification, Laurie pretended not to hear. There had been a few sharecropper children in school at Prairie- ville. It had always been some consolation that poor as the Fields were, they weren't croppers. Now even that was gone. The hardest thing she'd ever done was to walk into the school.

"You're a new pupil?" The teacher's black hair was bobbed and her sharp black eyes, quick motions, and the way she kept her head tilted reminded Laurie of an inquisitive bird. "Do you have last term's report card?"

"Yes, miss, and I have my brother's too."

"I'm *Mrs.* Evans. Call me that or 'ma'am.' "

Laurie dipped her head, fumbling for the cards tucked in her reader. "Yes, Mrs. Evans. And Belle here, she's starting school this fall."

Mrs. Evans scanned the cards. "Kansas," she sniffed. "Al- most Yankees. Well, we'll have to see where you fit here. Ac- cording to this, you're ready for seventh grade, but since you're the only one, you'll have to either do eighth-grade work or drop back to sixth. Your brother's grades aren't very good. I'll begin him in third but if he can't keep up, he'll have to take second over."

"He'll keep up," Laurie promised. Buddy didn't like school anyway. If he were put back a grade, he'd completely quit trying.

"Put your lunches on the shelf at the back and find desks that aren't taken," said the teacher. She jerked the rope that rang the bell that hung from a crossbar on the roof and a swarm of children streamed into the room.

Some were smaller than Belle but the two biggest boys were taller than the teacher. They sat in the largest desks at the back of the room. The girls Laurie had overheard slid into desks in front of the boys. After she saw Belle settled in one of the little desks at the front, Laurie took the only empty large desk, which was across the aisle from the girls. She tried to control her anxiety by counting the students and looking for someone with whom she might be able to make friends.

Her heart sank as she saw that the only girls near her age were those who'd talked as if croppers were some kind of animals. Most of the twenty children looked to be about the ages of Everett and his brothers. Several of the boys didn't have shoes and wore heavily patched overalls. They were sure to be croppers, but if they had sisters, they were among the younger girls.

Laurie's hope that her new dress, shoes, and anklets would make her acceptable withered like a plant in the blasting sun. The girls across the aisle were all friends. One of their fathers owned the land Grandpa farmed, even the tarpaper house, and they thought croppers had lice and itch. There were no possible friends here and it was clear that the teacher didn't like having two more cropper children in her school. The knot of misery tightened in Laurie's chest.

If only Daddy had taken them with him! Whatever California was like, it had to be better than this! Of course she was used to not fitting in at school. Those long stockings and belonging to the tabernacle had made her different in Prairieville, but she'd gone to school with mostly the same children since first grade, and she had a definite place, as they all did. Hers was as the smartest, poorest kid in the class who wore long stockings because of her religion. Thinking of her class back in Prairieville deepened Laurie's misery, though she wouldn't want to live there now, not without Mama.

Woodenly, Laurie stood up with the others and mumbled the Pledge of Allegiance to the Flag. Then they sang "My Country 'Tis of Thee" and "Dixie" before Mrs. Evans called the roll, separated a few of the boys who had already begun to whisper, and told everyone to study their readers and then work the arithmetic problems on the pages that she'd write on the blackboard for each class.

Except for three first-graders, Buddy and Laurie were the only new pupils. Mrs. Evans called Buddy to the recitation bench at the front and frowned as he stumbled along in the third reader. After a few minutes, she said curtly, "You'll be in second reader. Go to the board and work some problems."

Head hanging, Buddy seemed to shrink as the sharp voice rapped out subtraction and addition. Laurie was sure he knew most of the answers he now got wrong. No wonder, having to stand up at the board right after being set back in reading!

"You'll be in the second grade," Mrs. Evans ruled. "Take your seat now and study this second reader."

Poor Buddy! His mouth trembled and he kept his brown head ducked as he took the reader and went back to his seat. Laurie scourged herself for not having made him study that summer. When they hadn't been working, he'd gone off with the boys, but she should have just made time to get out his old books and drill him.

"Laura Field!"

It took Laurie a moment to realize that she was being summoned. Instead of the seventh reader Rosalie had bought for her, she was handed the teacher's eighth-grade reader. As she finished the third page without making any mistakes, Mrs. Evans snapped, "That'll do. Go to the board."

She gave Laurie long division, fractions, and decimals and finally shrugged. "You will start in eighth. If you can't keep up, you'll be back in sixth."

Dismissed to her seat, Laurie saw the startled looks on the faces of the landlord's daughter and her friends change to annoyance. They'd have had more use for her if she'd been stupid. At recess, Laurie was glad to see that Belle was being tugged to the swings by another little girl and Buddy had joined in a game of red rover. His setback might weigh on him but the other boys didn't care so long as he was tough and quick in playing. The four biggest boys played softball, monopolizing the center of the dusty playground.

Sylvia Hart, the blond landlord's daughter, strolled arm in arm with her friends, pig-tailed Bonnie MacAfee and Janice Redmond, whose lower jaw thrust so far forward that it gave her a bulldog look. Though she was in sixth grade and Janice in eighth, Sylvia was plainly queen of the school just as her older brother, Dan, led the boys. His fair hair, eyebrows, and eyelashes, were bleached silver and he had pale green eyes. The only boy who wore Levi's and boots instead of overalls, he had, according to enviously teasing remarks, driven Sylvia and Bonnie to school in the new red truck parked at the edge of the playground.

Too old for the swings, Laurie walked along the edge of the clearing, pretending great interest in the sunflowers, purple gayfeather, and rust and orange Indian blanket that bloomed in a swath of uncut buffalo grass stretching between the schoolgrounds and surrounding fields of cotton. A meadowlark winged up, yellow breast catching the light, and bees hummed at the violet flowers of tall owl clover. The grass rippled in the wind, now rosy, now lightest, softest green.

Daddy had told her that much of the prairie had still been like this when he was a boy before the war. Far as the eye could see, the different kinds of grasses stretched, grama and bluestem and buffalo grass, and in spring, the buffalo wallows were spangled with flowers, black-eyed Susans, lilylike wild onions, Johnny-jump-ups, and daisies.

In hard years, Daddy had picked up buffalo bones around those wallows and in the draws and sold them in Dodge City, where they were shipped east to make buttons and corset stays. Daddy had never seen a wild buffalo but twenty-five years before he was born, they had covered the plains from Canada to Mexico. Grandpa had been Buddy's age when his parents came to homestead in western Kansas in 1873, the year of the greatest slaughter. Great-grandfather had become a skinner to earn some cash money. By the next year, only a few scattered beasts were left on the southern plains, though those in the north lasted a while.

Along with the herds vanished the Plains Indians' whole way of life—food, shelter, clothing, and household goods. Their world had ended, just as the farmers' world was now blowing away in the dust of those once grassy, flower-scented prairies. Only here and there was a patch left. Like this one.

Laurie closed her eyes, imagining. That grass and flowers covered all the broken, ruined powdery earth, the cotton and wheat fields and all the plowed land; that great-humped buffalo roamed the gentle slopes, pronghorn antelope skimmed them, and no house or fence or road or town broke the sweep of a prairie vast as the sky, free as the wind.

She would never see it. But she opened her eyes to this small strip, this one piece of deep-rooted, lasting sod. Maybe someday people would let it grow back, reclaim the pulverized ground. Maybe—

The bell pealed harshly. Laurie tried to capture the little prairie in her mind, take it inside with her. As she turned, she saw Belle trotting from the GIRLS. Thirsty though she was, Laurie didn't fill her tin cup from the dipper when she went inside. She had to hold out till noon or undergo the humiliation of holding up the three fingers that Mrs. Evans told them would signify that they needed to be excused to go to the privies. Only one child could go at a time, she warned, and anyone who hadn't taken advantage of recess and lunchtimes would stay in and study fifteen minutes for each time they asked to go out.

Janice, Dan, and sandy-haired, flat-nosed Bob Matlock were the other eighth graders. They had reading and spelling before recess, studying at their desks when not called forward to perform for Mrs. Evans, and then worked arithmetic problems till noon.

The lunch period was an hour. Belle and the littler girls took their buckets to the swings. Loitering with the younger boys on the grassy plot around the pump, Buddy seemed to have forgotten his humiliation. Dan and his cronies sat in the truck and Sylvia's trio occupied the steps while Mrs. Evans brought her chair out on the small cement porch and lunched while keeping an eye on her students.

Rosalie said that she was the wife of a small independent farmer who was struggling to pay his mortgage. She certainly didn't seem to enjoy teaching and Laurie was sure that you could determine the standing of each child's family by the way the teacher spoke to him or her. It wasn't surprising that she smiled oftenest on Sylvia and Dan. Their father was president of the school board that hired the teacher, oversaw her work, and paid her salary.

Laurie carried her lunch to the little prairie and sat down in the grass next to sunflowers that were as tall as she was and cast nodding bits of shade. This was how it was going to be, she knew, with a bitter taste in her mouth. She'd been silly to think the new dress and anklets might make a difference. There wasn't going to be anyone to walk or talk or play with.

She told herself severely that if she had liked Sylvia or Janice or Bonnie, it would have been a whole lot worse. As it was, she'd keep out of their way and study hard so she could do the eighth-grade work better than Dan and the others and have at least that satisfaction. She hated to tell Rosalie that she couldn't use the seventh-grade books and needed texts for the eighth.

If only Daddy had at least sent enough money for books and shoes! Rosalie was nice but Grandpa behaved like they were beggars in spite of all the work they did. It wasn't right of Daddy to leave them here. Mama wouldn't have let him, not for a minute. . . .

That thought brought a guilty rush of other things Mama wouldn't have allowed—anklets, puffed short sleeves, movies, reading Rosalie's magazines. In a crushing flood of grief, of longing for her mother, for the way they used to be a family, Laurie fought back tears.

She'd gladly never see another movie or magazine, gladly wear the hated long stockings, if Mama could be alive again. All the rest of her life, there would be that big empty place, there would be that tablet with Mama's dreams of a nice house, the tormenting knowledge that Mama would never have a set of Blue Willow dishes, a washing machine, a soft, warm, new coat to replace the threadbare maroon one.

Laurie swallowed hard and blinked. She mustn't cry. Her eyes would be red and that nasty Sylvia would think it was because of her. Laurie gazed at a swaying purple-red gayfeather and Morrigan's voice filled her the way it did, all of her, not just her mind. *"You've got to walk that lonesome valley, you got to walk it by yourself. . . ."*

No, I don't, she thought, chin going up. *You're with me in that valley, Morrigan. You and your songs, you're always with me.* She got up then and marched to the privy like a soldier, ignoring the whistles and laughter of the boys in the truck.

That afternoon, as her class was called to the front for geography, Danny crowded her so that the front of his Levi's pressed against her hip. "Gettin' some titties on you, cropper girl?" he whispered, staring down the front of her dress. "I'll squeeze 'em for you to make 'em grow."

Bob Matlock heard and laughed. Janice heard, too, but instead of frowning at the boys, she gave Laurie a look of disgust. As they sat down, she pulled her skirt away so it wouldn't touch Laurie's. Mrs. Evans didn't seem to notice and Laurie suspected that even if she had, she wouldn't reprimand the son of her most important patron.

In geography, as in her other subjects, Laurie discovered that she knew as much or more than her classmates. This didn't please Mrs. Evans, since it cast a suspicion that her teaching wasn't as effective as that of Laurie's Kansas teacher.

On the way back to their desks, Dan pushed against Laurie again. Ready for him this time, she brought her heel up between his legs. Crowded as she was, she didn't kick him very hard but he yelped and swore, grabbing at Laurie, who dodged him.

"Laurie Field!" shrilled Mrs. Evans. "What are you doing?"

"Dan bumped into me," Laurie said.

"That's not what it sounded like. You'll stay in at recess and dust out the erasers and wash the blackboard."

Dan didn't physically molest Laurie after that but he missed no chance to whisper dirty suggestions. Laurie never mentioned this persecution to Rosalie. A cropper complain to the teacher or school board about the landlord and board president's son? What would happen if in a year or two he forcibly did to her the things he whispered about? It was pretty clear that no one except Rosalie would care or believe it wasn't her fault. If Daddy knew how awful it was here, surely, surely, he'd send for them, but Laurie didn't know where to write to him.

She made flash cards to drill Buddy in addition and subtraction but he fussed and complained and said she wasn't his mother or the boss of him. At a scold from Rosalie, he sulkily gave answers but it was clear that being set back had quenched the little enthusiasm he'd had for study. That made him fit in perfectly with the boys of his age and since the other first-graders were from cropper families, Belle had made friends and now prattled eagerly all the way to and from school.

Laurie's salvation was the little prairie, remembering Morrigan and his music, and study. She soon read her way through the small school library and, grudgingly, Mrs. Evans exchanged these books for different ones from the county library. The teacher had been nicer to Laurie since Laurie offered to help the first- and second-graders with their lessons. She worked with Belle at home anyway, and this was one way of making sure Buddy learned a little.

The first cotton bolls ripened by mid-September. After school and on weekends, the children joined Grandpa and Rosalie in the fields. Laurie had a full-size ducking sack and dragged it along the row by the wide strap slung over her shoulder. Belle had her own small sack, which she'd been given last summer. Before then, she told Laurie, she'd picked into a lard bucket and dumped it into Rosalie's bag. The boys had bags of varying sizes. Babe played or slept on a blanket at the end of the field and Rosalie picked in sight of her so that if the child woke, she could be tended to, or brought to ride along on her mother's sack.

Even through canvas gloves, the tough, pointed bolls rasped Laurie's hands. Where all the bolls on a stalk were ready, splitting to show white fluff, you could clean it quickly by placing both hands on the stalk and pulling upward. Most of the stalks, though, had only a few ripe bolls. On windy days, and nearly every day was windy, Laurie learned to pick fast till she got enough weight in the bag to keep it on the ground. Otherwise, a gust might send it billowing like a sail, spilling what was in it and almost hauling Laurie off her feet.

Sometime in November or early December, all the cropper children would stay out of school to pull cotton. It would be the end of January before the last sack was weighed and sent to the gin. Naturally, the kids got way behind with their lessons. It was no wonder some of them stayed in the same grade for two or three years and that most never considered going to high school.

So there you had your next bunch of croppers, Laurie thought, as she dragged her full sack to the scales. Not able to get a better job because they don't have an education and not able to get an education because of this kind of work.

Buddy wasn't going to grow up like this. His natural dislike of school was made worse by his cousins' similar feelings but Mama had wanted both her children to finish high school and Laurie was determined that they would—or at least that they wouldn't be sharecroppers.

Grandpa weighed her sack and jotted "50" on the notepad weighted down by a root. After emptying the bolls into the trailer that would haul the load to the gin, Grandpa tossed the sack at her without a smile, a word, or anything. She might as well have been a machine, and she supposed that was how he felt about everyone except Rosalie and perhaps Belle and Babe.

Dust stung Laurie's face and the sack blew upwards, buffeting her. She dragged it down and began to pop bolls. What was that song of Morrigan's, almost a jig?

Jump down, turn around, pick a bale of cotton,
Jump down, turn around, pick a bale a day—

Oh Lordy, pick a bale of cotton,
Oh Lordy, pick a bale a day.

It was mid-October when a letter came from Daddy. Laurie held her breath while Grandpa tore it open. *Let him send for us. Oh, Mama, help him do that.* Before Grandpa read the letter, he unrolled three one-dollar bills that were folded in the sheet of tablet paper. Laurie's heart plunged. That wasn't enough for train tickets—wasn't enough for much of anything! Grandpa thought so, too. He scowled at the bills and put them in his wallet before handing the letter to Rosalie.

"You read it, wife. You're a sight better at figgerin' out Ed's hen-tracks than I am."

Daddy might write and spell better if you'd have let him go to school past fourth grade, Laurie thought. It was just like Grandpa to blame Daddy when the truth was that Harry Field could barely read and never wrote letters at all. Puckering her eyebrows, Rosalie read slowly:

Dear Pa, Rosalie, and Children,

I am sorry that I am still not fixed to send for the kiddies. Cut my hand so bad I almost lost it and for three weeks I could not work. That and the doc I had to see when the cut got infected took all the money I had. But I am working now and, kiddies, I hope the good Lord will help me earn enough to buy your train tickets and have a fit place for you to live by spring so we can be together then the way your mother would want.

Rosalie, this isn't much but maybe it will help buy the kiddies' school shoes and school books. Pa, if you will get them what they need, I will pay you back with interest. Kiddies, you earn your keep and always act the way your mother taught you. It's getting dark. No electric lights in this fancy hotel (hah) so I will close, open up a can of pork-and-beans and hit the hay so I can be in the field at daylight.

"Ed's been awkward his whole life," Grandpa said disgustedly, spitting tobacco from the step. "Three dollars when we've fed his young'uns all summer and into the fall! And here he's talkin' about spring!"

"Harry!" Rosalie's eyes flashed. "They're your grandchildren! What's more, they've worked hard and Laurie's been a wonderful help to me."

He spat again and went inside to rest while Laurie helped Rosalie get supper. Disappointed beyond measure by the letter and mortified that her own grandfather grudged her keep, Laurie kept blinking at tears.

"Don't mind your grandpa," Rosalie soothed. "You more'n earn your board, honey, and he knows it."

A sick, bitter certainty that had turned Laurie's bones to water since the reading of the letter suddenly turned them to iron. To start with, Daddy had hoped to send for them before school started. Now he was talking about spring—then he'd probably talk about fall. If he ever did send for them, they'd have been separated for so long and Buddy would have changed so much that they'd never really be a family again—if that was even possible without Mama.

We've got to go. Go on our own—or we'll never go at all. She said to Rosalie, "Is there an address on that letter?"

7

There must have been forty men in the boxcar, some old as Grandpa, others only a few years older than Laurie. At first Laurie had been scared when they started tossing their bundles or cheap suitcases into the car and ran alongside, catching hold of the ladder or door to swing up as the train started slowly after stopping for water several miles out of town.

Some of the dirty, mostly bewhiskered men reeked with whiskey and tobacco. All stank of sweat and grime, but they were laughing about outwitting the railroad bulls who'd patrolled the railroad yards in Altus. There was a holiday mood about them as if they were going on vacation. A brawny, dark-haired tramp spotted Laurie and sauntered up.

"First time on the rails, kids?" Laurie was afraid of something in his eyes. She wanted to shrink from the whiskey smell of him but knew that would make things worse. "You're gonna need a jocker—someone to show you the tricks."

"Thanks, mister, but we don't need any tricks. We just want to go to California."

Grinning, the man started to sit down. "That gives us plenty of time to get acquainted. You got nice skin, kid. Just like a girl's." He touched her cheek.

Laurie struck his hand away. "You keep your hands to yourself!"

"Why, you little punk! I'll—"

"There you are, kiddos!" A tall, scrawny, loose-jointed man pushed through the men and dropped his bundle beside Laurie. "Thought I'd lost you for a minute."

The grin faded from the younger man's face. "You their jocker?"

"Nope. I'm their granddad."

The dark man stared at Laurie. "I bet they never saw you before, old man."

Suddenly, there was a butcher knife in the newcomer's hand. "You know what I think, bub? You'll be a sight more comfortable in another car—and you better hurry before we start movin'."

Though they hadn't seemed to pay much attention, a knot of men began ranging themselves behind the scarecrowlike man with the knife. "We don't want any yeggs in this car, Jake," a bull-chested redhead growled at the dark man. "What happened to your last sweetie, that freckle-faced kid who'd run off from an orphanage? Burned his arm with lye, you did—made great big running sores so's he could beg for you!"

The brawny man stood up. "That damn little punk greased the track—served him right! After all I done for him, he ran off with another jocker. That weren't lye I burnt him with, either. It was Spanish fly."

"What we oughta do," said the redhead, "is wait till this train's makin' fifty and let *you* grease the track!"

The jocker—whatever that was—hurried to jump off the car. The men moved off and began making themselves comfortable, except for the tall man, who put away the knife and settled down against his bundle. He had crinkly gray hair, dark eyes, and a moustache that almost hid his lower face. The right side of his cheek had a pale scar like a patch.

He asked gently. "Sure you don't want to hop off and go home, boys?"

"We don't have a home," said Laurie, relieved that he'd taken her for a boy.

She wasn't sure what that other man had wanted but evidently being a boy hadn't mattered. She was wearing overalls and had hacked her hair off with Buddy's jackknife in one of the warehouses. Knowing that they could never catch a moving car, Laurie and Buddy had crept on while the railroad detectives flourished their billy clubs at the hoboes and told them they weren't going to ride. Huddled in the dark corner, Laurie and Buddy hadn't been seen by the brakeman who'd poked in his head to look for tramps just before the train blew its whistle, shuddered mightily, and began to chug.

"No home?" said the stranger. "You're mighty young to be ridin' the rails."

"I'm fourteen, mister," Laurie said.

That wasn't as whopping a lie as the one she'd written in her note to Rosalie, saying that she'd met family friends from Prairieville who were heading for California and offered to take her and Buddy. "You've been mighty good to us, Rosalie," Laurie had concluded on the note she'd written in the rest room before going back down the dark aisle of the movie and whispering to Rosalie that her stomach hurt and she was going to wait in the truck.

Collecting Buddy, whom Rosalie thought was sitting with the boys, Laurie hurried to the truck and left the note on Rosalie's seat before scrambling up in the back and tossing down her bundle and Buddy's, which she'd hid under gunnysacks the night before. The double feature wouldn't be over for two more hours and by then the westbound train should be roaring through Texas.

"We just have to go to Daddy," Laurie had finished the note. "Will you keep our books and things and the bird quilt and Mama's cedar chest till we can get them? We won't need our winter clothes so the kids can wear them. I want you to have the ruby glass pitcher and sugar bowl. Please don't worry about us. We'll be fine."

To the curious stranger in the boxcar, Laurie finished explaining. "Our mother died so we're going out to find our dad. He's working in California."

"Sho', young'uns, California's a big state." The stranger shook his head so forcefully that his moustache jerked. "Don't you know whereat he is?"

"A place called Eden."

"I bin there. Might be Eden if you owned one of them big farms but it's a sight more like hell if you're workin' on one."

Buddy looked scared. It frightened Laurie, too, but she shrugged. "Guess it can't be much worse than pulling cotton. Least if we were picking fruit, we could eat some."

"Sho'. That's why so many babies and little kids die out there. All they get to eat's fresh fruit and maybe some beans. Empties out their guts."

"We'll be with our dad," Laurie said. "That's the main thing."

"Sho'. He'll be glad to see you. What's your names?"

"I'm Larry Field. My brother's real name is Edwin but we call him Buddy."

"Pleased to meet you." The man put out a leathery hand and shook theirs in turn. Laurie noticed that both his hands had livid patches like the one on the side of his face. "I'm Wayburn Kirkendall, Way for short. First time you hopped a freight?"

Laurie nodded. She was already hoping it was the last. These men scared her. Several had produced bottles and a couple of card games were in progress. Murder and cursing God were the worst sins, next came stealing and adultery, lying, swearing, drinking, smoking, dancing, and playing cards. Less heinous were going to movies and reading worldly books and magazines. Most of the hoboes were committing as many sins as they could all at once, and in the dim light, with cigarette smoke curling around them and filling the air, they looked like denizens of hell.

"Well, you just stay close to me and I'll look out for you," the crinkly-haired man offered. He eyed their bundles. "Don't happen to have some grub?"

Ever since her decision to leave, Laurie had saved food that would keep, enough, she hoped, to get them to Daddy, because the only money they had was the nickel she'd saved last week and the one she'd kept today, a dollar that Buddy still had hoarded from his nickel-a-rabbit bonanza, and his nickel from today. She had been tempted to take three dollars from Rosalie's jar to make up for the three dollars Daddy had sent, but her conscience insisted that Rosalie had spent a whole lot more than that on them.

Now, at their self-appointed protector's hungry stare, Laurie got a lard pail from her bundle. The one in Buddy's things held the same assortment—buttered cornbread and biscuits, some smeared with jelly or molasses; boiled eggs; molasses cookies and gingerbread saved from school lunches; and several pieces of fried rabbit tucked away from last night's supper.

The rabbit wouldn't keep long and was intended for tonight's supper, but there seemed to be no time in this boxcar rumbling across the plains, and no place, either. In this curious passage between real places where there were real times, it didn't matter when they ate. Laurie offered the man the rabbit after handing Buddy a piece. By the time she'd put some biscuits and cornbread on the pail lid, the rabbit had disappeared.

It was stringy, Laurie told herself. Goodness, if the man was that hungry . . . She and Buddy ate a biscuit apiece while their guest demolished four and longingly gazed at the pail. Their food wouldn't last to California at this rate, but she and Buddy had eaten big hamburgers that noon, and big breakfasts.

Laurie got out some gingerbread, broke off a third for Buddy, and gave the man the rest before firmly putting the lid back on the pail and shoving it into her bundle between her new dress, which was rolled up inside her other pair of overalls and plaid shirt, and one of Mama's quilts—not the one with birds, which Rosalie had put away in her trunk to keep it nice.

A couple of washrags, an old towel, soap, toothbrush, comb, Mama's New Testament, Morrigan's harmonica—that was all Laurie had, and now the things she'd left at Grandpa's seemed many and infinitely dear, the bird quilt, books, ruby dishes, and the little cedar chest with the lavaliere, grandmother's tortoise-shell combs, and locks of hair.

How she'd ached when she brought them from the Model T and put them in the apple crate, saw everything left of their home packed into that box to be kept under the bed! She'd have felt rich if she had them with her now, just as it wouldn't have been quite so terrible to leave Prairieville if they could have taken the round table where the family had gathered for so many meals, and the carved rocker that had been Mama's mother's.

If you moved enough, like these men, you soon wouldn't carry any of the little things that made a home and reminded you who you were. Maybe some people, like Morrigan, could carry all they needed to stay real in their heads but most couldn't. In order to believe they were who they thought they were, folks needed a home with things you couldn't pack in suitcases—and a family, and a town or a piece of land.

This was just one boxcar on one train. How many other trains all over the country were carrying men like this, men scattered from their roots like the dead, powdered dust of the prairies?

"Can you play that mouth organ I saw in your stuff?" Way asked hopefully. Morrigan had ridden in many a boxcar. Certainly he must have played his guitar, and the harmonica, too.

"I can't play very well," Laurie said.

"It'll sound better'n the wind howlin' through the cracks and these guys' dirty jokes and cussin'."

Laurie suspected that Way was more concerned with protecting her and Buddy's ears than with the quality of her performance. That was nice of him. Besides, playing always summoned Morrigan, and that was the most comforting thing in the world.

As she played, one of the drinkers stuck his bottle in his things and moved closer. A card game broke up. Before long, everyone in the car was listening, humming, or singing along to the songs they knew. When Laurie stopped to rest, they praised her and clamored for more.

"You know 'The Ludlow Massacre'?" Way asked.

"No, but if you sing it I can probably get the tune pretty close."

"Ain't got much of a voice, but it's a song you'd ought to know 'cause it sure happened." Way glanced around at the men. "You older fellers should've heard tell of Ludlow."

"Hell, yes," shouted one grizzled man over the chorus of assent. "That was when John D. Rockefeller hired scabs to break the miners' strike up in southern Colorado in 1913— brought in gunmen and militia with tear gas and machine guns. Somethin' touched off fightin' and when it was over, there were thirty-three on the miners' side shot dead or burned to death."

That had happened in the United States? Just over in Colorado? Daddy would have been about Buddy's age then, but he'd never mentioned it. Well, maybe a person wouldn't. Maybe it was something to forget as quick as you could.

"Half of 'em were women and kids, and there was a hundred more hurt bad," growled a big redheaded man in stained clothes that smelled like oil. "My uncle got shot in his tent, and his wife burned to a crisp when the camp caught fire."

"I was there, too." Way held up his scarred hands and touched the pale scar on his face. "I was eighteen. Worked with my dad in the mine. We wanted shorter hours, wanted to buy groceries wherever they were best and cheapest, not at the company store. Wanted our union recognized. But John D., he said it was against his principles to do that. Wasn't against his principles to kill us, though. Well, here's the song."

It was long, it was bitter and Laurie still didn't want to think such a thing could happen in this country. But she saw Way's scarred hands and face, heard grief and rage in the thready, rasping voice, and had to believe, so she locked the words in her mind.

A scrawny man in bib overalls who had a slower drawl than

Oklahomans asked if she knew "Seven-Cent Cotton and Forty-Cent Meat." After that, a chubby blond kid who said he was from Arkansas sang "Cotton Mill Colic" and they wound up with the songs colored folks had made to ease their hard times, "Ain't Gonna Study War No More," "Swing Low, Sweet Chariot," "No More Mournin' "—all the ones Laurie knew and the others could remember.

It had been dark a long time when Way said, "Larry's tired, boys. Reckon it's time to turn in."

Most of the men came up to thank her, looming shadows, who weren't so scary now that they'd sung together. The music that had joined them for a while gave them weight and substance the way rain might gradually get that pulverized dust to cling to other pieces and turn into real earth again, earth that would stay where it belonged and grow things.

A man she'd heard boast about the farm he used to have in Tennessee gave her a bottle of orange pop. One who'd talked about all the wheat he'd raised in Nebraska gave her a whole Milky Way candy bar. There wasn't much of a way to brush teeth and Mama had trained them not to eat at night after that chore, so Laurie stowed the treats away in her bundle.

She and Buddy each had a quart jar of water but they'd drunk most of it so Laurie didn't squander any by washing. From the sounds, she knew men were going to the boxcar door and urinating. Way took Buddy over and held on to him so he wouldn't fall out while trying to squirt past the train. Laurie couldn't do that though she felt ready to burst. She'd just have to wait till she could get off the train.

It was warm enough to do without cover so she doubled her quilt and Buddy's, spread them on the floor, and mounded their extra clothes under the top quilt for pillows.

After taking off her shoes, she lay facing the side, figuring that Way would bed down on between Buddy and the rest of the men, which, in fact, he did. Long after he was snoring, Laurie dozed only fitfully, afraid that if she really went to sleep, she'd lose control of her bladder.

After what seemed forever, the train lessened its speed and churned to a jerky stop. Laurie tested each step before she put her weight down, making her way as quietly as she could to the door. A few lights far up ahead looked like a small town.

She scrambled down to the cinders. Not daring to go far in case the train started, she let down her suspenders and squatted a little way from the door. Feeling much better, light enough to float, she got hold of the door, swung up one leg and dragged herself into the car as the train lurched into motion.

Blessedly comfortable now, lulled by the sound and Way's presence, she smiled to think of how glad Daddy would be to see them. Of course, he'd worry about not having a nice house for them, but once they were together, he was bound to see that was what mattered most. They'd be a family again, the way Mama wanted. Curling up with that thought, she slept more peacefully than she had since the night Morrigan camped with them.

Sometimes the train pulled onto a siding to let what Way had called a highball, a train with the right of way, thunder past. In different railroad yards, some cars were shunted onto sidings and others added. The population of the boxcar changed, too, as hoboes got off or jumped on. As it got light, Laurie saw that the way they got on a moving freight was to toss in their gear, run along by the car, and then grasp the door or ladder and spring aboard. One inexperienced boy tried to jump on from where he stood and was knocked backwards, sprawling in the cinders.

"He's lucky," Way said at Laurie's cry. "Could've gone under the wheels."

That started the men telling of gruesome deaths they'd seen along the railroads, men hanging between cars till their numb hands gave way and they fell, leaping from car to car and missing, catching a door wrong and getting jerked beneath. Laurie began to shiver. Way cut in at the next pause.

"Say, any of you fellers ever attend the Hobo College in Chicago?"

"I got a diploma from it." A big, burly, white-haired man brought out a shabby wallet and carefully produced a ragged piece of paper that was split at the creases. "Why, I was on the debating team that whipped the team from the University of Chicago—what chance did those kids have against guys who lived by their wits?" He peered at the diploma though it was too dark to read. "Says right here I 'attended the lectures, discussions, musicals, readings, and visits to art galleries and theaters.' "

"Yeah," drawled another man. "And you pledged yourself 'to lead a clean, honest, manly life.' That why you're here, brother? How are bums like us going to abolish poverty and misery and build a better world?"

The white-haired man folded up his diploma. "I'm still glad I had a chance to listen to those hotshot professors from the University of Chicago and read all those books and think about something besides just keeping alive. They didn't have easy chairs at the college, sonny. You sat on hard benches with no backs and paid attention."

"I didn't stay long enough for a diploma," said Way. "But I lived at Ben Reitman's Kingdom for Hoboes that one month it lasted before the landlord took it back." His voice deepened. "Why, we had concerts and community sings—even the cops who hung around lookin' for trouble joined in that singin'. Best I ever heard in my life."

"I didn't live at the kingdom," said the big white-haired man. "Worked for Mother Greenstein for my board and room, but I came to the concerts and singing."

"Mother Greenstein!" Way's tone was reverent. "Don't know how she kept that restaurant goin'. She fed anyone who was down-and-out—helped 'em get jobs or medicine or a place to stay. 'Member her Feast of the Outcasts she gave every Thanksgiving—a free dinner for—for—" The kinky eyebrows ridged. "She said it was for everyone the government, church, and society had forgotten. A saint she is."

"And Ben Reitman, how about him?" asked the graduate of the Hobo College. "A real doctor he was, and could've had a soft life, but he threw in with the hoboes, started the college, worked to give us a chance."

The younger man who'd derided the diploma took a swig from a bottle. "Never was in Chi but it sounds like some folks there had hearts—not like President Hoover and General Douglas MacArthur when us Bonus Marchers camped in Washington."

"Hey, I was there, too," called a wiry little dark man in the corner. "Me'n my wife and kids slept in a packing case for two months that summer—thirty-two, it was—hopin' Congress would go ahead and pay us the rest of the bonus veterans was voted in nineteen twenty-four. Last payment wasn't due till nineteen forty-five, that's so, but that was in the worst of the Depression, millions out of work and we figgered if Congress could send us overseas to fight, they could pay us our money sooner."

The man with the bottle laughed bitterly. "That was something to see in America—cavalry, tanks, infantry with tear gas and bayonets charging in there to run out men who'd fought for their country—kids and women, too—and then torching the shanties. Can't have that kind of thing messing up Washington, D.C.! MacArthur, he was the big cheese, under orders from Hoover, of course, but there was a couple of majors mixed up in it, too, Dwight D. Eisenhower and George Patton. Wonder if they're proud of themselves?"

"Hell, son, it's always that way," said the Hobo graduate. "I fought in the Spanish-American War. You're a hero while the war's on. Then if you can't settle down or there's no jobs, you're a no-good bum—busted, disgusted, can't be trusted."

"A hobo's not a bum," Way said. "He'll work when he can get a job."

"Dandy jobs, ain't they?" grunted the Bonus Marcher. "Hard, low pay, and they don't last long. My wife and kids are livin' with her folks while I flip freights lookin' for a job of work." He took a deep breath. "I've dug ditches, rolled logs, sunk telegraph poles, harvested, picked, pitched hay, pruned, plowed, cut wood, drove teams—longest I could ever stay in one place was a month. Most I ever got paid was two dollars a day."

"What this country needs is that one big union of workin' stiffs Joe Hill talked about before that Utah firing squad shot him twenty years ago," said the graduate. "Ought to be a way of gettin' men and jobs together and fixin' it so migrants can support their families and live decent. Migrants get treated worse'n most slaves ever did. Sho', they're free. Free to starve, with the sheriff and law hustlin' them on when some crummy job's finished."

"What we need," said Way, "is the Big Rock Candy Mountains. You know that song, Larry?"

Everyone else did. They sang it with gusto and after a couple of verses, Laurie could play the tune. Mama would have been scandalized at the words, but after all, Laurie wasn't singing them.

At the next stop, the Hobo graduate yelled, "Here come the bulls!" Men started jumping off, but Way shoved Buddy into Laurie's arms. "Set tight!" he hissed. "Buddy, you just keep your eyes closed, and let me do the talkin'."

A big, stout detective with a pistol on his hip and a billy club in his hand swung into the car. "Pile out of here, you bums!" he shouted, threatening the remaining hoboes with the club. As they grabbed up their belongings and jumped down, the detective saw Way and the children.

"Hey, you old bonebag! Up and out, or I'll kick you all the way."

Way spread his hands. "Officer, my little grandson's sick."

"He won't get no better ridin' a freight. You might as well get off here as anyplace."

"Beggin' your pardon, officer, but we wouldn't. We're headin' for my oldest daughter's. She and her man got a vineyard close to Sedona."

The big man rubbed his wide jaw and squinted, bending to look closer at Buddy and Laurie. She held her breath and didn't have to fake a look of distress. "How come you've got the kids?" he demanded.

Way sighed and swallowed hard, brushing an arm across his eyes. "My woman and me raised Bud and Larry when their folks got killed in a wreck, but my poor old lady, she took pneumony and died last month after the bank foreclosed on our little farm. My daughter'll give us a home."

The detective scowled. Way snuffled. "Please, officer. God'll bless you for your kind heart."

"God don't pay my wages." The man hesitated. "You may be a lyin' old scoundrel," he said with a ponderous shrug. "But the kid does look done in. Reckon it won't hurt to leave you be." Reaching into his pocket, he pulled out a package of gum and gave it to Laurie. "Take care of your brother, kid."

He grinned, lifted his club in farewell, and went out the door, bellowing. "Clear out of here, you deadbeats! No use hangin' around! You ain't goin' to ride!"

Feeling guilty over Way's lie and for staying on when the others couldn't, Laurie whispered, "Maybe we—we ought to get off."

"You daft?" Way squawked. "Wouldn't help nobody and make it a sight harder on us. How's about a stick of that gum? Not much of a breakfast but it kinda sweetens up your mouth."

They had just passed a third night on the train. With Way's assistance, the lard buckets had been emptied yesterday noon, but thanks to some new riders who'd appreciated Laurie's songs, they'd had a supper of pork and beans, salmon, raisin bread, and a 3 Musketeers candy bar.

There was some bread left. Laurie divided it, two slices apiece, and gave their shares to Way and Buddy along with a stick of gum. With no one being allowed on, they could get pretty hungry today, but according to Way, they'd be in Eden sometime tomorrow. And in California where you could pick fruit right off a tree! It was going to be so good to get off this boxcar after four days. She'd only gotten off to relieve herself. Way had taken charge of filling the water jars so that was one thing she hadn't had to do. She didn't grudge him food. He'd gotten rid of that awful jocker and he'd slept between them and the other men and made her feel a lot safer just by keeping them company.

At the next siding, the car in front of them was unhitched and joined to another train. "Shuckins," grumbled Way. "I picked this car 'cause it was between two loaded ones that'd hold it on the track. Now if we hook on to an empty—"

They did, and Laurie quickly learned what a difference it

made. The car jolted till it was impossible to lie down or sit up because you kept bouncing an inch or so into the air. "Try squatting," Way suggested.

That was better but still so rough that he showed them how to stand with their knees bent to absorb the shock. When Laurie got used enough to this posture to hope she wouldn't fall down, she got out Morrigan's harmonica and began to play the tune that chugged through her head with the revolving pistons.

> Gettin' off in California, pickin' fruit fresh off a tree;
> Out in California, life is fine and free.
> California! California! You're the place for me!

Eden looked like a nice town from the glimpses Laurie caught of the dwellings on the slopes above the business district. Such grass, velvety rich green that didn't seem possible after parched Kansas, Oklahoma, and Texas! White houses with red-tiled roofs sparkled amidst the first palm trees Laurie had seen outside her geography book and luxuriant bushes that flowered crimson, rose, and pink. It was so beautiful she simply stared, spellbound, as the train whistled and the clack of the wheels began to slow.

"We're a long way back from the passenger cars," said Way. "Soon as this baby stops, jump down before any railroad bulls come snoopin'. The squatters' camp's over there by the river. Reckon that's the best place to start huntin' your daddy."

Shacks of cardboard that would melt to sludge at the first rain; car fenders and doors wired to tree limbs; willow branches interwoven with scraps of carpet, old clothes, and cardboard. One family had fetched tin cans from the dump, flattened them, and nailed them to crooked boards and parts of orange crates.

Back in the bushes, canvas was draped here and there. A woman came out of one shelter, straightening her dress. Laurie glanced quickly away from a man squatting among the bushes. Flies that would crawl on babies' eyes and mouths swarmed around stinking places where folks who must have just completely lost all pride had gone outside their shelters. A scrawny child rising from beside a cardboard shack kicked a little dirt over his mess as a dog might.

There were more kinds of bugs than Laurie had known existed, crawling or buzzing everywhere—plain ordinary flies, great big green blowflies, gnats, beetles, caterpillars, millers, fleas, ticks, and mosquitoes like the one shrilling in her ear. She swatted at it.

"Watch you're steppin'," Way cautioned. "There's camps like this all over California. Scariest thing is these folks for the most part aren't shiftless bums or hoboes who like to drift. They're families who lived in houses, had farms or little businesses or worked steady for someone. They came out here to save money and get back on their feet, but they're lucky if they earn enough to eat and buy gas to the next job."

"But Way, it's so dirty and awful!" Laurie whispered. Compared to this, the little house in Prairieville and Grandpa's sharecropper's shack were palaces. Daddy living like this! What would Mama have said?

"Some big growers say California's got to have peons—lots of cheap labor with no power or rights," Way growled. "Well, the growers made peons of the Filipinos and Mexicans, Chinese and Japanese, and when that supply started to dry up because of emigration laws, here's the Okies."

Keeping an eye out for Daddy but half-afraid now that they *would* find him here, Laurie said, "Daddy hoped he'd earn real well out here—enough to send for us and have a home again."

"I sure hate to cast you down, but look at how it is. Only takes about twenty year-round workers to look after a big peach orchard that needs two thousand pickers as soon as the fruit's ready, and nary a one the minute the fruit's packed." Way shook his head and went on bitterly. "No way migrant workers can ever belong to a community. Folk's who've been good members of the grange, who've always voted on local and state affairs, don't have a thing to say about how things are run. It's a—"

"Look!" cried Buddy. "There's our flivver!"

It was indeed, with a clothesline stretched between it and a tent, a patched, stained tarp held up by poles canted at odd angles to tie it down over waist-high walls of scrap metal and wood. Outside the tent, a thin, yellow-haired woman in a faded dress jounced a fretful little boy on her hip while she stirred something in a kettle set on an old car grill spanning the small fire that sputtered sullenly in a shallow trench. At the approach of strangers, the woman pinned a strand of hair into the knot at the back of her long neck, the curving, graceful kind you'd call a swan's neck if it hadn't been so thin.

At her questioning look, Laurie said, "Please, lady, we're looking for Ed Field. Are you Mrs. Halsell?"

The woman dropped the spoon and stared. "Oh, dear Lord!" Her face crumpled. She came blindly toward Laurie. "You must be Ed's kiddies. Your Daddy talked about you so much—"

Dread gripped Laurie. Her insides turned to water. "Is—isn't he here?"

The woman shook her head. "Children, I hate to tell you this. Your Daddy's—gone."

"Gone?" shrilled Buddy.

"He—he drowned." Mary Halsell began to sob. "He went in to pull our baby out, little Rob here. We—we tried our best but by the time we got him out, your daddy was gone. Didn't know how to get in touch with you, though he sure talked about you children a lot." Her eyes widened and she studied Laurie. "Wasn't there—?"

A girl, she was going to say. Her woman's eyes had picked up what men's hadn't. Laurie gave her a warning look. Mrs. Halsell turned and pointed. "There's some big eucalyptus trees down the river—see, over there—and we buried him where he'd have shade and sweet air." The haggard woman broke into tears. "Ed was such a good man! Can't tell you how much he helped us and now it's our fault he's dead. Bob thought I was watching the baby and I thought the kids were. Just no way to tell you how sorry we are."

Sorry! Laurie felt as if she'd been kicked in the stomach and went all hot and sick. To come all this way . . .

The pot-bellied toddler on Mary's hip didn't look to Laurie like much of a trade for her father but of course he'd had to try to save him. It stabbed deep that Daddy must have kind of made the Halsells his family instead of Laurie and Bud. It wasn't nice, but Laurie stepped back when Mrs. Halsell tried to put her arms around her. Buddy had turned against Way and was hanging on to him, shoulders heaving. Little strangled sounds came from him. Laurie was glad Way was there. She didn't have any comfort for her brother.

It didn't seem possible, it was a bad, wicked joke, that they'd come all the way out here when Daddy had drowned the day before they climbed into the boxcar back in Altus.

"My husband, Bob, got real sick and he's just now getting well enough to work," Mrs. Halsell went on. "For a long time, we've been getting by on what I made picking cotton and the half-dollar a day Ed paid for his meals. Hated to take his money but he said we'd looked after him when he cut his hand and fed him when he couldn't work." Mary smiled tremulously. "Ed always had a joke. He said, 'The Lord'll take care of the poor folks and us rich devils will look after ourselves.' We met Ed down in the Imperial Valley where we were all picking lettuce and tomatoes. He drove into camp and saw me brushing Bernice's hair. Guess it made him homesick for you children because he parked the flivver a little way from our tent." Mary blinked and swallowed hard. "He looked nice, and real lonesome so I sent Bob over to invite him to supper. After that— well, we just sort of helped each other out."

"I know," said Laurie. "He—he wrote about how good you were to him."

"Poor folks have to help each other," Mary said. "The way growers like it is to have two or three times as many workers as there are jobs so folks'll hire on for two dollars a day or even a dollar since that beats nothing. We don't dare ask for toilets or water close to the fields when there's plenty waiting to take our jobs."

"Plumb wicked!" said Way. "Growers got to have pickers at just the right time or they'll lose their cauliflower and cabbage, peaches and grapes, apricots, apples, plums, and artichokes— all their crops. If workers ever organized—"

100

"Can't," said Mary flatly. "We *have* to work for whatever we can get."

"But if you didn't, you could force growers to pay decent wages or lose their crops."

Mary shrugged. "Growers have you coming and going. You need to get to a farm before picking starts so as to get hired, but if the crop's not ready, you have to wait for it to ripen, four, five days, maybe a week."

"So you get credit at the farm store where everything costs double what it should," said Way.

"That's how we lost our jalopy. We picked our way north from the Imperial Valley into the great Central Valley—that's the San Joaquin and Sacramento valleys. Got just enough work to buy food and gas to get to the next job and then we hit a string of bad luck. Neither Ed nor Bob got work for a couple of weeks. We were flat broke when we chugged into a big peach orchard more on fumes than gasoline. The men were hired but we had to live in one-room shacks that cost five dollars a month. Over a hundred people used the faucet at one end of the street and the single dug toilet at the other. Well, the peaches weren't ripe and there were five Halsells who had to eat. Bob was starting to get sick. He couldn't keep up with the pacer who picked a tree ahead of him, and you have to keep up even if the pacer's trees lots of times have to be done over. The pusher kept ridin' Bob. On the second day, he fired him. So there we were, in debt for the shack and groceries. The sheriff attached our Model T."

The woman's voice broke. Way nodded. "Single guys can hitchhike or catch a freight to the next crop but a family can't."

"I don't know what we'd have done without Ed. He quit his job and loaded us in his flivver, tied the mattress and tent on top, and we headed for here." Giving herself a little shake, Mrs. Halsell said, "Ed had a little money saved and I know you children will want your mother's Bible."

She hurried into the tent, came back with Mama's red-letter Bible, and held it out to Laurie. The leather binding was worn from Mama's hands—and Daddy's, hands that would do no more work, ever, or caress the faces of loved ones. Laurie didn't recognize the cry of grief as her own, but when Mary Halsell drew her against a thin bosom, this time Laurie didn't pull away.

8

Mary Halsell walked with them to the eucalyptus grove. Thin, rose-gray bark peeled from great trunks and the oval, silvery-backed leaves murmured in the breeze that freshened with the coming night. It was still light enough to make out the words carved and charred on the end board of an apple crate:

ED FIELD
Gave his life for a child
October 28, 1935

Daddy might have been alive if he hadn't met the Halsells, but they had gone to a lot of trouble to bury him in a pretty place and mark his grave. Only—he shouldn't be dead! Not him and Mama both. If he *had* to die, if he had to be buried, it ought to be where he had lived, where people knew who he was. He should be with Mama near the honey locust tree in the Prairie-ville cemetery, not here where he was just another Okie.

There was no way to fix that. *This* was how it was. But she could play for Daddy. She got out the harmonica and Morrigan's voice sounded in her head. *"You've got to walk that lonesome valley. . . ."* She played "Amazing Grace," "Swing Low, Sweet Chariot," "Will the Circle Be Unbroken?" and finished with "So Long, It's Been Good to Know You." Maybe it wasn't exactly fitting, but the dust had blown them here, and now Daddy was dead, she could forget how he'd acted since Mama died and remember when it had been good to know him, to be his child.

Kneeling, Laurie touched his name, which was carved roughly into the wood. Poor Daddy. He'd come a long way to die. It didn't seem right just to leave him here. More than likely neither she nor Buddy would ever come back. The marker would fall down and rot. In a few years, the grave might sink in a little more than the soil around it, but that would be the only sign that here a man's body was becoming part of the earth.

Laurie had brought the Bible out of a vague feeling that it retained some essence of her mother. Something valuable— something that meant a lot to Daddy—Laurie stared down at the Bible. It was the only thing that was not an absolute necessity that he'd brought to California, Mama's Bible, comments neatly written on almost every page with the purple satin ribbon bookmark worn threadbare where she'd used it.

Laurie supposed the dead couldn't know what was buried with them, that such a sacrifice was useless, and yet it seemed right to leave the volume with Daddy. She drew Buddy out of earshot of the others.

"Buddy, would you mind leaving Mama's Bible with Daddy?" His eyes, swollen from crying, widened as much as they could and she explained quickly, "We'd dig down a ways and leave it. We—we wouldn't try to put it in Daddy's hands or anything like that."

Buddy considered. "Do you think he'd like that?"

Laurie nodded.

"All right." Buddy dug his heel in the soft ground. "Guess I'd rather leave it. If we carried it around with us, you'd probably want to make me listen to the whole thing. The New Testament's bad enough—I mean, it's plenty."

Using the strong part of fallen branches, with Way's help they dug down a couple of feet above where Laurie reckoned Daddy's heart would be. It didn't seem respectful to just put the Bible in the hole. Laurie padded the space with eucalyptus bark and leaves, and placed the much-read book on the fragrant lining, covering it with many long strips of bark.

In a way it seemed wicked to leave a Bible like that, especially Mama's. Laurie's heart pained at losing her mother's dearest possession. Yet it seemed fitting. They gently scooped the silty earth over the tiny burial and pressed it down. Burrowing against Laurie's shoulder, Buddy sobbed, and so did she. All the months at Grandpa's, Laurie had held on to the hope of being with Daddy again, being as much of a family as they could without Mama.

That hope was gone. Kids couldn't be a family without at least one parent. All she was sure of now was that she had to take care of Buddy and get out of here. There was nothing for them in California. But what could they do? Go back to Grandpa's and grow into sharecroppers if they were lucky enough to find a farmer who'd take them on when they grew up?

"You'll want to spend the night." Mary Halsell touched Laurie's cheek with fingertips callused from pulling cotton bolls. "Your daddy's quilts are in the Model T. That's where he slept. The stew's ready."

Laurie turned instinctively to Way. It would be rude not to eat with the Halsells but she couldn't sleep in Daddy's bedding. Way said, "We'd appreciate a bite to eat, ma'am, but then we'd better get over to the railroad yards and catch a ride east." Laurie didn't realize that she'd been holding her breath till it came sighing out.

We, he had said. That sounded like he was staying with them, at least for a while. Maybe he'd eaten their food, but he'd looked out for them. He put one hand on Buddy's shoulder, another on Laurie's, and as they walked back to the camp, Laurie didn't feel quite so alone and desperate. But it seemed wrong, sad and awful and strange, to walk away from Daddy's grave, to leave him here for always so far from home.

Jimmy and Bernice Halsell were fair-haired, nice-looking, and hazel-eyed like their mother, but their clothes were rotting off, long past what patches and a needle could fix. They had just gotten home from school and Bernice, who looked about seven, was crying.

"I don't wanna go to school! No one'll play with me and the teacher says I'm stupid and—"

"You got to go to school," Jimmy told her roughly. He was older than Laurie, maybe thirteen. "Playing's not what matters, silly. You've got to stay in school and learn all you can so when you grow up—" He broke off, flushing, with a guilty look at his mother. "School's the only chance folks like us have, Bernie," he finished a bit lamely. "So just you pay attention to your books and not to those stuck-up California kids."

"But I got put back to first grade with the *babies!*" Bernice wailed.

"That's because you wouldn't let me help you with your reading and arithmetic." Jimmy's tone was unsympathetic and Bernice wailed louder.

"You—you got to go to school back *home!* Back where we had our nice house and our store and—and everything. It's different here. None of the other kids in camp have to go to school."

Mary rested her scratched, sunburned hand on Bernice's thin shoulder. "I know it's hard on you, sugar, but you've got to get your education so you can have a nice job teaching or keeping accounts or—"

"I don't care about when I grow up!" Bernice's narrow, freckled face screwed into wrinkles. "I—I want someone to play with now, at recess and noon!"

"Hush!" said Mary Halsell. "Wash your hands and get the bowls and spoons. Mr. Kirkendall and Larry and Bud don't want to listen to your fuss."

When the thin stew was dished up and a bowl carried in to Mr. Halsell, who was resting on a mattress on the ground, Mrs. Halsell turned to Way. "Are you some relation to the kids, Mr. Kirkendall? They're welcome to stay with us. We'll sure do our best for them, though you can see we don't have much."

The words snapped Laurie from a daze. She'd been trying not to smell the camp but the stench permeated her now, urine, feces, grime, and despair. Despair had an odor, like rotting fungus. She'd smelled it on some of the men in the boxcar and it rose from all over this camp.

"Thank you, Mrs. Halsell," she said, mechanically polite. "But we—we'll go back to grandpa's." She said it so Daddy's friends wouldn't worry, but she didn't see how she and Buddy could go back—or what they could do if they didn't. She just knew they weren't staying here.

Way said, "I'm not blood kin to the young'uns, ma'am, but I'll look after 'em."

"Guess you'll want to take the Model T." Mrs. Halsell glanced toward her husband. "Bob's able to work again. We were fixin' to start for the Sacramento Valley as soon as the cotton finishes, but—"

Her voice trailed off. "I can drive," Way said. "But we'd have to buy gas. Best thing to do is sell the flivver in Eden."

Daddy had written that the Halsells had lost their car and were traveling with him. Without the Model T, the family would be stranded. They'd been good to Daddy, took care of him when he cut his hand.

"You keep the flivver," Laurie said.

The Halsells' faces brightened, but then Mr. Halsell shook his head. "We can't pay for it, sis. It's worth at least fifty dollars, maybe more, with them good secondhand tires Ed put on it before we came here."

"You can send some money later." Laurie knew well that hope of "money later" never came true but the Halsells needed the Ford worse than she and Buddy did.

It was strange. Folks pitied orphans, the way that railroad detective had, but if kids had parents, the parents were sort of blamed for not being able to take care of their young.

Tears suddenly burned Laurie's eyes and her throat felt raw and swollen. It didn't seem quite fair for her to give away what was also Buddy's, the only thing of value Daddy had, but she was the oldest, she was responsible for her brother now, and she was going to have to make decisions concerning them both. "You can send the money to Buddy and me in care of Rosalie Field. I'll give you her address. Maybe—maybe you'd write her about Daddy and tell her we're all right." At Mrs. Halsell's puzzled look, Laurie flushed and added lamely, "It may take us a while to get home."

"Oh, it shouldn't." The yellow-haired woman almost smiled. "Your daddy had some money saved. He had me keep it for him. Ought to be enough to get you home. We didn't touch it, hoping he'd get a letter with your address so we could send it to you. And since Bob's picking again, we've got a few dollars ahead."

Her husband nodded. "We can pay four dollars on that Model T and still have enough to last us till we get to the next job."

The envelope with Daddy's savings held seven dollars. Mrs. Halsell gave them four more, pressing out the bills. After cups of coffee that must have been made from grounds used over three or four times, Laurie and Bud let Mrs. Halsell hug them again. She cried but they tried not to. Then they were on their way.

They moved through the yards, jumping across rails and switches, waiting as a train passed going the other way, so close it spewed cinders into their eyes. "There's one just startin' east," Way breathed. "Got to get on while it's movin' slow. Look, there's an open top car. I'll boost you onto the ladder. You climb on up and see if you can drop onto the load. If you can't, hang on till I get down there and can give you a hand."

He tossed their belongings over the side and started them up the ladder. Laurie hung from her hands inside the car. Her feet touched something hard and cold as Way dropped beside her and eased Buddy down.

"Mess of cast-iron machinery!" Way said in disgust. "First time this baby stops, we're findin' something better. Right now we better hunt a place where the load's wedged tight enough not to shift around and smash us if the engineer taps his air brakes."

The train chugged sluggishly enough that they didn't fall around while they searched for a secure nook. They found one behind the head end of the car, where the wind from the open top didn't hit full blast. At least the heavy load kept the car on the tracks and they could sit down on their bundles and huddle together with the quilts around them.

Wheels hummed, picking up speed. The train's long, lonesome whistle mingled with the rush of the wind. The only warm parts of Laurie were the side next to Buddy and her shoulder and back where Way's arm rested, but the *clickety-clack* was hypnotic and she was so exhausted that she drowsed.

"Doggone it!" Way's voice roused her. "Startin' in to drizzle.

107

Let me root around and see if I can find some cardboard or somethin' to put over the quilts. If they get wet, Lord only knows when they'll dry out again."

Fortunately, it was only a few minutes before he was back with a big smashed carton. Doubled, spread out between the end of the car and some machinery, it sounded like a real roof beneath the pattering rain till it began to get soaked and the playful drumming turned sullen before, blessedly, it stopped.

"One thing about going fifty miles an hour," chuckled Way, flipping the sagging carton on top of the machinery, "you can sure outrun a lot of weather—head into it, too, naturally. Wisht we'd stop so we could get a better roost."

Laurie drowsed again till they pulled onto a siding to let another train go by. "Okay, kids!" Way helped them roll their things into the quilts and tossed the bundles over the side. "Scoot down the ladder and watch out for bulls!' "

Keeping close to the train, Laurie and Bud waited while Way climbed up the ladder on a couple of cars. "Full of ice," he muttered, descending.

"Why don't we just get in a boxcar?" Laurie asked. It was cold. She'd been a fool to leave their winter coats at Rosalie's. *"California, where you sleep out every night . . ."*

"I'd like to find a nice empty ice car where we can get warm and cozy," Way said as he climbed up again. There was a metallic clunk. He called down softly, "This one's empty. Hand me your stuff and get yourselves on up here."

They clambered to the top. The tattered remains of a rising moon gave light enough to show the lid raised above a cavity in the middle of the car. Way jumped into it, helped them down, and settled the lid in place, taking care to wedge it open a little with the handle of the lock.

"Got to be mighty careful about these reefer lids so you don't get locked inside," he said. "Two kids crawled into an ice car a year or two ago. Brakeman didn't know they were there and locked the lid. Guess the poor little devils starved. But the wind can't hit us here and it's clean. You can roll up in your quilts and go to sleep. But first, now we can hear ourselves, maybe we'd ought to talk about what you want to do."

"I—I don't know," said Laurie. Maybe he didn't want to bother with them. If she only knew where Morrigan was! But he certainly wouldn't want to have a pair of kids to hamper him. Biting her lip, she made herself busy, spreading out a quilt.

"Reckon the natural thing would be to go to your grandpa's but I kind of got the notion you wasn't too happy there."

"We're not going back if there's any other single thing we can do," Laurie said. "Rosalie's nice to us but—"

"Well, then, would you like to throw in with me?" Way sounded apologetic, maybe a little scared. "Might head for Texas, look for work around them oil boomtowns."

"What kind of work? Buddy needs to get back in school but I'll have to earn us some money."

"I don't want to go to school," Buddy whimpered.

"Rather grow up ignorant like me?" demanded Way. "You're goin' to school and so's Larry, leastways through eighth grade."

"We can't sponge off you, Way!" Laurie argued.

"Let's not hear that kind of talk! Share and share alike, that's what we'll do, just like we're sharin' your quilts. If I hire on for a roustabout, I ought to get five-six dollars a day." When Laurie sucked in her breath at the fabulous wage, he added quickly, " 'Course, everything's sky-high in a boomtown, but a fella can save if he don't blow his pay on booze, cards, or women. I don't drink 'cause when I start, I can't stop. Never had an itch for gamblin' and women—" He chuckled. "It'd take more money than I'll ever have to get a decent one to look at me and I'm too old to fool around with the others."

"It still wouldn't be right for you to earn our whole living," protested Laurie. "You're not our kin and you've already been real good to us, running off that jocker and helping us get to California and everything."

"Sho'. I reckon I'm choosin' to be your kin, if you'll have me." Way hesitated. "I had a family once. Wife and a baby girl. They both died of influenza durin' that big epidemic in nineteen-nineteen. Been on the road ever since, workin' at one thing or another." He sighed and went on in a low, shamed voice. "Last couple of years I went from hoboin'—takin' a job of

109

work when I could find it—to just bein' a tramp. I'm sort of a painter, I can paint kids or dogs or signs. I've still got my brushes but I got so I wouldn't paint a sign for a meal if I could scrounge it. I'm sick of that. Sick of bummin' around. You kids give me a reason to buckle down."

Helping them might help Way but Laurie was determined not to be a burden. "Maybe I can get a job doing dishes or helping the cook in an eating house."

"Maybe." Way's dubious tone exploded in laughter. "Say, Larry, money's free and easy in the oil patch. I'll bet you can play that harmonica and folks'll slap down their dimes and quarters to hear you. Shucks, I bet some days you can earn more'n I do!"

"Oh, I'm not a musician! It wouldn't be right to take money."

"You are what you do," shrugged Way.

"But I *like* to play. If folks enjoy it, I'm glad, but I'd do it for me anyway."

"Sho'. You don't have to *sell* your songs. Give 'em away. Pleasure whoever wants to listen. But if they want to thank you, wouldn't it be plumb rude not to let 'em?"

"Morrigan gave me the harmonica. He gave me his songs."

"Sho'. But didn't he eat with you and ride in your flivver?" Way tousled Laurie's hair. "Don't you reckon he'd be tickled to death if he knew he'd given you a way to feed yourself?"

"Well—I still don't think anyone'll think my music's worth paying for."

"We'll see." This time, Way's sigh was contented, not regretful. "Know something? This is the first time I ever enjoyed ridin' the rails. We're snugged down warm and comfy, we're out of the weather—and we're together."

They were together because Daddy was dead. Together because none of them had anyplace to go, anyplace where they belonged. The enormity, the finality, of her father's death crushed in on Laurie. She stifled her sobs against her arm but couldn't keep her shoulders from heaving.

Way reached over Buddy to pat her shoulder. "You go ahead and cry, boy. Nothin' sissy about that."

"I'm not a boy," Laurie wailed. She had realized, as they talked, that Way had to know that. It wouldn't be fair for him to take on a girl without consenting to it.

Way's hand jerked back as if scalded. "Then what in the Sam Hill are you?"

"I-I'm Laurie, not Larry."

Was he angry? Would it make him not want to be their family? True, it was a patched up, makeshift, leftovers kind of family but it was worlds better than none. Besides, kids couldn't manage on their own, even if they had the means, because someone would turn them in to the sheriff or the orphanage or even the reform school. Daddy had a couple of times threatened Buddy with reform school. The very idea struck terror in Laurie's heart. They had to have a grown-up or the best thing that could happen to them would be to be sent back to Grandpa— and how he'd carry on now that Daddy wouldn't send for them ever or mail any more dollars! No matter how kind Rosalie was, Grandpa would make them feel like no-account beggars. On top of that, they'd grow up stuck in the rut of sharecropping— and in the squatters' camp Laurie had seen what happened when even that way of making a living got taken away.

She wouldn't cry and plead. Gulping down the salt taste, she explained. "I—I wasn't trying to fool you, Way. Catching a freight like we were, I just thought it was better to look like a boy. It was easier, too, wearing overalls and not having to comb my hair much."

When Way spoke after a long pause, his voice was soft. "Bet you've got purty hair, Larry. I want to see it all grown out and curly some day. But you was right. Won't do for a girl to flip freights. I reckon you'd better go on bein' Larry till we save up enough to settle down proper."

"Then—it's all right?"

"Larry-Laurie, it's downright wonderful!" There was no mistaking his amazed joy. "I can have my baby girl again and a mighty fine boy, too." He considered. "You had a daddy, a real good one. Sho', I wouldn't have the brass to try to fill his shoes." Way cleared his throat. "But maybe—maybe you'd have me for a grandpa or uncle."

"You're a lot nicer than the only grandpa we've got alive," said Buddy.

"What do you want us to call you?" Laurie asked.

"How about Gramp when we're around strangers? Rest of the time, just call me Way."

Laurie raised up and leaned over to give him a hug. "Goodnight, Gramp."

"Goodnight, Larry-Laurie. Better stick to Larry or I'll forget. Night, grandbud."

"Aw—" Buddy squirmed happily at the tease. Though he hadn't let Mama kiss him for a year, he threw his arms around their self-ordained kinsman. "Good night! Sleep tight! Don't let the bedbugs bite!"

Giggling, he snuggled in between the others. The train's whistle blended with the wind, the clack of the iron wheels. It seemed a year ago, rather than just hours, that they'd knelt by that heap of sandy earth in the eucalyptus grove, but the father they had known and thought so strong and wise and wonderful had really been buried with Mama. Still, he had been strong and wonderful for the Halsells. Jealous and hurt as she was that he'd befriended and helped them instead of sending for his own children, Laurie was glad that he hadn't been all alone—that he, too, had found a sort of family. And surely, even if he'd been backslid at the time, God wouldn't let him go to hell when he'd given his life for a child. He was with Mama now, not having to worry about paying off the doctor and undertaker or how to feed his family.

Laurie wept softly, the anger she'd felt at him mostly washing away as she remembered how hard he'd worked, how hard he had tried. But he's all right now, she kept telling herself, ignoring what Jesus had said in red letters in the Bible that had its own small grave above Daddy—that in heaven there was no marriage or giving in marriage. *He's with Mama and it's like they were young again and just married, all happy and well, and starting out together.*

What was that song of Morrigan's? *"No more weeping, no more weeping, no more weeping over there . . ."* At last, holding to that comfort, lulled by the sound and sway, Laurie drowsed and then she slept, deeply and heavily with no kind of dream.

She woke to the now familiar jerk of being switched to a siding. The slit where Way had propped the lid open made a thin sliver like a gray new moon. Way stood up, listened, raised the lid a bit more, and peered out.

"Doggone, they're unhitchin' this bunch of cars—prob'ly goin' to leave 'em on the siding. Gotta tumble off, kids, and hunt another car."

After the snug warmth of their car within a car, the early morning wind cut to the bone. Way had his old jacket but unless they found a mighty warm town, Laurie and Bud were going to have to get some kind of wraps. Shivering, staying close to the train so they wouldn't be seen by the crew, they moved along the row of cars still attached to the engine.

"Gondolas," Way whispered disgustedly as they stooped to creep by low-sided open cars. "We'd bounce right out if we didn't freeze, fry, or get tossed off by the crew or bulls. We don't want an open top, either, if we can help it. Hmm. This one's got manure and hay all over the floor."

Wishing he wouldn't be so particular, afraid of being caught and left out here in the desert, Laurie stumbled along with her bundle. The sky was getting lighter every second. Way peered into one car. "Loaded to the gills."

He hurried to glance in the next car and fairly sprinted to the one ahead, returning with a grin they could see even in the faint light. "Just the ticket! Empty car between two loaded ones that'll hold her on the rails. All abo-o-o-ard!"

Buddy and Way could relieve themselves out the door. Laurie couldn't. She scooted between a couple of cars and squatted on the tracks. Feeling much better, though her stomach cramped with hunger, Laurie grasped Way's hand and scrambled up. The Halsells had offered them some biscuits but it had been out of the question to take their food.

"Way," said Laurie as they stowed their belongings in a corner and wrapped up in the quilts. "The next town we stop at, let's—"

She broke off, shocked at her daring, but they were famished and they had eleven dollars. She decided then and there that

---

113

she'd pay her debts the way Mama and Daddy tried to do, and would never squander money, but there were times when you needed something good, something special and extravagant, and these treats were worth some pinching on either side.

Taking a deep breath, she finished. "Let's find a café and eat anything we want—lots of it, good and hot. Then we'll go to a grocery store and get some traveling food."

Way scratched his head. "Don't seem right to spend your money thataway. 'Specially not to feed me when I'm supposed to be takin' care of you. You and Buddy eat at a café. I'll go knock at some back doors."

"No." She wouldn't have said so, but now they were family, she didn't want Way to ask for handouts. She had persuaded herself—almost—that it wasn't stealing to ride a freight since the cars were running anyway, and besides, railroads had been given fortunes in public land so they'd build across the West and provide public transportation. You couldn't get more public than forty, fifty, sixty men sharing a boxcar. She touched Way's hand. "You're our Gramp. You eat with us."

Way's crinkly eyebrows puckered. "By grannies, I got my brushes, the best Russian sable. Bet I can rustle up a job or two paintin' signs on windows—that don't take long. Then *you* can eat with *me.*"

"Can't we eat first?" asked Buddy wistfully.

After another eyebrow pucker, Way grinned. "Sure we can. My backbone's knockin' on my front ribs and I'll bet yours is. That mulligan Miz Halsell gave us was thin enough to read a newspaper through. We'll have a bang-up feed and then I'll get some work. Better try to earn enough to get you kids some sweaters or coats. We're slidin' into November. It sure won't get any warmer."

"We'll look for wraps while you're painting," Laurie said, and an idea struck her. "Maybe if I played my harmonica—"

They got off at the next town and slipped through the railroad yards till they came on a tarpaper shed full of junk. "We'll leave our stuff here," Way said.

He got out his carefully wrapped brushes and a comparatively clean shirt. Laurie dug out shirts she and Buddy had just worn once. They all washed off at a faucet and dried themselves with their dirty shirts before putting on the cleaner ones. Way slicked water over his hair and combed it back, rubbed at his whiskered chin. "Got to buy a razor. Man with a family can't look like a bum."

Laurie, parting and combing Buddy's hair in spite of his wriggles, frowned at Way's brogans. They were held on more with broken and reknotted laces than with leather. "You need some shoes, too."

Way stared at his peeping toes as if he'd never seen them before. "Why, I reckon I do. Well, kiddos, if I can find enough jobs, we'll leave here stuffed like Thanksgiving turkeys and duded up like real people!"

Real people with homes, people who belonged someplace, Laurie thought with a pang before she lifted her chin. She had the harmonica, Way had his brushes. They might have to move around a while but someday they'd have a home.

And for now, for the first time in her and Buddy's life, they were going into a café and order exactly what they wanted and as much as they could hold!

9

Tarry was a discouraged-looking town in the California desert. One paved Main Street, Highway 66, was fronted for a couple of blocks by a bank and two gas stations, and more stores were boarded shut than were open. Main Street was angled by dirt roads that trailed out into thirsty sand. Small adobe houses and wood shacks scabbed one side of the railroad track that paralleled the highway. Three churches, two school buildings, and the better houses were on the other side of the tracks. Most of these buildings were stuccoed and pretended to get some shade from straggly palm trees with dead lower fronds drooping down like a witch doctor's skirt Laurie had seen in her geography book.

CAFE—CABINS—HOME COOKING—ALL YOU CAN EAT FOR TWO BITS!! read a crudely lettered sign pointing to a blistered white frame building with half a dozen little oblong buildings behind it. The spicy aroma floating from the door was a lot more enticing than the establishment's looks. A Chevrolet pickup and five cars were parked in front, all of them old except for one beautiful blue Packard.

"Let's go, kiddos," said Way.

The four tables were full so they climbed on stools at the counter that ran the length of the room. The gray-haired waitress looked tired, though the wall clock showed it was only seven o'clock. Her white apron was fresh and starched, though, and she had kind gray eyes. When she looked at the children, the lines around her mouth disappeared in a smile.

"Got big appetites this morning? There's cinnamon rolls and biscuits right out of the oven and we serve real maple syrup with our pancakes." At a nod from Way, she filled his cup with steaming coffee, scooted the cream and sugar closer, and said to Laurie and Bud, "You'll have milk."

Laurie's mouth watered. Everything smelled or sounded good. Rosalie had bought them hamburgers but this was the first time in Laurie's life to really eat in a café, decide what she'd like. Buddy asked at once for pancakes and bacon. Way ordered sausage, biscuits, gravy, and two eggs over easy. The cinnamon roll Laurie got was as big as a saucer, lavished with raisins and nuts and oozing from every coil with caramelly cinnamon and sugar. In between waiting on other customers, the lady kept their milk glasses full till at last they had to tell her they couldn't drink any more.

Way finished his third cup of creamed coffee and got out the dollar Laurie had slipped him back in the railroad yard. "Now, ma'am," he said to the woman, "We can pay cash or maybe you'd like a new sign painted. The one out front sure don't do justice to your food."

The lady looked in surprise at the dollar and then laughed merrily. "Goes to show! I figgered you were the ones I was feedin' today for the Lord. I've been after my husband to do that sign—even bought the paint—but by the time he cooks from dawn to dark, he's wore out. Sure, mister, hop to it. But the only brush we've got is gaumed with old paint."

"Don't fret your head about that." Way pulled his wrapped brushes out of his coat pocket. "I got the best there is right here. If you have a can and some turpentine, I'll get to work. While the background coat's drying maybe I could mosey around and pick up a few more jobs."

"You can if you're any good, mister. My brother has the garage at the end of town. I know he'd like a nice sign and I bet there's others."

A square-bodied man by the window looked up from his cigarette and newspaper. He had a thick, straight thatch of lusterless hay-colored hair and yellow-brown eyes. Laurie judged men's ages by whether they looked younger or older than Daddy. This one looked older, maybe as old as Way, though Way at forty looked fifty. The stranger's face was as square as his powerful body, his jaw was actually wider than the middle of his face, and his nose looked like someone had squashed it into his face.

"You folks on foot?" he asked in a lazy voice. He sure wasn't from Kansas. More like southwestern Oklahoma.

Way nodded. "Headin' for Texas."

"I'll take you as far as Holbrook, Arizona, if you'll paint some catchy signs for three truck centers I own along the way on sixty-six. I got business to attend to here." The man glanced at a wristwatch. "Plan to leave town after dinner, say one o'clock. My truck centers have cabins. You can bunk in one tonight if they're not full up with payin' customers, and if they are, we can rig you some cots in the gas station."

To ride in a car instead of scrambling onto a freight—be welcome instead of fearful of being caught? Laurie sighed with relief as Way said, "Suits me right down to the ground. Want we should meet you here?"

"One o'clock." The yellow-eyed man resumed his cigarette and paper.

While Way sandpapered off the old paint, Laurie got out the harmonica. She was embarrassed to stand on the sidewalk and play but this was like keeping Way company. The chunky man strolled out, listened to "Bury Me Not on the Lone Prairie" and said, "Know something snappier, kid? How about 'Begin the Beguine'?"

"Can you hum it, mister?"

"No, but I can whistle it." He did, melodiously, and they wound up doing the tune together. "We'll make some great music on the road," he said, and dropped some change into the bib pocket of her overalls. It sounded like a lot but she glimpsed dimes, nickels, and pennies. He got into the shiny Packard and drove off.

Way gave a whistle of his own. "Boy howdy, that buggy cost two thousand bucks if it cost a nickel! We're leavin' California in style, kiddos!"

He dipped his Russian sable brush in the white paint and began to cream it across the board, gaily in rhythm with Laurie's playing while Buddy held the bucket within easy reach. Most of the people coming out of the café stopped to listen. Dimes and nickels joined the coins in Laurie's bib, but it was the skinny little man in the battered pickup who listened till Way finished the background and then tucked a spindled dollar bill in her pocket.

"Just keep a-workin' and a-singin' and you'll be all right," he said, ruffling Buddy's hair.

While the board dried, they went down Main to the garage. The café lady's brother, Seth Hanna, who had her nice gray eyes, grinned at Laurie. "If I can get music and a good big sign that'll stop the highway traffic, it's sure worth a dollar. I'll go over to Lem's Hardware and pick out the paint. Why don't you come along and see if he'd like a sign?"

Lem, a pot-bellied, hairless man, wanted to work a trade, so Way agreed to decorate the show window in return for pints of turpentine and red, blue, and black paint. "I can get more jobs and finish 'em faster if the customer doesn't have to rustle up the paint," he explained to Laurie and Bud. "Sho', I'm beginnin' to feel like a capitalist with this here 'means of production.' "

"What's a cap-capitalist?" Buddy asked the question Laurie was about to ask.

"A capitalist owns a factory or a mine or a big farm or a railroad, somethin' like that. That's the 'means of production,' see? And then he hires, cheap as he can, folks to work for him. They got nothin' to sell or invest *but* their labor. 'Course the capitalist has to have 'em, or his 'means of production' don't produce. What he likes to have is ten or a hundred people wantin' a single job. He can pick the best workers and still pay next to nothin'. But without workers, all the means of production in the world would just be junk."

"What kind of Red talk is that?" demanded Lem with an infantile hairless wrinkling of his brow. "You sound like a damn Wobbly."

Way drew himself up. "I held a card from the Industrial Workers of the World for a couple of years. Mister, you tell me what's wrong with workers gettin' decent wages, decent hours, and a decent place to work?"

"Yellow-bellowed Wobblies wouldn't fight for their country!" growled Lem. "Get outa my store and go paint winders in Roosia!" He spun on Seth. "You ain't goin' to hire this goddam communist, are you?"

The garage owner shrugged. "I don't give a hoot about this guy's politics just so he makes me a good sign. You want to sell me the paint, Lem, or shall I mosey across the street to Armstrong's?"

"Hell, I'm in business!" As Way started out of the store, Lem rung up the prices of the yellow and red paint Seth had selected. "About as soon lose the sale as have to look at these here colors every time I look out the window."

"Reckon Armstrong's has 'em, too," Seth drawled as the screen door's bang dulled on strips of innertube nailed to it. He said to Way as he caught up, "Can't you mix yellow and red to make orange?"

"Sho'. Onliest way I know of to do it."

Seth's lean, long, rather sorrowful face split open in a grin. "Okey-dokey, let's just give ole Lem an eyeful!" The owner of the corrugated tin building pointed to the side facing the road. "I'd like you to paint a big yellow circle there, outline it with orange and red, and then do the letters the same way."

"What do you want it to say?"

Seth scratched his ear. "Seth's Garage, I reckon."

"How's about a little more pizazz? 'Best break for your brakes?' Or I could paint you a kitten with 'Your motor can purr like this!' "

"All of 'em can't. I'm not Jesus. But I am pretty good with motors *and* brakes." After a moment's quandary, Seth's face split again. "Paint it all on. I'll pay you another dollar for the idea and the extra work."

"I better get after it then so the circle'll dry," said Way. "Got some rags to clean the wall? And the cat'll show up better if it's black."

It was a marvel how he made that circle using the swing of his long arm like a compass. Laurie played, and flivver after flivver passed with suitcases wired onto the fenders, mattresses tied on top, piled full of kids and whatever could be crammed inside. The licenses read OKLAHOMA, TEXAS, KANSAS, ARKANSAS, GEORGIA, TENNESSEE, NEBRASKA, the litany of states that couldn't feed their people.

Laurie's heart swelled. She made a tune to go with the chant in her head. It was the wail of a train whistle, wind howling through the open machinery car, the rattle of a loaded-down jalopy, air hissing out of a flat, patched tire, the smell of the camp outside Eden, the loneliness of Daddy's grave under the eucalyptus. When her grief and anger had poured themselves into the new music, she switched back to Morrigan's songs.

Passersby stopped to listen. Most of them asked for tunes. Laurie learned some and by the time Way was ready to look for another job, her bib pocket clinked cheerily.

"Let's buy your paint in that Armstrong store if they don't need a sign," she suggested.

Mr. Armstrong's general store had a nice sign but his paint was cheaper than Lem's and he threw in an old canvas bag to carry it in. Buddy insisted on this task. As they proceeded down the street, he strutted a little.

"We're cap't'lsts now, ain't we, Way?"

"Aren't," Laurie corrected. If she couldn't get Buddy back in school soon he was going to backslide from education the way Daddy did from religion.

"Sho'." Way dropped his hand on Buddy's shoulder. Yellow crusted the cuticles of his fingernails and he smelled of turpentine. His cleanest shirt had a yellow smudge, but there was a lift in his gait and he held his head higher. "Let me tell you, kiddos, it makes a sight of difference to know you've got everything you need to earn your keep most anyplace you light."

"But Way!" protested Laurie. "You had your brushes all the time!"

He slanted her a wry grin. "Yeah, but I'd got to where I didn't care if I used 'em. I was just goin' where the wind blowed me, rolled up tight so's not to knock off more of me than I could help. But that's no style for a family man—any man a-tall."

A shoe repairman was pleased to swap a sign for a pair of good work shoes that had been half-soled the very day their owner keeled over with a heart attack six months ago. "No one around here's got feet that big," said the little shop's middle-aged owner. A small, humped-over man, he looked like one of Santa's gnomes with his ruddy face and canvas apron. "Don't like seein' them doggone flatboats 'cause Hank was younger'n me and my heart acts up sometimes."

Way adorned the window with the name of the owner, a cowboy boot, a child's sandal, a lady's high-heeled fancy shoe, and the beautifully lettered promise: REPAIRS WHILE YOU WAIT. Admiring the window, the repairman handed Way the sturdy shoes and glanced at the shoes Buddy had inherited from Everett. They were split open on the sides and a toe peeked through the left one.

"I could stitch up them shoes," said the gnome. "But there's some secondhand ones over there got a lot of good wear left in 'em. You can have 'em for a dime."

The shoes fit fine and weren't the least bit run over. Must've belonged to some rich kid. The old shoes were so worn out that the gnome shook his head over them and tossed them in the waste barrel. While Way went back to the café to finish the sign, Laurie asked the repairman to sew over the loose stitching on the shoes Rosalie had bought her for school.

"Sure, son, and I'll throw in new heels and laces if you'll play that french harp while I'm working. You know 'Oh, Dem Golden Slippers'?"

Leaving the repair shop in shoes that ought to last till she outgrew them, Laurie took Buddy into the dry-goods store. He picked out two pairs of red socks, which would protect his feet and the "new" shoes. Way had no socks. She bought him three pair of the largest size heavy black cotton ones. Her own needed darning so she bought spools of white and black thread and a card of needles as well as cards of bone and black buttons to replace those that had been shed off their clothes. Boys' flannel shirts were on sale for twenty cents, almost warm enough for a jacket.

"What color would you like, Buddy?"

His blue eyes widened. "We can get one?"

"Sho'!"

He giggled at her imitation of Way, then peered at her anxiously. "Will you buy one, too?"

The dollar bill would be left after paying for the shirt, but she wanted to keep that for the journey. "I want a different pattern," she fibbed. "But that blue would look nice on you, Buddy."

"I like the red better."

Laurie nodded at the storekeeper, who held the shirt up to Buddy to make sure it was long enough in the arms. Glowing with the heady power of buying things with money she'd earned herself, Laurie felt very grown up as she paid for the purchases.

In a way, she'd worked for Rosalie's nickels, but those were also a gift. The money going into the merchant's till was a return for music, though it still didn't seem quite right to get paid for doing what she loved. Counting the dollar windfall from the man with the pickup, she'd taken in almost as much that morning as Way had. She wished Morrigan could know that along with his songs, he'd given her the means to at least partly earn a living.

The nice gray-eyed lady had come out to admire the café sign as Way finished the lettering. A scalloped blue border edged the white background. A Blue Willow cup and saucer and plate were painted in the upper left corner above CAFE and a bed with a blue coverlet decorated the bottom right under CABINS.

"You'll have to eat dinner for that," said the woman. "It's lots prettier than what I expected." She looked from Buddy's red plaid shirt to Laurie's patched one. "Some tourists left a sweater in the café a couple of weeks ago. Reckon they'd have written for it by now if they were going to. Come in and let's see if it fits."

The sweater was sort of a flecked gray, not pretty, but clean and warm. The cuffs had to be turned up and it hung below Laurie's hips, but that just made it warmer. "Didn't cost me a cent," said the lady with a brisk shake of her head at Laurie's offer to pay. "It's too little for me or my daughter—might as well do somebody some good." She eyed them keenly. "You kids ought to be in school. Not to speak against your grandpa, but he strikes me as sort of footloose. May be up to you to remind him that you need your educations." She shook her head. "So many families on the road, nothin' ahead, nothin' behind. Don't know what's going to happen to this country. Guess folks have to help each other the best we can. Could you boys fancy some milk and a cinnamon roll split down the middle? Come get it and take your grandpa some coffee. I'll put it in an old jar so the paint on his hands won't matter."

It was half-past twelve when Way finished Seth Hanna's sign with a playful black cat curled along the red-and-orange lettering. "People can see it from the other end of town," Seth bragged. "Bet I get enough extra business in a week to more'n pay for it." He winked as he opened his dilapidated wallet, carefully extracted two dollar bills, and handed them to Way. "Lem hates cats. He's going to be mighty tired of this one before it wears off."

They detoured by the railroad-yard shack to pick up their bundles. What a lot had happened since they left them there that morning! They didn't even look like the same people, Way striding along with pride in the set of his head and shoulders, Buddy in good shoes and his red plaid shirt, Laurie with her shoes sewed up and snug in the good sweater. Its pretty carved wood buttons almost made up for the drab color. They'd had good hot food for the first time in the ten days or so they'd been on the road, had dinner coming, and they'd earned real money. Way had Seth Hanna's two dollars and Laurie had garnered more coins while Way finished the garage sign.

"How much were my socks?" asked Way, peeling out his dollars. From the way his fingers touched them, it had been a long time since he'd had that much. "I owe you for the paint, too."

Laurie backed away. "We owe you for breakfast and dinner, then. Please, Way! Families share."

"Well—But I'm supposed to be lookin' out for you kiddos!"

"I hate to think about what might've happened to us without you." Laurie shivered. "If you hadn't run off that jocker—"

"If you'd hollered and made a fuss, some of the other guys would've helped. Tramps and 'boes learn to mind their own business but most of 'em got hearts."

"All the same, we're lucky you decided to be our—our family."

"Not as lucky as me." He put the money back in an inner pocket of his coat, maybe where he kept the butcher knife. "Okay, I'll keep it for now but it's yours much as it is mine. We better shake a leg so we can eat that dinner we have comin' before we pile into that fancy Packard. And say, I'm goin' to buy a razor and see if that nice lady at the café won't let me borrow a washbasin and some soap."

She was happy to oblige and supplied a mirror to prop in the window above the outside bench. With his jaws scraped clean, the burn scar on Way's cheek was less conspicuous. He had trimmed his shaggy moustache, too, and looked years younger, in fact he now didn't really look much older than the forty years Laurie had figured out must be his age.

"Good gracious, Way!" she said so softly that no one else could hear. "If you keep looking handsomer and younger, no one's going to believe you're our grandpa."

He beamed and smoothed his crisply waving hair. "Reckon I've got a ways to go before anyone takes me for your big brother, kiddos. I may look better'n I did but no one's goin' to call me a liar if I say I'm fifty." He gave a startled whistle as the café lady put a huge steak in front of him with green beans and a mound of mashed potatoes and good-smelling gravy. "Ma'am, I'd have to paint your whole building, inside and out, to deserve this!"

"Beef's cheap because of drought and there's lots of apricot cobbler." She smiled at Laurie and Bud. "What would you like? My husband's chili is the best you'll ever taste. There's chicken and dumplings. Or you can have steak."

Buddy took the chicken and Laurie decided on chili. It *was* delicious, spicy beans with chunks of beef, altogether different from the thin concoction Mama had made by shaving slivers off a block that was more orange suet than meat. The soda crackers were good, too, and Laurie demolished a bowl of them. Just like they were paying customers, the lady kept their glasses full of iced tea, and Way's mug topped off with fragrant coffee.

They were starting on their cobbler when the big, square-faced owner of the Packard came in. He ordered sirloin steak without even looking at the gray-eyed lady. His chunky fingers drummed the counter, one wearing a gold ring with a glittering diamond—did men wear diamonds? Laurie had never seen a man with a ring before. You'd expect yellow eyes to be soft, but this man's were hard as they drilled into Way.

"Say, fella, are you some kind of goddam Red?"

The bald man who stuck his head through the service window of the kitchen rapped to get attention. "You watch your language in front of my wife, mister."

"I can sure find someplace else to eat."

"You sure can," agreed the cook.

"No offense, lady," muttered the yellow-eyed man. The cook went back to his stove and the big, square-bodied man turned back to Way. "Well, how about it?"

"Guess you been talkin' to Lem," drawled Way. "How'd you like the sign I did for Seth Hanna's garage?"

The broad, powerful, ringed hand made a dismissive sweep. The top of it and the bottom finger joints were furred with coarse black hair. "Short and sweet, mister. You one of them crazy radicals?"

Way wiped coffee off his moustache and unfolded from the

stool. Laurie remembered the knife in his pocket and sucked in her breath, but his tone was easy. "If it's radical to think there ought to be work for everybody at decent pay, I reckon I'm a radical. And I'm a radical if that means believin' that in this great big country of ours, the wonderfulest one in the world, there hadn't ought to be families camped under railroad bridges and kids that don't get enough to eat. Shouldn't anyone in this whole United States have to go to bed hungry."

"Includin' bums and tramps?"

"Ought to be some way they could work for a meal. Anyhow, Jesus was a bum and a tramp."

A lady with bluing-rinsed hair jumped up from a table. "You—you're blaspheming!" she sputtered.

No one paid her any mind. The dark pupil spread over the heavy man's yellow eyes and the skin at the curves of his flattened nostrils pinched white. "You don't want a ride much, mister."

"We'll manage."

Way turned his back deliberately and finished his coffee. "Thank you, lady," he said to the kind-eyed woman. "Best cobbler I ever sunk a tooth in. Come on, kiddos."

"Say, mister," said a lanky old man at the end of the counter, "I'm headin' east soon as I've et the last of crumb of this cobbler. Only goin' about eighty miles but the kids don't take up much room so you shouldn't have too hard a time catchin' a ride—and if you don't by nightfall, you can bunk down in the barn."

"I'll fix you a sack for your supper," the café lady said. She gave the flat-nosed man a scornful look as she vanished into the kitchen.

Suddenly, the square-faced man laughed and shrugged. "You're a tough old vinegaroon but I kind of like that. Besides, I want those signs." He smiled at Laurie and Buddy. His teeth were big and white and looked hungry. "Bet you kids'd like a ride in my Packard. I've even got a radio."

Laurie looked at Way. Riding in the big blue car would be almost as magical as having enough dimes to ride the merry-go-round as long as you wanted during the county fair. She'd never had more than two rides, clinging rapturously to the pole as the spirited horse she'd picked with such care to make sure he was the most beautiful plunged up and down with the music. Oh, if she was ever rich, she'd ride just as long as she wanted to, hours and hours of the dreamlike canter that carried her to an enchanted world. But she didn't like this man and hated how he'd talked to Way. It was up to him to decide. Buddy had his mouth open. She gripped his arm and gave him a fierce stare.

"We're much obliged to you, mister," Way said to the lanky old man. "Mighty good of you to offer, but we're headed for Texas and Holbrook is a good chunk of the way."

"Why, sure," their would-be benefactor nodded. "You better ride far as you can at one crack, 'specially with the kids. Good luck."

"Same to you," said Way.

The lady came out of the kitchen with two sacks that gave out delicious smells and a bottle of milk that she handed to Laurie. "Cinnamon rolls and fried chicken," she said. "You folks be careful now!"

"That's way too much!" protested Laurie, reaching in her pocket. "Please, we'd like to pay."

"That pretty sign's worth every bite," said the woman.

"Let me give you a song, then," Laurie said. She got out Morrigan's harmonica and played "So Long, It's Been Good to Know You." The lady didn't know the words, of course, but they were true.

10

It seemed almost sacrilege to deposit their scruffy bundles in the spacious carpeted floor of the back of the Packard, or sink down in seats covered with butterscotch-colored suede leather so soft it felt like velvet. Laurie's awed delight was penetrated by the stranger's hearty voice.

"Guess it's time we got acquainted." It must have been a

trick of the light but those yellow eyes seemed to blaze as the man settled heavily behind the wheel. This buggy didn't need cranking. It was the first car Laurie had ever ridden in that had a starter. As the motor throbbed eagerly, the driver swung the big, fancy car onto the highway. "I'm W. S. Redwine."

"I'm Wayburn Kirkendall and these are my grandkids, Larry and Bud Field."

"Their mother must be your daughter."

Laurie squirmed and waved a last time at the nice café lady. She hoped Mr. Redwine wouldn't get too curious. She wasn't good at lying. It was a bad sin and till she'd taken on a boy's identity, she had seldom even fibbed. Buddy lied a lot to escape punishment but always gave himself away and got spanked for that on top of his original misdeed. Way, however, nodded easily.

"My onliest child," he said in a mournful tone. "She died of dust pneumony. Her man went to pick crops in California and got drowned." Laurie filled with scandalized admiration at how he mingled truth with invention. Probably that was the secret of lying convincingly—stick to the truth as much as possible so it wouldn't be hard to sound sincere, like Way did. "So now the kiddos are with me. I'm all they've got. My wife and their other grandparents are dead."

"That's quite a burden, especially since you seem to be having a hard time of it. Lots of men in your fix would put the kids in an orphanage or find some good family to adopt them."

"Not while there's breath in my carcass," Way said fiercely.

After a pause, Mr. Redwine asked, "So you're headed for Texas? Got family there?"

"No, but I've worked in the oil fields. There's generally some kind of job in a boomtown. We'll get along."

"I started my truck centers in Texas," W. S. Redwine said idly. "Spread into New Mexico and kept going west. I may put one in back there in Tarry."

"What's the need?" asked Way. "There's a café, cabins, and garage already."

Mr. Redwine gave his shoulder a negligent hitch. "A modern center—everything new and all together—would close down those hick outfits inside a month. Local folks might go on using them but it's the highway trade that counts."

"And I reckon you could cut prices." Way's tone was dry. "Raise 'em again once you didn't have any competition."

"That's business."

If Mr. Redwine owned the café, Laurie was sure no traveler would get a bag of food like the one the lady gave them. It hurt to think of her and her husband and Seth Hanna being forced out of business in spite of the beautiful signs Way had painted. Kids weren't supposed to cut into grown-up talk, but even if it imperiled their ride, Laurie had to say, "That's a mighty mean kind of business!"

"Only kind there is." Mr. Redwine chuckled, not the least bit upset. "Let's hear a tune on your harmonica, sonny."

Laurie didn't want to play for him. She couldn't very well refuse when they were riding in his car but she played songs he wouldn't like and *thought* the words at him—"Ludlow Massacre," "Seven-Cent Cotton and Forty-Cent Meat," and "You'll Eat Pie in the Sky."

"I'm not partial to church songs," interrupted Mr. Redwine. The pie song used the tune of "In the Sweet Bye and Bye." "Let's see what we can get on the radio."

He fiddled with knobs, swore at the static, and finally located a music station that suited him. He tapped his fingers on the wheel to something called "The Music Goes 'Round and 'Round" and said over his shoulder, "Get the tune to that one, kid."

She wasn't his slave. It was a silly song, but she did like a couple of the songs that followed, "Red Sails in the Sunset" and "Tumbling Tumbleweed," though she didn't think whoever made up the last one had ever been caught out where the wind was whipping tumbleweeds across the plains. There was nothing lazy and melodic about that. She was getting the tunes in her head when Mr. Redwine switched off the radio and said, "Okay, Larry. Play it."

She played the songs she'd liked. "Fine," said the man, whose square shoulders bulked twice as wide as Way's. "Now how about the one I asked you to pick up?"

Laurie's mouth felt dry. "I couldn't."

They were traveling through desert country that looked as bad as the Dust Bowl. The only cheerful thing about it was the Burma-Shave jingles on signs along the way. She didn't want to be the cause of the three of them getting thrown out by the side of the road but something told her it would be dangerous to buckle in to W. S. Redwine. Besides, Morrigan had given her his music; it seemed unfaithful to let Redwine tell her what to learn.

"Pay attention," he said. "I'll whistle it."

"Whistle all you want." Way's voice was soft and drawly but something in it made Laurie think of the knife inside his coat and turned her cold. "But Larry don't have to play songs he don't like. Music's not a paid kind of thing."

"Didn't see him turning down any cash when he was playing outside the café."

"Larry gave his music. It was free. Anyone could listen. Folks who liked it and could afford to gave him money."

"Since I'm giving you this ride, you'd think he could give me a song."

"He gave you a bunch of 'em."

"But not what I asked for."

"That's how music is," said Way. "Anyhow, you ain't exactly givin' us this ride, Mr. Redwine. I'm goin' to paint you a bunch of signs." He chuckled. "Now that is business. I'll paint exactly what you want 'long as it won't get me throwed in jail."

Redwine turned on the radio.

Snaking, twisting, hairpin curves that made Laurie's stomach lurch. She had thought the bleached Mojave Desert looked the way the world would after the angels dumped out all the vials of God's wrath but these Black Mountains of western Arizona were even worse, rock melted in hell and spewed out to harden in fantastic monster shapes.

Surrounded by layers of what Way explained were mine tailings, the old mining town of Oatman clung to a hillside. Stores and offices shaded by wooden awnings were built on one side of the highway, which was also the only street. Wooden steps led up to a plank boardwalk supported by stilts to make it level. Houses perched wherever they found a flat space, many on steep hilltops ribboned by a road or trail. Some were neatly painted but the majority were weather-beaten gray.

It was a relief to reach desert again and see a few stunted trees with small, delicate leaves a little like those of honey locusts, growing along sandy watercourses. She had seen cactus before, of course, but not some of these kinds, nor did she recognize a scrubby bush with tiny, dark green, glossy leaves and little yellow flowers, or tall, thorny wands covered with small leaves and tipped with brilliant red blooms.

"Must've rained lately," said W. S. Redwine. "The creosote and ocotillo are blooming. Good thing we didn't get caught in it. The desert's so rocky that rain just runs off into the washes and sends a flood crashing along so fast it can catch a car and sweep it right along with it. I've sat here for a couple hours waiting for a flash flood to go down so's I could get across. And I remember when the desert road was just planks laid across the sand. If you met another car, you each kept the tires on one side up on the planks so you wouldn't get stuck."

The road edged a range of mountains of dark rock patterned with light that glowed crimson, azure, and gold in the sunset as the Packard slowed down a little for Kingman. Here the highway passed an inspection station, where they were waved on after Mr. Redwine genially told the man that of course he wasn't carrying any California fruit. Merged with the highway, Front Street ran past warehouses, businesses, and the depot for the Santa Fe Railroad. Buddy nudged Laurie.

"Aren't you glad we're not sneakin' around the yards looking for a boxcar?" he whispered.

Laurie smiled and nodded but she wasn't sure. Even if it had been scary coming through the mountains, the Packard was a lot more comfortable than any car, truck, or train she'd ever ridden in. The cushions were so deep that they sort of hugged you so you didn't jounce around and Mr. Redwine was a good driver even if he went faster than Laurie liked, especially on those terrible curves where you looked down and saw the road coiling dizzily beneath you.

But there was something about Mr. Redwine that made her determine never to play "Begin the Beguine" or learn the songs he tried to make her play. She'd learned all of Morrigan's that she could, and had been glad to pick up tunes from tramps and hoboes, but a fear deep inside her warned that he'd take over her music if she didn't fight him, and then it wouldn't be hers anymore or Morrigan's either.

Where was Morrigan? Would she ever see him again? If it weren't for the harmonica and his songs, she'd think that she'd imagined him, dreamed him into flesh and blood during that awful trip from home to Grandpa's. Usually she wouldn't let herself yearn for him because it seemed ungrateful to want more luck in her whole life than that he'd come along the way he had, traveled with them for that day, and given them his music. It still seemed to her that he was a kind of angel Mama had sent to help them through that journey. But it would be so wonderful to see him at least one more time and he'd been heading for work in the Texas oil fields just like they were. . . .

W. S. Redwine swung the Packard left off the highway and parked to the side of a long stucco building with four gas pumps in front of it, a big garage on one end, and about ten cabins behind it. A metal sign over the garage, where several men were working on a truck, said TRUCK CENTER—CAFE—CABINS. A neon sign rearing high above the center said DUB'S TRUCK CENTER.

"Bet you can improve on that, Wayburn." Redwine jerked his head toward the plain white sign with black lettering. "The neon catches folks at night but I need something good for daytime. Seth Hanna said you thought up that cat sign of his."

"Well, Mr. Redwine—"

"Call me Dub."

"Well, sir, I'd like to think it over some but how about 'Square meals—square deals' and something about what a good rest a trucker can get here? Maybe you'd ought to think on a name for your centers so's drivers could wait for the next one. If they take a cabin, maybe you could give a discount for one at the next place."

"That'd be a good idea where I have competition, like here. No use offering cut rates where they've got no choice, though." Redwine stretched his blocky shoulders and got out. "Let's see if there's an empty cabin for you. Wayburn, you can do some sketches to show me before you turn in tonight. I'll pick out the best one and get you started early in the morning. I'd like to make Ashfork Junction in time for you to do that sign tomorrow evening. We run out of paving a little piece out of Kingman and it's a long day from Ashfork to Flagstaff even when the washes aren't running."

Way grinned as he unfurled his gangly body from the Packard. "If you want the same thing on all the signs, I'll only have to think that up once."

"Guess that café woman gave you plenty of food for supper. You can have breakfast at half price."

Way folded his arms. "If that's how it is, then I guess you better think up what you want on your sign. You want me to figure that out, we'd ought to get our meals."

"You think your signs are worth a ride in a Packard, a place to sleep, *and* food for the three of you?"

"Reckon you thought so or you wouldn't have offered the ride."

"You better think up something good!" Mr. Redwine poked his head in the café. "Martha, are all the cabins full?"

A frowsy plump redhead with beautiful green eyes glanced up from pouring coffee for two men in stained khakis. "There's four empty, Mr. Redwine."

"Okay, I'll need one and these folks'll take another."

She hurried to the cash register and got two keys from a drawer beneath it. "There's a big bed and a cot in Number Seven," she said, glancing curiously at Way and the children. "Cot's not made up, though."

"No need." Mr. Redwine didn't thank her for the keys. "They can all sleep in the bed. Save getting more sheets dirty."

"We'll need the cot," Way said. "My back won't take the boys' thrashin' around."

"The brass you've got, you'd ought to be a millionaire." The glint in W. S. Redwine's eyes seemed more appreciative than annoyed. "All right, Martha, you or Helen bring a sheet to Seven when you get around to it." He led the way around the building to the cabins and opened Number 7 for them. "This good enough for you, Wayburn?"

Way ignored his sarcasm. "Suits us right down to the ground." He set down his bundle as if he owned the place. "Now if you'll get me a pencil and tablet or wrapping paper, I'll start on your sign."

"Martha'll bring you some." Redwine turned to Laurie. "You ever had an ice-cream soda or sundae, Larry?"

She never had, but she had watched longingly as rich kids sipped through straws from tall, frosted glasses or savored slow, ecstatic mouthfuls scooped with sensuous deliberation from silver sundae dishes. The banker's daughter often had three scoops of ice cream—chocolate, vanilla, and strawberry—with butterscotch sauce on the vanilla, strawberry sauce on the choc-olate, and hot fudge on the strawberry, each mound peaked with whipped cream, chopped nuts, and one of those bright red cherries.

"I don't like fancy things like that."

Mr. Redwine laughed. "You can go to hell for lying, son. But if you like plain ice cream better, the shop down the street has about any flavor you can imagine. I never can decide which is best, peach or toffee or chocolate chip. Why don't you and Bud come give me your opinion?"

Buddy's eyes cast an anguished plea at Laurie. "Thank you, sir," she said in the polite way Mama had taught her to use when declining something. "But we'd be too beholden."

Buddy couldn't stifle a disappointed groan. "Aw, Lau-Larry!"

"It'd be a fair trade if you'd listen to my phonograph and learn some catchy tunes like 'Beer Barrel Polka' or Cab Callo-way's 'Minnie the Moocher' and play for an hour or two in the café tonight. Be good for business."

"I'll play the songs I know for nothing."

The yellow eyes seemed to swell. "You're the hardheadedest kid I ever ran across."

Her insides shriveled. What if she lost all of them this nice cabin? It even had a bathtub! She and Buddy had never been so dirty in all their lives and their hair was stringy and smelled like moldy hay. What if she lost them a ride halfway across Arizona?

Buddy's gaze implored her. He must think she was mean and crazy to refuse to do what W. S. Redwine asked but her deepest instincts made her more determined than ever not to let him take charge of her music.

"Why don't I play what I know, Mr. Redwine?"

She felt trapped and seared by the tawny heat of his stare. Exerting all her will, she managed not to let her eyes waver. Finally, he shrugged.

"Try it if you want but if my customers act bored or fed up, get yourself out of there—and don't panhandle them."

Laurie flushed. "I never panhandled anybody, Mr. Redwine."

Buddy said hopefully, "But if someone stuffs money in Larry's pocket—if they really want him to keep it—then that'll be okay, won't it, sir?"

Mr. Redwine seemed to lose interest. "No skin off my nose so long as there's no cup or hat salted with coins. But don't you hang around in the café, kid." He turned to Way. "I'll be in Cabin One when you've got something on paper. Get there before nine. I'll have a visitor about then."

He left the cabin. Somehow, the way he shut the door made Laurie run to see that it wasn't locked. Relieved, the full wonder of the bathroom struck her.

"Buddy, you take a bath and wash your hair while I get our supper out—that is, unless you want to clean up first, Way?"

He shook his head. "I'll be thinking about that sign. You don't cotton much to Redwine, do you, Larry-Laurie?"

She shivered, though the room was warm from the afternoon's sunlight. "He scares me."

Way whirled. "He-he's not bothered you, has he? Tried to feel around on you?"

It took her a moment to understand. Blood heated her face. "He doesn't know I'm a girl, Way."

"Sho'. He thinks you're an uncommon pretty boy. Remember that jocker on the train?"

Laurie blushed even deeper. Her speculation about what and how men and women did with each other was confused enough. Now Way was saying a man might—well, do *something* with a boy. She couldn't for the life of her imagine what.

Way sighed. "Listen, kiddos, the main thing you got to remember is that some guys would rather mess around with each other or a boy than with the most beautifulest woman in the world. Some are turned that way natural-like. Some, I guess, kind of learn it. Anyhow, don't let a man get too chummy." He pushed at his crinkly hair. "I can generally tell when a man's like that. Didn't pick it up with Redwine."

"Why wouldn't you learn those songs, Laurie?" Buddy grumbled. "We could've had a sundae or soda!"

Feeling silly, Laurie helplessly shook her head. "I just can't let him be the boss of my music. Maybe it's because Morrigan gave me the harmonica."

"You get a gut feeling like that, there's a reason," Way said. "He wants me to do his signs—and if he changes his mind, shoot, I saw some places here where I bet I could get a painting job. Hold your ground, Laurie."

She took a deep breath and squeezed Way's hand. "Thanks, Way. I—I'm real glad you don't think I'm acting crazy."

He chuckled. "Sho', you got the best sense I ever saw in a young'un—and plenty of old'uns, too. If you'd rather not go on to Holbrook with this bird, we can part company soon as I do his sign."

Laurie would have been glad to see the last of W. S. Redwine, but it was something to have a sure ride that far and a roof over them at night. "He's taking us the way we want to go," she said. "As long as he doesn't get mean, we might as well travel with him."

There was a rap on the door. Without waiting, a long, lean blond girl several years older than Laurie stepped in with a sheet she tossed on the cot, several pencils, a small box of Crayolas, and a Big Chief tablet.

"What do you need Crayolas for?" she asked, staring at them

136

as she popped her bubblegum. "Mr. Redwine sent me to the dime store to get them and it was time for them to close so I had to run. I got a stitch in my side and—"

"Wait a second, sis." Way sat down at the small table. In a couple of minutes, he tore out the top sheet of the tablet and handed it to the girl. "Here's how you'd look if you got your mouth clear of that cud."

It was a good likeness, only prettier than the lanky girl was. She stared at it and smiled. Then she was pretty. "Gosh, mister, you're an artist! Gosh, thanks! Gosh, wait'll Mom and Dad see this!" She blew a joyous bubble and bolted, hugging the sketch to her washboard bosom.

"You really are an artist, Way!" Laurie was impressed. "Why, I bet you could make a mint doing rich folks' pictures!"

"Most I ever got for a por-trait was a good chicken dinner and a five-dollar bill from an old lady who was so crazy about her Siamese cat that she wanted a picture to remember him by."

"Can you do me?" asked Buddy.

"After you've scrubbed off a few layers of grit."

Buddy dashed for the bathroom. The clothes he and Laurie were wearing were the cleanest they had. Laurie held her breath as she unrolled their grimy, odiferous things, put them by the bathroom door, and spread the quilts over a chair to air out. They were dirty—not a hint of Mama's lavender remained— but they couldn't be washed till there was a place to hang them out a day or two till they dried.

"Do you have some clothes to wash?" she asked Way.

Way's frizzy eyebrows writhed in horror. "Honey girl, I wouldn't let you touch my socks with a pair of pliers! I'll take care of my duds when I have a bath, but I better not do that till I get Redwine's sign figgered out."

Laurie had to take a washcloth to Buddy's ears but he looked clean otherwise. He and Way attacked the chicken and cinnamon rolls while Laurie, after scrubbing away the ring Buddy had left, reveled in the first bath she'd ever had in a real bathroom with running hot and cold water. First she soaped and rinsed her hair and body of the worst filth before she let the tub fill up to her waist, washed her hair thoroughly, and scrubbed with a washrag till her flesh glowed pink except where the sun had browned it.

How good it felt to be clean! She could understand, almost, how people who had bathtubs in their homes and could stay clean got to where they looked down on folks who didn't have much of a way to wash. It was a real comedown to have to put on clothes that were soiled but at least she had the clean sweater. She didn't like or trust W. S. Redwine but she was mighty glad his cabins had bathrooms!

In the mirror, she saw her eyes widen at a sudden unwelcome thought. It would be harder to stand up to Mr. Redwine now that she'd, well—truly *wallowed* in a luxurious bath. She would, of course, she'd have to, but it was going to take more will-power. That must be how folks got led into doing what they didn't think was right, because they got used to comfort and nice things and didn't want to give them up, like the rich man trying to drag his possessions through the needle's eye. She'd have to be careful not to get so spoiled to her body's being clean that she let her heart get dirty.

After Laurie put their clothes to soak in her soapy second bath water, she had a drumstick and cinnamon roll. She washed the comb and stood on tiptoe in the bathroom to see herself in the mirror as she worked the tangles out of her hair. *Good gracious grief!* This was the first time she'd looked in a mirror since leaving Rosalie's, the first time she'd seen how raggedly she'd shorn off her hair. It was fluffed up from being washed but that didn't disguise the butchery.

How much did scissors cost? Way and Buddy needed hair-cuts, too. She hated to spend the money, but Way couldn't cut their hair very neatly with his butcher knife. She didn't want to use the money she'd earned in Tarry but maybe, in spite of what Mr. Redwine said about catchy tunes, some people in the café would like her songs well enough to give nickels and dimes— and enough of those added up!

She got Buddy to help her make up the cot, took her sweater, harmonica, and courage, and stepped out into the twilight. The mountains crouched outside of town like drowsing beasts and the wind, cool now, fanned the hair away from her face and neck.

Was she really here, way out on the desert, so far from home? Was Daddy really dead? She couldn't believe yet that Mama was. Everything that had happened since then seemed like a nightmare. Except for Rosalie. Except for Way. Especially, blessedly, except for Morrigan.

Through the big window, she saw a long counter with men in work clothes occupying every stool and booth in the smoke-filled room. A steady genial roar of talk and laughter was punctuated with occasional howls of glee. The only women were Martha and a hefty blond who had about her face something of the look of the skinny girl Way had sketched.

Laurie's knees actually quaked and her stomach felt all gone in spite of the good food she'd just had. How could she go in there and start playing? They couldn't even hear her! And they certainly seemed to be having a good time. More than likely, they weren't in any mood to hear songs like hers.

She almost beat a retreat but Morrigan got in her way. *Not even goin' to try?* he seemed to chide. *I gave you credit for more guts than that.*

She closed her eyes, summoned up the flash of his smile, the lilt of his voice, tightened her fingers on his harmonica, and stepped into the café.

Two hours later, she shifted one of two hot-fudge sundaes to her other hand and opened the door of Number 7. A pair of scissors was in her side pocket, another hot-fudge sundae was in her blissful stomach and the chink of coins in her bib pocket was muffled by several dollar bills.

"They didn't ask me to play those songs Mr. Redwine likes!" she exulted as she set the sundaes on the table. The drugstore lady had put them in round cardboard containers and stuck in little flat wood spoons. "Go on, eat the sundaes while the fudge is still hot! I had the lady put an extra nickel's worth on each one, just the way I had mine." She sighed happily and perched on the bed. "A trucker from Tennessee taught me some old mountain songs—'Sourwood Mountain' and 'Old Dan

139

Tucker'—and another man who was in the war in France hummed 'Mademoiselle from Armentières' and Martha—she's the head waitress—has a real nice soprano and sang the songs she knew while I played. We had a real good time—just like a party!"

Buddy eyed her in wonderment. "I don't see how you can do it, Laurie. Go in where you don't know anybody and just start in to play. Weren't you scared? What if they hadn't listened?"

"That would have been pretty awful." Even with that danger past, Laurie shuddered at the very notion. "And yes, I was so scared I almost didn't try. But I thought about Morrigan when I went in and, of course, once I saw everybody liked the music, it was—" She paused, considered, and said wonderingly, "It was the best time I've had in my life, except when Morrigan was with us." That made her feel guilty about their parents and she added hastily, "Except for Christmas mornings, I mean."

That sounded like all she cared about was candy and presents but when she stopped to think about it, the truth was that there hadn't been a lot of laughter and gay good times around their house. Mama had been sick so much and there were so many things Christians shouldn't do and there was always worry about money.

But oh, even if they hadn't joked and laughed much, home was safe and full of love. Laurie ached unbearably when she thought of Mama. She thought that no matter how old she got, there would always be a wound that would never heal, that would bleed slowly and quietly till she died and could see her mother again. Daddy had been the last part of that protected life that was gone as surely as if Black Sunday really had brought the end of the world.

That must have been how Way felt when his wife and baby died. How Rosalie must have felt when her father died and her stepfather hurt her. How Daddy must have felt when Mama died. How Mary and Bob Halsell must have felt when they lost their home and store and future. All those tramps and hoboes on the trains, all those migrants in hundreds of camps like the one at Eden, all the people on the road in old trucks and flivvers—the worlds they'd grown up in had ended. If they were lucky, they might build another, but lots wouldn't be lucky. As lucky as she and Buddy were to have Way and the music and memory of John Morrigan.

Swallowing hard and blinking, Laurie said, "Do you have the sign done, Way?"

11

Next morning, Martha kept flipping hot buckwheat cakes onto their plates till they begged her to stop. So full they could scarcely wiggle, Laurie and Buddy sipped their second glasses of milk while Way got started on the sign, which had been taken down from over the garage so he could do a better job than if he were hanging on a ladder. Last night, he'd painted over the old lettering so the background would be good and dry today.

Laurie had cut his hair and he had shaved and shaped his moustache so that he looked like a different person, years younger and, if not exactly handsome, interesting. He'd evened up Laurie's hair and she'd trimmed Buddy's. The clothing they'd washed and rinsed in the tub and draped around the bathroom was now on a clothesline Martha had said they could use. The desert sun should dry even the overalls before it was time to go.

W. S. Redwine wasn't to be seen, and that increased Laurie's appetite. As soon as she and Buddy drank the last of their milk, they thanked Martha and went out to see how Way was doing. Of his several ideas, the one Mr. Redwine chose was:

> DUB'S TRUCK-INNS
> FOR THE REST OF YOUR LIFE
> Square meals—square deals
> Your truck will be glad you stopped!

Way had used a pencil to mark the words and rough in a cloud cradling a pillow with a smiling, slumbering man's head and shoulders. He was painting the cloud now. It looked soft and fleecy against the light blue background, trailing off fluffily behind where some of the black lettering would be.

"It's going to beautiful, Way!" said Laurie.

He stepped back, cocking his head. "It'll do."

Martha came out with a cup of coffee for him and a rag he could hold it with. "That cloud and pillow would make anyone sleepy, much less a trucker coming in off the dirt stretch of sixty-six." She shook her frizzy red head admiringly and widened her green eyes. "I declare, Mr. Kirkendall, you got a talent."

Why, she was flirting! And Way was grinning, shy and pleased as a youngster. Laurie tugged at Buddy's sleeve and hustled him off. "Buddy, if you'll go to the post office—see, it's right over there with the flag flying—and get me a stamped three-cent envelope, you can have a dime to spend."

"A dime!"

Poor Buddy, fallen from the glory of his nickel-a-rabbit days! Probably, in a boomtown, he could run errands after school or find some way of earning a little spending money. Laurie smiled at him, digging a dime and nickel out of her pocket. "You can keep the two cents change from the envelope nickel, too."

"Why do you need an envelope?" Buddy's mouth quivered. "We-we ain't got anyone to write to."

"*Don't* have anyone," Laurie corrected. "Goodness, Buddy, try to talk right or you'll get put back when you start school. We do too have someone to write! Have you forgotten Rosalie, how nice she was to us?"

Buddy scuffed his almost new shoe on the gravel. "*She* was. But Grandpa didn't like us worth shucks."

"Well, I'm not writing to him. But in case Halsells didn't get to write, I have to tell Rosalie about—about Daddy." Tears welled suddenly in Laurie's eyes and her throat ached. *Oh, Mama, is Daddy with you? He must be even if he was backslid because he kept that little boy from drowning. If we'd just got there in time to see him—if he hadn't left us—if you hadn't died—*Getting hold of herself, Laurie gulped and rubbed her sleeve across her eyes. "I want to let Rosalie know we're all right. It's not fair to worry her. Now you go get that envelope."

Writing about Daddy was one of the hardest things Laurie had ever done, only it seemed there'd been lots of hard things since Mama died so you'd think she'd be getting used to it. Her eyes kept blurring. She tried to keep her face wiped, but tears still spotted the tablet paper.

At the end of the second page, she wrote that they'd been sort of adopted by a real nice man who'd lost his family and that she and Buddy would soon be back in school. Taking the three dollar bills out of her bib, Laurie smoothed and folded them carefully. She had seen some beautiful plaid shirts in the mercantile yesterday evening and both pairs of her overalls had sprung holes in the knees during the journey. If people at the Ashfork truck center were as generous as the ones last night, she could send Rosalie money from there.

But she still couldn't believe that the harmonica was a reliable way of earning anything. Just because she'd been lucky so far, she mustn't count on it. "Pay God first," Daddy used to say, setting aside the ten-percent tithe from his wages. Laurie figured God could take care of himself, no better a job than he'd done looking after her family and plenty of other folks, but Rosalie was different.

Laurie sighed and poked the dollars in the envelope. "This is to pay back a little of what you spent on us," she finished. "I'll send more when I can and write sometimes. Thanks for being so good to us when we weren't really any kin, and don't worry about us, we're going to be just fine. Please save the bird quilt and cedar chest and books and Buddy's things, but it's all right for the kids to read the books. We'll come see you sometime and get them." But not till she was grown up enough that Grandpa couldn't make her stay there and be a sharecropper and fight off his landlord's son.

Buddy dropped the envelope on the table and scooted off to spend his money. Laurie sealed the letter, cupped cold water to her swollen eyes, and started for the post office. As she passed Cabin 1, W. S. Redwine stepped out. Before he shut the door, Laurie glimpsed a dark-haired woman in the bed, sprawled out buck naked. Laurie had never seen a naked human except when she'd helped Mama change Buddy's diapers or bathe him. The hair on the woman's crotch was dark, too, which shocked Laurie as much as the large purplish nipples on the big breasts. Did all grown-up women have hair on that place? Rosalie hadn't said anything about that. Had Mama—?

Ashamed at even wondering, Laurie ducked her head and hurried past, muttering a response to Mr. Redwine's yawned greeting. He caught up with her in a long stride. His shadow blocked the sun. He wasn't as tall as Way or Morrigan or Daddy but he was a lot heavier. Somehow he reminded Laurie of a mass of rock.

"Martha told me you had quite a concert last night. Truckers gave you a bunch of change."

Laurie didn't want to talk to him but she couldn't resist saying, "They liked my music."

He raised a thick shoulder. "Hell, kid, they liked *you*. Most truckers are family men."

"Daddy was a trucker after we lost our farm." Of course Daddy had carried food Mama packed for him and slept in the truck. He couldn't afford to eat in a café, much less rent a cabin. Those sketches of Mama's dream house had made Laurie achingly aware of how much her mother had gone without, but she hadn't thought much about Daddy.

Now, with a flood of grief—and guilt, too, for having hated him when he hit her and left her and Buddy at Grandpa's, she understood a little of how hard Daddy had worked for them, how desperately he had tried to take care of his family.

She wished she could tell him that. Wished she could hug him and say that she loved him. Laurie averted her face so W. S. Redwine couldn't see her tears.

"Well," he said, "just like your pa missed you boys, other truckers miss their kids. That was part of why they filled up your pocket even if you didn't know the latest songs." He stroked his stubbled boxlike jaw. "But the other part is you're good—you could make a musician."

Laurie's heart leaped. She didn't like this man but he was a good enough businessman to have centers spread out over several states. He was probably richer than the banker or anyone else back in Prairieville and he'd been a lot of places. Mama would have called him worldly but that meant he should pretty well know what people liked even if he'd guessed wrong about the truckers.

What kind of musician? she wanted to ask. Good enough to play on street corners or— He couldn't mean she could ever be like the *real* musicians you heard on the radio or phonograph, Jimmie Rodgers, Gene Autry, Kate Smith, Jeannette Mac-Donald, stars like that.

Before she could figure out a way to find out what he thought without making a fool of herself, he said, "You can all have your lunch at the café. Be ready to leave right after that." Without looking at her, he turned toward the café and moved over to see how Way was doing.

Laurie went to the post office, wishing he had said more. Maybe he would on the way to Ashfork. She didn't know what she wanted to do when she grew up. She loved to read and learn things but you couldn't get paid for doing that unless, maybe, you went to college and became a teacher. You could teach even if you were a married woman. It would be wonderful to have a job. That way there might be enough money for things a family needed and if a husband was mean or took to drinking like Floyd, you could move out and support yourself. Even Mama had said it was a shame Margie couldn't do that.

Apart from teaching, women were clerks and waitresses and secretaries, or they took in ironing or sewed. If you married a farmer, you raised chickens and had a big garden and helped with the milking and crops and cooked for harvest hands if the land was planted to wheat. That kind of life would be fine if you had your own farm—*not* mortgaged—and had a good husband, but you wouldn't have any money of your own unless your husband let you keep the butter and egg money.

Was it possible that she, Laurie Field, blown like the dust clear across the country from the little town of Prairieville, could make her living with music? Wouldn't that make Morrigan proud of her? She was so excited at the idea that she floated to the post office, but came down to earth with the reality of the holes in her overalls.

Ignoring the lovely plaid shirts in the mercantile, she bought blue ticking remnant that would serve for patching. As she left the mercantile, Buddy trotted out of the drugstore licking a chocolate ice-cream cone and hugging a Superman comic book.

"Come back to the cabin," she said. "We're going to read the New Testament before you get into that funny book."

"It ain't—it's not Sunday!"

"We missed Sunday because we were on the train. We'll make it up now."

Buddy scowled but evidently remembered he wouldn't have the comic if Laurie hadn't given him some money. He consoled himself by running his tongue around the cone so none of the ice cream would drip and be wasted.

Laurie recited Daddy's favorite Psalm, the Twenty-third, which she knew by heart, and read Daddy's favorite story about the Good Samaritan, and the place where Jesus said, "Greater love hath no man than this, that he lay down his life for his friend."

Buddy snuffled a little. "Is this a kind of fun'ral for Daddy?"

Laurie shook her head. "No, it's just—remembering." She didn't feel able to make up a fitting prayer so she prompted Buddy through the familar chant of the Lord's Prayer.

He sprawled then on the bed with Superman. Laurie took the butcher knife out of Way's inside jacket pocket, which he had lined till it was sort of a sheath. She sewed on the buttons and mended the frayed cuffs before fetching their clean clothes from the clothesline and starting the patches.

Mama had always kept their clothes in repair but Rosalie never got past fixing Grandpa's garments, so that summer Laurie had progressed from awkward, pigeon-track, quarter-inch stitches to smaller, neater ones. What her patching lacked in delicacy it made up for in strength. She stitched till she was sure the patches would outwear the surrounding cloth. And all the time her head churned over Mr. Redwine's careless remark.

A musician! Was it possible—could she be a *real* one?

Way finished the sign well before noon so W. S. Redwine had him paint a new menu board to go above the counter and retouch the faded numerals on the cabins. "Eat up, kiddos," Way urged, sliding into the booth across from them. He smelled pungently of the turpentine he'd used to clean himself and his brushes. "Redwine owes us a good feed!"

"He sure does," agreed Martha. She'd done something to her hair so it wasn't nearly as frizzy and her green eyes were a bit wistful. "That's a wonderful sign, Mr. Kirkendall. If Dub weren't as tight as shrunk rawhide, he'd pay you some cash on top of your board and a ride to where he's headed anyhow."

"We'll take it out in chow." Way twinkled at her. Laurie thought again how different he looked with a haircut and shave. That wasn't all of it, though. Instead of slouching, he walked proud and his voice was confident instead of apologetic. "While I was paintin' that menu, I had plenty of time to figger out that I wanted chicken-fried steak with gravy and smashed potatoes, green beans, lots of coffee with cream, and a big chunk of pecan pie. That is, if it won't get you in trouble?"

"Dub'll never know it," Martha said.

"Where is he? He said he wanted to take out of here by one o'clock sharp."

"He's having dessert in his room." Martha gave Way a slow wink and Laurie blushed, guessing that the naked woman with that interesting patch of hair was still in Cabin 1. "He'll be raring to go at one, though," Martha warned, "so I'll tell Jim to hurry that steak. Now, boys, how about you?"

They were waiting outside the café when a somewhat battered green Pontiac swung up beside them. "Hop in," called Mr. Redwine.

These seat covers were a scratchy kind of checked fabric and there wasn't much room after the bundles were stowed in back with Laurie and Buddy, but it was still far ahead of the old Model T and it didn't have to be cranked.

"Swap your Packard?" Way asked, folding up his legs.

Mr. Redwine jerked his head toward the garage. "That's my California car. This one's for Arizona and New Mexico, where there's lots of unpaved roads. In the rainy season, from July to September, I've got an old Chevy truck that can get through most of the washes unless they're flooding."

This car either didn't have a radio or Mr. Redwine was too busy steering the car once the paving gave out. In either case, Laurie was grateful that he wasn't exhorting her to learn his music. She wished he'd say more about her becoming a musican, though she didn't want to ask. Maybe the conversation would lead around to it.

Only there wasn't much conversation beyond Mr. Redwine's cussing. They couldn't go much more than ten miles an hour on the bumpy road, which seemed to be either sand or jaggedy rocks or both at the same time. A tire went flat about an hour outside Kingman.

"Guess you know how to change a tire, Wayburn." Mr. Redwine had looked tired when he picked them up. Now his face was red and dripping sweat where it hadn't caked with dust. "There's two spares in the trunk."

"Never had a car," said Way. "Reckon you'll have to show me."

Mr. Redwine said some words Laurie hadn't heard before, even from hoboes on the train. "Have to drive and change tires, too! That's a helluva note! Get out, you kids. No use having to jack up your weight, too!"

Way fixed the next flat while Mr. Redwine smoked cigarettes and didn't even wave back at families packed into ancient trucks and flivvers that rattled past with everything from trunks to a piano tied on top or lashed onto the running boards. This might be a highway but it was about the worst road Laurie had ever seen, through the harshest country. The desert stretched to sawtooth mountains and what looked like ancient gray volcano peaks. The banks of the washes were streaked with red and green and gray. God might live here, or the devil, but it wasn't for humans.

Nor was the cliff-edged mesa country into which they ascended, a vast high tableland where wind whipped dark evergreens into tortured shapes, yet Mr. Redwine told them the highway ran through the corner of the Hualapai Indian Reservation. What had to be pronghorn antelope skimmed through the high grass, flashing white rump patches. There had been herds of them on the Kansas and Oklahoma plains, Daddy said, till they were hunted out or died because they wouldn't jump fences to get to water or feed. The prairie must have been beautiful then—forever stretches of grass and wild flowers like that tiny strip between fields and schoolyard she'd called the Little Prairie.

"Mountain sheep." Mr. Redwine nodded at white creatures poised along a precarious rock ledge.

Just around the curve, a Model A was pulled over to the side. A blond lady nursed her baby while several little ones ran and squealed as they gathered pinecones. A skinny, sunburned man in overalls was struggling to jack up the front.

"Let's stop and give him a hand, Mr. Redwine," urged Way.

"He'll manage."

"But the woman and kids—"

"Oh, some other Okies'll come along and help them," shrugged Redwine. He sent Way a hard glance. "It's my car and I'm driving. I'll decide when we stop."

" 'Cept when you have a flat."

Mr. Redwine slewed his head toward Way as Laurie, looking over her shoulder, cried out in relief, "A truck's stopping."

"I told you," shrugged Redwine. "That kind look out for each other."

"Now ain't it damned lucky they do?" said Way dryly.

When it seemed they would never see another human being, they came to a little village called Peach Springs and pulled in at the trading post from whence dirt tracks ran off in all directions. A couple of old trucks were parked beside mules and ponies. Dark-skinned men in overalls, trousers, and ordinary shirts lounged in the shade.

"Shucks!" sighed Buddy. "They're dressed just like anybody else."

Laurie was disappointed, too. These were the first "real" Indians she'd ever seen—people like Rosalie and Morrigan who lived like everybody else didn't seem Indian, though Laurie wasn't sure exactly what Indians could be like in these times. Daddy had worked with Indian cowboys up in South Dakota, and there were lots of Indians in eastern Oklahoma, but she hadn't realized that some groups still lived mostly on reservations and didn't mix with whites the way they had in Oklahoma. It began to dawn on her that Indian tribes could be as different from each other as European nations.

"How do the Hual—Indians make a living?" she asked Mr. Redwine.

He snorted. "Government handouts mostly, you can bet. But there's deer and antelope and mountain sheep to hunt, and rabbits, naturally. Their agent says they even eat porcupines and badgers and gather nuts and acorns, berries and grapes, and they use a lot of kinds of cactus. Down in the canyons, they grow little patches of corn, squash, melons, beans." He spat out the window. "About twenty years ago the government started giving them cattle so they could build up herds." He added grudgingly, "The agent says they're doing pretty well with that."

The white trader ordered a young Indian helper to patch the innertubes of the two tires in the trunk. Redwine selected a Coca-Cola from a tub of water-cooled soft drinks. "Want one?" he asked Laurie.

"Thanks, Mr. Redwine, we've got some money." She said to Way, "Let me pay for our drinks, Gramp. You've been working for our food and ride and room."

She got a 7UP, Buddy chose a Hires root beer, and Way pulled out a pale green Coke bottle. Laurie looked around for something the Hualapai had made, but except for some pitch-daubed baskets patterned in red and a blanket that looked like it was woven from strips of rabbit hide, the shelves and counters were piled with bolts of bright cloth, ready-made garments, shoes, felt and straw hats, blankets, canned foods, farm implements, tools, dishes, pans, and lamps—everything people would need from the outer world that ran through this edge of their high, wild one.

Seligman, with its ore cars and cattle pens and loading chutes near the railroad, was the only town till they pulled into Ash-fork with the road winding up the great hill above it. Laurie stared at a long, two-story building with arches supporting a balconied roof that stretched all along the front. "Is—is that a palace?" she whispered.

150

Redwine laughed. "Nope. It's the Escalante—a Harvey House. There was one smart Englishman. When he took the Santa Fe out west back in the 1870s, the food was so awful that he made a deal with the railroad. The Santa Fe would build the fancy restaurants and furnish 'em, bring in food, and pay the help's wages. Harvey hired French chefs and saw that every restaurant served the best of everything. The pretty waitresses got married so fast that he took to hiring plain ones, but they all had to be decent women and I guess they were watched after stricter than nuns." Redwine grinned. "I don't have to compete with the Escalante. After all, they can't service trucks."

Way got the sign painted before dark while Buddy roamed and Laurie washed out their dirty clothes and finished patching the dry ones. She'd never expected to treasure scissors, needles, and thread, but now she did, and kept them in the paper bag the store had given her. It gave her a good feeling to acquire things she'd taken for granted at home but which made all the difference in keeping respectable looking. Mama always said a patch or darn was no disgrace but a hole was.

There weren't many customers in the café that evening, but several tanned young cowboys taught Laurie a rollicking song about some cowboys riding home drunk from Prescott who met the devil, roped and branded him, and tied knots in his tail. "Gail Gardner made it up while he was bound for Washington, D.C., on the Santa Fe, fixin' to join up in the World War," said one of the men. "My daddy worked cattle with him on the Mogollon Rim and Gail was one of the best. Postmaster over to Prescott, he is now."

The song delighted Laurie. She got them to sing it till she had the words and valued the lesson more than the quarter and half-dollar they left for her when they jingled out. As Way and the children walked to the last cabin in the row, Buddy started singing the song. He had learned it, too! His boy's voice thinned here and there but it was clear and sweet.

Laurie gave him a jubilant hug. "Buddy! If you can sing while I play, we'll be twice as good!"

Wresting free, Buddy protested. "I can't learn all them songs, Laurie!"

"Those songs. Of course you can—most, anyway. We can practice in the car if Mr. Redwine doesn't mind. If he does, we'll practice at night. Just think! You'll have your own money again."

That brightened him considerably. "Do I get half?"

Laurie thought a minute. "Yes, if you buy your clothes and a share of groceries and whatever else we have to spend."

Buddy groaned. "I don't want to worry about all that! How much can I have to spend on good stuff like funnies and gum and candy and drinks and ice cream?"

Laurie glanced up at Way but he just grinned. "Well, Buddy," she thought aloud, trying to impress him with the facts of existence, "we all need clothes. We have to eat once Way's job with Mr. Redwine's over. When we get to Texas, we'll need to rent a place to live. It depends on how much we earn, too. The Kingman truckers gave us four dollars and ten cents. Tonight we only got a dollar and a quarter." Hastily, she added, "But that's good—and we have to be real grateful—when a man can work hard all day for a dollar."

"How much do I get?" Buddy persisted.

Way whooped. Aggravated, but giving up on educating her brother anytime soon, Laurie said, "Let's try fifteen cents."

That would have been riches to Buddy before the recent windfalls but now he wheedled. "What if we get—oh, *five* dollars? What if someone puts money in *my* bib pocket?"

"You've been spending some they put in mine."

"Yeah, but you're a lot older than me!"

"That's why I have to look out for you and why I can't let you blow money we need."

Buddy pouted as they entered the cabin. "Why should I sing when you'll give me almost as much if I don't?"

"You ought to like to sing! You should want to earn your money—and if you won't, then I'm not going to give it to you!"

"You—you're a mean old—" Buddy groped for a name bad enough and came up with one W. S. Redwine had hurled at their flat tires. "You're a mean, stingy old sow bitch!"

"Buddy!" Way caught the boy's shoulders and stared down

152

at him till Buddy stopped trying to twist away and hung his head. "You think that's the way to talk to your sister?"

Reddening till Laurie's outrage turned to pity for him, Buddy finally, reluctantly, shook his head. "Then," said Way, stern with either of them for the first time, "don't you reckon you'd better tell her you're sorry?"

Tears glinted in Buddy's eyes. As Way released him, he rubbed his sleeve across his face. "I-I'm sorry," he snuffled. "I didn't mean it, Laurie. You're not a—"

"Don't say it," she cut in swiftly. "Mama would hate to hear you talk that way."

"I'll sing," he promised in a small voice. "We can practice right now if you want to learn me some."

"Teach," Laurie sighed. "You learn and I'll teach." She sat down on the cot and got out her harmonica though she was so tired that she wanted to go right to bed. "All right. Let's try it."

Before they turned in, they had the words and music sounding right together, and if Buddy wasn't having fun, his zest was deceiving. Apparently, he'd picked up parts of Morrigan's songs, too, and it wasn't hard to work up "So Long, It's Been Good to Know You" and several of the spirituals.

"Sounds mighty good," nodded Way. "Why, you kiddos might get as famous as the Carter Family!"

Somehow, Laurie couldn't imagine Buddy singing as a career but she couldn't picture him doing anything else, either, except hunting rabbits. She was asleep the moment she stretched out on the cot.

12

Grassy meadows grazed by deer and antelope overlay ancient lava flows that here and there spread in terraces or jutted up like frozen waves. Pines, some bearing scars of lightning or fire, reared tall and straight into the sky, often so close together that there were no or few branches till close to the top, where they at last found the sun. A few yellow leaves still clung to graceful silver-trunked trees that were surrounded by a golden carpet.

"Is that a *bear?*" Buddy gasped as a dark hulk ambled unhurriedly into a thicket.

"Plenty of them up here," said Mr. Redwine. He had vanished into a cabin last night and they hadn't seen him till they were finishing breakfast when he came in the café, bleary-eyed and unshaven, to drink three cups of black coffee. "Mountain lions, too, but you could live here all your life and never see one."

A little east of Williams, cinder cones rose against the sky, their fervent heat extinguished millennia ago. Had that been one end of the world? Did it end over and over and make itself again all fresh and new?

This high world was so beautiful, so green and cool and different from the desert and plains, that Laurie feasted her eyes, unwilling to practice songs with Buddy while they had all this to see and admire.

"San Francisco Peaks." Mr. Redwine flicked his thumb toward a vast mountain with three separate crests thrust into the clouds, glistening with snow. "It's an old volcano. Fire and ice wore down the crater edge till it looks like that."

It was a shock when the forest abruptly gave way to substantial buildings of brick, stone, and wood fronting the wide streets of Flagstaff. It really was a city, the biggest Laurie had ever seen, except from the train. Signs announced a teacher's college, an observatory, and a museum. There were many church spires, a depot for the Santa Fe Railroad, an imposing Harvey House, and all kinds of nice big stores.

"Do you have a Truck-Inn here, Mr. Redwine?" Buddy asked hopefully.

"Too much competition." The man grinned at Buddy's remembering to use the name Way had coined. "This has been a big cattle and timber center ever since the railroad came through in the eighties. I like to find a place where there's plenty of traffic and not much choice for travelers. Put good food, good beds, and gas and repair service in one place and you can make a mint without being fancy the way you'd have to here."

They got the morning's flat tires patched at a gas station, where they used the rest rooms and got soft drinks. Laurie wished mightily to see the museum but she was resolved not to ask Mr. Redwine for any favors. If he knew you wanted something, she was sure he'd use that to get you to do things, like a dog does tricks for a bone. She wasn't going to be his dog. That was why she hadn't come right out and asked him what he'd meant about her becoming a musician.

The sights to the left and the right quickly made her forget her disappointment. Cinder cones; a gigantic gash in sandstone that was a solid rainbow of shadings from yellow to a brownish red the color of dried blood; far to the south the rim of what Mr. Redwine called Meteor Crater. Laurie shuddered at the notion of what sounded like a giant cannonball from space plunging into the earth with such force. She preferred to look the other way, where clouds and the slanting afternoon sun deepened every shade of crimson, violet, gold, and amethyst on distant buttes.

La Posada, the Winslow Harvey House, was a handsome Spanish-style building that awed Laurie, and she longed for just a peek inside. They passed it to eat at a roadside diner while the afternoon's flats were being patched.

"Can I buy your sandwich, Mr. Redwine?" Way asked.

Redwine gave him a tough glance from those cat's eyes. "No need," he said curtly, but he didn't offer to buy their sandwiches, either. "Make it snappy. Want to get to Holbrook before dark."

They got stuck twice in the sand of the Little Colorado River crossing and had to dig out to the tune of Mr. Redwine's cussing. As they neared Holbrook, the setting sun dyed sandstone ledges and mesas every hue of vermilion and purple.

"You can get the background painted before supper, Wayburn." Mr. Redwine pulled in behind a gas station–café and nodded at the sign above the pumps. "Then you can finish up before noon."

Way stared at the mesas, hazed purple now, fading into the distance. "Guess there's no rush. We're not fixed for campin' out in this high country. More cars are headin' for Californy

---

155

than the other way. Might take us a while to hitch a ride, there bein' the three of us."

"Asking for a free night in a cabin?"

"Reckon I know better'n that. We'll pay."

Laurie tugged at his sleeve. "Way! We can't afford—"

"Sure we can," he promised jauntily. "Bound to be some more painting jobs around town." He cocked a bland smile at his employer. "Why, I bet just as soon as that other gas station–café sees your new sign, Mr. Redwine, they're goin' to want one, too. Not to mention that tourist court on the edge of town."

"Trying to squeeze me?" growled Redwine.

"Tryin' to look out for my family."

The sun was down but Mr. Redwine's eyes caught light from somewhere and glowed pale orange. Way met his stare. After a long moment, Redwine shrugged. "We'll talk about it after you finish my sign, Wayburn. Dump your stuff in that last cabin and do the background coat before supper."

Without looking back, he strode into the café. As soon as Way had gone to the garage, Laurie turned to her brother. "Buddy, if Mr. Redwine's going to act mean, we don't have to sing in his place. Let's get cleaned up and go see if that restaurant down the road won't let us sing and play for their customers."

"They've got a big neon cowboy sign," said Buddy. "I bet they'd like our Sierry Petes song."

"I bet they will. Now hop in the tub and don't leave a ring."

Laurie shook their overalls out the window to jar loose as much dust as possible and got out clean shirts. When they stopped at the garage to tell Way where they were going, he frowned. "Why don't you go ahead and have your supper, kids? You must be plumb wore out. No need to go about this singin' like it was a have-to rain-or-shine job."

"How long will this take you, Way?" asked Laurie.

He was still scrubbing dirt and flaking paint off the metal. "Oh, maybe an hour, hour and a half."

"We'll come back then and we'll eat together."

They cut across the highway. The red neon cowboy topped

a bucking bronco on top of the whitewashed adobe building. A buzz of laughter and voices grew almost deafening as Laurie pushed open the door. The room was full of tables and the tables were full of people. Three waitresses hurried in and out of the swinging doors, skillfully levering their trays past heads and shoulders. Each time the kitchen doors opened, tantalizing aromas floated out but Laurie was so abashed that she'd lost her hunger.

This was a real restaurant, not a café for truckers who were glad of any diversion. These well-dressed people were tourists or town folks who wouldn't understand or like her music. Had Laurie been alone, she'd have bolted but she didn't want Buddy to guess her fears.

A chunky, gray-haired man behind the cash register was watching them. As she forced herself to approach him, he came out from behind the counter with its display of candy, gum, and postcards. "If you kids are hungry," he said in a low-pitched tone that still seemed echoing loud, "go around to the back and I'll tell one of the girls to feed you."

He thought they were begging! Flushing hotly, Laurie dug her harmonica from her pocket. "We-we'll be having supper across the road, mister. But—well, sometimes folks seem to like hearing us sing and play."

"I won't have anyone panhandling my customers." The big man's voice sounded louder than ever.

"We don't panhandle!" Laurie flashed, defending Morrigan and his songs and whatever talent she and Buddy possessed. "You just listen to one song, mister, and see if you don't think we're good enough to sing in your place."

She set the harmonica to her lips and launched into the rollicking gallop of "The Sierry Petes." Buddy, wide brown eyes fixed on her, sang in his high, sweet boy's voice the bibulous exploits of Sandy Bob and Buster Jigg. By the time the devil came prancing down the trail, the crowd was listening, and when he was finally branded and got a knot tied in his tail, there was thunderous applause.

"Say, Jed," called a prosperous-looking gentleman in a suede jacket and polished boots. "Let's scoot tables till those boys can stand in the middle and we can hear 'em better."

Jed, the gray-haired man, scanned his customers. "That suit all of you?"

"Tickles us plumb to death," drawled another man in boots, who rose to move his table.

Jed lowered his head to speak in Laurie's ear. "Okay, you can go ahead and sing but don't you stop and stare around between numbers like you expect money. Quit as soon as folks start talking like they'd rather do that than listen. I'll give you a dollar when you leave. Reckon we'll get enough extra pie and coffee orders to afford that."

The man in the suede jacket ordered root beer for them and taught them the haunting, wistful "Colorado Trail" when they had, to considerable applause, done all the cowboy songs Buddy knew. By then it was time to join Way. Laurie guessed these folks could put up with one Dust Bowl song so she moved into "So Long, It's Been Good to Know You."

As she and Buddy started for the door, the man in suede put a dollar in Buddy's overall bib. Someone else thrust a dollar in Laurie's. These were joined by half dollars, quarters, and more bills—no dimes or nickels.

Jed stepped out from behind the cash register. "Maybe you ought to give *me* a dollar," he said wryly. "But you didn't hint for anything and a deal's a deal." He gave Laurie another bill as the door swung open. "You boys going to be in town a while?"

"No, they're not." W. S. Redwine loomed against the door. "We're traveling east tomorrow." He gave a curt nod and held the door, following Laurie and Buddy outside.

"What's the big idea?" he demanded, striding across the highway. "You damned ungrateful little devils! I got a good notion to let all of you hunt other beds tonight."

"Then you won't get your sign," said Laurie, speaking up boldly though his anger scared her. "We've got money to rent another cabin. And we went across the street because if you're not giving us a room tomorrow night there's no reason to try to help your business."

"Your granddad's in the café," growled Redwine. "Come along in here and let's get some things settled."

"We've got to wash our hands first," said Laurie.

When she and Buddy entered the café, Redwine didn't even glance at them but finished what he was telling Way. "—so you might as well ride with me to Texas and do signs for my places there. When you're finished with that, you can get work easy in Black Spring, what with the oil boom." His gaze flickered toward Laurie. "There's a school. That's where the boys ought to be."

School? To go to school you had to have a home, even if it was a shack or a tarp stretched from a car to a post. You had to have a *place,* if only for a little while. Way's dark eyes searched Laurie's face.

"What do you think, kiddos?"

"Texas is where we want to go," said Laurie.

It was a real big state, the biggest, and there were lots of oil fields, but wasn't there a chance of someday meeting up with Morrigan? Wherever he was would feel like home—she wouldn't have bad dreams—even if it was along the road beneath a cottonwood the way it had been last time, that magic, never-to-be-forgotten time when Mama talked God into sending an angel.

Sun and shadows crimsoned the Painted Desert, hazed it in every tint of blue, purple, and gray, or drenched the white and yellow with stark brilliance. Dead rainbow trunks and stobs of the Petrified Forest twisted or sprawled from warped masses of hardened red clay. Buttes, lava flows, earth gashed with ox-blood or leached dull gray. Reservations and trading posts, Gallup, New Mexico, Grants.

Redwine didn't own any truck stops in this state so they drove right through the night. Laurie had already discovered one interesting habit of W.S.'s. Heading downhill, he'd speed up, then throw in the clutch and coast in neutral as long as he could. "Saves gas," he said, but she thought what he relished was getting a free ride where most people didn't.

Just as stingily, he saved sleep. He wouldn't let Way spell him. Dozing as she sat in the corner of the backseat and cuddled Buddy, who was stretched out with his head in her lap, Laurie roused when the car stopped and Mr. Redwine turned off the lights. He sort of wrapped his arms across the wheel and rested on them. Laurie drowsed off again so she didn't know how long he had napped when she woke to the sound and movement of the car. That happened several times before dawn, when they ate at Los Lunas and headed north for the mountains and Santa Fe.

"Be glad when they straighten the highway," Redwine grumbled. "When they run it through Albuquerque like they're talking, they'll cut off ninety miles."

Santa Fe! The name—all Spanish names—enchanted Laurie, and so did the adobe buildings with pole ends sticking out of the upper walls. The golden-brown walls were smoothed as if with loving hands and looked as if they'd curve like bodies to fit the people who lived in them. They weren't hard and unchangeable like wood or stone or brick. Laurie yearned to look at the jewelry, moccasins, pottery, and other things the Indians had spread on blankets along the streets but of course she couldn't ask.

Mexican food in Las Vegas that afternoon, a bowl of steaming chili that night in Tucumcari. It was morning but still dark when they stopped at a string of cabins and a truck center with a neon sign that glared at them: WELCOME TO TEXAS—GOOD FOOD—GOOD BEDS—GOOD GAS. From the opposite side, it proclaimed: LAST CHANCE AT TEXAS PRICES.

W. S. Redwine got out and stretched, his blocky shoulders looking solid as granite, his legs like pillars in the sand. "It's good business to rake in money off 66." He yawned heavily and his thin seam of a mouth stretched in a grin. "West Texas is my stomping ground, though, where I've really sunk my money. Pile out. When you wake up in the morning, Wayburn, you can start my sign. There'll be fourteen of them to do between here and Black Spring—hotel and café signs, too."

Lifting a metal box from under the seat, Redwine got out a huge ring of keys, each shaped differently but with no other means of identification. He selected one, opened the café, and got a key from one of the nails spaced on a board beneath the cash register.

"Last cabin," he told Way, before, without knocking, he went through a door marked PRIVATE.

"Dub!" came a woman's voice. The woman was surprised for certain, but whether glad or sad, Laurie couldn't guess.

W. S. Redwine and his party drove through the Llano Estacado, the high, wind-scourged Staked Plains, perhaps named for the yuccas spiking lance-straight from the seared earth, yuccas much larger than those Laurie remembered from the Oklahoma Panhandle. Dust had blown here, too, especially where the prairie sod had been broken to farm. Dunes banked against buildings, heaped around yuccas, half-buried fence posts.

Most of the flivvers and trucks they met were headed the other way, mattresses and chairs roped to the top, suitcases and boxes tied to the running boards, kids stuffed in amongst the bedding and household gear. Laurie ached every time they passed a family with a broken-down vehicle but there was no use asking Redwine to stop. He even seemed to drive faster past these stranded folks, churning up more dust. If I ever have a car, she thought, I'll carry extra innertubes and tires and food and water and I'll always stop. Meanwhile all she could do was pray someone like Morrigan—well, not like him, for no one could be—but someone kind and cheerful would come along and get each family on its road again.

"Dust never got as bad here as it did in that hundred-mile circle around Liberal, Kansas," said Redwine, as if he, personally, had gentled the storms. "But come the blowin' months in spring, lots of this country moves over into New Mexico."

They stopped in two places where a Dub's Truck-Inn was all there was. Even so, Laurie and Buddy collected $1.75 for their singing in the first café and $2.60 in the other. They didn't keep it, though. While Way was finishing up the sign at the second truck stop, a jalopy pulled in for a few gallons of gas. The tall, raw-boned driver and his yellow-haired wife must have been

161

young—she held a baby and the towheaded twin boys couldn't have been more than three—but lines were graved in their faces and they looked *old,* worlds older than Grandpa Field.

The woman took the children to the rest room and took advantage of water and soap because when they came out, faces and hands were much cleaner. Smells of bacon, coffee, and biscuits floated from the café. "Hun'gy, mama!" One boy tugged at his mother's faded skirt. "Billy hun'gy!"

"I'll give you a cracker," she said, urging him along.

"Want some milk!"

"We don't have any," the woman whispered in a desperate, embarrassed way. "Get in that car, Joey, and quit makin' a show of us!" Her husband was digging into his pocket, adding to the change in his hand. It was with clear relief that he found a nickel and three pennies that finished paying for the gas.

Laurie glanced at her brother. He nodded and delved into his bib pocket for his share of the money. Laurie got hers. Catching the woman's raggedy sweater sleeve, she thrust the money into her hand. "Please take it, lady," she whispered. "We're from the Dust Bowl, too."

It was the first time she'd said it but now she had, she knew for the rest of her life it would be a kind of password, a bond with everyone blasted from their roots, blown with the dust along the lonesome roads. They were her people, they were her kin. The woman gazed at them warily.

"How'd you boys get this kind of money if you're Okies?"

Laurie's mortification changed to pride. "We didn't steal it, lady." She got her harmonica out of her pocket. "Folks gave us money for our music."

"Your ma and pa—"

"They'd want us to help." Of that Laurie was sure. "Please, lady, get your kids some milk and good things and sometime, when you're able, help someone else."

The worry lines in the woman's face melted into a smile. She looked years younger, almost pretty. "You're angels!" She kissed Laurie, patted Buddy's cheek, and took Joey's hand. Trailed by the other children, she hurried to the grocery store up the road while her husband got the Model T to cough and start.

" 'Preciate it, boys!" he yelled at them, waving.

"I ain't no angel!" Buddy grumbled.

"Aren't, Buddy! You *aren't!*"

Laurie could scarcely see the family for the mist in her eyes. Wasn't it funny the woman called them angels when that was what she herself had thought about Morrigan? It was a good feeling, but it ebbed as Laurie stared at the old jalopy that carried a family and all they had on earth.

Four dollars and thirty-five cents. That would feed them a couple of days, buy gas to get them a little farther on that long way west. And then they'd be just as broke and just as hungry. She kept her share of the music money separate from Buddy's. Running to the cabin, she hauled the old sock out of her bundle and took out the bills.

Eight of them. And here were five half-dollars. She'd been hoarding them for school clothes and things they'd need to set up housekeeping, but she and Buddy could always earn more. If the man worked anytime he found a job along the road, if they were lucky and found a farm where they could have a house and some of their food on top of a small wage, if . . . if . . . if!

Why did poor people's lives depend on so many *if*s they couldn't control? At least this money would buy gas, buy food, buy a little hope. Laurie ran all the way to the store and gasped up as the family came out of the grocery with two big sacks.

The woman shifted the baby in her arms and fumbled in her pocket. "If you want your money back, all we've got left is two dollars."

Laurie shook her head. "Keep it. And—and Mama sent this." She stuffed the rolled dollars and coins into the sweater pocket and got out the harmonica. "Is there a song you folks like? Songs help on the road."

"Play your fav'rite, son," the man said.

Laurie did, "So Long . . ." Then the family piled in the Model T, Joey guzzling milk right out of the bottle. They waved till the mattress-crowned flivver jounced out of sight.

"What the hell you up to?"

Laurie jumped. W. S. Redwine had told Way he tipped the scales at two hundred pounds but he could be soft-footed as a cat. She hadn't done anything to be ashamed of; why was it so hard to meet his eyes?

"I was just telling those folks good-bye."

"You gave them money." He said it like she'd committed an unspeakable crime. "Emptied your overall bibs, but oh no, that wasn't enough! I saw you stick a wad of bills in that tramp woman's pocket. And all the time I'm givin' the lot of you free beds and meals, not to mention transportation!"

"Well, you have mentioned it, Mr. Redwine, and the cabin and meals haven't been free. Gramp's painted your signs. What's more, he thought up that catchy slogan about 'the rest of your life' that would've cost you plenty if some big advertisement outfit had done it!" The man scared Laurie just by being so big and rocklike. Why did the sunlight drain the color from his eyes, leaving them the shade of dirty ice? Laurie's stomach knotted but she said boldly, "Buddy and I earned that money— maybe we didn't *earn* it, but folks gave it to us. If you don't like what we do with it, I reckon we can take off on our own and get along just fine. You can find someone else to paint your signs in Black Spring."

His body seemed to swell, completely blocking off the sun. If he tried to shake or slap her, she'd go for his wrist, bite in as hard as she could. A breath went out of him, almost a sigh. He chuckled suddenly. "You got a big mouth, Larry, but it's kind of interestin' to see what you'll do next. Toss your stuff in the car. Time we was going."

Her knees started to shake as she walked away. Strangely, she didn't feel exhilarated about facing him down. It was as if he were keeping accounts and every mark by her name would have to be paid for sometime. But that was crazy! This was a free country—free to starve anyhow. She and Buddy and Way could leave Redwine whenever they took the notion. She just mustn't ever let him guess how he scared her.

13

The high plains looked like a vast rumpled carpet dropped carelessly from the doming sky, faded yellow-brown worn bare where the grass was gone, pegged down by yuccas or by derricks that looked from a distance like towers made of Tinkertoys. Pump jacks worked up and down, huge mechanical birds bobbing heads and tails as they sucked oil from beneath the exhausted soil. It reminded Laurie of draining blood from a dead body. The highway in New Mexico had been a mix of pavement, dirt, and gravel, paved from Tucumcari to the Texas border. From there it was unpaved almost to Amarillo, the biggest city Laurie had ever been in and the most important one for hundreds of miles in every direction.

"Those grain elevators may be empty and ranchers aren't shipping many cattle," said Redwine. "The dust gets bad here, too, busts ranchers and farmers, but it can't hurt what's underground. Pipeline and tank cars run out of here with gas and oil for Kansas and Missouri, even far away as Michigan and Wisconsin and all the oil fields get their supplies and equipment here. Don't see how Amarillo can go any way but rich so it's one city with competition where I'm investing pretty deep."

To Laurie's relief, they didn't see much of him during the three days Way painted signs for Redwine's restaurant and hotel and two Truck-Inns on the west and east ends of town on 66. She and Buddy sang at the restaurant during the noon rush. Close to the bus station, courthouse, and post office, it was clean but not fancy and served good food at moderate prices so that it drew regulars as well as bus travelers and those stopping at the junction of 66 and 87, the city's main thoroughfare.

The big contributors were people in the oil business. From their talk and what the waitresses said, Laurie began to sort them out. A tool pusher in for equipment might wear work khakis but his laced boots were of the best quality and the hat he tossed on a peg would be a Stetson. Producers wore dark suits with polished cowboy boots. Speculators emulated that attire but added tooled belts with inlaid buckles and turquoise rings, even silver and turquoise wristwatch bands, and usually smoked cigars. Roughnecks didn't eat here, preferring places nearer to their other entertainments. Speculators either didn't leave any money or they made a show of stuffing a dollar into an overall bib. Producers usually gave a quarter. Drillers always left fifty cents or a dollar and one, who'd asked Laurie if they could do "Yellow Rose of Texas," left a wadded five-dollar bill in her pocket.

Three musical noons at the restaurant and three evenings at the truck stop filled the sock again. Laurie's fingers trembled as she counted out the money and Buddy divided it into even shares. "Twenty-one dollars, Buddy! That's ten-fifty each. We can get school books, the clothes we need worst, and set up housekeeping."

Way sighed. "Don't seem right for you kiddies to buy our pots and pans but in return for my paintin' his signs at Black Spring, Redwine's going to give us a house for a month and credit for groceries at his store."

"Which'll cost more than they do anywhere else," said Laurie. At Way's crestfallen look, she jumped up and gave him a hug. "I bet we get enough from singing to buy our groceries till you get a paycheck from the job you're going to find!"

"I bet you will," chuckled Way, touching her cheek with his rough, paint-stained, turpentine-smelling hand. "Far as that goes, before I hunt a job in the oil patch I might better pick up any other paintin' jobs I can find. Shucks, might even be some fellas want their pictures painted to send their old mothers for Christmas. Most men'll do anything to get out of writin' a letter."

"And when they do write, they likely don't get it mailed." Laurie thought aloud, remembering with a pang how seldom Daddy wrote, wishing she had those scrawled cards. "You get addresses, Way, and we'll wrap and mail the pictures."

"We'll sell a bunch more doin' that." Way's eyes lit up. "Say, Larry-Laurie, it's a sight easier to come up with good ideas

166

when there's someone to help. When we get to Black Spring are you goin' to be my granddaughter?"

Laurie didn't understand it, but she didn't want W. S. Redwine to ever know she was a girl. "I better stay a boy for a while. It's easier that way to go in places and make music."

"S'pose you're right." Way looked wistful and she remembered his dead little daughter. "But I'll be tickled when you can wear some pretty dresses and let your hair grow out all curly and soft."

"What'll you do about going to the toilet at school?" Buddy asked. "I don't want somebody finding out you're a girl and then trying to see if I am!"

"They won't find out if you don't tell them," snapped Laurie. "I-I'll watch and go to the boys' toilet when no one's there and they're busy playing or something."

Buddy curled his lip. "I'll still be glad when you go back to bein' what you are."

Skirts would feel funny now and so would curls. The time was coming when bib overalls wouldn't hide her breasts but as long as she could pass for a boy, she was going to. Guilt smote her over that dress Rosalie had made for her, the only garment in her bundle that she hadn't worn during the journey. She ought to send it back to Rosalie so she could make it over for Belle.

"Better tuck in, kiddos," said Way, yawning. "Mr. Redwine wants to leave real early so we can get to Black Spring before dark."

It had been wonderful to see that high, wild mountain country in Arizona and New Mexico but Laurie was worn out with traveling, especially with Mr. Redwine. Still, now their long road was ending—the road that ran all the way back to Prairieville—she felt nervous, wondered if the teachers and kids at the school would be as mean as those in Oklahoma. "I wonder if we'll like it there," she muttered.

Way's answer was simple, short, and beautiful. "If we don't, we'll move on."

Of course! Of course they could. Way had his paintbrushes, she and Buddy had their music. But a little pang tainted the heady sense of freedom. She wanted a home, a place to belong. But with Mama and Daddy both dead and Way used to wandering, she thought she'd better not count on staying anywhere very long.

It was dark outside when they went in for breakfast. A big black Cadillac hulked in front of the café but no one was in the narrow, glaring white room except a hefty waitress with kinky brown hair who rubbed her eyes sleepily as she took their order. By the time she brought their pancakes, several truckers had come in. Their banter woke up the waitress. She started sloshing coffee into Way's cup when she refilled the truckers'.

"Hold it, Sal." Redwine stepped inside. "You'll give Wayburn coffee nerves." He laughed and dropped a thick hand on Laurie's shoulder. "Ready to go?"

"Yes, sir." She slid out from under his hand. He wasn't pressing down, not really, but she felt as if he were.

He stared at her a minute. She pretended not to know it and made for the door. "Toss your stuff in the Caddy," he said. "That's my car for Texas where there's paving."

"Is Black Spring paved?" Way finished his coffee and left the waitress a dime.

"It is through town." Redwine's voice followed Laurie as she ran back to the cabin for her bundle. "I've got two trucks there. One's usually running."

Was he a little crazy? Surely no one else in the world would think of keeping a Packard for California, an old car for dirt roads, a Cadillac for good Texas roads, and a couple of trucks. She could understand being stingy all the way or always extravagant if you could afford it, but she guessed W. S. Redwine was the only person who had plenty of money but threw the clutch into neutral to coast far as he could without burning gas. She wondered what kind of a house he had. It was hard to imagine him living anywhere.

The Cadillac whizzed by so many oil derricks before they got to Black Spring late that afternoon that Laurie didn't see how there could be that much oil beneath the sandy drifts or the scoured underlying hardpan. Hadn't she read in her geography that oil formed from decayed plants and animals buried ages ago? At first she sort of liked the smell of oil but by the time they stopped for chili at a Dub's Truck-Inn, the oil stank like something dead to her, like the guts of the earth had rotted after men finished gashing and stripping and killing it. She felt sick at her stomach and paid for a Coke. Redwine let her and Buddy order milk but announced at the start that he wasn't providing soft drinks.

She still felt so bad that she rolled down the window for air. There was no telling what anyone as peculiar as he was might do if she threw up all over his soft leather seat and thick carpet. As soon as he stopped, she got the door open and stumbled to the side of the road. Fortunately, it was outside town. Nobody saw her except the others in the Cadillac.

Way was bending over her in seconds, awkwardly holding her head, supporting her. As soon as her stomach emptied, she felt better and stopped sweating. Way wiped her face and mouth with a raggedy handkerchief. "You all right, Lau-Larry?"

"Yes. I-I'm sorry—"

"Comes of swillin' pop." Redwine got out of his car, which was not so shiny now. "Get your stuff and I'll show you your house." He peered down the rutted track. "You're in luck. Hasn't been rented. See that first house after the tents, the white one?"

"Don't look no color to me," said Way. "And it don't look very big for a family."

"It's a three-roomer," Redwine said indignantly. "Rents for five dollars a week furnished."

"May be why it ain't rented," Way grunted.

"You can start walking. I'll get the key and a truck and be there by the time you are."

The old main part of town lay just ahead on either side of the pavement, the solid frame, stone, and brick businesses and buildings that Redwine said were raised by cotton and cattle money. Church spires rose above substantial dwellings and a turreted courthouse dominated a square. Well, that was for folks who belonged to Black Spring. But a block from the highway was a yellow brick school with a fenced playground where some boys were playing baseball. School was for everybody—at least, if you lived in a town, they had to let you come even if you got called a dirty cropper or Okie or oil-field trash.

Laurie picked up her bundle and trudged beside Way. "Coldblooded sucker!" Way growled. "You sick but he wouldn't get his damn Caddy in the dust!"

"I think he was more scared I'd upchuck in it," Laurie grinned. "Don't fret, Way. I feel better walking."

Rows of tents stretched along both sides of the road, which splayed out widely in places to avoid bumpy hollows that must have been impassable after a rain. Trucks and wagons clunked and rattled past, piled high with all sizes of pipe, with barrels and tanks, engines, wheels, and all manner of mysterious gear. Some of the tents were reinforced waist-high with boards. As a couple of shouting boys burst out of one, she glimpsed a wooden floor. Chimneys stuck out of the tent tops and smoke came from some of them.

Laurie shuddered at the thought of how fast a fire could jump from tent to tent. The shacks couldn't be much sturdier but the playing youngsters and the women chatting with each other or going in and out of the half-dozen stores and cafés looked well fed and wore good clothes.

These people were on the move, just like the Okie pickers in California. Laurie had scarcely learned the names of some of the oil kids who went to school in Prairieville before they moved away. But though this was a tent-and-shanty camp, it wasn't a bit like that awful, despairing, starving place where Daddy had wound up with the Halsells.

Where were they now? Would the Model T get them to the next job? Would the little boy Daddy died to save grow up and have some kind of chance for a decent life? What would happen to Jack, who was smart, and Bernice, who hated to go to school because the town kids were mean? How come President Roosevelt didn't make the growers stop sending those lying handbills to the Dust Bowl and other places where folks were losing their jobs or farms? How come the government didn't warn people there weren't steady jobs in California? But if most of them swarmed to the oil fields, there wouldn't be enough work. It just wasn't right! If folks wanted to work, they ought to be able to, and they ought to earn enough to live decent even if the work kept them moving.

Almost as much as food and shelter, though, Laurie wanted a real home, a place to belong. Black Spring wasn't it, at least not while it was booming. When it went back to being a cattle and farming town—if it ever could, what with drought and dust—they'd have to move on to make a living. Still, there was a school. She and Buddy could go on with their educations the way Mama and Daddy had wanted.

A Chevy truck with a few muddy patches of pocked maroon rusted metal swerved around them to park by the shack with the FOR RENT—FURNISHED sign. About all you could say for it was that it didn't look any worse than most of the houses scattered two or three deep along the road. It was at least all made of boards, not like some that were cobbled together out of old crates, rotting wood, sheet iron, and buckets and oil barrels cut open and pounded flat. It had two cracked glass windows. One had a hole stuffed with a rag but some windows didn't have panes or screens, only gunnysacks or pieces of tarp. The roof was corrugated tin.

Redwine unlocked the door and entered the cabin. He almost filled the narrow room that was crowded with a kerosene cook-stove, a packing crate stood on one end with a couple of shelves that served as table and cupboard, and apple crates for chairs. "Plenty of houses have dirt floors," Redwine said. "You've got wood *and* linoleum."

It looked more like tarpaper with cracked enamel showing under the stove and close to the edges where it didn't get walked on. Plasterboard walled off two even narrower rooms with spaces between it and the outer wall left for doors. A lopsided army cot took up most of one room and a double bed with rusty springs but no mattress fitted tight against the wall in the end room, leaving less than a foot between it and the plasterboard divider. A half-dozen nails hammered into the solider wood of the framing served as the wardrobe.

"Like I said, this fetches five dollars a week, but you can have it for a month for painting my signs."

"How many signs?" asked Way.

Redwine paused as if to count but Laurie thought that if you'd roused him from deep sleep and he'd wanted to, he could say exactly what he owned where, what it cost to run and what it brought in. "Well, here there'll be the hotel, a Truck-Inn, the lumberyard, and hardware store. Selkirk, Tyson, and Cross Trails have Truck-Inns, hotels, and hardwares. Cumberland and Rimrock have Inns and hardware stores."

Way's eyebrows bristled together. "Whereat are them towns?"

"Oh, they're all within a hundred miles," Redwine said easily. "I'll see you get rides back and forth, no charge."

"Big of you. Sounds like you got about seventeen signs you want painted. I reckon you'll want me to think up something catchy for your hardware stores. Fella at Holbrook told me he got ten dollars a day for paintin' signs." Way rubbed his chin. "Tell you what, Mr. Redwine. You get decent mattresses on the bed and cot, lend us sheets and pillows and enough dishes and pans to get by on, put in a heating stove, and I'll do your signs—the ones you mentioned—for the house and three dollars a day."

"Why, you broke-down old tramp—"

"We got to eat."

Laurie put her hand on Way's sleeve. "We've got enough money to go someplace else, Gramp." She spoke to him but it was for Redwine's benefit.

"You kiddos need to be in school."

"There's schools in other towns." But how tired she was of being on the road, on the move, a different place each night. Repressing a sigh, she picked up her bundle. "Come on, Buddy."

Redwine's hand dropped to her shoulder. She felt it like a giant paw—maybe the sphinx's—clamping her down. "Ride over to the hotel with me and pick out what you need, boy." To Way, he said, "Three dollars a day, then, if you think up a good slogan for the hardware stores."

Laurie shrugged out from under Redwine's hand as soon as they were outside. She still felt as if he had hold of her. She climbed into the truck and he slammed the door. "None of my business," he said after he got the Chevy running and yanked it around, narrowly missing the shanty across the road. "But you better get that kid brother of yours in school before he gets so used to bein' on the tramp that he can't settle down."

That was Laurie's fear, especially since getting put back a grade that fall had further disgusted Buddy with school, but she said hotly, "We're not on the tramp! Mama and Daddy died and—"

Redwine held up a square, dismissing hand. "Son, I admire your stickin' up for your grandpa but if he's not a tramp, or anyway a hobo, I've never seen one. He may try to stay put for you kids' sake but wandering gets in the blood. You're quite a bit older than your brother. It's up to you to see he has a chance to amount to something."

"Gramp hasn't had any reason to settle down before," Laurie defended though she couldn't help but think back to how Way had been when they met—eating up their food, ready to panhandle rather than work.

But he *had* changed. He'd got out his paintbrushes and earned their lodging, food, and transportation all the way from California. He and she and Buddy were a family. Tomorrow was Thursday and Laurie had been thinking she'd wait till Monday to take Buddy to school and get enrolled. The truth was that much as she wanted to get them in class, her stomach knotted tight when she remembered how they'd been treated at the Oklahoma school. Mr. Redwine was right, though. She was responsible for Buddy. Tomorrow morning, no matter how he fussed, they'd cross the highway to that yellow brick school.

The Redwine House was the largest, handsomest building in Black Spring, two-story red brick with a long veranda where guests could sit and watch the doings up and down Main Street. Its owner drove around in back and parked by the black Cadillac.

"We'll go in through the kitchen, Larry," said Redwine. "You can pick out the stuff you need there while the manager's wife decides which mattresses and bedding you can use. Clem'll drive you back. I've got business to attend to." He paused at the back door. "When you starting school?"

"Tomorrow morning."

"Fine. The county superintendent of schools is a friend of mine. I'll find time to call him so he can tell the principal at this school that I'm taking a special interest in you and you're not just oil-field brats."

"You don't need to do that, Mr. Redwine." Instinct warned Laurie that it wasn't good, being beholden to him, no matter how nice—and different—it would be to have an important citizen vouch for them.

"I will, though." Redwine's chuckle was hearty but it didn't warm his yellow eyes. "You've got guts, Larry. The way you've made a good thing out of that old harmonica sure makes me suspect you could do real well in music if you got the right breaks."

It was the first time he'd mentioned that since way back in Arizona. What did he mean? Surely not that she and Buddy could ever be like Jimmy Rodgers or the Carter Family? Bemused, Laurie followed him into the kitchen.

"Edna," he said to the skinny, gray-haired woman who was frosting a huge cake. "Larry here needs a few dishes and pans for three people—old stuff you can spare. Might give him a chunk of that cake, too."

"All we got to cook with is stuff Noah left on the ark, Dub," said the woman tartly. "I been tellin' you I need some stainless steel instead of cast iron that's so heavy it puts my back out to lift it and dented old aluminum that's worn so thin a body can well nigh see through it and—"

Redwine threw up his hands and made for the swinging door to the restaurant. "All right, Edna, all right! Go over to the hardware and get what you want. Damn fine thing when I can't walk in the door after a long trip without your bellyachin'!"

"That's what I say!" she shrilled after him.

As soon as he vanished, she cackled, did a kind of jig step, and peered over her wire-rimmed glasses at Laurie. "Lord bless you, child, pick out whatever you want so long as it's not the good china and silverware on those shelves by the door! Never thought I'd get new cooking gear out of Dub. Unless somethin' shows, he's tighter'n new bark on a green tree, you savvy." She larruped a broad spatula across the cake, scooping up a luscious slather of chocolate frosting, and handed it to Laurie. "You need a glass of milk with that," she said, pouring one. "Your folks renting one of Dub's shacks down in Sludge Town?"

The frosting didn't taste quite as good as it had before Edna said that, though her tone was kindly. Laurie put down the spatula, though there was still frosting on it. "Is—is that what town people call the oil camp?"

"When they don't call it B. S. Flats," Edna laughed. At Laurie's puzzled stare, she explained, "You must be new to the oil patch, lad, not to know that B. S. stands for bottom settlin's or sediment, same as bullshit."

Laurie gasped. She'd never heard a woman use that word. Edna didn't notice. "You'll want a dishpan." She took a big one off a nail by the sink and set it on a stool. "Pile your things in there. How many in your family?"

"My kid brother and Gramp and me."

Edna gave her a long look. "That all?"

Laurie's throat ached. "Yes'm." *Don't let her ask questions.* "Can you spare this teakettle? And a couple of knives?"

"Help yourself." Edna flourished with her ruffled flour-sack apron. "More you cart off, the more new things I can get. Fact is, I reckon I'll put everything I plain detest on this cabinet top. I'll give Susie—she's Clem's wife—her pick of what you can't use. Lord knows she earns twice what she gets paid for keepin' this big hotel clean with only them two scatterbrained girls of hers to help. Clem washes the windows and dumps the wastebaskets but anyone except Dub Redwine would hire more help when he's got every room rented most any night."

"We don't have anyplace to keep more than what we really need." Laurie tucked in a cast-iron skillet and deliberated over sizes of pots. She added one big enough for a mess of beans and found a lid that would fit it and a chipped enamel saucepan for cooking oatmeal and potatoes.

While she rummaged through the growing heap of bent, broken, or shoddy utensils, Edna took time from her orgy of gleeful discarding to wrap four plates, saucers, bowls, and cups in flour-sack dish towels and clean rags. "The fourth's in case you have company," she said, and filled a jar with sugar. "Screw the lid on tight between meals so ants and flies can't get in. Better take these mixing bowls. This is the best eggbeater. Here's some glasses. . . ."

A horn sounded. "Drat that Clem! Always in a toot 'cept when there's something I need him to do! Late in the day to start cookin', child. You might as well take this leftover chicken and mashed potatoes, I can't feed 'em to the customers."

"Hold your horses!" Edna yelled out the window as the horn blasted louder and longer. She cut off a good quarter of the cake and put it in an empty shoe box she got down from a shelf in the pantry. "You folks have a good supper, Larry. If you think of somethin' else that'd come in handy, just come by after school and we'll see what we can do."

Putting the food in a crate that still held some apples, Edna lugged it outside and Laurie followed.

14

Clem, a staved-up cowboy whose red hair was fading to white, helped put the mattresses on the cot and bed and set the kerosene heater where it wouldn't get tripped over when someone opened the door or shove easily against the wall. "Be careful with this thing," Clem warned. "These shanties burn like tinder 'cause that's what they are." He eyed the interior with disgust. "Five bucks a week for shack! No wonder Dub's rich. If he don't have me hoppin' all day tomorrow, I'll bring over some chairs and a little cupboard that're just rottin' away in the hotel basement. Bring a tin bathtub, too."

"Thank you kindly," said Way, filling the coffeepot from the old bucket that had been setting on the cookstove and shaking in some Arbuckle's. "Got time for a cup?"

"There's plenty of cake," added Laurie.

"Much obliged but Dub wants I should wash and wax his Caddy right away." He limped to the door. "Pleased to meet you folks. Hope you do all right in Black Spring and find better diggin's before too long." His dappled face creased in a wide grin. "Wouldn't be real hard, would it?"

While Way heated up their supper, Laurie got Buddy to help make the beds. Clem's wife had sent two quilts and though they were faded, they brightened the narrow little rooms. The biggest dish towel was made from a hundred-pound flour sack splashed with giant sunflowers. Laurie smoothed it over the crate-table and put on the plates and forks.

It was wonderful, absolutely wonderful, to sit down at their own table again. She hadn't been saying grace out loud in the Truck-Inns, just bowing her head and making sure that Buddy did. Now she reached for Buddy's hand on one side and Way's on the other. "Father, we thank you for this food and for a place to live. Thank you for bringing us safe—and be with all the folks out on the road and flipping freights and in the camps. Amen."

Neither Laurie nor Buddy had clean shirts or underwear and socks for school, so as soon as the dishes were done, Laurie carried the pan to the faucet behind the shack next door that served the six households that paid rent to Redwine. They were entitled to share two privies set back about a hundred feet from the road. Laurie needed to go but hoped she could wait till dark even though she was scared of the spiders and snakes that frequented such places.

Relieved to see Buddy scrambling after a football across the road with some other boys, Laurie filled the pan as full as she could carry it without splashing and started home—what a lovely word! The back door of the nearest shanty banged and a girl about her own age came running out. Her perm-frizzed brown hair made a scant frame for a round face with a snub nose and hazel eyes. "Want me to open your door?"

"Sure."

"What's your name?"

Laurie had an impulse to confide in this seemingly friendly stranger but decided it was too risky. "Larry Field. What's yours?"

"Catharine Harris. We just got here yesterday from Wichita Falls." She held the door till Laurie passed through, hesitated till Laurie said, "Come on in. I've got to wash out some clothes but the water has to heat first."

"Don't your mother wash your things?"

Laurie bent lower than necessary to light the kerosene burner beneath the dishpan. The wicks were shielded by tall canlike flues that had little isinglass-paned doors to open for lighting. "Mother's dead." She could say it now without sobbing, though her eyes stung. "So's Daddy. My brother and me live with Gramp."

"Did I hear my name?" Way came in with a box that he set on the table. "Hi, sis," he said to Catharine. "How about a Coke?"

"Thanks, mister. I'd split one with Larry."

"Catharine's last name is Harris," Laurie said. How lovely to be able to offer a visitor half a Coke! Laurie dismissed alarm over how much Way must have spent for groceries—there were bags of beans and potatoes, sugar and flour, but there was also Eagle Brand, peanut butter, grape preserves, tinned meats, and apples and bananas. After all, they didn't have to buy sheets and pillows and dishes, though she wanted to get their own things as soon as they could afford it.

She took two glasses from the top of the oven that rose to the right of the three burners on the stove. She had scrubbed off greasy dust so dishes could be stacked there till Clem brought the cabinet, bless him. "She just moved in next door yesterday. Catharine, my Gramp's name is Wayburn Kirkendall."

"Pleased to meet you, Mr. Kirkendall." Catharine bobbed her head. "My pop's already got on as a roustabout. You had any luck?"

"Oh, I won't be lookin' for an oil job right away. Doin' some sign paintin'."

178

Catharine's anxious smile broadened to a laugh. "Gosh, Mr. Kirkendall, I'm glad you're not a driller or tool pusher! Pop's last driller was nice but his kids were real stuck up, wouldn't play with me and my little brother or even walk to school with us."

"Buddy and I'll be glad to walk with you," said Laurie, moving the dishpan to a box and unwrapping a big bar of Ivory.

"I got cheese and bread and cookies for your lunches tomorrow," Way said. He went off to the bedroom as if to leave them private, though a word spoken in one corner of the house would reach to all the others. Catharine puckered the almost invisible down of her eyebrows.

"You don't care if the other boys call you a sissy?"

That was better than the things Dan Hart, the landlord's son, had whispered to her. "As long as we're friends, I don't give a rip about the rest of them," Laurie said. Maybe, though, it wasn't fair to let Catharine think she was a boy. Rubbing away at Buddy's shirt, afraid to look at Catharine, Laurie blurted out the truth.

There was shocked silence. Laurie wrung out the shirts. "If you don't want to be friends—" she began.

"Oh, I do!" Laurie found herself embraced, soapy arms and all. Catharine's eyes shone like green jewels. "Why, this is lots better, Larry—I guess I better call you that so we won't get mixed up. The girls will be jealous because I have a good-looking boyfriend and you won't care if the boys think you're a sissy because you are!"

She hugged Laurie again as a voice from across the way called wearily, "Cathy! Get yourself home and tend to these dishes!"

"I'm so glad you moved in." Catharine finished her Coke and made for the door. "Mom let Billy and me stay home today but says we have to start tomorrow. We'll come by for you about eight-thirty. We can loan you paper and pencils till you get your own." As she skipped out the back, she shouted, "Thanks for the Coke, Mr. Kirkendall."

He was in the kitchen when Laurie came back with rinse

water. "Looks like you've got a pal. Make it easier, won't it?"

"Lots easier. Isn't it funny, Way, what a difference one person can make?"

He was looking at her and yet he wasn't. His gaze reached far back, far away. "Honey, sometimes it only takes one person to turn the world into heaven or hell." She thought of Morrigan and knew that was true.

Bill Harris had his sister's round face and snub nose but his hair was yellow. He and Buddy raced ahead of their sisters while other Sludge Town children eddied around them or dallied behind. There were a few jeers: "Look at the lovebirds!" "Hey, why don't you kiss each other?" and the inevitable: "Sissy boy!" but Laurie and Catharine laughed and chattered as if they couldn't hear anyone else until they neared the school. Catharine's feet began to drag.

"What grade are you in?" she asked. "I'm in seventh if this school's not too different from Wichita Falls."

"I was in eighth." As her friend's mouth trembled, Laurie added, "I really belong in seventh, though."

"Goody! We might even get to sit next to each other. If the teacher seats according to the alphabet, *F* and *H* only have *G* between them."

Laurie scarcely heard. What if the principal made a fuss over where she and Buddy had gone to school that fall? She had their cards from Prairieville—the Oklahoma teacher had given them back—but how was she going to explain September, October, and most of November? She didn't want to lie, and if she did, Gramp wouldn't sound like much of a guardian for keeping them out of school a third of the school year. She had managed to change "Laurie" to "Larry" on the card and hoped that wasn't *really* lying.

Billy and Buddy were waiting inside the big double doors and outside the door with a frosted pane lettered PRINCIPAL. It was still early. The other Sludge Town kids had spilled onto the playground so the broad hall was empty. Catharine hung back. "I—I think I better go to the rest room."

Did you knock on a principal's door? Laurie didn't know. At

180

Prairieville, the door had always been open. It couldn't be *wrong* to knock, she told herself. And it seemed that she was going to have to do it. She was lifting her knuckled hand when the door swung open.

"Good gracious, in trouble so early?" The erect lady was plump but corseted so her front and back looked solid as concrete. Her blue-gray hair was clipped short in back and waved deeply on the front and sides. Her black eyes swept over them quickly but Laurie believed she'd noted down everything about them. "You're new, aren't you, and come to get enrolled?"

"Yes, ma'am," said Laurie, and Catharine nodded.

"I'm Mrs. Parrish." Her smile showed neat white teeth. "Two of you are Larry and Buddy Field?"

"Yes, ma'am."

"Mr. Redwine called about you. Ordinarily, we require a parent to enter a child but he explained that you're orphans and he's taking an interest in you."

"We live with our grandfather." It didn't seem a lie. Way had certainly done more for them than Grandpa Field. "But he's working for Mr. Redwine."

"So Mr. Redwine explained. You have your report cards?"

Laurie handed over the Kansas ones and held her breath. Mrs. Parrish scanned them. "Seventh for you," she said to Laurie. "Third for Edwin." Buddy winced at his real name. The principal lifted a steel-gray eyebrow. "Mr. Redwine explained that you've been out of school because of family difficulties. You'll need to do some makeup work and study hard to catch up, but I'll give you the chance to be in your proper classes."

"Thank you, Mrs. Parrish."

The principal smiled and turned to Catharine, who mutely extended two grubby cards and a folded sheet of tablet paper. "Neither of your parents could come to enroll you?"

Catharine shook her head. "Pa's working, ma'am. And mama's got the baby. She said to tell you if you have to see her that she'll come after I get home from school. That way I'll tend the baby and—"

Mrs. Parrish raised her hand. "I suppose this signed note will do," she said. "Step in the office while I see if we have textbooks

---

for you. Since there was no cotton crop to speak of this year, most of the farm children are in school though they're usually out picking till Christmas. Oil-field families are always coming and going and we have a rule that no child gets a report card till they've turned in their books."

So they wouldn't have to buy texts! That meant that after school while she and Buddy were buying their Big Chief tablets, pencils, crayons, and such, they could get enough clothing to stay decent without washing things out every day or two. Mrs. Parrish pulled books off shelves in a big long closet, placing them in four stacks. "Edwin, you and Billy will have to share a speller. Larry, you and Catharine will have to share geographies with other students till someone leaves. Come along. I'll take you to your teachers."

Buddy's teacher greeted him and Billy with a smile as if she'd been waiting for them and was glad they'd finally come. She was young with a merry laugh and soft brown eyes. Miss Larson, the slender, gray-eyed seventh-grade teacher, didn't act delighted to have two latecomers in her room that was already crowded full of one-armed desks, but she wasn't mean about it, either, and when the janitor brought their desks, she told him to put them next to each other.

"So long as you don't whisper or carry on," she warned. "My father was a railroad man so I know all about new schools. If it turns out you're behind in some subjects, let me know so I can work with you after school."

The playground hierarchy wasn't much different from Prairieville. Grades had recess at different times. Only younger children lined up for the slides and swings or bumped each other off the teeter-totters, or swung across the jungle-gym bars by their hands. When the eighth grade boys made for the ball diamond and the girls strolled off in pairs or collected in giggling bunches, Laurie and Catharine walked together—and what a difference *together* made.

"I just hated my last school," Laurie said, burning to remember how new shoes, anklets, and the pretty dress Rosalie made hadn't saved her from scorn. "It was a one-room country school and everyone could see when you had to go to the privy.

The girls were mean and snooty and the landlord's son—well, he said nasty things to me and the teacher didn't even seem to notice."

Catharine bobbed her head. "Country schools are the worst, where the other kids know each other. Towns are better, especially close to an oil field where there's your own kind. You can kind of ignore the town kids." She shrugged philosophically. "When I start new, I watch and try to find a girl I think I'd like, one who doesn't have a lot of friends. Then I just go up to her and say something nice about her hair or dress or whatever fits."

"Isn't that hard?"

"Sure. But it's not as hard as hanging around by yourself." Catharine sighed. "The worst part is when you really, really like someone and have to move. I've had friends I missed so much that I didn't try to find one at the next school." Her face scrunched up and she blinked. "But after a while, a new girl would come in and if I could tell she was lonely, I couldn't help being nice. I guess it's better to care about people than not to, even if it hurts to lose them."

"Oh, yes! There was a man we only knew one day, but it was a bad day. He sang us songs and made us laugh and gave me his harmonica. I never will forget him."

"Was he good-looking?"

Startled, Laurie thought, trying to summon up Morrigan's dark face, his smiling mouth, the green-gray eyes. "I don't know. But if he was in a room of handsome men, he's the man you'd notice."

The bell shrilled. "Darn it!" said Laurie. "I meant to get to the rest room before the bell rang. Now I'll have to wait till all the boys are through."

Using the boys' rest room turned out to be her worst problem at Black Spring Elementary. As Catharine had said, it was easier to be new in a school attended by a shifting majority made up of oil-field children. Of the thirty-two children in Laurie's class, only twelve were from town or nearby farms and ranches. Among them, there was a definite pecking order from the biggest rancher's and doctor's daughters and the banker's son down to farm workers' kids and several from town whose mothers were raising them alone by taking in laundry or doing housework for the few families that could afford it.

The oil-field kids didn't fit the niches. They lived in shacks, tents, or boxcars and didn't own their homes or have more furniture or belongings than they could load in or onto a car or truck. Still, those dusty wayfaring mud- and oil-splashed vehicles included late-model Chryslers, Packards, Lincolns, and Studebakers as well as Pontiacs, Dodges, Chevys, and Fords. The children either bought lunch in the cafeteria or carried light-bread sandwiches, cookies, and fruit in their lunch pails or sacks. Only the poorest farm kids hid out with their cornbread and molasses or fried side meat. Laurie wished she could offer them some of her nice lunch but she knew from experience that they'd rather no one noticed what they were eating.

Some of the Sludge Town boys wore belt pants just like the richer local boys, and most of the girls' dresses were as nice as anyone's outside of those the doctor's wife bought for their daughter in fancy Dallas stores. It aggravated Laurie that she had to stay in overalls when, once Buddy had the clothes he needed and Way was outfitted, she could have afforded a few pretty dresses.

She made the best of it by picking out some beautiful plaid flannel shirts that felt soft as a kitten's ear. She also bought a warm wool jacket, green and brown tweed lined with gold satin. These purchases and things for cooking and housekeeping took all their savings except for what Buddy hoarded, but that was all right because Way earned enough cash for their daily needs and she and Buddy were singing and playing again, just on Friday and Saturday nights since Buddy had to study hard to catch up the third-grade work he'd missed and Laurie was helping Catharine with her lessons.

Because it was just down the street, they started in the Black Gold Cafe their first Friday night in town, but on Saturday night, W. S. Redwine came in and drank cup after cup of coffee, yellow eyes brooding, face like a squared rock. The oil-field men from drillers and producers to tank-builders and pipeline layers applauded each song, shouted for more, and stuffed bills in

Laurie's and Buddy's pockets as they left, but Redwine's eyes pressed on Laurie till her mouth went dry and her lips and fingers turned awkward.

Nodding to Buddy, fixing her gaze on a dark man in stained khakis who reminded her a little bit of Morrigan, she launched into what had become their ending number. As Buddy's voice trailed away with "I've got to be drifting along," the shouts and clapping literally shook the flimsy building.

Laurie smiled and bowed to the audience, though she was filled with unreasonable panic. "Let's get out of here," she muttered to Buddy. Grabbing his arm, she tugged him toward the door, but the way was blocked with men who wanted to thank them for the music and give them some money.

Redwine didn't hurry. Some of the other men were taller but there was a weight about him that caused an uneasiness as if a mountain were moving. When Laurie and Buddy finally made it out the door, he loomed beside them.

"When you didn't show up to play at the Truck-Inn or Redwine House, I figured you needed your evenings to study. That was okay. But then I heard you played here last night. How come, Larry?"

His voice was hurt. That shook Laurie more than anger. He *had* brought them all the way from California and, according to his lights, he'd been good to them. "The Truck-Inn's on the other side of town and the hotel's a mile away." It was a perfectly good excuse. Why did it sound lame?

"Clem can pick you up and drive you home."

"That's a lot of trouble."

"He's paid for trouble."

Buddy said, "I don't think we'd make as much in the hotel, Mr. Redwine. These oil-field guys—they act like they're not happy till they've got rid of their money."

"How much did you take in tonight?"

"We haven't counted."

"Well, count it up. I'll guarantee you that much."

"Guar—guaran—what?" asked Buddy.

"If my patrons don't give you whatever you got tonight, I'll make up the difference."

185

There was no way to refuse. On the following Friday, Clem picked them up at six-thirty, right after supper, and brought them home around nine. Mr. Redwine had never needed to make up the guarantee of twenty-three dollars. An auburn-haired lady in a clinging black dress and shiny, high-heeled, patent leather sandals had been playing the piano in the Redwine House when Laurie and Buddy ventured in that first night. People were talking so loud above the lady's soft, dreamy music that Laurie thought it must be wretched to make music against so much noise. She was sure she and Buddy wouldn't be able to perform in such circumstances and was about to retreat when the woman brought down her hands in a crash that hushed the diners.

While they were momentarily quiet, she rose, swept out her skirt in a curtsy so exaggerated that it looked like mockery, and walked to the children with a graceful sway that drew more attention than her music had. Intensely blue eyes scanned the pair. Her eyelids were smudged with purple and tiny creases rayed from the corners of her eyes that had such long lashes they couldn't be real. She was a pretty, pretty lady and she smelled like roses. Laurie was glad when she smiled and said, "I'm Marilys and you're Larry and Buddy."

Standing behind them, a manicured hand resting on a shoulder of each, Marilys spoke into the lull her crescendo had demanded. "Ladies and gentlemen! Thanks for your kind attention. The management of the Redwine House is honored to present Buddy and Larry Field in their first professional engagement! Years from now, you can say you heard them at the beginning. Most of their songs weren't written by a single person but were passed around and added to and changed—they grew from this country. Here they are—The Field Brothers!"

More warmhearted clapping than you'd have expected from such a well-dressed, well-fed bunch. As at the Black Gold Cafe, there were many more men than women. The women at Black Gold were the wives of the oil-field workers, or maybe not their wives, and the life had aged them, faded and dried their hair and skin, left them fat or scrawny.

These women were different. Their hair was carefully bobbed

or waved, their complexions looked unnaturally fair and rosy, their clothes must come from Dallas at least, and jewels glittered from throats, wrists, ears, and fingers. Quite a few of the men wore rings or tie clasps that sparkled against their dark suits but others wore the required coats over khakis that added the smell of oil and sweat and maleness to the ladies' perfume.

At the back of the room, shadowed by their distance from the gleaming crystal-pendanted chandelier, three nicely dressed but unspectacular couples shared a table. The men's faces were baked a few shades darker than their women's, and even in the dim light, their eyes wrinkled at the edges as if staring through sun at a distant range. By chance, the eyes of the five people Laurie could see were varied shades of the prairie sky—mist gray, dark gray, smoky blue, light blue, and a color in between.

Ranch folks. Hanging on through the oil boom, maybe surviving from royalties they got when it was pumped from their land. The ones on this land before them, wandering Comanches, had long been banished. According to Morrigan, most of them ranched or farmed in southwestern Oklahoma—also part of their once vast nomadic domain that stretched from northern Kansas to Mexico, where they had raided for decades in the autumn at the time fearfully known to Mexicans as the Comanche Moon.

Laurie didn't know any songs of the Comanches but a tune came to her, of wind soughing through the rain-freshened September grass, of rolling plains with purple mountains crouched on the horizon, of cantering horses with wind bannering their manes and tails. Laurie heard women and children laughing, smelled their cook fires, heard a lover playing on his flute to his maiden. They passed with immense herds of buffalo beyond her sight, passed with the waving bluestem and grama and rose-rippling buffalo grass.

She played that song, a wild, lonely wind song of fading hoofbeats, and then, though it wasn't an Indian song but was at least about them, she played the start of "Pretty Redwing" and Buddy cleared his throat, fixed his eyes on her, and sang.

"That was for the Comanches," she said when the clapping subsided. "Now for the cowboys."

Some of the ranchers joined in on the choruses of "Old Chisholm Trail." "Streets of Laredo," and "Bury Me Not on the Lone Prairie." Laurie told how Gail Gardner had written "Sierry Petes" on a train bound for Washington during the Great War. It was a new song, apparently, to these folks, but they chuckled and cheered the devil's discomfiture.

Redwine came in and took a small table in the back. Laurie felt her spine ridging like a cat's arched back but she didn't change the program. She moved to the songs she and Buddy knew best, songs that gave voice to what had happened to them, to Daddy, the Halsells, and Way and millions all over the Dust Bowl. These diners in the Redwine House might not like to hear them and Redwine would probably demand that she play popular songs like "The Music Goes 'Round and 'Round" or "Beer Barrel Polka." She'd just tell him if she couldn't play what she wanted to in his hotel, she'd go back to the Black Gold.

"A young musician named Woody Guthrie was living north of Amarillo when that worst dust storm hit last April," she said. Her voice stuck in her throat but she thought about Mama and Daddy and Morrigan and she spoke strong. "Woody wrote this song about it. I learned it and some of the others you'll hear from Johnny Morrigan."

"On the fourteenth day of April of nineteen thirty-five
There struck the worst of dust storms that ever filled
    the sky. . . .

Our relatives were huddled into their oil boom shacks,
And the children they were crying as it whistled
    through the cracks. . . .

We saw outside our windows where wheat fields they
    had grown
Was now a rippling ocean of dust the wind had blown.

It covered up our fences, it covered up our barns,
It covered up our tractors in this wild and dusty storm. . . ."

No one left, in fact no one left all evening except reluctantly when folks were waiting at the door for a table. As the diners passed Laurie and Buddy, they smiled and nodded thanks. There was a crystal bowl on the piano and it gradually filled with crisp or crumpled bills.

When Laurie and Buddy got tired, Marilys played while they slipped out in the hall and savored the fizzy ginger ale the waitress brought them.

"Marilys plays better than anyone we've heard on the radio," Laurie said, scowling as the buzz of voices and laughter blurred the music. "It makes me mad that those people don't listen to her."

"Maybe she just sort of comes with their dinners," Buddy ventured.

Laurie snorted. "They listened to us."

"We're new. Maybe when they've heard us a few times, they won't pay us any better attention."

"If they don't, we'll go back to the Black Gold."

"Aw, Laurie, who cares as long as we get paid?"

"We're not paid!"

"What else would you call it?"

Laurie floundered. But there was a difference, there was! "We give our music—that's a present. Whatever folks give us back, that's a present, too. They don't have to, they're not being charged."

"Yeah," said Buddy doubtfully. "But if they didn't give us anything, we'd have to find some other way to make money. The grocery won't swap us grub for a song and we can't buy clothes with one."

Laurie retreated to the superiority of older-sisterdom. "You just like to argue." She glanced at the gilded foyer clock. "Come on. If we're going to do a few more songs before nine, we'd better get started."

At nine o'clock, Way stepped quietly in. He had changed from his painting clothes, was shaved, and looked real nice. He stood at the side of the room, beaming, and joined in the applause as the harmonica's notes and Buddy's high, sweet voice trailed away—*"and we've got to be driftin' along."*

"Thought I'd catch the end of your show and walk you home," Way said, unfolding from the wall. "Clem's rheumatics give him fits of an evening and I told him he didn't have to stay up in order to drive you."

Marilys had come over and the little lines around her mouth and eyes disappeared when she smiled at Way, tilting up her head. "So you're the Field Brothers' grandfather! You must be proud of them."

"I am." Way's dark eyes shone and though his laughter was soft, it came from deep in his chest. He suddenly looked younger, just like Marilys did. "But I'm sure sorry I didn't get to hear you play the piano, ma'am. Clem says you sound like an angel."

She lifted one slim shoulder. "Clem's sweet but I don't know how he could hear me over the racket. Folks seem to think the piano's just to make enough noise to keep people at other tables from hearing what deals they're cooking up." She smiled without rancor and her long, graceful fingers brushed Laurie's cheek and Buddy's. "Your boys really held the crowd."

"But you—you're a real musician, Miss Marilys!" Laurie cried. "All I know is what John Morrigan taught me and what I've learned myself. I—I'd give anything to play like you!"

"Would you?" None of them had heard or seen Redwine till he bulked at Marilys's side. His big square hand closed on Marilys's blue-veined wrist. The sparkle and life went out of her. She shrank into herself like a trapped creature that realizes there's no use in fighting. "Marilys, you studied at all those fancy schools. You could teach Larry a few hours a week, couldn't you?"

Some of the life came back. "I'd love to. Why don't you come by after school, Larry, as often as you can? I don't start work till five."

Laurie ached to accept but even though Marilys seemed eager, Laurie still didn't like to take favors from Redwine. "Not much use my learning the piano. I don't have one, probably never will."

"It would still be good for you to learn to read music, know your scales and notes." Marilys's eyes pleaded. For some reason, this was important to her. "Besides," she added a trifle bitterly, "you don't have to own a piano to play one, God knows, I haven't had my own since I was a kid but I've made my living banging away on them."

"You don't bang!" Laurie cried. "You—you play like all the feelings and things in the world are shut up in the dark inside the piano and you're bringing them out in the light."

Marilys blinked. After a moment she said, just to Laurie, "You'll come then?"

"Yes. I'll come."

15

That began a pattern. After school let out at four o'clock, Laurie and Buddy walked four blocks to the hotel. Edna fortified them with cookies and milk—she was still elated over all the new cookware she'd been able to acquire—and Buddy got his homework done while Marilys taught Laurie. "I don't see why I can't stay and play at school," Buddy grumbled.

"The boys who do are all older, and town boys to boot."

"Well, I could go home with Billy."

That caused Laurie a guilty pang. Catharine had to walk home by herself now. So that the kids wouldn't notice, she stayed ten or fifteen minutes and dusted erasers for Miss Larson. When Laurie got home, Catharine hurried over, usually bringing the baby, a wizened little thing that cried a lot and burped smelly white curds on Catharine's shoulder.

While Laurie got supper, she tried to respond wholeheartedly to Catharine's chatter about school that day, but her mind was full of what Marilys had taught her. She heard the notes of the composition she was learning rather than Catharine's remarks about how the banker's daughter looked like a barrel in plaid and what a pretty dress Miss Larson had worn. What with music and study, Laurie didn't need a friend so much. As if sensing this, Catharine clung tighter. Laurie tried to be extra nice but she would really have rather gone quietly about her work and pondered Marilys's lesson.

Now, to Buddy, Laurie spoke sharply. "You can't go home with Billy because Mrs. Harris has enough on her plate without trying to keep track of you." She softened her tone. "But look, Buddy! This way when we get home your lessons are done and you can play till supper."

That didn't entirely reconcile him, but Edna's cookies did, especially when she added a dish of ice cream or a chunk of her gold-crusted pie. With her children grown and scattered and her grandchildren far away, she enjoyed having youngsters around, as did Clem. They had known W. S. Redwine since his days as a roustabout in the Permian Basin farther south and east, and of all his employees, they alone didn't seem afraid of him.

"I was lookin' for a job when I found this one, Dub," Clem told him once when Redwine swore at him over some trifle.

Marilys was afraid of him. Just as her color brightened and the blue eyes grew bluer when Way happened in, she went still as a creature feigning death when Redwine rested his hand on her like a big cat claiming its prey. She never talked much about her past but from things she dropped, she came from an East Texas family that could afford a piano and lessons for her, and later some kind of fancy girls' school in Dallas. It was hard to guess her age. Around Way, she looked young, almost a girl, but when Redwine's eyes touched her, even when his hand did not, she seemed to wither and shrink.

It was almost time for school to let out for Christmas when Way finished painting signs in Cumberland, Selkirk, and Cross Trails, hotels, Truck-Inns and DUB'S HARDWARE FOR HARD WEAR stores. He'd been able to come home every night, but now Redwine wanted him to finish signing his other Texas businesses, which stretched as far east as Abilene and south to Odessa.

"Dub's going to loan me one of his old trucks," Way said. He'd started calling Redwine that since most all other grown-ups did. "That feller has every durned car or truck he ever owned. Most of 'em don't run, of course. They're just rustin' away a few miles out of town on this farm he foreclosed on. I asked him to sell me a pretty good old Ford truck on credit but he wouldn't."

Laurie thought with a moment's regret of Daddy's Model T before she shrugged and just hoped it was holding up, getting the Halsells from one job to the next. "It sure would be nice to have our own truck or flivver," she said. "How much would one cost, Way?"

"Feller over at Cross Trails is askin' two hundred dollars for a thirty-three half-ton Chevy pickup with good tires. Figger it's a pretty fair deal. They cost about six hundred fifty dollars new and this one only has thirty thousand miles on it."

Two hundred dollars! It seemed a fortune. Laurie's first dismay subsided a bit, though, when she considered their position. Just as soon as they'd bought necessities and clothes, she'd figured out how much cash Rosalie had spent on them—the Saturday movies, hamburgers and ice cream, school supplies and clothes. The two of them had certainly worked hard enough to pay for their food.

The sum was close to twenty dollars, all of it taken from Rosalie's butter, cream, and egg money. Overcome afresh at how kind Rosalie had been to them when they were no real kin of hers, ashamed to compare how many eggs and how much cream and butter and work it took to bring that much when she and Buddy got that much or more for a night's music at the Redwine House, Laurie next day swapped all her hoarded dollar bills and half-dollars to the pretty blond restaurant cashier, who handed back three tens, a five, and several dollars.

"Going to start a bank account, Larry?" the young woman asked. "You're getting to be a real plutocrat!"

A bank account? That was for rich people. The idea of having more money than was needed to get by on struck Laurie with jarring force. Someday, though . . .

Sticking the bills in her pocket, she grinned at the cashier. "I owe this to a lady, Beth. Guess it'll be a long time before we have money in the bank."

"May be just as well, the way so many closed and took folks' savings," Beth said. "My dad was a carpenter. Had enough put by to take it easy the rest of his life, even take Ma to Wales so she could look up her great-greats' gravestones in the little village her grandparents left eighty years ago. His bank closed in 'thirty-two. He's still working, and glad he can at seventy-eight. At that they were luckier than lots of people. Owned their home and car free and clear. Doubt if Hank and I ever will."

"Hank makes good money in the oil field, doesn't he?" Laurie asked.

"Sure. But everything's sky-high in an oil town, kid. Rent on a shack Ma wouldn't keep hens in sets us back thirty bucks a month and we've got to keep a good car to get from one boom to another. If Hank could get a job where we stayed in one place, we could get ahead on half the money and start buying our own house, too. But—" She sighed philosophically. "We're lucky to have work. When I see Okies going through in their old jalopies, well, I just ask the Lord to look after them."

Laurie wrote Rosalie as much of a letter as she could without giving away where they were or what they were doing. "The money's honest-earned," she explained. "The man who sort of adopted us got a real good job." She trusted Rosalie but if Grandpa found out that she and Buddy were making as much money as they were, he'd certainly try to channel their earnings into his pockets.

So Rosalie had back her money with interest and Laurie would send more now and then. She wished she knew how to share their good fortune with the Halsells or some of the others in the camps or on the road. Way, now that he had some cash wages in his pocket, had bought tires, gas, or groceries for stranded families he met at the Truck-Inns. That was why Laurie insisted he take five dollars a week from the Field Brothers' earnings. Even so, five weeks after their arrival in Black Spring, Way had no savings while there was close to fifty dollars in the peanut-butter jar Laurie kept under her bed.

Two hundred for a truck didn't seem so impossible when she cast up some quick sums and reckoned that she and Buddy had made close to that at the Redwine House. She had trouble believing that folks were always going to be generous, especially when they'd heard the Field Brothers several times, but they always were. The crystal bowl had never held less than twenty dollars and had yielded as much as thirty-five, which seemed incredible, even wicked.

This Christmas, Laurie had vowed, was going to be a happy one in spite of the grief that flooded her when she thought of last year—the plates with oranges and candy Mama and Daddy had put out so she and Buddy saw them first thing Christmas morning, and the few gifts under the little tree that brought so much delight. As long as Mama was alive, Laurie had never really felt poor. Now that Mama and Daddy were both gone, Laurie didn't think she'd ever *not* feel poor even if she had a million dollars.

Christmas could never be the same again but they had Way and he had them. Morrigan was surely alive somewhere in the world and she had his music and could share it with others. Buddy was back in school and at least not failing. Instead of paying a lot for one of the scraggly wilted trees leaning against the Sludge Town grocery store, Laurie had captured a huge tumbleweed. With Catharine's help, she'd strung popcorn and cranberries and covered pasteboard cutouts with pretty paper and foil from gum wrappers. They'd have Christmas dinner in the afternoon so that Marilys and Clem and Edna could come. They'd been so happy when Laurie invited them and Edna was bringing the turkey, Marilys some pies—yes, this would be a good Christmas even if it was a new kind of one in a new place with new people.

Buddy had wanted another .22 but Laurie had suggested that she and Way contribute half toward the shiny red bicycle in the window of the hardware store, and Buddy pay the rest out of his saved money. After some argument and tears on both sides, Way's intervention had settled that Buddy got fifty cents a week of their earnings and the rest of his half went in another peanut-butter jar for clothing, school supplies, maybe even college someday. Laurie had paid her share on the bicycle and it was safely put away in the store's back room. She'd got Edna and Marilys pretty scarves and pretty blue bottles of Evening in Paris. For Catharine, there was a heart locket, and for Miss Larson a gray paisley scarf to match her eyes. Clem loved cowboy stories so the newest Zane Grey was wrapped for him.

Ticking off the gifts, Laurie discovered that the only money she owed on presents was five dollars to finish paying for the stylish hat she was getting Way—not a Stetson, he wasn't the type, but a broad-brimmed, fine-quality fedora in dark gray with a black grosgrain band. Holding back ten dollars for the Christmas feast and any unforeseen expenses still left thirty-five. She hurried to get it and handed it to Way.

"Why don't you telephone that man in Cross Trails and see if he'd take this down on the truck? We should be able to pay it off in a couple of months, 'specially if Buddy's willing to pitch in."

Way balked. "Let you kiddos same as buy a truck? I'd feel like I was takin' advantage of you."

"You're paying for our house and food, Way. We'll ride in the truck, too." When he still scowled, she let her eyes mist and her lip quiver. "Oh Way, let's do get the truck! There are things I'd like to get for housekeeping like pretty dishes and our own bedding, curtains, some pictures—things like that there's no use buying unless we can take them along when we move."

"We-e-ell—if you're certain sure—"

She tucked the bills into his scarred hands and closed his fingers over them.

One thing haunted Laurie and tainted her joy at being able to buy nice presents. She couldn't get anything for her mother, not now, not ever. She couldn't give Daddy a hat like the one she was buying Way, or the red wool muffler and mittens she'd wrapped for Clem. For most things, there was hope. For this, there was none. Till now, she had mostly grieved simply her loss of her parents. Now she grieved all they had missed, what she would never be able to do for them, and thought she could not bear the finality. And then a boiler blew up right next to Sludge Town and with it the man who tended the fire to keep the steam engine running.

He left three children, one of them a boy in Buddy's class. The widow needed money to pay for the funeral of what was left of her husband and move the family back to her parents' farm in Arkansas. They could give their daughter and grandchildren a home but had no cash money. The boiler man's driller took up a collection and a coffee can for contributions sat next to the cash register in the Black Gold. When she heard about it, Laurie took her whole share of that weekend's earnings—it came to forty dollars because folks were extra generous at Christmas—waded through the mud to the café, and put the money in the can. *For you, Mama and Daddy.*

She felt they knew. She felt their love reaching her, warming her through the wall of death. Then she was able to throw herself wholeheartedly into Christmas.

Buddy's bicycle was too big to wrap but Laurie tied a big red bow on it and leaned it against the wall beside the decorated tumbleweed. A star Way had cut from the bottom of a five-pound molasses can adorned the top of the "tree" and gifts were heaped to its middle after Edna and Clem and Marilys arrived with their arms full of bright packages.

The box table and stove were filled with food so after Clem gave the blessing, everyone heaped their plates and held them on their laps, sitting on chairs or crates while they feasted, finishing with Edna's deep-dish apple pie, so redolent of spice and aromatic juices that it made your mouth water even when you could scarcely make room for it.

"Let's get the dishes out of the way," said Marilys, rising. She wore a midnight blue velvet dress that made her eyes glow even deeper blue and a matching bow held her waving dark hair in a soft coil at the back of her neck. "I'll wash."

"Not without you having an apron over that pretty dress," Way objected. There weren't any aprons so he fetched one of his clean shirts and tied it around her waist while she held her arms out of the way and laughed at him as he awkwardly made a knot.

More flushed than the exertion warranted, he got the dish towel. "I'll dry."

"I'll help," said Clem.

Edna scraped plates and put them in the dishpan. Buddy took the scraps out where stray dogs and cats could get them. Laurie stored away food and then took newly dried dishes from the men and put them where they belonged.

A chill, high sun slanted through one of the house's two windows, gilding the festooned tumbleweed as they gathered around it. The Field Brothers had been playing Christmas songs for the last few weeks so they were in practice. Laurie started off on the harmonica with her favorite, "We Three Kings of Orient Are," moved into "Oh Come All Ye Faithful" and "Joy to the World." Marilys had a rich alto. Edna's soprano carried Buddy's sweet, high voice when it quavered, and Clem and Way had deep, pleasant tenors. It was pure delight to weave the harmonica's music in and out of theirs. When they had sung all the carols any of them knew, they pulled seats close to the bush and Buddy handed out the presents.

Edna's scarf and perfume; Marilys's. Clem's mittens and muffler, Way's hat, Buddy's red sweater—another round of gifts, and another. Still Laurie had nothing. Her smile began to feel tight and strange. She'd loved buying presents. It had been wonderful to ask to look at things and know she could pay for them. But all the same—

It couldn't be they thought her too old for presents. Edna had embroidered initials on handkerchiefs for all the grown-ups, Clem had hand-tooled a billfold for Way as well as for Buddy and made Marilys some moccasins. Marilys had a warm, fringed, green plaid shawl for Edna, and house slippers for the men.

Laurie didn't understand. One person might have forgotten but not all of them. Then, when the smile on her lips felt as if it would crack, or worse, dissolve in the tears she was fighting, Buddy picked up the big package next to the bicycle and brought it over to her.

"Here!" he said, brown eyes sparkling. "From all of us! But first, guess what it is!"

Stunned, Laurie moved the package. Star-patterned paper concealed a box about twice as tall as it was wide. It could have been almost anything. Helplessly, she shook her head, so glad they hadn't forgotten her that she didn't care what the present was.

"Come on, Lau—Larry!" Buddy urged. "If you could have

anything in the world you wanted—well, almost anything—what would it be?"

Her parents. Morrigan to be where she could see and hear him. A home. A place to belong. Those wouldn't fit the box. But of things that would—Something she dreamed of having one day, sometime—

"It—it just can't be!" she almost pleaded. She was afraid to put the private wish into words, afraid of embarrassing her friends and herself.

"It's a guitar!" Buddy exploded. "Clem bought it in Amarillo. We all went in on it. Sufferin' cats! Open it!"

Trembling, Laurie obeyed, but Way had to help her pull out the box flaps. Light shimmered on mellow wood, the graceful curves and roundings of the instrument. The wood wasn't cold to Laurie's hands. It felt warm, responsive, almost alive.

"Ohhh—" Her sigh of wonder trailed off. "It's beautiful! I don't know how to thank all of you and I'll keep it forever! B-but I can't play it."

"I'll teach you," said Marilys. "The way you've picked up the piano, it won't take you long to feel just as easy with this as you do with your harmonica."

Unable to believe the guitar was real, Laurie traced it reverently with her fingers. If only Morrigan could be here! If only he could teach her— She gave herself an inward shake. That was silly, ungrateful, to always be wanting more. She handed the guitar to Marilys.

"Please, will you play something?"

"Just one. Then we've got to get back to the hotel."

Edna nodded. "I did all the cooking I could this morning but I need to be back in that kitchen *muy pronto.*" She and Clem had worked for years on a South Texas ranch and they flavored their talk with Spanish phrases that fascinated Laurie. She thought it a musical, lilting tongue and determined to get Clem to teach her some of the songs he sang a few lines of now and then.

Marilys plucked strings and tightened the ivory pegs till she was content with the sound. Then she played and sang a song Laurie had never heard before but immediately loved. The boy

Jesus begged his reluctant mother to let him go play with the other children. They made fun of him for being only a poor carpenter's son. To win them over, he worked a miracle that frightened their mothers so that they demanded Mary call him home: ". . . and when she asked him why, said he, 'Oh, I built them a bridge of the rays of the sun so they would play with me.' "

Eyes downcast and half-closed, Marilys looked so beautiful and the song was so sad and lovely that Laurie's heart contracted. They were clapping when a knock on the door made the wood vibrate.

Laurie was closest. She opened and quickly stepped back. W. S. Redwine stood there, filling the door. He held an unwrapped guitar. In the flicker of an instant, his gaze took in everything.

"Didn't know you played the guitar, Marilys."

"You never asked."

"It's your job to entertain patrons. They might enjoy a change."

"This is Larry's guitar."

"Then he won't need this one. You can use it." He looked aggrievedly at Edna and Clem. "It's time the whole bunch of you were over at the hotel. We'll have a big crowd tonight."

"Don't twist a knot in your tail, Dub," Clem advised. "We were just fixin' to trail out of here *muy* pronto."

"Make it snappy! Marilys, you ride back with me."

The fresh, young color drained from her face. It seemed she might argue. Then something bright left her body, just as it had her face, and she gave the guitar to Laurie. Redwine already had Marilys's gray coat off the bed where it had been placed with the other wraps.

The way he helped her into it wasn't a courtesy. It was a claiming. Hand gripping the doorknob, he swung back toward Way. "You've finished the towns you can do from here. I'll lend you a truck so you can go to Lubbock tomorrow and get started over around there. You can stay at the Lubbock Truck-Inn, get your gas and meals, and I'll still pay you seven dollars a day."

Seven dollars with no expenses coming out! Redwine must

really be pleased with Way's signs. But for Way to stay in Lubbock— Way rubbed his chin. "I don't know, Dub. The kiddos are pretty young to stay alone."

"You can come back every weekend."

"Maybe I better look for a job in the oil patch."

Thinking about the dead boiler man and the other awful accidents she'd heard about, Laurie touched his arm. "We'll be all right, Gramp. The Harrises are right next door."

Way's smoky dark eyes searched her. "You sure?"

She nodded. "Oil workers get drunk and fight each other but they'd never bother kids."

With a truck to pay out, it didn't make sense to turn down such good money. "All right," Way said, but without enthusiasm.

"Clem'll have a truck ready for you in the morning." Hand under Marilys's arm, Redwine looked at the rest of them. His mouth turned down. "Merry Christmas."

It sounded like mockery. Was he hurt that he hadn't been invited? He had, for just a second when Laurie opened the door, looked like a kid realizing he'd been the only one left out of a party. That he'd brought the guitar for her made Laurie feel both guilty and resentful. It wasn't right to bring her such a present and not give anything to Way or Buddy—and she doubted if he had gifts for Clem and Edna. Marilys? Probably there was something for her but Laurie was sure it wouldn't be what Marilys wanted. They weren't married, yet Redwine acted as if he owned her.

After the door closed on Clem and Edna, Laurie and Way stared at each other. Finally, blushing, Way said, "Kiddos, I don't know exactly how to say this, but— You remember that jock on the train?"

They nodded. "Well—" Way cast his eyes toward the ceiling. "Men like him hanker after boys instead of women. You got to be careful if a man's too nice to you. Redwine hasn't acted like that kind—he's sure had women all along the road—but maybe he likes boys, too."

Laurie tried to joke to hide her nervousness. "If he does, he'd sure be disappointed if he finds out I'm a girl."

Way didn't smile. "He's got some special feeling for you, Laurie-Larry. Could be you're the son he never had. Could be it's ugly. But don't let him get either one of you alone."

Buddy snorted. "He never even looks at me!"

"All the same," insisted Way. He frowned, which made his eyebrows bristle even more. "You kiddos sure you don't mind staying alone? Miz Harris would most likely let you make up pallets over at her house."

"The baby squalls all the time," said Buddy.

"Catharine says she's cutting teeth," Laurie defended. "But it'd be real crowded over there, Way. We'll be fine here, honest!"

His eyebrows wrinkled like a caterpillar on a hot pavement. At last, he sighed. "If that's what you want, kiddos. But if you get scared or there's any kind of problem, promise you'll get right over to Miz Harris, or tell Miss Marilys or Clem or Edna."

Laurie went to him and kissed him on his scarred cheek. "Don't worry—we've got lots of friends! We've got to get that truck paid for, and then let's head down the road away from Mr. Redwine."

"But you've got your piano lessons, honey, and you're both doin' good in school."

"Well, maybe we can stay till school's out," Laurie conceded. Almost more than she hated to give up piano lessons, she shrank from losing Marilys.

It struck her, with shock, that Way felt like that, too. He watched Marilys as if she were precious and really, though he looked so much older, he probably wasn't, not when you figured in those little lines around Marilys's eyes and mouth.

Wouldn't it be wonderful if— Laurie quelled the bright hope as it dawned. Redwine behaved as if he owned Marilys. Did he love her? Did she love him? Laurie couldn't guess but just as he never let loose of a car he'd used, she doubted if he'd allow a woman to leave if he'd ever had a hold on her. He had one on Marilys.

Maybe, for Way's sake, the sooner they left Black Spring, the better. Maybe in the next town, they could stay. But a piece of her heart would stay with Marilys, with Catharine, with Edna and Clem. A sense of loss crushed her heart with such physical force that Laurie couldn't breathe for a moment.

Blindly, she reached for the guitar, touched the strings. *Oh, Morrigan, all these roads, all these miles!*

Way left early next morning for Lubbock. Before she went to school, Laurie took the decorations off the tumbleweed till it stood as naked and forlorn as she felt. A weed dressed up like a tree! But oh, Christmas had been lovely! And there was the marvelous guitar just waiting to yield its music.

She carried the tumbleweed to the verge of the buildings. *Good-bye, tumbleweed. Thank you for being beautiful, for stopping a while.* She closed her eyes, thought again of Morrigan, and released the bush into the wind, which would sweep it out to the open plain.

16

The first evening Way was gone, Clem drove Laurie and Buddy home from the Redwine House. "Reckon I could have a cup of coffee?" he drawled as Buddy escaped with a whoop to join Billy and the other boys. "This sharp weather's nibblin' at my bones."

"I'll have a cup, too," said Laurie, though she didn't much like coffee. Clem never came in like this; he was doing it so the house wouldn't feel so lonesome.

"No lock on the door?" asked Clem as Laurie opened it and led the way in.

"When the walls are thin enough to kick in, locks aren't much use." She'd left the guitar on her cot that morning. When she saw it, her heart leaped. She wanted to hold it, listen to the strings. Suddenly she wasn't fearful or anxious and almost wished Clem hadn't come in so she could right away practice the way Marilys had suggested that day. Marilys said not to bring the guitar to the hotel—Mr. Redwine was upset about it—but she, Marilys, would come over when she could and teach Laurie. Turning to laugh up at Clem, Laurie added, "Anyhow, folks in Sludge Town may live in shacks and tents but they don't steal or break into each other's homes."

"Guess not," chuckled Clem. "Takes a higher type of society to do that."

He got the heater going while she lit a burner on the cookstove, set on the coffeepot, and got out sugar and evaporated milk. They had a companionable cup of coffee, hers mostly milk.

"The Harrises know your Grandpa's away?" Clem asked as he rose to leave.

Laurie nodded. "Mrs. Harris promised to keep an eye out for us and she said we could come stay with them anytime we want."

"Then I guess we'll see you tomorrow." Clem grinned. "You can quit fidgetin' now, Larry, and get at that guitar."

He left, chuckling. Laurie blushed at being so transparent but the second the door closed, she had the guitar in her arms.

It was strange that night to eat supper without Way, and worse to get ready for bed. Laurie debated about leaving a lamp burning but since there were no curtains, that would let any passerby see in, and it was foolish to increase the risk of fire in the flimsy building. No, the best thing was to turn off the heater, blow out the lamp, and go to bed as usual.

Only it wasn't usual. She had got out of the habit of saying her prayers at night. The God she had grown up fearing while trying to love didn't seem very real since she'd left Prairieville. In the dark, kneeling beside her cot, she prayed that night, but her asking that Way be all right and that she and Buddy would be safe till morning seemed to reach no higher than the Sheetrock ceiling and mockingly return.

The guitar leaned against the cot. She had the harmonica beneath her pillow. Holding it, she fixed her thoughts on Morrigan. If they met again, wouldn't he be pleased that she had a guitar? Maybe they could play together and he'd teach her some new songs. . . . She jumped at a groping touch on her ankle and gave a smothered gasp.

"Laurie?"

"Oh." She went limp with relief, then fired up. "Good grief, Buddy, you almost scared me to death!"

"I *am* scared, Laurie! It—it's creepy without Way."

She sat up and he let her put her arm around him. That proved he really was upset. "Gracious, Buddy," she cajoled. "At home you slept by yourself in that little den on the back porch."

He sniffed. "Yeah, but that was at home, and Mama and Daddy were there."

She didn't have any answer to that, except to hug him. They sat on the cot a few minutes. She was the oldest. It was up to her to comfort him. And herself. "Buddy, I'll come tell you poems till you go to sleep."

He sighed, snuffled, and trotted to the other room. Gathering her blankets around her, gripping the harmonica, Laurie followed. Propping Way's pillow upright against the wall, she delved into her memory. Kipling's "The Ballad of East and West," Alfred Noyes's "The Highwayman," Longfellow's "The Skeleton in Armor," Stephen Vincent Benét's "The Ballad of William Sycamore," and Vachel Lindsay's "The Chinese Nightingale." How wonderful that these men, most of them dead, had made up poems that she could invoke now against fear in the night! And songs like Woody Guthrie's would be played and sung long after he and all of them now alive were gone. The songs and poems would always matter, not that a girl and boy were scared one night in a boomtown shack.

Calmed by the rhythmic words, by the time she was sure Buddy was asleep, she could scarcely hold her eyelids open. She padded to her cot, hugged the harmonica, and was asleep before she could start worrying about the sounds and creakings of the floor and walls.

It wasn't so bad after that. For a while before bedtime, she played the harmonica or chorded and crooned to the guitar. Then she sat on his bed and told Buddy stories or poems till he was drowsing. When Way came home Friday night, it was like Christmas all over again.

"We own a quarter of that truck over to Cross Trails," he boasted, hugging them both and producing Tootsie Rolls for

Buddy and a Butterfinger for Laurie. "Soon as we own the whole thing we can take off in style anytime we need to. Hope you kiddos can finish out the school term, though."

Laurie did, too, and felt a pang at the prospect of leaving Catharine, Clem, Edna, and Marilys. Still, Sludge Town couldn't be a real home and she'd breathe easier when they were a long way from W. S. Redwine. Blessedly, he'd been away since Christmas, but that couldn't last.

Buddy, thrilled at owning part of a truck, had agreed to contribute half of the savings part of his half of the Redwine House money and Laurie's share that weekend came to twenty-eight dollars. Between them, they gave Way thirty dollars to apply on the truck when he left on Monday morning.

"Boy howdy!" he laughed exultantly. "We keep this up and we'll own that baby inside of six weeks! You kiddos take care of each other and I'll see you Friday night."

This time it wasn't quite so hard to smile and wave as he left. They *had* gotten through last week. He *had* come safely home. It just took a little getting used to, that was all. But after school that day while Laurie was having her lesson with Marilys, Redwine came silently into the restaurant, sat down, and listened.

Uneasily conscious of his gaze, Laurie fumbled and made a lot of mistakes. Redwine came over to lean on the piano. "You must not be much of a teacher, Marilys. I better find someone else for Larry."

"No!" Laurie took a deep breath and sent a message to her fingers. *Do what you know! Do it right!* She played an easy little exercise without a bobble, the harder one she'd been succeeding with until Redwine paralyzed her, and then dared the first real song Marilys had let her try, a simplified "Mexicali Rose."

Redwine's yellow eyes moved from the woman to the girl he thought a boy, back again, with a faint smile. "Reckon you are a pretty good teacher after all, Marilys." He brushed her shoulder with his furred hand as one might negligently pet a dog. "Come along with me for a minute, Larry. I want to show you something."

Laurie tensed. Was he going to be like that jocker on the train? Buddy jumped up from his books. "Can I see, too?"

Redwine shrugged. "Sure, might as well."

Exchanging relieved glances with Marilys, Laurie followed Redwine into the foyer and up the stairs with the ornate fluted, knobbed banister. They went down the carpeted hall, past heavy mahogany doors with brass numerals, to the very end. Redwine unlocked the last door and held it open.

It wasn't just a room—this must be what was called an apartment. A fire crackled cheerfully in the stone fireplace along one wall with big windows on either side. The dark green plush divan and easy chairs matched and the round low table in front of the divan held shiny new magazines and a box of chocolates. The rich jewel-toned rug was patterned in flowers and leafy tendrils. A piano gleamed in the corner, facing into the room so the light from a third window burnished the wood and streamed like glory on the keyboard and music rack. Through an arched door, Laurie saw twin beds with striped bedspreads and matching curtains at the window. Beyond a chest of drawers was a bathroom.

It was by far the most elegant abode Laurie had ever seen, though she would have expected Redwine to have a big bed and the landscapes on the walls weren't what she'd have thought suited his taste.

"Gee whiz!" Buddy gasped. He shouldn't say that. Mama said that *Gee* was short for Jesus and almost as bad as swearing. "This your place, Mr. Redwine?"

"No. My apartment's across the hall. This is for you boys during the week while your granddad's out of town."

"Gee whiz!" Buddy's awed delight faded as he looked around more carefully. He caught Laurie's sleeve. "There's nowhere to sit down 'thout being scared of getting it dirty. And the rug's too nice to walk on."

Laved in gold, the piano seemed to float in a magic cloud. The bedroom looked like a picture out of *Ladies' Home Journal.* They couldn't stay here, of course. It would make them beholden to Mr. Redwine. But this was a glimpse of a gracious way of living that made Laurie think with a kind of shame, and with shame at being ashamed, of the shack in Sludge Town. She didn't aspire to anything this luxurious but neither did she intend to spend her life in shacks, stopovers along the road, the long road of her life that vanished into unfathomable distance.

"Edna'll feed you in the kitchen," Redwine said, turning. His heavy body exuded triumph. "I'll take you over to your house now so you can get your things."

"No."

"What?"

Laurie's blood chilled as he slowly looked around. "I mean, no, thank you," she amended, her voice scratchy and tight in her throat.

They stared at each other. He seemed to swell, blocking the hall, but he was solid mass. He frightened her so that her knees actually knocked together. She had to constrict her muscles against a spurt of urine.

He sucked in air and thrust his hands behind him. "You crazy?"

"We've got a place." She swallowed but her tongue still felt like a boll of cotton with seeds still in it.

"That shanty! It could burn down so fast you'd never get out."

Laurie had her knees under control, though the urge to urinate made her fight the need to wriggle. "Well then," she said hardily, meeting the yellow eyes, "since you own it maybe you ought to fix it up."

"Your granddad would rest easier if he knew you weren't alone down there in Sludge Town."

"Mrs. Harris keeps an eye on us. We can go over there anytime we want. Gramp wouldn't want us taking up a fancy place you can charge a lot of money for."

"Leave your granddad to me."

"Thanks, Mr. Redwine, but we've got to get home now. Mrs. Harris will be worried if we're late."

Redwine's hand fell on her shoulder. The blunt fingers dug in but it was the sensation of being grasped, crushed, that panicked Laurie. Struggle was useless, would only challenge him. She stayed quiet, still as death, even her heartbeat slowing.

"Damned hardheaded kid! I bring you all the way from California, give your granddad work, fix it for you to have piano lessons, let you play in my restaurant, offer you the suite the governor stays in when he's out this direction, and you don't have the brains to appreciate it or act the least bit grateful!"

In spite of her marrow-deep distrust of him, Laurie felt guilty. "We—we do appreciate it, Mr. Redwine! But Gramp's painted real good signs for you and thought up slogans you'd have to pay a bunch for if you'd hired someone like whoever does the Burma-Shave jingles. And it was you who wanted Buddy and me at Redwine House." Laurie's chin came up. "I can pay Marilys for lessons. If you'd rather we went to playing at the Black Gold—"

"You'll play here! And Marilys already gets more than she's worth." Redwine stepped over to the door across the hall. In the shadows, his eyes glowed like sulphurous fire. "All right, go to Sludge Town! Maybe that's where you belong."

He went in his apartment and slammed the door. Laurie and Buddy looked at each other. Then they raced down the hall, down the steps, and into the kitchen where Clem looked up in surprise from a faucet he was fixing.

"You boys want a ride home?"

Laurie nodded. Edna hugged her. "Good for you, dear. I'd love to have you close, goodness knows, but you're a sight better off to be as independent of Dub as you can be." Behind the steel-rimmed round spectacles, her gray eyes showed worry. "It must be that Dub kind of sees as you as the son he'd like to have."

Clem spat into the waste can. "He had a son."

"Had?" asked Laurie.

"Will was a nice kid—when he was sober. Dub picked at him all the time, cut him down every time he tried to do anything on his own. So Will drank and drove fast and reckless—guess it was the only way he had of getting away from Dub."

Edna shuddered. "He lived through three wrecks. Fourth one, he was pinned under his new Lincoln."

"It blew up," finished Clem. "What was left of him was burned so bad they had the funeral with a closed coffin."

"Just turned seventeen," Edna mourned. "He had wavy yellow hair and the prettiest blue eyes. Good-hearted he was, too."

"What happened to his mother?" Laurie probed reluctantly.

Edna sighed. "Rosemary was a sweet lady but she couldn't stand up to Dub. He just ran her right into the ground. She was sickly after Will was born and took lots of medicine. The day he was buried, she swallowed a lot of pills. She was dead when Dub found her."

"What it comes to is he killed 'em both," growled Clem. "You don't want to be his son, Larry. Anyone he gets close to, he smashes the life out of 'em. Look at Marilys—"

"Clem!" warned Edna.

Clem spat again. "Come on, boys. I'll take you home."

To Laurie's vast relief, Redwine was gone the rest of that week. When Way came to walk them home from the Redwine House on Saturday night, he came early, shaved and all spiffed up in a new shirt. While the Field Brothers entertained, Marilys sat with him at a little side table. She always looked nice, but Way's admiring gaze brought a sheen to her. When it was time to leave, Way hesitated, twisting his new hat's brim.

"Thought I'd take the kiddos to the matinee tomorrow," he said. "Maybe you'd come with us, ma'am?" You'd never know him for the tramp they'd met in the boxcar not quite three months ago. Laurie warmed with as much pride as if he had been her grandfather. He looked handsome and respectable and spoke courtly enough to flatter any woman.

"I'd love that." Marilys didn't even ask what the movie was. Her eyes glowed like summer twilight. "I don't have a kitchen but Edna lets me cook when I want to. Let me make spaghetti and garlic bread to have for dinner at your place."

Way grinned. "Didn't know Christmas came twice a year but I'm all for it."

"I'll make a burnt-sugar cake, too," planned Marilys. Her brow furrowed. "I haven't made one in so long it may be a failure."

"No way it can be that," Way assured her.

Next afternoon, Laurie and Buddy sat with Bill and Catharine Harris, whom they had invited, and blissfully munched Cracker Jacks through a Donald Duck cartoon and the last part of Gene Autry's serial, *Phantom Empire*. Laurie was glad it was the last part so Buddy wouldn't fuss to see every install- ment. They sipped Cokes during *Mutiny on the Bounty* with Clark Gable and Charles Laughten.

Afterwards, supper was delicious. Marilys asked Bill and Catharine to join them. As she whisked about the kitchen, Laurie watched her with adoration. It seemed so right and happy for Marilys to be with them that Laurie wasn't the least bit jealous of her taking charge.

As they lingered over the caramel cake and hot chocolate, Marilys's brightness faded. Glancing at her watch, she said, "I'll have to go as soon as we do the dishes."

"Looks like you could have a night off now and then," Way objected.

Her soft, full mouth curved down. "Dub never lets me forget that I'm paid enough to live on for just playing the piano three or four hours an evening."

Way rubbed at the scar on his cheek as if dead nerves were coming back to life and he couldn't decide whether it pleasured more than it pained. His dark eyes compelled her to look at him. "You still got a right to a life of your own."

She stiffened and started clearing the table. "You don't un- derstand."

"Dub don't own you! All you need to do is walk out of there."

"People don't walk out on Dub." Marilys shrugged. "Die, maybe, but they don't walk."

"If he hurt you—"

She caught his hands. "Way, please! Stay out of it. Things could be a lot worse—they were when I met Dub. I owe him something for giving me this job."

"Way, why don't you take Marilys home?" asked Laurie. She and Buddy didn't always call him Gramp in front of Marilys. "Buddy and I'll do the dishes and bring the restaurant pans back tomorrow."

Marilys brushed a kiss on Laurie's forehead. "That's sweet of you. I'll see you after school tomorrow, then." Way helped her into her coat, turned the collar up to cover her ears, and tucked his arm beneath hers as they went out.

After his obligatory grumbling about how many dishes there were, Buddy said almost under his breath, "Laurie! Wouldn't it be swell if Marilys lived with us? When she and Way are both around, it's—it's—" He broke off, reddening.

Laurie finished for him. "It's like we're a real family, honey. You don't need to feel bad for liking it. We'll never forget Mama and Daddy but they'd be glad we've got grown-up friends who care about us."

When Way came back, he acted funny, smiling dreamily one minute and scowling the next as he packed his cardboard suitcase for the next week. "I can't pay any on the Chevy this week," he said shamefacedly when Laurie brought him twenty-nine dollars to apply on the truck. "Two of Dub's old tires blew out and part of our deal is I replace any that can't be patched. But next week—"

"That Chevy's more than half ours right now," Laurie reminded him. "Only ninety-one dollars to go!"

Way frowned. "Don't seem right for me to get the title to the truck when you kiddos have put in most of the cash."

"If you'd rather, we'll pay you rent and groceries," Laurie teased.

Way chuckled at that before he sobered. "Laurie—Buddy— you like Marilys real well, don't you?"

Buddy jumped up and grabbed Way's wrist. "You—you're going to get married?" he asked eagerly.

"Well—maybe." Way grinned and pushed back his hair. "I asked her tonight."

"What'd she say?" Laurie blurted.

"Didn't say yes—but she didn't flat out say no. Just had a bunch of fraidy-cat reasons why we shouldn't, but no real good ones."

"She'll do it, then!" Laurie hugged Way and Buddy tangled in somehow though he generally wouldn't let anyone touch him. Laughing through tears, Laurie exulted, "When we leave Black Spring in *our* Chevy, we'll be an honest-to-goodness family!"

"We'd have to leave," Way said, troubled and apologetic. "No way Marilys could stay in town if she walks out on Dub. Don't want to take you kids out of school, though."

"It would be nice to finish this term but it'd be a lot nicer to have Marilys with us."

"We'll see how it goes." Way nodded.

Laurie was so happy that she got out the harmonica and launched into Jimmie Rodgers's "T for Texas." It was late when they went to bed, early when they rose, and then Way was gone for another week.

As they waved him off this time, though, Laurie didn't have to fight tears. In three or four weeks, they'd own the truck, could go where they wanted when they wanted. Her throat tightened at the thought of leaving Catharine and Miss Larson and Edna and Clem, but it was going to be mighty good to see the absolute final last of W. S. Redwine. If only Marilys would—could—go with them! The only possible thing more wonderful than that—no use wishing that the dead could rise—would be to find Morrigan again.

Way didn't come in the Redwine House Friday night while the Field Brothers were entertaining, nor was he waiting in the hall when they came out of the restaurant. Redwine was. He looked grave, angry, and at the same time kind of satisfied.

Trouble. Laurie's insides froze. Her legs turned wooden and couldn't move her feet. "Wh—where's Gramp?"

"Skipped the country is all I know."

"He—he wouldn't!"

"He did. And stole a bunch of expensive tools out of my hardware at Lubbock."

Laurie's heart contracted. "You're a great big fat liar, Mr. Redwine!"

He smiled but there was no warmth in his yellow eyes. "Better not talk that way to your guardian, Laurie."

While her brain clicked at the name, he chuckled. "Yes, I know now you're a girl. Smart of you to pass for a boy on the road. I had quite a talk with your real grandpa a few days ago. Told me how you'd run off, how your mom and pa are dead.

He was plumb tickled that I was willing to take care of you kids. Want to see the paper he signed at the lawyer's that makes me your guardian till you're eighteen?"

"You gave Grandpa Field some money!" Laurie accused.

"Not much."

"You the same as *bought* us!"

"It's for your own good. Inside of six months, you'll thank me." Redwine reached into his inside vest pocket and brought out a rumpled envelope. "This is from Wayburn. He left it for you at the hardware he robbed."

The seal was broken. "You read it," Laurie accused.

"Sure I did. I'm your legal guardian. County judge just confirmed that this morning."

Feeling trapped, desperate, and bewildered about Way, but wildly intent on breaking free, Laurie pulled out the page of folded tablet paper. She had never seen Way's handwriting but the neat script was a small version of that he used on signs where he didn't need big block letters.

Kiddos—

I got a snoutful of booze and like I told you, once I start, there's no stopping. I'm not fit to be around you. I know you don't like Dub much but he can give you a good home and education. With your music, you can earn more than I can. I'd just be a detriment to you. Don't think hard of me, Larry-Laurie and Bud. And don't worry your heads, neither—this old tramp knows all the roads. I love you like my own. That won't change. Bart Rogers at Cross Plains seems like an honest feller. If Clem or Marilys was to talk to him, I'll bet he'd give back at least your money that's paid on the truck and you're sure welcome to any of mine he offers to refund. Good luck, kiddos. Knowing you has sure been the best thing in my whole life.

So long, it's been good to know you. . . .

"What does he say?" demanded Buddy, a quaver in his voice.

214

"He says he loves us." She gave Buddy the note.

"I don't know all the words," he said after a moment's scowling. "Does—does it mean he—he's gone away?"

Unable to speak, Laurie nodded. Buddy let out a wail like one of the rabbits he used to shoot and burrowed his face against her. "Won't we ever see Way again?"

Holding him, Laurie sort of rocked her brother and said, "Yes. Don't you worry, Buddy. We'll see him again."

She looked up into Redwine's eyes. They were flat and sheenless as dried paint. "Come on," he said. "We'll get your things."

17

Redwine stood where the tumbleweed Christmas-tree had reigned and swept a quick glance around the shanty. "Clem'll come over tomorrow for the mattresses and heater and kitchen stuff," he said. "Won't take long to rent the place."

Stripped of its flour-sack tablecloth, the packing crate was only a box, not the center of many happy meals, just as this was a shack again, not a home. Laurie had known from the start that this couldn't be their always place, hadn't wanted it to be, even, but she felt nearly as sick and robbed as when Daddy sold the rocking chair and old oak table—as when she caught a last glimpse of the brave, battered little cherry tree as they pulled away from the house in Prairieville. *Oh, Way! Why did you leave us, too?*

Maybe they'd been more trouble than he let on. Maybe he hadn't really wanted to be stuck with a couple of kids. But—did Marilys know? Had he just gone off and left all three of them? What made him start drinking again?

As if she might find an answer, Laurie ignored Redwine's impatient order to hurry and went back to the room Way had shared with Buddy. Everything he owned had gone with him in that old cardboard suitcase, except for the nice fedora she'd got him at Christmas. She took it off its nail and held it against her cheek. It smelled like the hair oil Way started wearing after he met Marilys.

How could he leave them, all of them? Laurie couldn't believe it. "No use taking that hat," Redwine said.

Laurie held it, careful not to crush it, picked up her guitar, and followed Buddy out to the truck. Grandpa Field, an Oklahoma lawyer, and a Texas judge had handed them over to Redwine. Way had vanished somewhere out on the road. Didn't he know that even if he was drinking, they loved him and would try to help him stop?

As Redwine shepherded them up the stairs, Edna came out of the kitchen. "Boys, would you like some milk and cookies?"

Laurie's stomach was tied in a knot and for once even Buddy shook his head no to a treat. "Well, kids, if you need anything, our bedroom's right under yours," Edna said, staring at Redwine through her steel-rimmed glasses. "Just pound on the floor and Clem or I'll be right up."

That made Laurie feel a little less crushed and deserted. "Thanks, Edna."

"And I'll make you buckwheat cakes for breakfast," Edna promised. "With sliced bananas and a lot of maple syrup."

"That—that'll be real nice."

"Good night, boys. Don't you worry, everything's going to work out fine."

How could it, with Way gone God knew where, boozing again, tramping? Besides, Laurie knew in her marrow it couldn't be fine to have Redwine for a guardian. Now that he knew she was a girl, she felt as if he had stripped away her clothes, as if he'd seen her naked. She couldn't say this to Edna, though.

"Thanks, Edna," she said again, and moved on up the stairs.

Redwine unlocked the door of the apartment and switched on a lamp before he put bundles down on the sofa. "I'll lock the door so no drunk can come bustin' in," he said.

Panic flooded Laurie. "Can't we lock it from the inside?"

"This is safer."

"But locked up—with someone else having the key! It—it's like being in jail."

"You've never been in one or you wouldn't say that," Redwine snorted. "You don't have any sense, Laurie Field, or you'd appreciate what I'm doing for you and your brother." He checked, spoke in a kinder tone. "I know it's a jolt to have Wayburn light out on you but it really is for the best. I know he was good to you as he knew how to be but he was just an old tramp—"

"He wasn't!" Laurie whirled, spitting outrage, trying not to cry. "You hired him yourself!"

"Yes, and what did he do?" Redwine's words clubbed her. "Went back to the bottle. Even he knew he had no business keeping you kids with him. I'm your guardian now. That's the luckiest thing that's ever happened to you. So settle down and we'll get along just dandy."

"Like you did with your son?" Laurie burst out.

Redwine's arm drew back. She cowered instinctively before she straightened and glared at him. He moved to the door. "I'm going out of town but when I get back, I'll talk to your teacher and the principal about how you're really a girl," he said. "Marilys will take you shopping tomorrow for some dresses. Maybe she can figure out something to do with your hair till it grows out."

"I can't be a girl here," Laurie cried. The kids would tease her so unmercifully that maybe even Catharine would avoid her.

"The sooner you start, the better. Go on to bed."

The door closed. The key turned in the lock. "Laurie!" Buddy whimpered. "What are we going to do?"

Things had happened so fast and Redwine had taken charge so firmly that Laurie hadn't thought beyond not breaking down in front of him. Now, gripping Buddy by the arms, she didn't have to think, the words rose out of her without a twinge of doubt.

"We're going to find Way."

Buddy's eyes widened. "How?"

Laurie had no idea but now that she knew what to do, her mind started working. "We'll watch for signs that look like he made them. We'll ask after him in hobo jungles along the railroad. We'll just plain hunt for him till we find him—or he finds us."

"He's not looking for us," Buddy objected, pulling away. "He went off and left us, didn't he?"

That stabbed, but Laurie stoutly denied her own qualms. "He didn't want to go, Buddy. He left because he got drunk and thought he shouldn't be around us if he was liable to do that. He knew Mr. Redwine wanted us to stay with him and that Marilys and Edna and Clem would take care of us. But if Way knew we were out on the road by ourselves, you bet he'd come after us."

"Yeah, maybe he would."

"You know he would."

"But how're we going to hunt for him if Mr. Redwine locks us up?"

"He can't lock us up all the time. We can take off on the way to school or afterwards." She sighed. "I wish we could drive that truck over at Cross Trails or at least get some of our money back but no owner's going to deal with kids. Maybe like Way said, Clem or Marilys can get some kind of refund. It's too bad he didn't have enough money to pay the Chevy off and travel in it."

"That would've been taking our money!"

"Not if you figure our share of rent and groceries. Anyhow, Buddy, it just makes me sick that he paid in that much and lost it."

"Well, he shouldn't have got drunk!" Buddy rubbed angrily at his eyes. "Why'd he go and do that?"

"I don't know," Laurie admitted. "It must have been something awful because you know he never drank all the time we knew him."

She stared at their bundles. More than they could carry, and she wouldn't leave her guitar—or Way's hat, either. She was going to find him and put it on his head. They only had five dollars and a little change. Maybe they should wait till after they'd gotten more money that Friday and Saturday nights or until Clem or Marilys could get some of the truck money back.

But every day would carry Way farther, make it harder to pick up his tracks.

"Are we going to run off tomorrow?" Buddy asked. He didn't sound eager. Laurie remembered the train, the jocker, the railroad police, the awful, filthy camp outside Eden, and shrank from striking out again, especially without Way. Whatever would have happened to them if he hadn't made them his business? Should they hitch rides or stow aboard trains or what?

She'd have to decide for them both. What if she made the wrong decisions? What if Buddy got killed or hurt because she hauled him away from this nice apartment where Clem and Edna and Marilys would look out for them?

"Buddy." She wet her lips and gulped. "Maybe you ought to stay here. You could probably live at Harrises and I'd send money for your keep."

"No!" He dived for her and held on as if she might disappear and began to sob. "Mama died. Daddy went away and then he died. Way's gone. If—if you go anyplace, Laurie, I'm going, too!"

She kissed his wet cheek and hugged him. "All right, honey. All right, I promise. Cross my heart and hope to die, I won't leave without you. Let's say a prayer that Way's safe and then we'd better get to bed."

Buddy regarded her skeptically. "Does it do any good to pray?"

"I don't know." Laurie's feelings about God had always been more fear than anything till Mama's dying. Since then, anger usually smothered the fear except when guilt for the anger roiled her emotions into an unidentifiable mixture. "I don't know if God can hear, or if he cares if he does. But when I pray, I feel closer to Mama, like *she* hears, and that makes me feel better."

Buddy snuffled. "I don't feel like anybody hears me."

"Well, let's pray together."

"Out loud?"

"Sure. Then *I'll* hear you anyway." She grinned, hoping to make him laugh, but he watched her so solemnly that, stricken, she took his hand and squeezed it as she knelt by their heaped belongings. He came down beside her.

"Dear Lord," she pleaded, "Take care of Way. Help him not to get drunk. Don't let him get run over or fall under a train or get beaten up by railroad bulls. Please, help him get work and shave and change his clothes so he'll keep his self-respect and won't be a tramp. Let him know we love him, and help us find him. We ask this in Jesus' name. Amen." She prayed more to Jesus than to God because he was human once and surely understood better, so it seemed peculiar to make her request in his name, but if he could hear her, she was sure he could figure it out. "Now, Buddy, you say your prayer."

"Uh—Our Father who art in heaven—"

Laurie poked him in the ribs with her elbow. "Buddy, the Lord's Prayer is fine but it doesn't say anything about Way."

"Mmmhm." Buddy was silent a long moment. Then he blurted, "I want the same things as Laurie. Amen."

He jumped up. So did Laurie. "Buddy Field, that's lazy! It's—it's like putting ditto marks instead of spelling out a word. What if—"

A metallic click came from the bedroom door. They spun toward it. "Larry? Buddy?" came a voice, barely audible, from the other side. Barely audible, but it was Marilys!

Laurie ran to open the door and Marilys stepped in from the next room. Bending, she scooped them both into her arms. "Edna told me about—about Way." Tears glittered in her eyes. "You can bet Dub's behind that!"

Laurie dug the crumpled note from her pocket. "Way says he got drunk."

"Men do it every night. It's not the end of the world."

"Way says he can't just take one drink and stop. All the time we knew him, he never had a drop."

"There's some reason why he did." Marilys's mouth twisted. "Somehow, Dub set up the whole thing. He's mighty good at setting traps."

"Way didn't write to you?"

She shook her head and then, even in the yellowish electric light, she went pale and flinched. Straightening, she turned away. "That's what Dub did!" she whispered. "That lowlife bas— I'm sorry, kids—Dub told Way about me."

"About you?" Laurie puzzled.

Marilys colored. "I've done some things I'm not proud of. I—I've tried to tell Way but he always stopped me—said it didn't matter." Her head drooped like a flower on a broken stalk. "I guess it did. And Dub could have made it worse than it was—which was bad enough."

That sounded like one of the grown-ups' mysteries about which Laurie wondered but didn't really want to know.

"I expect Way thinks he's not good enough for you since he got drunk," Laurie comforted, tentatively laying her hand on Marilys's arm. "Anyhow, we're going to find him."

"How? Do you have an idea of where he's gone?"

"No. But we'll watch for his signs and hunt in the hobo camps. If we don't find him, he'll find us."

"I'll go with you."

"Marilys, you can't!"

"I can if you can."

"But you're a lady, a pretty one! You can't flip freights and hitch rides!"

"You've passed for a boy, Larry—I guess it's Laurie now. Maybe I can."

Laurie glanced from Marilys's delicate features to her bosom. "I don't think so." A sudden hope filled her. "Say, can you drive a truck?"

"Papa got me a Chrysler sedan for my sixteenth birthday," Marilys said. "I like to drive, in fact I used to wrestle those old trucks of Dub's around the dirt roads when he got tired of driving." Her thoughts jumped to connect with Laurie's. "Way said in his note that maybe Clem or I could get your money back on that truck at Cross Trails. How much do you still owe?"

"Ninety-one dollars." That was an awful lot, though looking at it another way, the ninety-nine dollars they'd paid on it was even more.

"I can pay it out and have a little money left for gas," Marilys said after a moment's silent calculations. "We ought to be able

221

to play and sing enough to pay our way. But we'll have to be careful and keep moving, probably keep trading vehicles. Dub'll have the law and highway patrol watching out for us."

"We haven't done anything wrong!"

Marilys shrugged. "You're runaways and he'd accuse me of kidnapping."

"Kidnapping!"

The word sent a shiver through Laurie. Three years ago, Colonel Lindbergh's baby had been kidnapped, held for ransom, and found buried a few months later only five miles away, probably killed the night he was stolen from his bed. Bruno Richard Hauptmann had passed some of the ransom bills in 1934. He swore he was innocent but if he was convicted, he'd probably die in the electric chair. After the Lindberghs' agony, kidnappers were hated and feared worse than murderers and Congress passed a law that gave the death penalty to kidnappers who took their victims across a state line.

Laurie caught Marilys's hands. "That's too dangerous for you, Marilys!"

"Dub has to catch me first," Marilys said with a wry chuckle. "If he does, I expect we could do some fancy bargaining. I know things that could get him into big trouble." Her blue eyes darkened. "We'll find Way. That's the main thing. And then if he doesn't want me around, I'll just keep going."

"But—"

Marilys raised her hand. "Don't worry, honey. However that works out, I'll be glad something gave me the guts to leave Dub."

Laurie stood on tiptoe to kiss Marilys and give her a warm hug. "I know—I just plain know—that if we can talk to Way, he'll see we all belong together no matter what anybody's done! Are—are we going tonight?"

Brow puckering, Marilys thought a moment, then shook her head. "Dub has to go to Oklahoma City tomorrow on business. He's buying an oil company if he can do it cheap enough. If he can't, he'll go on like he is, staking independent drillers as cheap as he can and claiming a hog's share of any oil they hit. Dub won't risk big money, that's why he'll never be a millionaire. It's

222

also why he's not broke. Anyhow, with luck, he'll be gone all week." Marilys grinned. "Clem and Edna just won't be able to track him down when they call to tell him you've disappeared."

"Won't he be mad at them?"

"He'll be mad at everybody, but for their own good, we won't tell Clem and Edna what we're doing. I'll leave them a note so they won't worry but the less they know, the better they can stand Dub off."

"I—I don't have to leave my guitar, do I?" Laurie would almost as soon leave an arm or a leg.

"I've got a friend who can pick me up here in the afternoon when Edna takes her nap and Clem's at the pool hall. We'll bring all your things and come by school for you just as it's letting out. With luck, we'll pay for the truck and be out of Cross Trails before dark." Marilys's words quickened as she planned, and her eyes glowed twilight blue. "I'll bring bedding so we can sleep in the truck. We'll have to buy a tarp to go over the back. In case Dub finds out about the Chevy, we'd better trade it the first good chance we get, but I hope we're a long way off by the time he gets back from Oklahoma."

"I hope we'll have found Way."

Again, Marilys gathered them close. "So do I, kids. So do I."

Twenty-four hours later, they were cuddled in the back of *their* Chevy truck, parked off a dirt road several miles from the blacktop. The seller, Bart Rogers, a chunky, bow-legged cowboy who'd turned to roughnecking, was so taken by Marilys that he threw in two spare tires, a jack, some tools, and an oil-splashed but serviceable tarp with grommets. He even lashed it over the high board sides of the back of the pickup. Way had told him about his kid partners who were putting most of the money in the truck and Way had even phoned that day to ask Bart if he'd return the children's money.

"Didn't ask for his own," Bart said, as he took Marilys's five twenties and gave her back a dollar. "But this works out better for all of us, ma'am, and I'm tellin' you this is a mighty good truck for the money. I just kind of hankered for a new one. Bein' a bachelor, and not bein' a hand for booze or cards, I don't spend much." He watched Marilys shyly but couldn't keep pride from his voice. "Payin' cash for a brand new Studebaker. Sure couldn't do that if I was still cowboyin'."

"You have done well," Marilys praised, but when he asked if he could buy them supper, she'd smiled, shaken his hand, thanked him for everything, and said they had to be on their way.

Snug and warm between Marilys and Buddy, Laurie couldn't quite believe their plan had worked out so well, though she felt a pang at thinking that she hadn't been able to tell Miss Larson good-bye and thank her for being such a good teacher. She'd just had to be content with complimenting Miss Larson on her dress and the new way she was wearing her hair. Laurie had told Catharine good-bye right after school, saying she was going to live with a nice lady and explaining that was all she was allowed to tell. Tears had formed in Catharine's hazel eyes and in Laurie's, too. They had stepped into an empty first-grade room and gave each other a hard, fast hug.

"You'll always be my best friend," Catharine snuffled.

"And you'll always be mine," Laurie assured her, feeling guilty at leaving her but knowing they'd been close because they were Sludge Town kids starting at a new school on the same day. New families moved into Sludge Town all the time. It shouldn't be long before Catharine found a newcomer as eager to be friends as she had been. Were friendships mostly like that—a means of not being alone rather than because you really liked each other?

All the same, Laurie missed Catharine, and Miss Larson and Edna and Clem. She'd kissed Edna that morning, and thanked her for the hotcakes, laughed hard at one of Clem's jokes that wasn't really funny. The note she left under her pillow said, "Thanks for everything, Clem and Edna, and don't worry, we'll be fine. When we grow up, maybe we can come back to see you."

No notes for Redwine, though. While they ate breakfast, he'd had a cup of black coffee, standing in the kitchen. "When I get back," he said with what Laurie thought was a perfectly heartless grin, "we'll get you turned into a girl, Laurie. I've already told Marilys to take you shopping."

Laurie didn't answer. "Did you hear me?" he rapped.

"Yes."

"You won't get anywhere by sulling, girl. Make up your mind to that." He set down the cup so hard it cracked and went out the door.

"Oh my, oh dear gracious!" murmured Edna, examining the cup. "That's exactly the way he used to talk to young Will. Remember, Clem?"

"Yeah." Clem tousled Laurie's hair. "But this one's a sight different from Will. Have some more hotcakes, kids, they're the best in Texas!"

Buddy made a sound in his sleep like a lost puppy. Laurie put her arm around him and snugged the covers around their ears. "It's all right, Buddy," she whispered. "I'm here."

While they'd been driving, Way's hat was placed carefully on the back of the seat against the rear window. Now it set on top of their bundles and Marilys's suitcase, watching over them, sort of. Laurie said a prayer for him wherever he was, heard coyotes yodeling far away. Somehow that made her think of Morrigan. She drowsily said a prayer for him, too, and then she was asleep.

She woke to the aroma of coffee, stretched, blinked, and remembered. Rolled in a quilt cocoon beneath their shared blankets, Buddy burrowed deeper into his pillow. In the dim light, Laurie smiled at Way's hat and wished him good morning wherever he was. *And you, John Morrigan, good morning to you.* He was always ready to flash his grin from the back of her thoughts but being on the road again brought him powerfully to mind.

Pulling on her clothes and jacket, Laurie scrambled out of the truck. Marilys had brought a box of cooking things, including a dark blue enamel coffeepot. This belched contentedly on a grill set over a fire in a hole dug in the sandy earth. Marilys's eyes were hollowed but she wrinkled her nose like a kid and

225

grinned as she poured out two mugs of coffee, tipping evaporated milk into Laurie's.

"Sleep good, honey?"

Laurie nodded. "Did you?"

"Too excited." Marilys moved with eager expectancy as she
opened a white bakery bag and offered Laurie a cinnamon roll.
"When I think Way might be in the next town, or the next one,
I can't wait to get started."

"We can let Buddy sleep and go soon as you're ready,"
Laurie suggested. "If he wakes up to one of these cinnamon
rolls—boy, they're good, all chewy with lots of nuts!—he'll be
happy." She hunkered close to the cheerful flame, enjoying its
warmth. The heat of the rich coffee felt good slipping down her
throat to her stomach. She watched dawn streak the sky behind
some spiky yuccas on a gentle slope rising above the dry
creekbed. A nibbled moon still shone in the west. She sighed
with near bliss.

"Marilys, if Way were here, wouldn't it be perfect? To be out
like this together while the world wakes up? Of course, we'd be
on vacation or camping out for fun—we'd have a home somewhere."

"That would be perfect." Marilys took a deep breath and
threw back her head. "But this feels good, Laurie. You can't
know how good!"

They sipped more coffee, put out the fire with great care,
propped the rolls beside Buddy, and were on their way with the
rising sun pushing at their back and besplendoring the wide
plain before them.

18

No telling where Way would go, or how. He could be in a bus
or car or truck, passing them, or being passed. He could be in
any boxcar pounding along the tracks. Laurie racked her brain
for the name of some place he especially liked, but all she was

sure of was that he hated California and was uneasy traveling the high mountain country of Arizona. Nor, surely, would he head into the most blighted part of the Dust Bowl, that animal's skull Morrigan had sketched in the sand.

"Makes sense that he'd stick to oil towns where there's money to pay for signs and usually some kind of work," Marilys said. "That could take us all the way across Texas into Louisiana and Arkansas and back west through Oklahoma and Kansas. The trick is going to be looking for him without getting caught by Dub."

Laurie's heart jumped into her mouth. "He—he won't hunt us, will he?"

"Not himself. But when he gets back from Oklahoma, he'll alert the law all over Texas and probably the neighboring states." Marilys flashed a grin. Even with the prospect of Dub on their trail, she was merry and lighthearted as she'd been at their tumbleweed Christmas tree. "One thing sure, we won't stay at any of his Truck-Inns."

They picked up Highway 287 at Claude about thirty miles east of Amarillo and descended from the Cap Rock, the rugged, tortuously winding shelf that set off the high plains of the Llano Estacado from the sweeping lower prairies, the rugged country between cut by eroded canyons where angles of recent snow whitened the clefts. Scrubby mesquite and cedars tufted the wall of the escarpment wherever a seed had found soil enough to root and grow squat and strong to withstand scouring winds and blizzards.

Goodnight was a few businesses caught in a bent elbow of the highway. A few newer frame houses kept a respectful distance from what Marilys said was Colonel Goodnight's old ranch house. Behind the house, narrow-flanked, great-humped creatures roamed, horns protruding from what looked like kinky wigs.

"Buffalo!" Buddy yelled. "Hey, those got to be buffalo!"

They pulled off the road and went over to the fence to watch the big animals. "Goodnight was the first settler out here," Marilys explained. "He saw how in just a couple of years hunters killed off most of the southern herds just for their hides and

227

left the meat to rot. When the herds were gone, folks sold the bones east for buttons, dice, knife handles, collar and corset stays. Anyhow, the colonel hated to see all the buffalo gone, so he started a herd on his ranch."

These were the beasts that fed the Indians who once ranged the plains stretching from Nebraska to the Rio Grande. And the buffalo fed on grass, grass and flowers like that tiny strip near the Oklahoma school, Laurie's Little Prairie. At least much of this land had never been broken by the plow. Daddy, as a boy, had picked up buffalo and cattle bones after the wheat was planted, after the snow had thawed, driven a wagon around the draws where the tired creatures died. The market in Dodge City was between the river and Hampton's livery barn and the big boneyard was on the bank of the Cimarron River about three-quarters of a mile east of Boot Hill. Daddy had heard Billy Sunday preach once when the evangelist pitched his tent on the hill.

How quickly it had all vanished. That prairie world would never come again, never. The sod of a vast part of the Great Plains was powdered dust that couldn't nourish anything even if it hadn't swirled up to blacken the sky and fill the air anytime the wind rose.

"We'd better go," said Marilys. "The sooner we get to a place where we can swap this Chevy, the easier I'll breathe."

They camped that night by a diminished lake ten miles out of Childress and were in town by the time businesses opened. No used-car dealer would trade even and they found no signs that looked like Way had painted them.

"That's most of my cash," Marilys said as they paid for groceries after filling up with gas. "But before we try singing and playing, we need to be in a different vehicle. We'll do better in an oil town, too, where folks don't depend on cotton, wheat, and cattle for money."

Just in case, they went to the jail. Way wasn't there. But it was a place they'd have to check in every town that had one. Electra came in sight before sundown, prosperous-looking, with factories to make oil machinery and drilling tools. "W. T. Waggoner was drilling for water for his cattle back in 1911 when he struck oil instead," explained Marilys. "Named the town for his daughter. The field's still producing, not like some that boom and play out fast." She slowed down by Myrt's Roadside Cafe. "With a name like this, there's got to be at least one woman around. Why don't we see if we can sing for our supper here?" They had already agreed that the Field Brothers had to disappear, though Laurie still posed as a boy, and their signature song had to change. For a while, they'd be the Tumbleweeds, but they'd be switching names often. "We'll drive out of town to camp and light out early for Wichita Falls," Marilys finished. "For sure, we can trade off the Chevy there."

Myrt, an enormous blond woman with chins that undulated as she laughed, looked at them keenly over potatoes she was mashing into creamy peaks and glanced from the guitar Marilys held to Laurie with her harmonica and on to Buddy. "Can't say I ever heard of you, but if I had, you prob'ly wouldn't be in Electra. Sure, you can have supper for makin' music for an hour or so, and keep anything folks care to leave you. Kids make a big hit even if they can't sing for shucks and these oil-field hands don't get to see many pretty *ladies.*"

Two hours and a bowl of silver and bills later, The Tumbleweeds ended with "Tumbling Tumbleweed." Amid shouts, stamping, and whistling, Myrt urged them into the kitchen, not forgetting to pick up their money. "Try to eat out there and they won't give you any peace! I swan if you hadn't ought to be on the radio like the Carter Family." There were two chairs at a small table by a window and Myrt scooted over a stool for Buddy and started pouring glasses of milk. "Coffee for you, dear?" she asked Marilys.

"Milk for all of us, please, if there's enough."

"Oh, there's still a few cows on ranches that never got oil," Myrt chuckled. She brought meatloaf, potatoes, gravy, biscuits, and green beans and set three-quarters of a fluffy-topped lemon-meringue pie in the middle of the table before she went out to tend the cash register and tell her customers to hurry back while a brisk gray-haired waitress cleared tables while serving latecomers.

"Aren't you going to count the money?" Buddy demanded, eyeing the overflowing bowl beside the pie.

"After we finish eating," Marilys said. "There's no telling what kind of germs are on those bills. I'll bet your mama told you to always wash your hands after you touched money."

"Awww!" His eyes widened. "Boy howdy! There's a five-dollar bill on top!"

"I think that cowboy way at the back left it," said Laurie. "He just kept ordering coffee, Marilys, and watching you."

Marilys blushed. "Well, there's gas and groceries for a while." Her eyes sparkled, though she must have been tired after wrestling the truck down the winding road from the Cap Rock and singing while she played the guitar.

"You don't look old enough to be the boys' mother," Myrt said to her, returning now that she'd locked the outer door.

"I'm their aunt. We're hoping to run across my brother who's probably in the oil fields somewhere."

"His name Tumbleweed, too?"

Marilys ignored the hint for information. "He may not be using his right name. His last boss is accusing him of stealing some equipment, but I know he didn't. He's tall and skinny with real curly gray hair and dark eyes, scars on his cheek and hands. Anyone like that asked if he could paint you a sign?"

"If he had, I'd have a new one," said Myrt. "But if he passes through, I'll tell him his family tumbled through lookin' for him." She poured more milk. "Reckon you wouldn't want to stay a while? Between my cookin' and your singin', we could just about put the other eating places out of business."

"Thanks, but we really do want to find my brother."

Myrt filled one sack with big spice molasses cookies and another with biscuits. "Well, you be careful on the road," she said. "Can't say I like the notion of your travelin' after dark. If you don't want to spend money on a tourist court, you're welcome to my spare room."

"Thank you, ma'am." Marilys accepted the biscuits and Buddy hugged the fragrant cookies. "We'll be real careful about where we stop but we'd like to get a little farther to-night."

230

"Good luck, then." Myrt smoothed Buddy's head. "If you get back this way, stop and see me. I'll pray the good Lord to keep you from havin' flats and trouble, 'least when you're a long way from help."

She let them out the back door. They called a final thanks and good night and piled into the Chevy. Buddy was asleep before they spotted a dirt road that didn't seem to have any lights along it. Several miles off the highway, they pulled behind some mesquites, moved Buddy into the back, fastened the tarp, and were soon asleep.

Laurie woke to Marilys's, "Dammit, must have parked on a mesquite thorn!" As Laurie clambered out, Marilys shrugged and started collecting dead branches from trees that weren't any taller than she was. All the branches looked dead, of course, but you could tell they were alive if they didn't snap right off. "Might as well have breakfast before we change tires," Marilys said. "I knew we were being too lucky."

They had a patch kit, but since they had two spares and hoped to get rid of the truck that day, they jacked up the front of the truck. Marilys pried off the flat while Laurie got the spare that had the most tread. Buddy was up by then. While he slathered biscuits with peanut butter and jam, Marilys had more coffee and Laurie scanned the sparsely grassed earth for more thorny fallen limbs, clearing several out of the way.

Wichita Falls proudly announced its population to be 45,000, which made it almost as big as Amarillo. It seemed bigger with its oil refineries, huge flour mill, and scores of manufacturing plants. After checking the jail, the Tumbleweeds were the first customers at a used-car lot. In its rattling body, the Chevy held their savings, so Marilys insisted they go to every dealer in town.

"We'll get cheated," she said philosophically. "But we want it to be the best cheat we can get. Keep an eye out as we're driving around for any trucks that have a 'For Sale' sign."

Only three dealers offered an even trade. "Our Chevy's a long shot better than any of them," Marilys grumbled. It was noon and they were heading back for the first place, Jerry's Nu-to-

Yu, where they'd been offered the best trade, a dilapidated Chevy four years older than the one they had with no spare tire. "We might do better in Lubbock but I'm afraid to wait."

"Myrt won't tell on us," Laurie said.

"She won't, but there were plenty of people in the café. If Dub offers a reward—"

Laurie's stomach tightened. "You think he will?"

"I know it."

"It's not fair! Just because he the same as bought us from Grandpa Field, he shouldn't have the right to hunt us like criminals!"

"I'm the criminal," Marilys reminded her wryly. "All we have to do is drive fifteen miles north, cross the Red River into Oklahoma, and I'll be a kidnapper who could be sentenced to death under federal law."

Buddy yelped and Laurie chilled to the bone. "We wouldn't let them do that! We'd say how it was—that we were going to run away from Dub ourselves." She swallowed hard, fighting down the picture of Marilys strapped into the electric chair. "Anyhow, we can stay in Texas."

Marilys's delicate jaw tightened. "We'll go wherever we have to in order to find Way. At least I will."

"So will we."

Buddy nodded and then cried, "Look! Marilys, there's a 'Trade for Truck' sign on that Pontiac in the driveway!"

Marilys hit the brake and herded the Chevy in behind the maroon Pontiac. "We need a truck so we can sleep in it," she said. "But it aggravates me to let old Jerry steal us blind. The Pontiac *looks* good. If it drives that way, we'll try for a swap and trade it for a truck first decent chance we get."

"You can sleep in the back," Laurie said. "Buddy and I can manage in front."

"No, I'll sleep on the floor in back," Buddy differed.

The burly owner had just gotten a job at an oil field halfway to Electra on a dirt road and figured a truck would get him there better than an auto. The Pontiac had a good spare, and ran smoothly when Marilys tried it. She and the roughneck made out the titles to each other. She'd bought the Chevy under the name of Lila Meredith and now she explained to the man that she wanted her sister's name on the Pontiac's papers, Gloria Meredith.

After their things were loaded in the auto, Laurie gave the Chevy a farewell pat on the fender. It had carried them away from Dub, sheltered them by night, and she was sorry that Way would never get to drive it.

"How come we don't pick up hitchhikers?" Buddy asked after they passed several men with their thumbs raised.

"I hate not giving them a ride, honey," said Marilys, "but it's just not safe for a woman with two kids to take chances." At least, thank goodness, these roads weren't full of jalopies stuffed with homeless families and the little they could carry.

Leaving the valleys of the Wichita and Brazos rivers, driving through vast ranchlands and regions where cotton gins testified to the main crop, which hadn't been very "main" during the drought, they followed a crest that divided the cedar-studded ravines of the watersheds of the Brazos and Wichita rivers, spent the night on a ranch road, and pulled into Lubbock on Sunday, passing the tile-roofed brick buildings of Texas Technological College where shrubs and young trees, many of them evergreens, contrasted luxuriantly with the surrounding prairie.

"Way worked here and around here for a week," Laurie said, her heart speeding. "For sure we'll find his signs. Maybe one of us could ask about him at the Truck-Inns and hardwares."

Marilys nodded. "With luck, Dub won't be after us earlier than Friday but we'd better be well out of here by Thursday night. We'll scout after Way, earn some money, and trade off this flivver for another truck." Her cheeks were rosy and her eyes were like midnight with stars shining through. "Let's see who spots Way's first sign!"

Lubbock, a neat town of broad streets, was full of churches, and all of them seemed full of people in their best clothes who were just coming out, shaking hands with their pastors and pausing to visit. With a stab of guilt, Laurie winced at what Mama would say about her children not setting foot in a church since they left Prairieville. Laurie had thought about it several times in Black Spring but there wasn't any Tabernacle of Holiness. Even if there had been, she wouldn't have wanted to go. It was wicked and worldly and she was ashamed of herself, but it was a relief not to have to sit through Sunday school and two sermons on Sunday, prayer meeting on Wednesday night and every night of every revival meeting even when there was school next day. And that was besides family worship—a chapter of the Bible and prayers all around—every morning and every night.

Before she let Buddy go play, she mostly did remember Sunday mornings to read out of Mama's little white New Testament, grimy now that it was no longer nested in the small cedar chest among embroidered handkerchiefs, but now they just prayed under their breath and she suspected that Buddy only ducked his head and closed his eyes.

Well, thought Laurie, rebelling, if God expected them to be good like Mama, he should have left her alive. With the possible exception of Edna, who regularly attended the Methodist church, none of the people who'd been kind to them since the world of Prairieville ended were Christians. Not Rosalie or Way or Marilys. But they were good. According to Brother Arlo, that didn't matter. In fact, it was presumptuous to be good if you weren't a Christian and you'd go to hell as fast as a drunkard who'd murdered his wife, kids, and neighbors, too.

That had never seemed right to Laurie. It seemed at odds with what Jesus said about whatever you did for the sick or hungry or imprisoned, you did it to him. Jesus, when you came right down to it, didn't sound much like God. Maybe the only thing God noticed was if you were Christian. Mama said it was sinful to question his ways, but whether you were kind or mean made a mighty lot of difference to the people you knew.

Laurie swallowed a gasp of joy as she saw the scrolled letters painted on the store window and repeated on a sign above, but left it to Buddy to call out, "Look! 'Dub's Hardware for Hard Wear!'"

"You win," laughed Marilys. "Let's see what else we can find."

They discovered Way's unmistakable flourish on a restaurant, a hotel, a farm-machinery store, and a sign by the edge of the city park that featured a man with a paintbrush and a pretty woman kneeling by a tulip bed.

Cleanest town in Texas!
Winner of the National Clean-up and Paint-up Bureau's
First Prize
Every year since 1931!

Let's win
AGAIN
in 1936!

The same distinctive lettering ornamented another sign.

SITE OF SINGER'S STORE, 1879–1886
FOR MANY YEARS, ONE OF ONLY TWO
STORES ON THE SOUTH PLAINS***FIRST
POST OFFICE IN LUBBOCK COUNTY***
CROSSROAD OF MILITARY TRAILS***
*Though this was a frontier town, we are proud that
in its whole history, Lubbock has had only one
saloon which the owner voluntarily closed after
receiving a petition from fellow citizens.*

"Must be some bootleggers around," mused Marilys. "Or Way couldn't have gone on a toot. Why don't we have a picnic here and then find the Truck-Inn and a place for the Tumbleweeds to earn some money?"

The Truck-Inn was on the San Angelo highway at the edge of town. It would be the first place Dub would check so it was decided that Laurie would go in alone and say Way had left his hat at her house and did the Inn people know where he was? She didn't want to lie, but no one needed to hear that the house had been in Black Spring.

"No use worryin' about Kirkendall's hat, sonny," advised a heavy woman whose blond hair was pulled back in such a tight knot that it gave her a tilt-eyed look. "If it's any good, he'd just trade it for a pint of booze." Her snub nostrils belled with outrage. "I've never been so taken in as I was by that old hobo! Stayed here a week, worked hard, kept himself clean and polite, never had so much as a sarsaparilla bottle in his room. The next week he locks his door, stays drunk for three days, and then he's gone like smoke." Seeing Laurie's distress, the woman pitched her voice softer. "Friend of the family?"

Laurie could only nod. "Well, son," the woman said more kindly, "I'd guess there's not much use looking for Wayburn Kirkendall in La Mesa or Plainview, Tule Creek or Tahoka. He's already painted signs there. He's got grandkids in Black Spring, poor little devils. If you leave the hat here, next time Dub gets through here, I'll ask him to get it to the youngsters. Kirkendall bragged on them a lot, especially on the oldest one called Larry who could play the harmonica real good."

Laurie heart began to thump so loudly she thought the woman must surely hear. "Thanks, ma'am," she said. "Guess we'll wait and see if Way—Mr. Kirkendall comes by. My folks think a lot of him." They would, had they known him.

Back in the Pontiac, Laurie told what the woman had said, and added reluctantly, "Way talked about the Field Brothers here. We'd better not look for a place to sing."

Marilys flinched and suddenly looked exhausted. Hard on her to do all the driving and of course now she felt responsible for them. After a moment, she shrugged and gave a careless laugh. "Being it's Sunday, there won't be any car lots open and we don't have time to hunt for some reprobate who'll do a trade. Might as well get a start to San Angelo."

Wintry fields—thank goodness there was still some land in the Southwest that could be plowed and yield crops—ranchlands with cattle gathered at earthen tanks filled with water pumped by windmills; crumbling rock corrals; dry, white-bedded alkali lakes; a few towns crouched behind the upside-down funnels of cotton gins. They camped that night on the edge of the Cap Rock.

Big Spring had cotton gins, gas-storage tanks, stockyards, and the stink of oil refineries. The only trees were saplings that hadn't yet decided whether to live or die. There was no clue of Way. They did trade the Pontiac and most of the cash they'd raised in Electra for a Ford truck. The dealer surveyed them, scratched at a nimbus of graying hair that surrounded his pink scalp, and finally spat tobacco into the weeds.

"No way I could sleep nights if I turned you loose with these tires, lady," he said to Marilys. "I'll switch 'em with those on that truck over there."

"They'll still be bad tires," Laurie pointed out.

He grinned, showing stumps of brown teeth. "Shucks, sonny, I'll sell that truck to some young sprout who needs to learn how to patch tires. Be good for him."

Gas and groceries left them only a few dollars but sleeping in the car hadn't been too comfortable. "We should be able to keep this one for a while," said Marilys as they drove along the valley of the North Concho, where derricks reared everywhere. "Phew-ey! Smell that sulphur? This field has to be producing what they call sour oil."

Sheep began to outnumber scrawny cattle in pastures with tight fencing that Marilys said was supposed to keep wolves out. As they entered a rough region where cedar and oak showed the bare, white limestone bones of hills, cattle dwindled and goats and sheep browsed the hills and along the river bottoms beneath giant oaks and pecan trees.

San Angelo held no trace of Way. Abilene had several of his signs but none of the business owners knew where he'd gone. In Stamford, he'd done a sign for the headquarters building of the SMS Ranch, using the brand with two *S*'s backwards. Haskell had no trace of him but on the other side of Wild Horse Prairie in Seymour, on the Salt Fork of the Brazos, a café and farm-machinery store had brand-new signs.

"Yeah, miss, your brother did my sign last week," said the café owner, a middle-aged, gray-haired man whose belly protruded under his grease-spotted apron. "No, he didn't seem to be headed anyplace in particular. Said he was seein' the country, paintin' his way along." He sounded disapproving. As if to console Way's relations, the man added, "I guess a sign painter cain't rightly settle down, not unless it was in a big city where there'd always be work."

Instead of going north to Wichita Falls, they took 283 east

through rolling small-hilled ranch country and spent one night near the crumbling adobe ruins of Fort Griffin, the post from which countless sorties were made against raiding Comanches and Kiowas who had wandered this region time out of mind. An old man who turned up at the smell of their breakfast coffee, curious about them, shared their doughnuts and held forth in a quavering voice about how down in the flats, gamblers, wild women, and saloons emptied the garrison's pockets at payday and relieved hidehunters of their earnings from the slaughter of thousands of buffalo.

"My pap hunted buffler out of here till they was gone," he said, blinking watery, pale eyes. "Then he scouted for the army till the Comanches was all penned up in Oklahoma, and then he hauled freight and went to ranchin'. Got pushed off his land by the Circle X, a big English-owned outfit that moved in and took over. So he freighted full time till he married my ma and moved in to Abilene to run her daddy's store. I was born out here, though, and it's where I aim to die if'n they don't make it into a state park and run off the folks that's left—ain't more'n a hunderd and thirty-forty people."

"You ever see any buffalo?" Buddy asked. "Wild ones?"

"Sure, son." The old eyes blinked and looked far away. "Even shot a big bull when I wasn't much older'n you. Had to prop the rifle on some rocks to do it, use all my bullets. I was kinda sick when he finally caved in on his knees and went down, wished I hadn't ever started, 'specially since he was the last one ever seen around here."

Accepting another cup of coffee and filling it to the brim with Eagle Brand, he cackled. "Wish Pap could know the Circle X is deep in trouble. On account of the drouth, ranchers been sellin' off so much stock the price is low, and what with the depression, folks can't afford to buy much beef, anyhow. So the government's bought the best cows at twenty dollars a head to ship to better grazing lands, bought and shipped more to slaughterhouses, and I hear about twenty-five hunderd head of culls are goin' to be shot by the federal inspector right out by the pens."

Laurie's stomach roiled and she scattered the rest of her

doughnut for the birds. "Anyhow," she said, trying to find something good about it, "lots of people ought to get beef for the rest of the winter."

The old man shook his head. "Them cow's cain't be eat, sonny. The whole idee is to raise the price on what beef gets to market. I hear the Circle X's givin' its neighbors the hides for helpin' to drag the carcasses off to a little canyon by the pens. They'll heap 'em there and keep a fire goin' on top till there's nothin' left but bones."

Seeming nothing but loosely connected bones himself, he got to his feet. "Thanks kindly for the coffee and doughnut, folks. Good luck on the road. The pens are pretty close to it. You'll likely see the slaughter."

They heard the bark of the rifle before they saw the penned cattle. Dead ones were being dragged by cowboys on horses to where men were skinning them. The skinned bodies were hauled to a ravine and tumbled over into it. Not all of them, though.

"That federal inspector must be pretty decent," Marilys said. "He's paying so much attention to the shooting that he can't see how all those folks from town and around are loading quarters and sides of beef in their flivvers and trucks and wagons."

Laurie was glad some poor people were going to have food because of the killing but she was glad when the sound of the rifle faded. She didn't think she'd ever eat beef again.

19

Albany, Cisco, Brownwood, Eastland, Ranger, Weatherford. Farmers clumped in brogans, ranchers, and cowboys strode along in high-heeled boots, and oil workers wore laced boots if they could afford them.

No Way-signs, as they had started calling them. The Ford developed coughing fits so they stayed in Ranger three days, singing noons and evenings to pay for a good used carburetor.

"This was the wildest boomtown since Spindletop," their mechanic told them. "My dad came to work in the field back in 1919, when it put out over twenty-two million barrels. Must've been fifty thousand people here, most livin' in tents like us." He wiped his greasy hands on a rag and banged down the hood. "Ten years later, Ranger was only makin' something over two million barrels. But we've still got a producin' field, which is more than lots of towns do once the big boom's over."

They paid him and left town, the Ford purring as contentedly as a cat with a full belly of warm milk. When Weatherford had no Way-signs, either, they held a council. "We can try the East Texas oil towns," said Marilys. "We can swing up to Burkburnett and the Panhandle. Or we can head for the fields in the Permian Basin. Got any 'druthers'?"

"You're the driver," said Laurie. Buddy nodded.

None of them said what they must all have been thinking: that Dub was in Black Spring by now and could have the law after them; that Way might have swapped his Russian sable paintbrushes for some whiskey—that there might not be any new Way-signs.

"Let's try west," said Marilys.

From San Angelo, they drove through slopes covered with oak, cedar, and mesquite. "We'd better get a new name," Marilys worried. She frowned and sighed. "I guess we really ought to trade in the Ford but it runs so well with the new carburetor, I plain hate to take a chance on getting a lemon."

Buddy thrust out his lower lip. "I liked being a Tumbleweed."

"It's a dandy name," Marilys agreed. "Maybe we can use it again sometime if Dub loses interest in us—he could do that if he ran across someone he'd like for a son—or when you're grown up."

"Grown up!" echoed Laurie.

"That's only five years," comforted Marilys.

"But we can't—*can't*—stay on the road all that time, changing our names, changing trucks!" Laurie wailed. "If we find Way—"

"Only difference that'd make is he could be accused of kidnapping, too."

"That's wicked! *We* chose him for our family! We sure didn't pick W. S. Redwine."

Marilys patted Laurie's knee. "I know, honey. It's not right. It's not fair. But W.S. got to your grandpa, hired himself a smart lawyer, and to be fair to the judge, being adopted by Dub would seem to be real good luck for you kids."

Laurie shuddered. "It'd be about the worst thing I can imagine!"

Marilys shot her an anxious look. "He never—bothered you, did he?"

Remembering how Way had warned her and Buddy about men like that jocker on the train, Laurie flushed and shook her head. "No. He hardly even touched me. But he tried to make me sing songs he wanted, he the same as killed his own boy, I bet he had something to do with Way's getting drunk, and—and when I'm around him, I feel like he was sitting on my chest."

Buddy giggled. "If he was, you'd be one smashed patootie!"

They all laughed and Marilys said, "Why don't you pick out our next name, Buddy?"

He wrinkled his brow and thought a long time. "How about the Roadsters?"

"We're not cars," objected Laurie.

"No, but we're on the road."

"Why not?" chuckled Marilys.

At Texon, oil derricks reared in all directions and pipelines stretched across earth soaked and crusted with overflows from slush pits. McCamey was a few wooden stores surrounded by shacks, derricks, and red storage tanks. Every sign here looked as old as the town.

Red tanks accompanied the highway for a time through land that rolled like a bumpy carpet of sage, mesquite, and all kinds of cactus. Then the tanks stopped. The Ford crossed the Pecos River and climbed to a high tableland that was lonesome as God, stretching to dreamlike far-off azure ranges that faded into the sky. This wasn't the desolation of the Dust Bowl where crops had once flourished. This country belonged now, as it always had, to eagles, hawks, rattlesnakes, and their skittering prey. Sun and the tang of sage purified the air till it almost hurt human lungs accustomed to civilized poisons.

Fort Stockton's limestone and red stucco courthouse dominated a sprawl of adobe and stone houses and the ruins of the old fort. The stone guardhouse was inside the park, where springs gushed and a sign recorded that Comanche Springs had been a watering place for Indians on their annual autumn forays into Mexico. The army post was established in 1859. Gold rushers stopped here to rest on their way to California, and later, the stage line to San Diego.

But Way had not.

North against a bitter wind through thousands of acres irrigated by springs. Pecos's old cowtown buildings were jostled by new ones raised by oil and irrigated farming. A norther howled down with gusting wind and snow that made travel out of the question. All day, the hotel filled up with travelers refuging from the storm.

"Nothin' between here and the North Pole but a barbed-wire fence and that's blown down," several of them said, repeating the old saying as if they'd just made it up while they stamped off snow. When the Roadsters played that noon and night, it turned into a party, with those who knew the words singing to the music and a lanky, sandy-haired cowboy borrowing the guitar and nasally chanting songs Laurie had never heard before, "Strawberry Roan," "Bad Brahma Bull," "The Hills of Mexico," "Zebra Dun," and one about the Colorado Trail that was so haunting and lovely that she asked him to play it again.

> Weep all you little rains,
> Wail, winds, wail—
> All along, along, along
> The Colorado Trail.

The storm moved out that night. Next morning, the sun dazzled off the whiteness blanketing the plains to the sky's blue rim. By noon, big supply trucks had cleared the highway and the Roadsters were in Big Spring by night.

"We haven't seen any Way-signs since Ranger," Buddy lamented. "If he's stopped painting 'em, how'll we know where he's been?"

"I guess we won't," Marilys said.

Nothing in Sweetwater, nothing new in Abilene. They struck south. Ballinger, Paint Rock, Eden, Menard. Towns ran together in Laurie's mind. Texas was such a big state! Fredericksburg, Boerne, San Marcos, Austin, down to Laredo, up to the East Texas oil fields and towns, where they had to buy "new" tires and get the engine worked on. Back west across the northern rim of the state to the Panhandle, Pampa, Borger, Canadian, Perryton, swing down to Burkburnett, one of the roughest of the boom camps but calmed down considerably, though wells still pumped in the middle of town.

There, about the last place they could look in Texas, was a tourist court with a sign painted in Way's distinctive flowing style: SWEET DREAMS CABINS—YOU'LL THINK YOU'RE HOME TILL WE BRING YOU YOUR MORNING COFFEE! Nobody but Way could have painted that steaming cup so that you almost smelled it.

"Kirkendall's your brother?" asked the owner, a paunchy thin-haired man whose false teeth didn't fit. "Well, he paints a nice sign, and could've got more jobs here like I told him, but the last I saw of him he was hitchin' a ride north."

Burkburnett was right on the border. North was across the Red River into Oklahoma. Marilys swallowed but her eyes stayed lit up. "When was that?"

"Oh, must have been five-six days ago." The man clicked his teeth disapprovingly. "His clothes were stickin' out of holes in his old cardboard suitcase but instead of gettin' a new one, he had him a jug of booze. Hope you can get him straightened out, ma'am."

"You bet we will, mister, if we can just catch up to him."

Once back in the truck, they all looked at each other. "He's not far ahead," said Marilys.

"But he's across the river," Laurie objected. "He's in Oklahoma."

Marilys started the truck. "So that's where we'll go."

"But that's across the state line!" Fear tightened Laurie's throat and she caught her friend's arm. "Marilys, they could send you to the electric chair!"

"They've got to catch me first." Marilys laughed and threw back her head so that her dark hair caught waves of sun. "Anyhow, I know things Dub wouldn't like to have out in public. He won't want me to go on trial."

She couldn't talk if she was dead. Would Dub go that far? It was too late to worry. They were crossing the bridge.

Farmers were plowing, some with tractors, some with horses, turning up brown-red soil the color of their own skin, though sometimes Laurie glimpsed a weathered white face. "Do you know what kind of Indians they are?" she asked Marilys. Morrigan would know. Was he still in Oklahoma? Could they possibly meet up with him again?

"I think they're Comanches," Marilys said. "Kiowas and Apaches, too, I think."

"Apaches!" Buddy shrieked and watched as if hoping a man in overalls following his plow would suddenly change into a loin-clothed warrior with lance and bow.

"I thought Apaches were farther west," Laurie puzzled. "In Arizona."

"A lot are, I think." Marilys frowned in an effort to remember. "I'm not real sure, but it seems I've heard these Oklahoma Apaches—their parents and grandparents, of course, not the ones you see—were shipped to Florida with Geronimo after he surrendered. They got sick in the east. Finally the government sent them to the Comanche Reservation. The officer in charge got them started at raising cattle and they built up a real fine herd and learned to farm. Geronimo was an old man when he died up near Fort Sill. Not long after that, sometime before the Great War, the government decided the Apaches weren't prisoners of war anymore and let them decide if they wanted to take up land allotments here in Oklahoma or go live on the Mescalero Apache Reservation in New Mexico. Some went there. Others stayed here."

"How come there are still reservations in New Mexico and Arizona but there aren't any here?" Laurie wondered.

Marilys shrugged. "Oklahoma has good farming land and lots of oil. Even after every Indian got a one hundred sixty-acre allotment, there was lots of reservation land left to open up to white homesteaders. You look around the country, honey. The only reservations left are on land white people don't think is worth anything."

And land they had coveted, like the Dust Bowl, was dead now, dead as powdered buffalo bones. But this land they passed through now alternated fields with rolling hills that were covered with buffalo grass foraged by cattle that had wintered better than most they'd seen in Texas.

In Waurika, there were Way-signs but no one knew where he'd gone, not the owners of the gas station, the tourist court, or the café, which each had a new sign. The one at the café had been painted only three days ago.

Three days! "At least we're on his trail," Marilys said, spreading out the Oklahoma map she'd gotten at the gas station.

That was both *en*couraging and *dis*couraging. Would they always be a week behind, a few days, even a couple of hours after someone saw him hop a freight or hitch a ride? "I guess we'll try the oil fields," Marilys decided, folding the map. "Duncan first."

"Just so we don't get over around Altus where Grandpa Field might see us," Laurie said. When she grew up, when it was safe, she'd go to visit Rosalie.

That night they camped off a dirt road branching from the highway, parking beside a small creek. The winter-bare cottonwoods, ashes, and willows didn't completely shield them from view, but Marilys was afraid of getting stuck in the sand if they went farther.

Laurie and Buddy gathered fallen limbs and built a cheerful fire while Marilys made potato soup with lots of onions and baked biscuits in the dutch oven. This was the closest they'd been to Way yet. If they could just find him and get back across the border to Texas where kidnapping didn't mean the electric chair! Or maybe, with Way, they'd just head for the Louisiana oil fields, where Dub was much less likely to find them.

"We'd better get rid of these Texas plates tomorrow, maybe trade trucks if we can," said Marilys. "Dub will have the law watching for us. There'll be lots of vehicles with Texas plates around the oil towns but maybe not so many with a woman driver and two kids."

That was true but Laurie was sad at swapping off the Ford that had carried them so many miles. Sleeping in it as they did, it felt like home, the only home they had. As soon as the dishes were done, Laurie got out the harmonica and began to play.

All the roads, all the miles, rivers and plains, canyons and hills, all the people and all the towns . . . *Well, yes, Morrigan, you gave me a song for that.*

> I've been a-wandering early and late,
> Oklahoma to the Golden Gate,
> And it just sure looks like
> I ain't ever goin' to cease my wandering. . . .

Buddy started singing. Marilys got the guitar. They hadn't sang or played for several days and the music poured out of them now, hope and fear, loving people and places and losing them, and how it was to be human. They were finishing "Tumbling Tumbleweed" when two men stepped from behind the truck.

Pulled-down hats, light-colored and broad-brimmed, darkened their eyes. Fire glinted off their badges and pistols. "You sound so purty we hate to interrupt," drawled the shorter, stockier one. "But I've got a warrant here for Marilys Shannon, wanted for kidnapping two boys or one boy and a girl across a state line." He quoted from memory. " 'May play a guitar and harmonica and sing to raise money.' Hold out your hands, ma'am."

He pulled linked metal ovals out of his pocket. "Don't!" Buddy yelled, running to shield Marilys. "She didn't kidnap us!"

"We *want* to be with her," Laurie pleaded, grasping the man's arm. "Please, mister—"

He brushed her away. Marilys said nothing. She put down the guitar and got to her feet. Slowly, she put out her slender, graceful hands. The officer bent to slip on the handcuffs.

Laurie didn't really think. She caught up the guitar, stepped back, and crashed it down as hard as she could on the man's skull. From the corner of her eye, she glimpsed Buddy launching himself at the other lawman, hanging onto his arm, grappling for the gun.

The bottom of the guitar shattered but the man only fell to his knees, though his hat pitched to the earth. Marilys grabbed his gun. "Stay right where you are!" she ordered both men, and to the one trying to break Buddy's bulldog grasp, "Give the boy your gun, mister."

The officer shook Buddy like a pup, clouted him sideways so that the boy rolled over and over, but before the man could level the pistol, Marilys pulled the trigger. He staggered back, half-whirled around by the impact of the bullet, clutching his right shoulder while the gun dropped to the sand.

Buddy sprang for it and scooted to the side. "Let's tie them up," said Marilys. "Use the rope that holds the tarp over the back of the truck."

Laurie hurried to obey. Blood running through his fingers, which he held now at the back of his shoulder, the wounded man spoke through gritted teeth. "Aren't you goin' to stop this bleedin'? Let me bleed to death, woman, and it'll be murder of a law officer on top of kidnap."

"We'll bandage you up soon as you can't give us any more grief," Marilys said.

The stocky man, still on his knees, lunged at her. She swung the barrel of the pistol down on his head. This time he went all the way to the ground. Blood ran out of his dark hair, dripped to the sand. Laurie gasped, then swallowed and kept on tying the other man's hands before Marilys ordered him over to a young cottonwood and told him to sit down so Laurie could tie his feet together.

"Scalp wounds bleed a lot," Marilys said as Laurie started on the heavyset officer. "I don't think I hit him hard enough to crack his head. Here, let's tie him to this tree."

"We—we aren't going to just leave them out here, are we?" Laurie quavered.

"Oh, they could get loose after a while and it's not cold enough to freeze them, but because they were dumb enough to get shot I suppose we'd better let someone know about it." Marilys sounded so disgusted that Laurie didn't press further. "Get our oldest clean towel and a pillowcase," Marilys instructed as she checked Laurie's knots and added some of her own.

The bullet had gone out the back of the shoulder, making a much bigger wound than the neat hole in front, Marilys deftly plugged it with toweling and a pad and had Laurie hold the dressing in place while it was secured with strips of pillowcase.

"You bitch!" the man snarled. "You can't get away. Now you've pulled this, everyone'll be ready to shoot you on sight." His face twisted in a savage grin. "Maybe you ain't heard but that Bruno Hauptman's been convicted of murdering that Lindbergh baby he kidnapped. Sentenced to die next month in the electric chair. I'd sure like to pull the switch on *you,* sweetheart."

Laurie blanched. The hate in his eyes and voice was terrible and she understood that some of it was because he'd been bested by a woman and two kids. Marilys didn't answer him, but tied the last knot on the bandage carefully before going to the other man. Laurie helped pad and bandage the creased scalp while Buddy put their cooking things in the truck. He held up the splintered guitar.

"What about this?"

"Put it in." Marilys hugged Laurie as they got to their feet. "I'm sorry it can't be fixed, honey. You sure crowned that fellow. The sound board's broken, too. But we can save the strings, and we'll get you another guitar soon as we can."

"It's all right," Laurie said.

Only it wasn't, no more than shooting law officers and leaving them tied to trees. She quailed at what Mama would have thought of that. But what else could they have done? It was

W. S. Redwine's fault! Even if it was a sin, she wished he was dead so he couldn't keep causing them trouble, maybe even get Marilys sent to the pen if not the electric chair. And the guitar, the wonderful Christmas guitar, was broken!

Laurie blinked back tears. She needed music and thought Buddy and Marilys might, too. She brought out the harmonica and played it all the way to Duncan, where Laurie called the police from a gas station and directed them to "some folks who need help."

She hung up immediately and they drove on through the night, fearful every time a car passed them or as they drove through slumbering small towns. How long would it take the police to locate the tied-up wounded men? At least a couple of hours. How long would it be till sheriffs, police, highway patrol—gracious, maybe even FBI men—were watching for a Ford truck with Texas plates?

At last a wide dirt road turned off the highway. Distant lights blazed miles away, lots of them. What was such a big place doing so far off the main road?

"Got to be an oil boom." Marilys sighed with relief. "Lots of strangers coming and going, lots of Texas plates and trucks."

"But—"

"Stay on the highway and we're bound to get stopped." Marilys turned the Ford into the best tracks she could find among the ruts. They couldn't go better than ten jostling miles an hour. They could smell oil and hear the rumble of bull wheels and thud of drills pounding at rock and sand long before they drove into the sprawl of tents, shacks, and flimsy buildings that were surrounded on all sides by derricks, some only partly built.

Work-stained men came in and out of cafés, boarding places, hotels, and dance halls, most of which were only tents. The signs were crude, not Way's handiwork. Broken-down flivvers, trucks, and new autos that shone where they weren't splattered with oil or mud were parked wherever there was room. Plenty of Texas license tags. Arkansas, Louisiana, and Kansas, too, though most were Oklahoma.

Marilys's tight-held shoulders relaxed a little. She steered off the road around some tents and parked among vehicles from half-a-dozen states. Buddy was asleep, his head in Laurie's lap. They got him into the back of the truck, arranged the ropeless tarpaulin as best they could, and fell into sleep.

Next morning they traded the Ford for a Studebaker truck. It had more miles on it and the tires were worn but it had Oklahoma tags. Laurie fought back tears and gave the fender a farewell pat when no one was looking. The truck didn't know or care that it was being swapped to a redheaded roughneck. It was silly for her to feel they were abandoning it, and yet she did.

Avoiding highways, keeping to country roads, they rattled from oil field to oil field, but found no trace of Way. Laurie didn't say anything, but she watched for Morrigan, too. They were afraid to sing or play as a group but they blew a tire and replacing it took most of their dwindling cash. Marilys took a job waiting tables and Laurie played her harmonica in a different restaurant, jumpy, constantly on the alert for the law, while Buddy prowled to watch for police vehicles.

At the end of a week, they had enough money to put brand-new tires on the Chevy truck they traded the Studebaker for, stock up on groceries, and buy gas for a while. They hadn't seen hide nor hair of lawmen apart from harried constables who had their hands full with drunken roughnecks who were trying to kill each other or beat up their women. The newer camps didn't have jails so the rowdies were usually chained or handcuffed to heavy logging chains strung between two trees or poles.

"We haven't seen a Way-sign in a couple of weeks," said Buddy with a weary sigh as they headed out of town.

"Maybe he got rid of his brushes." Laurie hated even to say it. That would mean Way had slid all the way into trampdom, even worse than before, because then he at least had kept his brushes.

"Then how'll we find him?" Buddy's face crumpled. He turned his face away and scrubbed at a tear.

"We'll just keep looking," Marilys said.

"For*ever?*"

Marilys and Laurie laughed at that. "We'll find him before forever," Marilys promised.

"What if we don't?" Buddy persisted. Laurie felt a twinge of guilt. Buddy had been worried all this time and she'd been too full of her own fears to encourage him to say what was on his mind. His brown eyes were scared and solemn. "If—if we can't find him, Marilys, are you goin' to leave us somewhere?"

"What in the *hell* makes you think such a thing?" Marilys had never sworn at them before. Her cheeks burned and her eyes flashed blue fire. "Of course I won't leave you!" She swallowed and glared down the road.

"I—I'm sorry," Buddy mumbled.

She reached over and smoothed his cheek, gave his hair a tousle. "Listen, you're my family! You'll be the ones who leave me someday when you grow up." She thought a moment, then pondered each word as she measured it out. "If we don't find Way after we've looked all over Oklahoma and the near parts of Arkansas and Louisiana, then we'll settle someplace that we like. I'll be a widow lady. You kids'll go to school. Who knows? Maybe someday Way'll find us." She gave them a heartening grin. "Meanwhile, we're going to hunt him. We'll look around the railroad yards, we'll watch for his signs, we'll ask at jails. And where there aren't any jails, we'll look over prisoners they put on a chain."

That was where they found Way. In the next boomtown, handcuffed to a chain.

20

Five men were fastened to the chain, tarps and blankets beneath and over them. It was nine in the morning and none of them stirred. An enormous man with gummed yellow hair and a bruised, cut face snored with his mouth open. The thin dark one who looked Indian had a bandaged head. Two boyish, freckled, sandy-haired ones curled close together might be brothers.

At the far end, arms splayed above his head to where his wrists were cuffed to the chain, Way had only the side of his face exposed, but the old scar showed in spite of the wild, crinkly, gray beard and moustache.

Laurie dropped to her knees, not only to embrace him but because her legs wouldn't hold her and her head swam. "Way! Oh, Way!"

"Are you sure?" Marilys whispered.

"Sure! It's how he looked when we met him." How he'd smelled, too, of sweat and filth, except now the sour stink of whiskey overwhelmed the other odors.

Laurie didn't care. It was heaven to hold him, kiss the scar, lift him up. Marilys was down, too, cradling him to her breast, murmuring.

His eyes opened slowly. He blinked, groaned as if the light hurt, then stared, coming awake. "Marilys!" It was a croak. "Larry-Laurie!" He elbowed up, trying to move away. "Why'd you come after me? I'm just an old sot."

"You—you're our Way!" Buddy hunkered down. "We hunted for you all over Texas and the Oklahoma lawmen tried to arrest Marilys for kidnapping and—and she could go to the 'lectric chair! You—you *got* to take care of us!"

Way tried to shake his head, winced, and growled, "I'm not fit to be around you."

"We want you!" Laurie cried.

He turned away his face, spoke in a dull, low tone. "I traded my brushes for some bootleg last night—never did that before. I'm lower'n a snake's belly. I 'preciate you lookin' for me and all but you'd better rustle on out of here."

All this time he hadn't really looked at Marilys. She gave him a shake, heedless of his startled howl, and demanded, "What did Dub tell you to make you go off? What?"

He did look at her then. Something blazed from his eyes. "It don't matter."

"But it's why you won't go with us now." She got to her feet, looking tired and frail, brushed dark hair back from her forehead. "All right. I'll go on alone somewhere. But you, Wayburn Kirkendall, you get up your hind legs and take charge of these kids. The truck's full of gas and parked right over there by the

252

café." She turned. "I'll go pay your fine—drunk and disorderly, is it?—and we'll head off in different directions."

"Marilys!" Laurie and Buddy cried, jumping up and blocking her path.

Way couldn't stand but he hitched himself to one knee. "Marilys, it don't matter, what Dub said. And—well, what you think mattered, never did."

Marilys stopped in her tracks. "Then why—?"

"I left on account of he got me drunk. Figgered if he could anyways do that I wasn't any use to you or the kiddos—that you'd do better without me, girl, 'specially when he was ready to give the kids everything, even send them to college."

"You see how much they wanted what Dub could give them."

Way's head dropped. After a moment, he raised it. "I reckon what matters is that you're here."

" 'Course we are," said Buddy. "You're our family—and so's Marilys."

Laurie nodded, too full of tears and hope to speak. Way said, still on his knee, "Marilys, I don't have any right to ask you now—but if I stay sober—if I prove I'm fit to be a family man, would you—"

"Marry you?" She bent and kissed him, though he tried to turn his whiskered face away. "Yes, and we'll do it first chance we get. You won't have time to booze it up, Way. You've got a family to look after."

A deputy had come out of the little jail to see what was going on and let the prisoners loose except for the huge man who had to spend two more days on the chain for breaking a café table and window in a fight. Marilys paid Way's fine. He got his bundle from the jail office and they piled into the Studebaker's cab. Buddy recounted their adventures and how they'd kept trading vehicles.

"I'm sure glad you didn't take a loss on that Chevy truck at Cross Trails," Way said. "Just like that skunk, Redwine, to accuse me of stealin' from his hardware store." He looked like his head hurt. He hadn't argued when Marilys offered to drive.

"We're not too likely to get stopped now that we look like a regular family," she said. "But it's safer to stay out of Texas, and probably Oklahoma, too, since I'm wanted for resisting arrest and wounding two officers."

Way slanted her a grin. "And you look like such a sweet lady!"

"It was their fault," Laurie said. "They could tell we weren't kidnapped!"

Way touched her cheek. "We'll have to get you another guitar."

They stopped at the next town early that afternoon and took a tourist cabin with two rooms. Marilys and Laurie went downtown to buy Way some new clothes. They had baths, put on clean things, and then, with Way all shaved and neat, his hair trimmed by Marilys, they got a marriage license and located a justice of the peace. Marilys had her mother's wedding ring and that was what Way slipped on her finger. It was risky but they got married under their right names. The four of them had supper in the town's fanciest restaurant.

When they got back to the cabin, feeling strange and a little bit sad though she was entirely grateful and glad that Way was with them, Laurie started to shoo Buddy into their room and close the door. It was going to be different now that Marilys and Way were married. Laurie was glad, of course, but she didn't feel as close to either of them as she had.

Then Marilys smiled and said, "Why don't we have some music, a party just for the family?"

She got out Cracker Jacks and salted nuts, ginger ale, and tiny chocolate squares with green peppermint fillings. They ate and drank and sang and played till Buddy fell asleep and Laurie's eyelids kept drooping shut.

"Guess I'd better carry Buddy to bed," Way said.

"Let me take off his shoes," said Marilys.

"I'll wash the chocolate off his face." Laurie hurried for a wet washcloth. The three of them got Buddy snuggled into his pillows. Laurie turned to Marilys, hugged her and then Way, then both of them, while their arms went around her and each other. It was tangled up and hard to tell where one person's arms left and the other's began, but it was the warmest, safest, and happiest Laurie had felt since—well, she couldn't remember exactly but she hadn't been so glad and grateful since that terrible Black Sunday when Buddy and Daddy walked alive out of the lingering dust.

"Oh, please," she breathed against the shoulders of the two grown-ups, "Please be happy!"

Way chuckled softly. Laurie could hear it rumbling beneath her ear. "I'm the luckiest man alive!" He turned solemn, watching Marilys. "Anyone with good sense would have let me go, but I'm mighty glad you girls are both a little daffy."

"We're buying you some paintbrushes tomorrow so you can start supporting us," Marilys teased.

They left the room, laughing. Laurie could hear the sound of their voices, though not the words, as she got ready for bed. That was how it used to be with Mama and Daddy. She'd always believed as long as they were awake, nothing bad could happen, the world couldn't end. With the comforting murmur in her ears, she drifted off to sleep.

East of MacAlester—wasn't that the town Morrigan's mother lived close to?—through what had been Choctaw country on sometimes paved, sometimes graveled roads. The gentle Winding Stair Mountains were greening up, tree buds swelling, grass spearing through dead leaves. Farmers were plowing and planting. Many appeared to be Indian but there were some with fairer skin and black eyes Laurie took for Italian and others who looked just plain old mixed-up American, Scotch, Irish, German, English, what have you.

Over in the Arkansas Ozarks, they felt safer from Dub and the Oklahoma law. No one was watching for a family. Marilys wanted to get the children in school so they settled in Splitlog, a little town on the White River. They rented a big old house so embraced by honeysuckle and trumpetvine that the flaking white paint hardly showed. As spring came on, the yard was fragrant with lilacs and brilliant with orange and vermilion tiger lilies. Birds Laurie had never seen before flashed through the hickory, oak, and walnut trees shading the front yard. She looked them up in a bird book she found in the school library:

scarlet tanager, pileated woodpecker, a dozen kinds of warblers, the wood thrush and yellow-throated vireo. Her old prairie friend, the mockingbird, sang sweetly here from the magnolias that shielded the long porch where, as the evenings warmed, the family sat after supper, Laurie and Buddy in the creaking swing, Way and Marilys in spraddled old wicker chairs rescued from further dereliction in the backyard.

Buddy soon made friends and played outside till dark, but Laurie was so glad to have both Way and Marilys and be off the road, that she didn't mind much that the girls in her class already had best friends. She felt worlds older than any of them. They had their parents, grandparents, too, mostly, living in this town where all of them had been born and where the gravestones in the cemetery were engraved with the same family names going back before the Civil War. Laurie hadn't belonged in Prairieville because her family went to the tabernacle, were poor, and she had to wear those ugly long stockings and couldn't go to movies. She hadn't belonged in Black Spring but she and Catharine had sustained each other—poor Catharine! Had she found another friend? Laurie still wore overalls after school but Marilys had bought an old Singer sewing machine for a few dollars and made Laurie three pretty school dresses, a green plaid with ruffled sleeves; gold-brown sateen trimmed with yellow rickrack; and a blue-green paisley with a white eyelet collar. Anklets to match, new shoes. No one could laugh at the new girl's clothes. Marilys had trimmed her hair into a stylish bob that looked nicer than the haircuts most of the girls had.

"Laurie, your hair's growing out to where it's starting to curl," Marilys said, as she deftly scissored around Laurie's ears.

"It's darkening up," observed Way. "Doggoned if you aren't going to wind up pretty close to a redhead."

"Auburn," reproved Marilys. "Her hair's going to be a lovely dark auburn. My goodness, Laurie! You're almost tall as me."

"Which isn't real tall," grinned Way. "Five foot three. Laurie'll be looking down at you in another year."

The textbooks were different, but Laurie quickly caught up

with her eighth-grade class and drilled Buddy with homemade flash cards for arithmetic and reading till he was even with most of the boys in his class, which was as far as he could be pushed.

The depression had hit some parts of Arkansas hard, but farms around Splitlog produced thousands of broilers every year, stuffing the cooped chicks from the day they hatched till the day they were slaughtered at the chicken plant, picked, gutted, and sent to market.

In April, white apple blossoms covered the slopes. Some apples would be shipped away, but most would go to the vinegar plant, which ran all year, night and day, grinding fruit for several months starting in August, fermenting and oxidizing the juice into cider and then making vinegar. Way got a job there as soon as he'd painted signs for most of Splitlog's merchants. There was a sawmill, a silica plant, and a milk cannery, enough jobs for all of Splitlog's inhabitants who wanted them, though the work was hard, dirty, and low-paying. Rent was cheap in Splitlog, though. Families had died out or moved away and a half-dozen old homes, in varying states of dereliction, peered through broken windows at waist-high grass and pigweed.

Everyone except the two doctors, three lawyers, a dentist, and a banker had gardens, a few fruit trees, maybe a grape arbor, and a chicken house and pen. Way borrowed a hand-plow and they planted as soon as they moved in. Well before school was out, Marilys was making Way's favorite dish, fresh lettuce wilted with hot oil and vinegar served with heaps of fluffy scrambled eggs along with a plate of crisp radishes and green onions. They bought eggs from their next door neighbor, an old widow lady who clucked and talked as she fed her several dozen industriously pecking snowy white Wyandottes. Twice a week, Way picked up a gallon jar of milk from the dairy at the edge of town. Even after Marilys skimmed off the cream to make butter, the milk was rich and sweet from the lush pastures the cows grazed in.

Such a different world, such a different life, from Prairieville or Black Spring.

Three churches sat on three small hills, steeples vying to be the highest point in town. There was the limestone Baptist

257

church, the red brick Methodist, and the mortared rock Presbyterian. Laurie's conscience goaded her into dragging Buddy to each Sunday school in turn, but it was such a struggle to make him dress up and come and Laurie felt so out of place herself that she gave up and just insisted that they read out of Mama's New Testament every Sunday morning.

This hilly region had never been part of the plantation South, though a statue of a Confederate soldier stood in the courthouse square with the names of southern dead engraved on all four sides of the pedestal. There were no Negroes in town and white people did all the work that farther south or east would have been shared by what were locally known as colored folks.

That summer, Laurie picked strawberries for two cents a quart, stooping or kneeling along the rows of low-growing plants to search beneath the leaves for the succulent red fruits. The wooden carrier held twelve quarts and when she took it to the shed, Bobby Jay Ballard, the farmer's son who was a junior and captain of the high school basketball team, grinned at her each time he marked down her quarts. He had dark-lashed blue eyes, black hair, and was a lean, strong-muscled six feet tall. He picked, too, and she was flustered to realize that he was working on the row beside hers.

She wore a shirt under her overalls so he couldn't see her breasts, which had swelled in the past months, though they were still firm and didn't jiggle when she walked the way a few of the plumper girls' did. That was when some boys rolled their eyes and murmured things like "Shake 'em, don't break 'em!" and "Hey, one of them's hanging lower'n than the other one!"

Bobby Jay didn't whisper anything like that but she knew he was watching *her,* although several girls from high school giggled when they passed and one of the cheerleaders, Linda Merritt, swerved a hip against him. He gave it a pat, but kept picking next to Laurie.

When she finished her crates, no one was close. He straightened. Smiling, he held out a beautiful big red fruit. "Can I buy your love with strawberries?"

His eyes were bright and blue as the summer sky. He slipped the berry between her parted lips. Involuntarily, her teeth crushed it. Sweet, tart juice filled her mouth. Startled, lured, yet frightened, she gazed up at him.

"Meet me at the creek tonight," he said softly. "It'll still be warm enough to swim."

"I—I don't have a swimsuit," she stammered and immediately knew that was foolish.

"Neither do I," he laughed, and took her carrier, striding to the shed to mark down her crates and those of several pickers who were impatiently waiting.

She didn't go, of course. Next day, Bobby Jay flirted with Linda and marked up Laurie's crates as if he'd never seen her before. It stung a little, but not much. What stung more was that Bobby Jay had thought she might swim naked with him and then—

She thought of Morrigan and blushed hotly. It seemed almost blasphemous to think of him in connection with Bobby Jay's suggestion but grateful as she was for Marilys and Way, Laurie yearned for Morrigan almost in the way she did for her parents except with the hope she might someday see him again. Because he'd come to them the day they left Prairieville, the day that world had ended, and because he'd laughed and talked with Daddy, Morrigan was linked to her childhood, but she didn't want him for a father.

Laurie finished ninth grade in Splitlog, and Buddy the fourth. They came home with their report cards to find Way and Marilys loading the truck. "I'm sorry, kiddos, but we got to scoot," said Way, pausing to wipe sweat from his forehead and crinkly eyebrows. "Feller who works with me has a brother who's a deputy sheriff. Told my friend a private detective's nosin' around for someone who looks like me—wanted for theft in Texas. He ruffled feathers in the sheriff's office. They didn't tell him anything but Splitlog's not big enough to hide in."

Laurie's heart stopped, then pounded. She leaned against the truck to keep from falling. It had seemed so safe. She had almost stopped worrying. Marilys touched her cheek. "At least the detective didn't seem to know that we're all with Way. But it shows Dub hasn't given up. Change into your overalls, honey, and let's see how far we can get tonight."

Who would eat the good things from their garden, pick grapes from the arbor, plums and apples from the trees? Who would sit on the porch swing and hear the mockingbird when the honeysuckle and magnolia smelled so sweet that you ached with the beauty?

Buddy's face screwed up. "Can I tell the guys so long?"

"Sorry, son." Way dropped a hand on Buddy's shoulder. "Better not."

The back of the truck was heaped with bedding and belongings, though the only thing they were taking along of the makeshift pieces they'd acquired was the sewing machine.

"Reckon we'd better stick to the oil fields, maybe head for Louisiana for a spell," Way said as they rattled south.

Laurie got out the harmonica. As always, when starting for a new place, she wondered, Would Morrigan be there?

She launched into "Tumbling Tumbleweed," using her fingers to make a rustle like the wind, and in a minute, the others were singing. How lucky that no matter how light you had to travel, you could always carry songs!

21

The family moved around Louisiana for the next two years with occasional job forays into East Texas, living in tents, tarpaper shacks, lean-tos. They didn't want Way endangering himself by working as a roughneck or roustabout but he hauled pipe and other supplies, and helped build tanks and rigs. Painted signs, too, about the time they were fixing to leave a camp. That was when Laurie and Buddy would entertain in cafés while Marilys played the piano or guitar wherever she could briefly make "a star appearance." She did dressmaking, too, and gave piano lessons wherever there was enough of a permanent town for richer, settled folks to have pianos.

During the school year, they tried to stay a semester in the same town so Buddy's schooling wouldn't be too broken up.

With Laurie coaching him, he managed to pass. "But you don't go anymore!" he protested when she marched him down to register for seventh grade.

"I finished ninth grade in Splitlog," she reminded him. "When you get that far, you can decide if you want to go on so you can maybe go to college and be an engineer or something like that." She knew he admired the engineers, who, like drillers, always wore the very best boots and Stetsons, though most were careful never to be seen in new-looking hats. They got them oily and spanked them in some dust. Laurie let that temptation sink in and continued. "You're staying in school till you're through ninth if it takes ten years so you might as well buckle down and study."

He glowered at her triumphantly. "In ten years, I'll be twenty! You won't be the boss of me after I'm eighteen—not even that long if I run away."

"Run if you want to," she said, knowing he wouldn't, not for worlds. "But as long as you're home, you're going to finish at least ninth grade."

She hadn't felt right about being a burden on Marilys and Way while she finished high school. Besides, though she loved to learn, she was tired of always being an outsider, fearing to make friends she'd lose in a few months. She had another guitar and knew she could make a living from music. Marilys had taught her to sew and Laurie now made her own clothes. She liked cooking a lot better and she and Marilys took turns preparing meals. Several times, she and Marilys hired on to cook in boomtown restaurants. Laurie learned from Marilys how to banter with the oil-field workers while making it clear that none of them were walking her home. It was seldom necessary for Marilys to give an importunate roughneck or toolie his marching orders, but when it was, her tongue was so scathing that the man slunk away among the hoots of his companions—who, at that point, would have made sure he let the women alone.

These workers, many of them from ruined farms or ranches, ranged from one field to the next, Texas, Oklahoma, Louisiana, Kansas, working twelve-hour "towers," cleaning up, eating, then looking for some fun, which was usually a fight, before collapsing on a cot that was often warm from the previous occupant. Laurie saw so many tanned, joking, oil-stained men that it seemed Morrigan should have turned up amongst them.

"That driller, Jim Hartford, seems real nice," Marilys remarked one day as she put a row of pies in the oven and Laurie washed dishes in the open-sided tent restaurant where they were working. "And I've heard that movie he asked you to, *Algiers,* is really good—with Charles Boyer, it has to be!"

"Jim is nice." Laurie scrubbed at some hardened egg. "But—well, it doesn't seem right to go out with him."

"Whyever not? He can't be more than twenty-three or -four. It's true you're only fifteen but you're grown up."

When she really was grown up—and when Buddy was eighteen, so Redwine's custody order wouldn't count—then they could settle down. Way could start a painting business, Marilys could teach piano, maybe play in a nice restaurant, and Laurie and Buddy could perform without worrying about getting caught.

They could go visit Rosalie, too, and collect the books and things Laurie hoped she was still saving. Through the years, Laurie had sent Rosalie money now and then and let her know they were fine, but she always mailed letters from some town they were just passing through, or gave them to a worker who was heading for another field to mail when he got there. There mustn't be any way for Grandpa Field to track them and hand them over to Redwine. Of course he probably didn't want her now, but he'd cause Marilys and Way plenty of grief, maybe even get them sent to the penitentiary. All this passed through Laurie's head before she rinsed the last dishes and began drying them.

"Don't think I'm crazy, Marilys, but I keep hoping that—well, that John Morrigan may turn up."

"Good grief!" Marilys's jaw dropped. She wiped her hands on her apron and sighed. "Laurie, baby, am I right that this man was with you for just a day while your daddy was driving you to your grandpa's?"

Memories flooded back from those times she remembered no more than she had to, except for Morrigan. Leaving Prairieville and the brave little cherry tree, the desolate wasteland of the Oklahoma Panhandle, Buddy sick, Daddy wrestling with the flat tire, and Morrigan appearing, just when they all needed hope and comfort so much. As always, when she really allowed herself to think about him beyond being grateful daily for the harmonica and his songs, Laurie's gratitude mingled with a silent wail from her heart. *Morrigan, Morrigan, won't I ever see you again, won't I ever find you?*

"He came along at noon the day we left home," she said, blinking back tears. "He got Daddy to rest till it cooled off and made willow tea for Buddy. He helped Daddy drive and change flats and we let him off next morning so he could catch a train."

"So he was really with you less than a day."

"Yes, but you know how days are. Lots are just about the same. Some are real happy and others are pretty bad." Laurie groped to explain. "Some days are like—hinges. They can swing either way and shut you on that side. Black Sunday was like that, when Daddy went after Buddy and we all thought the world was coming to an end. That was the day when everything changed." Laurie could still hardly bear to think about her mother's last illness and forged ahead. "It was a hinge day when Buddy and I ran away and met Way on the train. If he hadn't been there—" She shivered even now to remember the jocker. "It was a hinge when we got in Redwine's car for the first time. And when you decided to come away with us and hunt for Way."

"But, honey, Morrigan only did what any decent man would have."

Laurie shook her head. "He gave me music."

"Yes, and that was wonderful—is wonderful." Marilys gave Laurie a helpless, worried look. "Listen, dear, all I'm trying to say is that you've turned this Morrigan into a hero. With you dreaming over him all these years, building him up, he seems smarter and handsomer and wiser and stronger than any man who's going to walk in here and stretch his legs under the table. But they're *here.*" She hesitated. "Laurie, I hate to say this, but you've got to face it. The oil fields're dangerous and so's a hobo's life. He could be dead."

263

"If he is, I don't want to know it." Laurie hugged the older woman and laughed. "Marilys, I'm only fifteen! The way you're carrying on, anyone would think I was an old maid! I'll bet if I wanted to marry Jim, you and Way would have fits."

Marilys grinned reluctantly. Marriage agreed with her. She was prettier now she ever had been, not so frail and wispy, with good healthy color in her cheeks. "You *are* too young to get married, but you're of an age when you ought to start getting acquainted with men, go out with some nice ones, fall in love a few times for practice."

"I don't think I'm going to do that."

Marilys scanned her closely. "Oh, Laurie, baby! You sure can't think you're in love with John Morrigan!"

Laurie colored. "I don't know what it is. He lives in the back of my mind, he's always there, just like his songs." She had never tried to pursue her feelings for Morrigan till she could put them into words. "He—he came to us when it was like the end of the world. Rosalie was nice to us, but if Morrigan hadn't come, if he hadn't left us his songs, I don't know what would have happened to Buddy and me."

"You'd have managed."

"Maybe. But it's like you would've managed without Way."

Way just then drove up in front of the café and got out of the truck. They looked anxiously at each other as they heard him coughing. "That asthma gets worse all the time," Marilys said soft enough for him not to hear. He got mad when they fussed over him. "I think it's the mold and damp. It didn't start till we moved to Louisiana."

Laurie thought about that. "Maybe we need to move to where it's dry."

"Maybe. But we can't get near the Panhandle in case Dub's still got the law or his detectives after Way and us."

"We could go to Oklahoma or central Texas."

"May have to." Marilys poured a mug of steaming coffee and handed it to Way as he sank down on a bench. Coffee helped relax his spasming chest muscles. By the time he swallowed a second mug, his skin had lost its pallor and he could speak.

264

"Sorry, gals," he said, with a twisted grin. "You better take me out and shoot me."

"Hush that!" Marilys studied him anxiously as she refilled the mug. "What we'd better do is move to where you can breathe!"

They had argued this before. It was a mark of how bad off Way was when he hunched his shoulders and then nodded. "Okay," he wheezed. "Soon as Buddy finishes school. Can't pull him out three weeks before the end of the term."

"All right," bargained Marilys, "as long as you'll lay off work and take care of yourself."

Three weeks and two days later, they picked Buddy up at school, stopped at the drugstore to celebrate with chocolate malts his passing sixth grade, and drove toward the setting sun.

They didn't get into the worst part of the Dust Bowl, but the fringe that the Fields had driven through on their way to southwestern Oklahoma four years ago had changed past recognition. It had rained enough last year in 1938 to finally break the drought that had begun in 1931 and produce something of a wheat crop. This year's rainfall was close to normal. Many farmhouses stood empty but around them, instead of oceans of fine, rippled dust, valiant spears of corn and wheat marched to the horizon and cattle grazed where buffalo grass had revived and ruffled softly in the wind, changing color like rose-gold velvet rubbed against the grain before it was smoothed again.

"Remember that story we read last year in *The Saturday Evening Post*?" Laurie asked. She loved the magazine for its good stories and usually managed a nickel for it. Because "It's Gotta Rain Sometime" reminded her so powerfully of her home region, she'd read it several times and remembered the April 9, 1938, date, and the author, Ross Annett. "I wonder if that really happened to some farmer out here?"

"Let's see," mused Way. "The bank took back two of the feller's tractors but another was buried so deep in dust it couldn't be dug out."

"Yes, and the granary beside it was buried, too, with some seed wheat," added Buddy. "Little Joe and Babe found the pipe of the tractor stickin' out and their daddy thought he'd plant the wheat and maybe get a crop but he couldn't borrow the money for gas so he got caught tryin' to steal some. By the time he got out of jail, the old bootlegger neighbor had bought gas and plowed and planted!"

Put that way, it didn't sound so edifying but Laurie could scarcely lecture Buddy for a story she had read to him. "Anyhow, it began to rain," she finished. "It finally did rain." She pointed at a blistered gray shack that stared at them from paneless windows. "I'm sure that's the house where the family was just starting out for California, after the bank foreclosed on them," she said. "We filled our water jars at their well. I wonder what happened to them." What happened to everyone who lived in these houses, who most likely never could come back to a home place?

"FDR's New Deal helped a lot of farmers hang on," Way remarked. "But of course, most of 'em bought tractors with the aid money and got rid of their tenants. Guess if it wasn't for those AAA checks, there wouldn't be any farmers left out here, 'cept for the Mennonites. They never took any government aid but they got along on account of they never did plant all their land to wheat. They planted big gardens and all kinds of crops, kept dairy cows and chickens—they could always eat."

"What's AAA?" asked Buddy.

Way scratched his ear. "Agricultural Adjustment Administration? Think that's it. There's such a passel of alphabet-soup outfits you can't keep 'em straight. The DRS—Drought Relief Service—bought up starvin' cattle in the worst years. Killed and buried some but shipped the rest to packing plants. Then the FSRC—Federal Surplus Relief Corporation—gave the beef away to poor families all over the country. Then there's the Farm Security Administration, FSA, that loans farmers money for seed, fertilizer, stock feed, and other such. There's the Farm Credit Administration, the Civil Works Administration, the Rural Rehabilitation Corporation and—"

"We saw cattle being killed and burned down in Texas," Marilys said. "Didn't the AAA and Soil Conservation Service buy a lot of 'blow land'?"

Laurie had talked about that in Current Events her last year in school. "They did and hired men to furrow it to catch the blowing dust and hold the rain and snow," she said. "They sowed it to cane and Sudan grass so the roots would hold the soil. They planted worn-out rangeland, too."

So pulverized, dead particles that had howled through the air, never resting long enough to bond with the earth, would be held together by living roots till at last they became nourishing soil. She doubted, though, that the plains would ever again look like the Little Prairie, with gayfeather, black-eyed Susans, and Indian blanket shining out of bluestem and buffalo grass. And the people that had blown away, blasted from their land like shriveled crops, where were they now? How many could ever take root?

"FDR's done things for the whole country, not just farmers and ranchers," put in Marilys. "There's the WPA and CCC to make jobs and the National Recovery Administration to help all kinds of businesses and industries. Lots of folks way out in the country got electricity because of the Rural Electrification Act. There's Social Security so most workers can pay in for their old age as they go along, there's a minimum wage for most workers, and John L. Lewis's made the CIO strong enough to make big companies like General Motors and U.S. Steel bargain with workers instead of just firing them."

"And there's Charlie McCarthy!" added Buddy. He loved to watch the apple-cheeked marionette sit on Edgar Bergen's knee almost as much as he'd been entranced with the funny little men in *Snow White and the Seven Dwarfs.* He'd sat through the movie three times and for weeks had gone around singing, "Whistle While You Work."

"Yeah, son," laughed Way. "There's old Charlie and Fibber McGee and Jack Benny. None of 'em will ever be a patch on Will Rogers, though. He was funny but he told the truth about things. He'd have liked what that British Parliament feller said at the World's Fair in New York this year—that there won't be any peace till Franco's widow tells Stalin on his deathbed that Hitler's been assassinated at Moos—moos-olini's funeral. Just about the time the country's gettin' over the Dust Bowl and the

Depression, doggoned if it don't look worse and worse across the pond. If you ask me, England and France should have jumped on that old Hitler the minute he invaded Austria last year."

"At least he got his comeuppance at the Berlin Olympics when our Negro track star, Jesse Owens, left all the Master Race in the dust," Marilys remembered.

Way sniffed. "That didn't slow Hitler down. I've read Jews can't marry Germans anymore, or be citizens, or own businesses, and they're getting shipped to concentration camps. Hitler's grabbed Czechoslovakia. And now he and that Moos-o-lini who took over Ethiopia three years ago have signed up to help each other for the next ten years." He whistled sadly between his teeth. "Nineteen forty-nine! There's goin' to be a lot grief before then."

"If there's another big war, it'll be a lot worse than the last one," said Marilys. "Airplanes just sort of dueled each other then. But look what happened in Guernica in the Basque country during their civil war a few years ago. No military excuse for Franco to get his Nazi friends to bomb it. It was the Basques' old, old holy city where their freedom oak grew. That's the first time civilians were heavily bombed on purpose."

"It won't be the last," Way said gloomily.

Thinking about the wars across the ocean knotted Laurie's stomach. She remembered that in Revelations the Beast, the Antichrist, rose from the banks of the Tiber. Couldn't that mean Rome and Mussolini? Guilt and fear flooded her. The family still had a chapter from The New Testament and silent prayer on Sunday, but none of them were saved, much less sanctified. Laurie wasn't sure what she believed. She felt guilty and disloyal to question Mama's teachings, yet frightened though she was, something at the core of her could not embrace what was preached at the tabernacle. Whatever her punishment, that was the way it was.

Derricks sprouted in the distance, dwarfing a sprawl of tents and shacks. Way turned off the highway on a rut-gouged dirt road with a pointing sign that read TO LUCKY. "Ought to be some work, with a name like that," he chuckled. "This dry air's already cleaning out my lungs."

He helped build derricks all summer, seldom missing a day because of asthma, though if he got too tired or worked up about something, he would start wheezing and had to breathe vapor from steaming water till he was better. Laurie and Marilys worked in a tent restaurant, and Buddy stocked shelves in the Lucky Mart and delivered groceries. There wasn't a school, though, so late in August, they moved to Reynolds, southwest of Oklahoma City. On September 1, 1939, the day that Hitler invaded Poland in a "blitzkrieg" lightning war, the family rented a trailer from a driller who had decided to build a house and stay in the area.

Buddy enrolled in seventh grade September 3, when Great Britain and France declared war on Germany. That evening President Roosevelt talked to the nation by radio as he had done so often in his Fireside Chats. He said the nation would remain neutral but that "even a neutral cannot be asked to close his mind or his conscience."

"Huh!" Way snorted. "If England falls, Hitler'll be over here. We better fight while there's still someone else left to help. If I was a little younger and didn't have this blamed asthma—"

"Helping produce oil is good as being a soldier," Marilys assured him. "But, oh, I hope someone stops that lunatic before he takes over all of Europe! Those poor people, never any peace!"

With such terrible things happening, it seemed strange that everyday life could go on pretty much as usual. Way got a job as a pumper on a forty-acre tract with four wells. He went around every two or three hours to check the gas engines and start them or shut them off, gauge the tanks, and keep track of production. He worked a twelve-hour day but it wasn't as hard and dirty as most oil-field jobs.

Marilys and Laurie got work in a hotel run by a shrewd but kind couple, Ross and Shirley Marriott. Marilys cooked and Laurie waited tables. While fending off what seemed to be all the single men in town and some of the married ones, Laurie wished she could play the guitar or harmonica instead. When she turned sixteen in October, she hugged Marilys and said, "Only two more years! Then Redwine can't bother me though he might still try to control me through taking charge of Buddy."

"He better not try!" Buddy's freckled face was getting thinner and sometimes gave a hint of the man he would be, with Daddy's chin and smile and widow's peak to his sun-streaked hair. "I'm going to be a soldier if the war lasts till I'm old enough!"

"Well, don't sound so happy about it," Laurie snapped. Surely no war could last that long but her heart contracted with fear for him and all the boys everywhere who might die in battle before they had even lived.

In a few weeks, Russia invaded Poland from the east. They divided Poland with Germany. Early in November, the neutrality act was changed to let Great Britain and France buy arms from the United States. For the first time in Laurie's memory, there were jobs for any worker willing to move near a defense plant. Nazi submarines sank ships twice as fast as U. S. and British shipyards could build them.

On Saturdays and Sundays, Buddy helped Way with the pumping. A week before Christmas, he came running into the hotel kitchen, where Laurie was picking up a tray with two plates of grits, ham, and eggs.

"Some—some detectives and Mr. Redwine drove up while Way was reading a gauge," Buddy panted. "They took him down to the jail!"

Marilys turned pale and leaned on the sink. Laurie set down the tray and gripped Buddy's shoulders. "Did Redwine see you?"

Buddy nodded, gulping convulsively. "Yes, but I don't think he recognized me."

Entirely possible. Redwine had never seemed to really *see* Buddy and that had been three years ago. "I—I've got to go down there." Marilys fumbled at her apron strings.

"No! Redwine's accused you of kidnapping. That's a lot worse than stealing. He may not know you're here."

They stared at each other. Laurie dreaded confronting Redwine but it seemed the only hope. "I'll go to the jail," she said. "Maybe Redwine will drop his charges if we pay him for his detectives and whatever he claims Way took."

"We don't have that kind of money."

"We can borrow against the trailer and truck and we do have a couple of hundred dollars saved." They kept it under the mattress. None of them trusted banks after the way so many of them had closed.

The tiny lines in Marilys's face seemed to have deepened. "This isn't about money. It's Dub getting even with Way."

"I know that. But if I beg Redwine and offer the money besides—We have to do something, Marilys!"

"What if he wants to make you and Buddy live with him?"

Laurie froze inside at the very notion. "I—I guess we'd have to. But he wanted a son. He can see now that I'm not that."

"He knew you were a girl."

"Yes, but now I'm almost a woman." Laurie tried to smile. "I don't think he'll want me."

"What if he does?"

Laurie shrugged. "I'll go with him and get away the first chance I get." She took off her apron and lapped it around Buddy. "You wait tables while I'm gone. I'll be back as soon as I can."

She pulled on her coat, more because it would shield her from Redwine's eyes than because the wind blew chill outside. The jail, she knew, was at the back of the courthouse next to the sheriff's office. Go with Redwine? Every fiber shrank. She remembered the women he'd had at his Truck-Inns and shivered. Maybe he'd be satisfied if she pleaded hard and offered the money. At the courthouse, she summoned her courage, turned the heavy brass doorknob, and stepped inside.

A dark-haired man stood arguing with Redwine and a thin, narrow man with a hatchet face. The dark one turned at the sound of the door and she looked into gray eyes with a shimmer of green. She forgot why she was there, forgot everything. It was Morrigan.

22

He stood there, black hair winging across his forehead, the cleft in his chin a little deeper like the sun lines at the corners of his eyes. But it *was* him, like a prayer, looking taller than he was because of the way muscle and bone fitted smooth and easy so that every move he made was graceful as if he'd practiced it yet was careless as his smile.

"Morrigan!" she breathed. "Johnny Morrigan!"

He tilted his head. His brow furrowed. "You have the advantage of me, ma'am." He smiled. "Not for long, I hope."

His voice filled her, spread into every nerve, every part, warming her, calming her fear. Then she knew, in the depths of her that were becoming a woman's, that it wasn't because he'd come to her at the end of one world and help her start in another that she hadn't forgotten him, that she hadn't been interested in any of the men who tried to get her attention. His voice and smile and image were sealed up in her heart. Only he could unlock it. Foolishly, desperately, she wanted him to remember her, at least just a little.

"Laurie!" Turning from a deputy whose pale brown moustache looked like a shaving brush, W. S. Redwine bulked larger than ever but he still had the same squashed nose above a jaw broader than cheekbones and forehead. Gray dirtied his straw-colored hair. His yellow eyes flickered like a cat's in a dark room with only a blink of light. "Damned if it's not Larry-Laurie of the Field Brothers, alias the Tumbleweeds and Roadsters!" Square white teeth showed as his lips peeled back. "I couldn't track you after you half-killed those deputies close to Duncan three years ago but I guess this means you kids and that slut managed to find old Wayburn and dry him out."

"Laurie Field." Morrigan studied her, frowning. Suddenly, he laughed. "Why, sure, you've gone and grown up on me! We shared a camp once. You still got the harmonica?"

All Laurie could do was nod. From the back of the jail, she heard muffled coughing. Well, this was more than enough to bring on Way's asthma.

"I've wondered about you folks," John Morrigan said. "Hope California worked fine for your dad."

"He—he died out there."

"And then she and her brother fell in with that old hobo locked up in the back cell," Redwine said. "I gave him a job, tried to straighten him out, but like I've been telling you, Johnny, he went on a bender and stole a lot of expensive equipment."

"He didn't," said Laurie. "You got him drunk—that's why he left us. But he didn't steal from you any more than Marilys kidnapped Buddy and me."

More to Johnny than to Laurie, Redwine said in an aggrieved tone, "I wanted to give the kids a chance, good educations, help with their music. If they'd stayed with me, they'd be making records by now like the Carter Family." He shook his head. "Must be in their nature—they ran off with a tramp woman. God only knows what tricks she's taught them."

"Here's one!" Laurie couldn't help herself. She kicked him as hard as she could on the side of the knee, hard enough to break the knee of an average man.

Redwine wasn't average. He lurched sideways and grunted. "So she's turned you into a tough little bitch just like her!"

"Marilys wasn't tough. You had her scared to breathe."

"She'll be scared a sight more when she's tried for kidnap across a state line. Wonder if a woman fries faster than a man?"

Morrigan stepped between them. "What kind of talk is that, Dub? I don't understand what all this is about but it's pretty clear Laurie's not a child now and she doesn't think she was kidnapped." He paused, catching and holding the older man's eyes. "Like I told you before, I can't see throwin' someone with bad asthma in jail for something you can't be sure he did. He didn't sound or look like a sneak-thief to me."

"Next thing you'll want to hire the old bum!"

"Guess I would, if he's been a friend to Laurie and her kid brother."

273

The two men dueled with their gazes. Way's coughing echoed along the corridor. The deputy said, "I don't want that guy dyin' in one of our cells. He better have a doctor."

"Please," Laurie said. "Please, Mr. Redwine!"

"Well, that's a change! To hear you saying 'Please' !"

Johnny cut in. "W.S., let the man go or start hunting another partner."

"Oh hell," said Redwine. "Let him go!"

The deputy went down the hall, selecting a key from the ring at his belt. Redwine dropped a dark-furred hand on Morrigan's shoulder. "All right, boy. Have it your way." He glanced dismissingly at Laurie. "It's too late to do what I wanted to for the kids. If they'd rather be oil-field trash, they're welcome to it."

"Guess I'm oil-field trash, too," said Johnny.

"You've been my partner in the company these past two years." Redwine's tone softened and there was a proud light in his tawny eyes. He gave Morrigan an affectionate shake before taking his hand off the younger man's shoulder. "What's more, Johnny, you're like a son to me." His eyes slued to Laurie as if he'd never seen her before. "Reckon you and this girl got some catching up to do. I'll see you out at the rig."

Johnny nodded. "Okay, Dub. May have to shoot that well to bring it in."

Redwine chuckled. "You're the one that can do that, son." He went out without speaking to or even glancing at Way, who was gasping for breath between fits of coughing as he labored along the corridor.

Laurie hurried to slip her shoulder beneath his arm and help him into the office. "Would you please heat some water?" she asked the deputy as she eased Way into a chair.

"Can I borrow a cup of your coffee, officer?" Johnny was already pouring a cup from the enameled pot steaming on a hot plate.

"Make yourselves to home!" The deputy's moustache fluffed as he vented sarcastic exasperation but he did produce a washbasin, fill it, and set it on a burner.

Two cups of coffee controlled the worst of Way's gasping. By the time he'd inhaled steam from the basin while Laurie held a towel around it and his head, his face had lost its bluish pallor and he regarded Johnny with frank interest.

"So you're Laurie's Morrigan. Walked on any water lately?"

Laurie blushed. Johnny laughed. "Only on slush and bottom settlings. Why don't we go get some dinner?"

"Got to get back to my job or I won't have one," Way said. He got up but had to steady himself against the wall.

"You drive over to the hotel and I'll bring you a sandwich and some lemon pie," Laurie commanded.

"Can I get the same?" asked Morrigan.

"You can have anything you want," she said, and took Way's arm in spite of his protests.

An hour later, Morrigan finished off his T-bone, glanced at his watch, and forked up the last delectable bit of lemon meringue. "Got to get out to the rig," he said. "After all the grief that hole's given us, it better make a one-hundred-barrel well! We've lost two strings of tools down it, had to fish for five days for the last bunch. And the bit keeps twisting off. If we don't hit oil this afternoon, it's time for a good charge of soup."

Nitroglycerin. Laurie didn't want to think about what an explosive that fractured rock formations could do to a human being. "If you're a producer, why don't you hire another shooter?" she asked.

"Because I'm the best." It was said with a grin and without bravado. "Anyhow, the way Redwine-Morrigan Production works is Dub takes care of wheeling and dealing and I stay in the field. Suits us both right down to the ground."

Laurie couldn't help but think it was risky to leave the finances and records to Redwine, but in the moments of talk they'd managed while she waited tables, she heard affection in Johnny's voice when he spoke of Redwine, so she forbore to fill Morrigan's ears with accusations against his partner. Redwine had wanted a son. Maybe he'd learned something since he drove his real one to suicidal recklessness. Anyway, Johnny was grown up. He'd have defenses against Redwine's possessiveness.

"Do you still have your guitar?"

"Hocked that one, but I have another. Say, I sure want to hear you play and sing."

"I want to hear you, too." She took the dollar he'd stuffed under the napkin and thrust it into his shirt pocket. "Don't try to pay for your dinner. It's a present from Marilys. She wants to meet you but she's been too busy cooking. Could you come by our place tonight? Bring your guitar."

"What I do tonight depends on that hole. But tell me where you live and when you're likely to be there. I'll come by first chance I get and we'll celebrate. If Crystal's not busy, I'll bring her."

"Crystal?"

"My girl." Pride and a hint of something else deepened his voice. "She's Dub's private secretary. Keeps the company's books." He shook his head and sounded abashed. "Don't see how anyone that pretty can be so smart with numbers and all, but Crystal can figure percentages faster than a machine. Don't know what she sees in me. I wouldn't know a decimal if it kicked me in the teeth."

Laurie felt kicked in her center. To find him after all these years only to have him crazy in love with this Crystal woman, a little awed by her. *I hate her—hate her!* It took all Laurie's willpower to hush that jealous wail. From things Johnny had said before, she reckoned him to be about twenty-five. He might well have been married by now. And she, Laurie, was going to have to try hard to like Johnny's woman because he loved her and his happiness was tied to her.

Still, Laurie's lips were so numb she could barely force a smile. "You'll certainly have to bring her to meet us." Giving directions to the trailer, Laurie pretended not to see Johnny's outstretched hand. She called good-bye and her thanks as she hurried to take an impatient diner's order.

"I got a peek at your Morrigan," Marilys said, spooning gravy over a mound of whipped potatoes. "Got a smile like sunlight breaking through a cloud. I like the way he moves— not brash or pushy but you know he's going wherever he starts."

"Mmhm," was as far as Laurie could trust herself.

"Isn't that something?" Marilys went on. "Imagine him being Dub's partner!" She made a face. "Your Morrigan's going to need all his guts and backbone."

"He's not *my* Morrigan!"

"Why, honey!" Marilys put down the ladle and stared. "What in the world's the matter?"

"He—he's got a girlfriend!"

"Well, of course! Why wouldn't he?"

Laurie gulped and blinked at the stinging in her eyes. "I—I just—"

"Oh, sugar!" Marilys's blue eyes darkened. In a way that said she understood everything, she held out her arms. Laurie ran into them and burst into tears.

Crystal wasn't pretty. She was gorgeous. Long, silver-blond hair rippled when she threw back her slender throat to laugh with a tinkling that reminded Laurie of tiny hail stones striking glass. Johnny had shot the well late that evening, bringing in an eighty-barrel-a-day producer, so he looked tired but satisfied when he brought his sweetheart to the trailer. Shedding her fur coat into Johnny's hands, she revealed a jade green knit dress that molded her narrow flanks, small waist, and high firm breasts. Three-inch heels made her almost as tall as Johnny.

She glanced around the trailer's kitchen–dining–living room, gave an almost imperceptible shrug, and occupied the edge of the big easy chair that had been the family's Christmas present to Way. The place was meticulously clean. Marilys and Laurie had made striped monks' cloth curtains to brighten the beige linoleum, walls, and built-ins. The second bedroom was divided with painted wallboard for Laurie and Buddy, her side done in white and yellow, his in blue. The small bathroom was painted sage green and the shower had a matching curtain and mat. There was water and electricity.

It was the nicest place Laurie had lived. They were all proud of it, of owning their own home even if they rented the space it set on. Crystal behaved as if she might get dirty, though, and when Marilys offered coffee, Crystal examined the cup before holding it out.

One of Laurie's favorite dreams had been showing Morrigan the use she'd made of the harmonica, how much she'd learned, and how she could play the guitar, too. Her most favorite dream had been to hear him again, hear in reality the voice that had brought her such comfort on the worst day of her life, the voice she tried to evoke before she went to sleep, or when she was afraid or discouraged.

It *was* lovely to hear him though he didn't play the spirituals or blues but stuck to songs like "Smoke Gets in Your Eyes," "The Very Thought of You," and "Just One of Those Things."

"Now it's your turn," he said, smiling at Laurie.

She looked imploringly at Marilys, who got their guitar. Laurie had never before been reluctant to play. Now she didn't think she could with Crystal's frosted green eyes on her. But Marilys strummed and when Laurie held the Hohner, fingers gripping the engraved metal, what she knew took over, and she followed Marilys into "Tumbling Tumbleweed." Buddy and Marilys sang, voices blending sweetly. Morrigan's foot started tapping as they moved into "Orange Blossom Special." When they swung into "Ramblin' Boy," Johnny joined in.

Finally, to play with him, weave her music in and out of his! "Do you know this?" he'd say, and then Laurie or Marilys would propose a song. Way beamed, moving his head in time with the tune. For a while, Laurie almost forgot Crystal was there. Johnny looked at Laurie and launched into "So Long, It's Been Good to Know You," taking her back to that afternoon beneath the cottonwood when he came along and changed her life.

I've sung this song but I'll sing it again,
Of the place that I lived in the wild windy plains. . . .

The others played or sang along but before they were halfway through, Crystal got out a pack of Camels and blew smoke toward Johnny. "For God's sake, Jackie, don't play that dismal old song! I've had enough of the Depression and Dust Bowl to last me ten lives."

That put a damper on the party. They played a few more

songs, but Crystal was swinging a long, silk-sheathed leg and fussing with the emerald pendant of the silver necklace that rested between her breasts. Her third cigarette filled the room with smoke. She tapped out her ashes in a saucer. Way started coughing, excused himself, and went outside into a cold north wind.

"Would you mind not smoking?" Marilys asked when Crystal shook out a fourth Camel. "I'm sorry, but you see, my husband has asthma—"

Crystal shoved the Camels back in her purse. "It's time we left, Jackie. Dub and I are driving to Oklahoma City tomorrow and we're leaving early."

He unfolded his legs reluctantly but without protest and helped her into her mink. Laurie wondered how many animals had died to make it and devoutly hoped that Morrigan hadn't bought it for her. "You make me real proud I left you that Hohner," he told Laurie. "I'll bet you and Buddy made more money off your music than I ever did."

"Holy cow, Jackie!" Crystal's tone was shrill. "A man's supposed to have a job or own a business, not vagabond around with a guitar! If you hadn't cut out that nonsense by the time I met you, I wouldn't have looked at you twice."

"All the same, my songs got me many a meal and bed when I was on the road."

"If I were you, I wouldn't be proud of it," Crystal said. She produced a smile for Marilys that was more a curl of the lip. "Thanks so much for asking us over, Mrs. Kirkendall. Jackie's always running into people he used to know."

"You're welcome anytime we're home," said Marilys.

"How sweet of you," drawled Crystal. "I do so admire women who don't mind being caught in a mess or at inconvenient times." She directed a bright smile between Buddy and Laurie. "So nice to meet you children. Jackie's mentioned you innumerable times, wondered how you were getting along. Thank goodness, he finally knows."

"See you soon," said Johnny, giving each of them a warm and special smile.

He did. He came to the hotel for breakfast or dinner almost

every day, and two or three evenings a week he brought Crystal in for supper. Now that Redwine couldn't bother them without getting in trouble with Johnny, Marilys and Laurie negotiated with the hotel owner to work their regular schedules except for Friday and Saturday evenings, when they played and sang from five till midnight and Sunday when they performed from eleven in the morning till three and from five till eleven. After the weekend cook and waitress were paid, Marilys and Laurie were entitled to a third of the profits. The first Friday, they split five dollars, by Saturday, they divided fifteen, and Sunday had people waiting for tables.

"What say I just pay you ladies ten dollars each a day for your music?" suggested the jowly owner, Ross Marriott. "That way you won't be taking any risks."

"Oh, we couldn't let you stand to lose money," said Marilys sweetly, accepting two tens and two fives from his reluctant hand. "This way we'll get exactly what we're worth to you."

Crystal would sit through their music while she dined, but the couple never lingered. They were always on their way to a movie or dancing at the Blue Light to a band that Crystal especially liked because there was a clarinetist who sounded "just like Benny Goodman," she said when Laurie stopped by their table. "White-type swing, you know, not like the coon-jazz Duke Ellington and Louie Armstrong play."

"I'd give an arm to see the day I could play half as well as either one of them," Johnny said. "They're as great as Mozart or Bach—and a damn sight more people enjoy their music."

"Don't swear at me, Jackie," pouted Crystal. "I don't know why you get so worked up when I forget to say 'Ne-grow.' After all, I was raised in East Texas where we called them—"

"I know what you called them," cut in Johnny. "But I don't want to hear it." He got to his feet. "Come on. I've been up since five and I'm sleepy if you're not."

"If you're not working, you're tired," she complained. When he still looked grim, she glanced up through her eyelashes and smiled coaxingly as she rose and brushed tapering plum-enameled fingertips across Johnny's mouth. "Don't growl at me, sweetheart. After a nice martini, you won't feel tired at all."

Oklahoma was a dry state, which only meant that folks who drank bought from bootleggers and carried their own brown-bagged bottles into nightclubs. Because of Way's struggle with alcohol, her own upbringing, and the havoc she had seen caused by heavy drinking in the oil towns, Laurie detested liquor but she didn't see much point in a law that was utterly ignored and that encouraged crime. She was afraid Johnny drank too much and wished Crystal wouldn't urge it on him, but Crystal herself carried a pint silver flask in her purse and poured it into her Cokes.

It hurt so much to see her with him, controlling him with silken twitches and the lure of her body, that Laurie sometimes wished she hadn't met him again if it had to be this way. She ached when he looked weary, which was too much of the time. Still, she lived for the moments when he came in the hotel alone and she could serve him, keep his coffee cup full, and talk with him a little about safe subjects.

Crystal and Redwine weren't safe. "Dub's been like a father to me, a good one," Johnny had said when explaining how their partnership began. "After I visited my mother—she's married again to a good man and busy raising a second family—the only work I could find that paid better than roughnecking was helping Houston Clay. Don't know if you've heard of him but he's about the best wellshooter in the business exceptin' maybe Tex Thornton."

"I've heard of Tex Thornton," Laurie remembered. "He tried to make it rain over by Dalhart the same spring we left Prairieville."

"Yep. Farmers and ranchers guaranteed three hundred dollars for TNT and nitroglycerin jelly. Tex was going to send the charges up to low-lying clouds by balloons tethered at a certain height. Dalhart was all set to have a big street dance to celebrate. Must have been a couple thousand local folks, reporters, newsreel cameramen, and photographers on hand. Then a humongous dust storm blew in. Everybody scampered to their vehicles 'cept Tex. Since the wind was too high for balloons, he set off sixty charges in the ground. The explosions just kicked more dust up in the air. Poor old Tex didn't try it again."

"You got a job with a shooter?" Laurie prompted.

"Sure did. Kind of enjoyed the way other trucks and cars cleared the road when they saw me comin' with those torpedoes fastened in my racks. I learned to mix the soup and pour it in the shells and Clay showed me how to send those babies down—showed me the way to run if gas or oil pushes one back up, too, you bet! He had a trailer—let me share it and we each bought half of what groceries we cooked, so I was able to sock most of my pay in the bank." He chuckled. "Sure, I know you can't trust 'em but I trust 'em more than I trust me! Saved till I could buy a Fort Worth spudder—you know, the drilling rig that starts a hole, spuds it in. Doesn't use a derrick to raise and lower the tools and drill, just has a mast, but you can move it around with a truck and it'll drill a shallow well."

He'd gone wild-catting with Gary MacIntosh, a driller friend who was willing to work for a share in any oil they found. Over in Kiowa County, they found some prairie where they liked the way the creeks and ridges ran and talked a farmer into letting them drill on his land for no payment unless they hit oil.

"Brought in three nice little forty-barrel-a-day wells, all at less than five hundred feet," said Johnny. "We didn't have trouble getting leases then but the nearest pipeline was fifty miles away so we couldn't sell our oil. Dub was in Hobart opening up a new Truck-Inn. He heard about our wells, bought us a steak, and after we talked a while, he said he'd put in the pipeline. That's how we got to be pardners, two years ago." He frowned slightly. "After about six months, Mac asked if I wanted to buy him out. He and Dub were always crossin' horns, and anyhow, Mac wanted his own company. He's done pretty well down in the Permian Basin. I got what you might call custody of the spudder. Use it for luck to spud in new holes. Besides, if the oil's ever all gone, I can dig water wells with it."

Redwine, thank goodness, was in Oklahoma City, Amarillo, or Black Spring most of the time, or making lightning appraisal raids on his Truck-Inns and other businesses. It was a great relief not to have to hide from him. Now that it didn't matter if Grandpa Field knew where they were, Laurie took a few days off work and, laden with gifts, rode the train to visit Rosalie.

How strange, to get off in the town where Rosalie had treated them to ice cream, movies, and hamburgers—where a thirteen-year-old girl and her younger brother had clambered into a freight car to go find their father.

Her heart contracting with pain, Laurie again saw the raw mound beneath the eucalyptus tree outside Eden. Would Mama's red-letter Bible still exist in its small grave over Daddy's heart? Had the Model T faithfully carried Mary Halsell and her family from job to job or had it broken down and been abandoned? Had those people Daddy had shared with, for whose baby he had died, ever found a home? If the Halsells had written Laurie in care of Rosalie, there was no way Rosalie could send a letter on. Laurie wished she knew how the Halsells had fared. If they were doing well, it would make her and Buddy feel their father hadn't died for nothing, and besides, he had thought a lot of that family.

Laurie had never ridden in a taxi, but she hired one at the station, agreeing on a price. She hadn't written that she was coming just in case Grandpa Field could think of some way to cause her trouble and she heartily wished she didn't have to see him at all.

The tarpaper shack looked forlorn as ever, sand blown away from the block foundations, but the loam of the fields was striped with the fresh new green of young corn and cotton, and the climbing rose by the front door had branched out, no longer struggling for life, but luxuriantly affirming it.

The hounds ran out— Were they the same ones? The driver got out to unload Laurie s gift-packed suitcases. "Want me to wait, ma'am?"

Rosalie stepped out, gold hoop earrings catching the light, shading her eyes in the nooning sun. "No, thanks," said Laurie. "I'll be staying a few days." She ran toward Rosalie, whose stare turned to disbelief and then to joy as she sprang from the step and held out her arms.

Rosalie still smelled of spice and roses and her body was firm, though it might have been a trifle fuller. "Oh, honey, it was sweet of you to send that money all these years but I'd have swapped it all for a look at you!" She held Laurie back and laughed delightedly. "Here you are tall as me! Same eyes but your face fits 'em now and your hair's darkened till it's more the shade of buckwheat honey than pulled taffy. Oh, I wish your mama and daddy could see how nice you've grown up! Come in and tell me what you never put in your letters." She gasped and snapped her fingers. Rosalie could do that. "Good gracious, speaking of letters, I have some here for you! From that Mary Halsell who wrote and told me about Ed and that you kids had been there and were fine." She went in the bedroom, rummaged in a drawer, and returned with four envelopes. "The last one just came a few weeks ago," she said, handing them to Laurie.

Laurie started with it. A twenty-dollar bill, a ten, and a five fell out. "This pays out the Model T," Mary Halsell wrote. "With five dollars' interest. I never can thank you enough for letting us keep that flivver. It got us from one picking job to another till Bob died. A man at that last camp knew a preacher in town who gave Bob a funeral and helped me find steady work in a laundry so we could settle down and the kids could stay in school. Tom's a good man and we got married last year. Now I've got a good job in a defense plant so things are looking better than they have in a long time except I'll always miss Bob and I'm sure scared of that awful war and hoping Jimmy won't have to go. I've never heard from you, Laurie. I hope you kids don't hold a grudge for your daddy's getting drowned. I think of him every time I hug Robbie because he wouldn't be here if Ed hadn't gone in after him. If you get this, please, please, let me hear from you." It was signed, "With love and thanks, Mary Halsell Weeks."

"What's the matter, honey?" asked Rosalie.

Laurie couldn't speak and her eyes were brimming. She handed the letter to Rosalie and opened the others. The first contained three dollars and was mailed two months after Daddy's death. The second held four dollars sent six months later, and the third, mailed early in 1937, contained nine dollars. With each payment was a letter in Mary's neat penmanship, telling where they were, how they were getting along, and asking for news of Buddy and Laurie.

"I—I'm so glad the family's doing all right," Laurie said when she could speak. "That makes me feel better about Daddy. They paid off the flivver, too."

"Mrs. Halsell sounded nice in that letter she wrote about Ed and this is sure a sweet one. Glad she's found her a good man." Rosalie handed back the last envelope. "Gracious, I've got to finish getting dinner. Your grandpa and the kids'll be in for dinner pretty quick."

"Aren't the kids in school?"

"Billy and Ernie and Belle are out to help with the crop work," Rosalie said. "I talked Ev'rett into finishin' eighth grade but he didn't want to go into town to high school and of course your grandpa can't see any use in a farm boy gettin' an education."

"Does Ev'rett want to stay on the farm?" As if she'd never been away, Laurie started setting the table, finding the dishes in a glass-doored cabinet Rosalie had finally got. The table had a blue-checked oilcloth and there was a new red-brown tile linoleum on the floor. The biggest changes, though, were piped water to the sink, electric light bulbs hanging from the ceiling, and a big white refrigerator. The old cast-iron range still ruled supreme but was flanked by a gas cookstove that would certainly keep the house cooler in the summer.

"Ev'rett's sick and tired of the farm, 'specially since it's not ours." Rosalie sighed. "If his pa won't let him work the wheat harvest this year, and keep some of his money, I reckon the boy'll just take off. Can't blame him."

Working around farm machinery was at least as dangerous as the oil patch. "I've got a friend who could probably hire him on as a roustabout," Laurie said. "He could live with us. Shall I talk to Ev'rett about it?"

"I'd a sight rather he was with you than off with a threshin' crew." Rosalie brightened. "Sure, ask him, but not in front of his pa or the boys. They'd want to come, and they're too young. All right, honey, before the gang comes bustin' in, tell me where you've been and what you're doing."

While they got dinner, Rosalie listened with head shakings, widened eyes, and laughter. "I could see why you wanted to find your pa," she said. "But when I found your note in the truck and knew you were gone, I prayed harder than I ever prayed in my life that the pair of you would be all right. Sure a good thing you fell in with that nice Way Kirkendall." Rosalie dabbed at a tear. "I'm glad he and Marilys got married. But that mean old W. S. Redwine—I sure hope he won't cause you any more trouble."

"Oh," chuckled Laurie, "Morrigan makes him a better son to brag on than I ever could have even if I'd been a boy and wanted the job. I don't see Redwine very often. When I do, he acts like he never laid eyes on me before."

She didn't voice her distrust of the closeness that existed between Redwine and Crystal and how she sometimes felt that Crystal kept an eye on Morrigan for Redwine's benefit. You don't like Crystal, she told herself. Fact is, you're green-eyed jealous of her so of course you're ready to think she's lower than a snake's belly. At least you can keep that kind of nonsense to yourself.

"Just think of you and Buddy making a living with that harmonica and your songs!" Rosalie enthused. "You did bring your harmonica, didn't you?"

"Sure, and I've learned a lot more songs since I left."

"Good. Maybe you can play before we go back to the fields after dinner."

"If there's a pair of overalls that'll fit me, I'll help."

"No. You're company. Besides you're not used to the work. You'll get blisters and sunburn."

"Lend me some work gloves and a big hat. Honest, Rosalie, I'd a lot rather chop out weeds with the rest of you than laze in the house."

Grandpa Field had shrunken a little but he still had the savage look of a one-eyed hawk. He snorted on seeing her and then shrugged as he sat down and switched on the radio. "If you'd had any sense, you'd have let that rich old boy adopt you," he yelled above the blare. "But you're mule-stubborn, just like your ma. Damn good thing you don't seem to be as puny and ailin'."

After that, he ignored her, which was fine with Laurie. He didn't like her and she didn't like him but he seemed to accept that he had no control over her. The boys stared at her from beneath sun-bleached thatches. Everett, who must be about fourteen, was taller than she, all arms and legs and blue eyes. Sandy-haired thirteen-year-old Billy had hazel eyes almost the color of hers. Ernie, a year younger, gazed at her with brown eyes that were on a level with Laurie's.

Belle, in overalls and barefoot like her brothers, was brown and fleet and soft-eyed as a fawn. She shadowed Laurie adoringly, touching her dress and hair. Babe, now six, was an elfin little blond, her hair drawn back into one plump braid. Her sagging dirty diapers, thank goodness, were long forgotten. She and Belle insisted on sitting next to Laurie. Instead of apple crates, there were chairs now for everyone. Rosalie's cream biscuits and gravy were delectable as ever and the juicy, gold-crusted plum cobbler brought memories of picking plums along the North Fork of the Red River in what seemed lifetimes ago.

After dishes were done, Laurie got presents out of her luggage, letting Belle and Babe hand them around after *ooh*-ing and *ah*-ing over the birthstone necklaces she'd brought them, with matching bracelets and adjustable rings. They could scarcely be dissuaded, dirty from field work as they were, from slipping on their quilted rosebud seersucker robes with padded house slippers. For Rosalie, there was a cut-glass bottle of French perfume, chocolates, a copy of *Gone With the Wind,* and silk stockings; for Grandpa Field, a nice striped shirt; each boy got a baseball cap and jackknife with an amazing array of blades and tools. For all the children, there was a chinese checkers game, animal dominoes, and books to take the place of those Laurie was at last reclaiming.

Then, in the heat of the day, Laurie played the harmonica while her grandfather snored from the couch. The boys liked cowboy songs, Rosalie favored church-house blues, and Belle sang the songs she knew in a sweet, shrill voice while Babe swung her scratched brown feet in cadence.

Grandpa Field woke himself up from his nap with a loud,

whiffling snore, swung his legs off the couch, and glared at his offspring. "Time to get back to them weeds!" he ordered.

Laurie slipped into patched overalls, long-sleeved shirt, hat, and gloves Rosalie unearthed for her, and put on the old shoes she'd brought for wearing around the farm. As she worked her way along a row, she chopped cautiously, turning the blade to hook out the tiniest roots of Johnson grass, and hacked deep at big, tough roots of pigweed without damaging the cotton.

The late April afternoon sun was hot, though nothing to what it would be in June, July, and August. Beneath the frayed straw hat, her hair plastered itself damply to her skull and forehead. Gnats got in her eyes and nose and a fat green horse-fly decided to buzz around her ears. She had to push to keep up with Belle. The others, except for Babe, soon edged ahead. Babe's little hoe wouldn't get the toughest roots. Someone else would have to clean up her row, but she was learning.

Learning what? To be a sharecropper, wear herself out on land that would never belong to her? Laurie swept a glance around at her cousins, doggedly waging their eternal, season-after-season wars with insects, weather, and weeds. If she could manage it, they were going to have a choice. Starting with Everett.

Almost under her breath, she started a song. Pretty soon, Belle and Everett were singing, too.

> "Boll weevil is a little black bug
> Come from Mexico, they say—
> Come all the way to Texas,
> Just lookin' for a place to stay—
>
> Lookin' for a home,
> Gonna find a home. . . ."

Two days later, Rosalie drove Laurie and Everett to the train depot. Grandpa Field had refused to let his son go till Everett desperately promised to send home half his wages. "You can hire good help for less'n that, pa," he argued.

"Yeah, and what am I gonna do when Ernie takes it in his head to go, and then Billie?"

Rosalie laid her hand on his arm. "They're all goin' sooner or later, Harry, and you're not gettin' any younger. I've been savin' butter and egg money and most of what Laurie's sent. What we'll do when Belle's high school age is buy a little place on the edge of town."

"What?" From Grandpa's tone, you'd think she'd proposed that they homestead the moon. "God-a-mighty, woman, how'd we make a living?"

"Well, for one thing, what we grow'll be ours, not half some landlord's." Rosalie spoke in the voice that meant she'd made up her mind. "Belle and Babe are goin' to get good educations so they can teach school or be secretaries or something nice and clean. We'll have a great big garden, fruit and pecan trees, chickens, and keep a few good milk cows."

"But—"

She pressed her fingers to his lips and smiled in that coaxing way that made it clear she loved this man, that for her he had a kindness he'd never shown anyone else but his daughters. "You deserve to take it easier, Harry. And *I* deserve to have my own house and fix it up the way I want it." She paused and looked him in the eye. "Harry, you've been a good man to me. I'm not sorry about a thing. But I don't want our kids to work their guts out sharecropping."

He stared at her a long moment. "All right, young sprout," he said to Everett. "But you send half your wages reg'lar till you're twenty-one or I'll have you back in the field."

Now, at the depot, Rosalie kissed her squirming eldest son. "Be good, son, and don't give Laurie and her folks any trouble." Hugging Laurie, she whispered, "Thanks, honey. Thanks for giving him a chance."

Laurie squeezed her tight. "I don't know what we'd have done if you hadn't loved us."

"Quit bawlin'," implored Everett. "Here comes the train!"

23

Helen's Babies and *Black Beauty* had torn loose from their covers but *A Wonder Book, A Child's Garden of Verses,* and *The Little Lame Prince* didn't look as if they'd been more than briefly opened since Laurie last put them in the crate. Mama had written inside each book Laurie's name, the date, and "Happy birthday!" or "Merry Christmas!" Each book was signed, "With love to our dear little daughter from Mama and Daddy."

Laurie probably wouldn't read the books again till she read them to some child, but she felt as if some missing part of her had been restored. The round oak table and rocking chair and brave little cherry tree were lost forever but it was wonderful to have these beloved things from that time of being a family. She put the books on the shelf with others she'd slowly ac-cumulated. The latest was John Steinbeck's *The Grapes of Wrath,* which had just won the Pulitzer Prize. Some Oklaho-mans didn't like it but Laurie thought it the truest book she had ever read. She planned to go the movie, which would star a young, long-faced actor named Henry Fonda.

It would be terrible for the bird quilt to wear out so she folded it at the bottom of the bed after examining each block and pressing it to her face to breathe in the smell of lilacs. Mama's little cedar chest went on the built-in dresser. It still held locks of baby hair, embroidered voile gift handkerchiefs, Mama's amethyst lavaliere, and Grandma Phares's jet brooch and tortoiseshell combs. Laurie wept while she arranged these things but they were happy tears. Of the safe, protected world she had lost, she now had something to touch, something of her mother's to give her own daughter if she ever had one.

Buddy hadn't wanted her to bring his Big Little Books—lucky, since they'd been read to tatters—but he put the coyote skull above his door and proudly hung the Sioux beaded belt and watch fob on the wall. Everett had declined to move into his tiny room.

"I'd as lief sleep on the couch," he insisted. Relief made Buddy ready to share his closet and chest of drawers with his older cousin. While Everett was putting away his things, Marilys drew Laurie into the kitchen.

"I think you ought to know, Laurie, so you won't think Dub's turned nice and charitable." Marilys frowned, looking away.

Fear gripped Laurie. "What, Marilys? Did he—" Surely not even he would try to get her back now she was married to Way.

But Marilys nodded. "First, he tried sweet talk." Her lips twisted. "He had the nerve to pretend he really cared about me. When that didn't work, he said he hadn't told Way all about me before. If some of the truth had been enough to send Way on a binge back in Black Spring, what would the whole story do?"

"Way wouldn't care!" Laurie threw her arms around Marilys. "He'll never forget that you hunted all over Texas and Oklahoma for him."

Hugging Laurie back, Marilys said, "Before we got married, I told Way everything there was to tell. He didn't want to hear it, but I made him."

Startled at the raw note in her voice, Laurie stared at her friend. "Marilys—"

"I held my baby once. Just once. Then I had to give her away because I wasn't married and there was no one at all to help." Marilys released a jagged breath. "I can't have another child." Laurie put out a comforting hand. Marilys squeezed it and managed a smile. "You're the age my daughter is, Laurie. I hope you don't mind that sometimes I've pretended you were her."

"I'm glad. Proud, too."

Laughing through tears, they embraced each other. People were like books with stuck-together pages, Laurie thought. There were always things you didn't know. She was beginning to have quite a few stuck pages herself.

"I'm mighty glad now I told Way," went on Marilys. "Because I looked Dub in the eye and said Way knew a lot more about me than *he* did and all he'd get with his tales was a good fight." Her blue eyes glinted. "I also told Dub I'd sooner get in bed with a dead, rotting rattlesnake than with him. Maybe I shouldn't have. He finds ways of getting back at people who hurt his pride. But it sure was fun to see him swell up and turn purple."

"I'm glad you set him straight." Laurie's grin faded and she sighed. "We'll have to watch out for him. Why can't he just leave us alone?"

Marilys's brow furrowed. "Well, he's never liked it if people got out from under his thumb before he was through squashing them. He wasn't through squashing me. And I think he's jealous of Way."

Laurie stared. "Why? Way doesn't have money or power or any of the things that matter to Redwine."

"No, but Way's got what Dub's money can't buy, Laurie."

"You mean he's happy? He's got a family?"

Marilys nodded. "And he's got the kind of self-respect you only get after you've sunk to the bottom and fought your way up again."

It was a strange notion, Redwine envying the man he'd patronized as a derelict, but when Laurie thought it over, it sounded true. "We'll just have to watch W.S.," she said. "At least now we know he hasn't got religion and he'll hurt us if he can without Johnny finding out about it."

Everett was so glad to "be off the end of a hoe handle" and earning real wages that he was painstakingly careful not to make extra work or cause any worries. Upon his insistence, he was allowed to chip in on groceries, but that was his only living expense so that he felt rich even after sending home half of the three dollars a day Johnny paid him while he was learning the various jobs around a rig.

Johnny became his hero, of course. His conversation was a litany of "Johnny says . . ." and "Johnny did . . ." till Buddy erupted. "I'm sick and tired of hearing about your old job!" he hollered, banging shut his arithmetic book.

Everett blinked. The slight stoop of his shoulders had straightened in the month he'd been with them and his blunt boy's features were firming into a handsome young man's. "Sorry, Buddy. I just—"

"It's bad enough I have to go to school without your rubbin' it in that you're earning wages, while all I've got's a paper route and this summer job delivering groceries," Buddy grouched.

"I finished eighth grade," Everett defended. "Gosh, Buddy, I'm a lot older than you!"

"Well, the second I get that ninth-grade report card Laurie says I gotta have, I'll never set foot inside a school again," Buddy glowered.

"You'll only be fifteen," said Laurie. "You'd do a lot better to finish high school, maybe go on to college and be a geologist or engineer."

Buddy snorted. "That's how all of you talk—all of you who never got past eighth or ninth grade except for Marilys."

That hurt. If it hadn't been for being a burden on Marilys and Way, Laurie would joyfully have finished all the school there was, including college. She would never stop reading and learning, of course, but Mama had so hoped that both her children would finish high school. . . .

"Finish eighth and then we'll talk about it," Laurie said, speaking briskly to cover how her younger brother's words had stung.

"If we get in the war—"

"Buddy, hush! I don't even want to think about it!"

"You got to think about it now that old Hitler's taken over Denmark and Norway and Belgium! That English guy—the new prime minister or whatever they call him—Churchill, he was lucky to get all those troops out of Dunkirk! But they had to leave their weapons, so what'll they fight with now?"

Just then, the radio blared out that German troops were marching into Paris. That was June 14, 1940. General Charles de Gaulle, leader of the Free French, vowed from London to fight till his country was free again. Chilling, Laurie closed her eyes, breathing against a crushing weight. Why did there have to be wars? Why did people kill each other when surely most of them wanted the same thing—a decent living and a chance for their children?

293

That thought prompted her to get out Mary Halsell's letters and look up the return address on the last one. Laurie wrote to thank Mary for paying off the Model T and included a receipt. She said she was sorry Mr. Halsell had died but was glad Mary had a good job, had found a man she could care for. She told Mary that she and Buddy were doing fine, though she was having a hard time keeping Buddy in school and she hoped he'd get over his ambition to be a well shooter like their friend, John Morrigan. Writing his name gave Laurie a warm feeling and she smiled as she closed the letter with an invitation for the Halsells to visit if any of them got out to Oklahoma. There was still a pang for Laurie in knowing that while she and Buddy had waited for Daddy to send for them, he'd been buying food for the Halsells and making over the kids, but the Halsells had taken care of him when he'd hurt himself and couldn't work. No, really, in spite of that little edge of jealousy, she was glad he'd been with folks he cared about, who cared for him. He could have died in plenty of ways without saving anyone's life. That he had been—well, yes, a hero—took away some of the bewildered pain and the cauterizing hatred Laurie had felt toward him when he slapped her and forced her and Buddy to stay at his father's.

As the summer of 1940 passed, life seemed split in two, normal everyday things going on in Oklahoma while the papers and radio were full of horrors. In September, Congress passed an act for the first peacetime compulsory military service, which required all men from twenty-one to thirty-six to register for the draft. That included Johnny. Though she knew it was selfish, Laurie hoped he wouldn't be one of those selected to serve for a year.

In spite of Hitler's persecution of Jews, the U.S. State Department refused to increase the quota for admission. Laurie wrote her first letter to the president and her congressmen after a ship carrying nine thousand European Jews was turned away from New York Harbor. "I'm surprised the Statue of Liberty didn't topple over," she wrote. "Where will those people go now? What will happen to them?"

In spite of shame, anger, and sympathy, life went on as usual.

Was that the way it always was till *you* were the tormented ones? If you felt the pain of all the world, even a fraction of it, you wouldn't be able to live. But not to care, not to feel—that was like the California growers in their big shady houses who somehow managed not to see babies dying in the filth of migrant camps.

Laurie's seventeenth birthday came during the prolonged Battle of Britain fought in the skies between the Luftwaffe and the RAF, which was outnumbered two to one. Battling to protect England from a land invasion, Spitfires and Hurricanes brought down double their own losses. The Royal Air Force men dueled as bravely as ever had Arthur's knights, but how long could they hold out? Laurie felt a bit guilty to be celebrating a birthday without fearing a bomb might explode amongst them, but she didn't feel guilty enough to refuse the little party Marilys had planned.

Marilys invited Johnny for cake and ice cream after she and Laurie got off work. Crystal, thank goodness, was off on business. Johnny came in, wearing clean khakis, fresh-shaved, hair slicked back till it almost didn't curl. The tiredness in his face disappeared as he crossed to Laurie and grinned, taking her hands.

His gaze reached to her heart and held it. "Do I get a kiss from the birthday girl?"

You're going to. At least, one time, she was going to feel his mouth on hers. Still holding her hands, he started to brush her cheek. She turned and took the kiss full on her mouth. His hands on hers tightened. For a startled instant their lips clung. She felt more than heard the swift, sharp intake of his breath before he stepped back, setting his hands on her shoulders as if to keep distance between them.

"Happy seventeenth," he said. Smiling ruefully, he shook his head. "Doggone it, Laurie, you're growing up on me." He might try to pass it off like that, deny it had happened, but with a thrill of woman-pride, she knew that for that naked, unguarded second, he had answered her as a man, he had returned to her at least a flash of what she felt for him.

That was birthday gift enough, her first kiss, bittersweet,

seized rather than given, but all the same, John Morrigan's. Even if it was wicked to turn a friend's big-brother kiss into a real one, she wasn't sorry. It might be the only time she'd ever taste his mouth.

"Buddy," he said, "Help me get your sister's present. Someone'll have to hold the door open."

"If it's that big, I hope we got room for it." Way glanced around apprehensively.

Johnny grinned at Marilys. "We measured. It'll fit right there between the sofa and the door."

"What on earth—" puzzled Laurie.

"You'll love it!" Marilys promised, and opened the door.

Buddy hefted up a square cabinet with doors and put it in the space Marilys indicated, then went outside. Morrigan carried a square boxlike case with a transparent top, placed it on top of the cabinet, and unwound a cord, which he plugged into an outlet.

"A phonograph!" Laurie breathed. She'd seen them in store windows and dreamed of owning one someday but there was always a more urgent need for money.

"When you want music but don't feel like making it yourself," Johnny laughed, eyes dancing with light she thought must be reflected from her own. "Got you a start of records—hope you'll like them."

Buddy staggered in with a crate of 78 RPMs. "Gracious Johnny, you must've bought out some Oklahoma City store!" Marilys cried. "Ohhh, look! Here's Louie Armstrong and 'My Blue Heaven.' And 'Blueberry Hill'!" She held up another record. "Duke Ellington with 'Mood Indigo.' I love that!"

There was "Fats" Waller with "Honeysuckle Rose," "Ain't Misbehavin'," "I Can't Give You Anything but Love," and more; Cole Porter's hits, including "Night and Day" and "I Get a Kick Out of You"; George Gershwin's "Oh, Lady Be Good!" and "Someone to Watch Over Me"; tunes from Rudolf Friml's "Rose-Marie" and Jerome Kern's "Showboat," half a dozen numbers along with Way's favorite, "Ol' Man River," sung by Jerome Bledsoe, the marvelous black baritone. Bessie Smith's records included W. C. Handy's "St. Louis Blues." There was

Leadbelly, who'd served time in Texas and Louisiana pens, at least once for murder, with "Pick a Bale of Cotton," "Irene, Goodnight," "Easy Rider," and other ballads with the twelve-string guitar. Jimmie Rodgers had died in 1933, but here was his music, magically preserved beside that of the Carter Family.

Laurie couldn't have been more stunned if a million dollars had dropped in her lap—or been anything as pleased. Once again Morrigan had given her music, picked out his favorites and songs he thought she'd like. She would treasure them forever. Unable to speak, she gazed at him.

"Hey!" His eyebrows raised as he thumbed a tear from her cheek and spoke softly. "Crying, honey? I thought it was a dandy notion but—"

Overcome, Laurie stammered. "It's—it's—I can't say how wonderful it is!"

"Don't need to, as long as you like it."

His smile flooded her like sunlight. Dazzled, she could only look at him. "Well, Laurie, let's try it out." He switched on the phonograph, selected a record, and put it on. Taking her hand, he set his other hand at the small of her back and took a gliding step to "Somewhere Over the Rainbow."

"I can't dance!"

He smiled down at her. "Sure you can! Just let yourself go with me and the music."

Melting her, his hand spread almost across her back, bringing her easily with him. He didn't hold her close but she was so near that the radiant warmth of their bodies fused, joining them invisibly. He laughed when she stepped on his toes, swung her as exuberantly as he could in the small space, and guided her back and forth, back and forth, till she stopped worrying about her feet and let herself flow with him. More than anything she'd ever experienced, dancing with him had the enchantment of floating up and down on a carousel steed, lost in the magic, wanting it never to end.

Marilys urged Way up for the next tune, which finished the record's three-and-a-half minutes. "You pick one, Marilys," Laurie said, wondering if Johnny knew he still had hold of her hand. Couldn't he feel her inner trembling, sense that as she followed him in the dance, she longed to follow him always? Fearing that he'd read her thoughts, she closed her eyes when he took her in his arms again. But surely, anyway, he could read her body?

They were dancing to Gershwin's "Rhapsody in Blue" when the door opened. "Hi!" Crystal moved between the dancing couples and sat down on the couch, crossing her long legs. "I got back early from Okie City and decided to crash the party." She got out a pack of Camels and started to shake one out.

"Crystal," warned Johnny. "Don't smoke in here."

"Some party!" she complained above the music. "No smoking, no drinking! Do we get birthday cake and pink lemonade?"

"There's Coke, coffee, or hot chocolate," said Marilys, dancing on determinedly though Way's feet slowed and tangled. He said Crystal always made him feel like he had egg on his face and holes in the seat of his pants.

As the rhapsody ended, Crystal unfolded her legs and bent to examine the records. "If I can't smoke or have a martini, I guess I'll dance," she said. She put on a record and smiled at Laurie. "Mind if I cut in?"

Claiming Johnny, she pressed her cheek to his, in fact, to "Body and Soul," she molded against him breast to thigh. Flushing, Laurie pulled the record crate out of the way and concentrated on going through them, forcing herself not to glance toward Johnny and Crystal. The woman plainly had his body, if not his soul, and Laurie couldn't believe she knew how to value either. But no good could come from that sort of thinking.

Johnny's in love with somebody else. That's all there is to it, she scolded herself. He brought you a wonderful present, and you'll have the music a long time after tonight. Besides, you *did* kiss him. You *did* have your first dance ever in his arms.

All the same, she could have wept with frustration at the way Crystal had sailed in and ruined her party. Not that she was going to let the nasty cat see how upset she was! When the record finished, Laurie stood up.

"Let's have the cake," she suggested. "Everyone has to get up early in the morning."

"You've got to have your special song." Johnny got his harmonica out of his jacket. He played "Las Mañanitas," the beautiful Mexican birthday tune, and grinned as Marilys lit the candles cupped in yellow roses on the lovely white-frosted cake. "Take a deep breath, Laurie," he advised. "Blow 'em all out first time and you get your wish."

Closing her eyes, she started to wish that someday, somehow, they could be together, but then she stopped that hope, drove it away, and willed with all her being. *I wish you'll be happy, Johnny.*

When she opened her eyes, smoke curled from all the candles. "Well," Johnny said, "You get your wish."

"I hope so." She took the knife from Marilys and began to cut the cake.

Johnny and Crystal came to the hotel for breakfast next morning. Crystal had a sleepy, sated look. Johnny's eyes looked sunken. He tossed aside a paper as Laurie brought their coffee. "I was never sure we belonged in World War One but we ought to be fightin' this one—now, not after England's smashed."

"I can't see why you get so worked up about it," Crystal said, yawning. "There's always a war on somewhere."

"This one's different." Johnny brooded for a moment. "At least the RAF has that Eagle Squadron—all the pilots are American volunteers. If I knew how to fly, I'd go in a second."

Crystal's eyes narrowed. "You've already registered for the draft. If you're called up, you'll have to go. But unless you are drafted, it wouldn't be fair to Dub to leave him without a working partner."

"If the Nazis start on us, he may lose a damn sight more than a partner."

"Oh, Johnny, they won't get over here!"

"They may if we let England go down the drain."

She looked at him, pouting. "What about me? You'd go off and leave me here biting my fingernails, worrying about you?"

"You stay too busy to miss me much," he said drily. "Hell, sometimes I feel like you're married to Dub instead of being his secretary."

"I *am* the company's bookkeeper," she reminded him. She smiled coaxingly at Johnny. "After all, darling, you're Dub's partner. What helps him is good for you."

In the next weeks, the RAF fought off the Luftwaffe so fiercely that Hitler had to postpone plans for sending his armies across the Channel. Besides, German armies were needed to aid Italy's assault on a desperately resisting Greece. In November, Way refused to vote for Roosevelt's third term. "I like most of what FDR's pulled off," he said before he and Marilys went to vote. "But no human ought to be head of a country that long. Gettin' too much like a king."

Marilys scrunched her nose at him. "He's got my vote," she said. "But I'd sooner elect Eleanor. There's a real fine lady."

Roosevelt won his third term. A German bomber scored a direct hit on Buckingham Palace. Princess Elizabeth was about Laurie's age, with Princess Margaret younger. Laurie was glad they weren't hurt. Japan was angry because the United States had stopped selling it the oil and scrap metal needed for Japan's war with China.

"You know what I'd like to do?" said Way late one night as they sat drinking hot chocolate. "Start a salvage business. Seems like a good time for it when the defense factories are usin' so much steel and iron. There's thousands of dollars' worth of pipes, generators, pumps, tools, boilers—all kinds of stuff that the big companies sell cheap when maybe it just needs a little repair. I'm a fair hand at welding. Reckon there should be a good profit in sellin' good used equipment to small operators who can't afford new."

"That sounds like a great idea, honey." Marilys still worried about Way's asthma and wanted him to get work that wouldn't keep him out on the dusty roads. "Guess the problem's getting started, but we have a little saved."

The trip to Rosalie's had depleted Laurie's hoard but it was building up again and she hadn't spent her share of Mary Halsell's payment for the Ford. "I can put in seventy dollars."

"I'll give my Ford money," Buddy volunteered, puffing out his chest with an entrepreneurial glance at Everett.

Sighing, Everett relinquished his weekly movie and chocolate soda. "It's not much, but I'll kick in what's left over from my board and what I have to send Pa."

"No, you won't," commanded Laurie. "You don't begin to eat what you pay for board so you're already helping a lot."

"That's right, son." Way looked from Buddy to Laurie. "You kiddos sure you want to sink all your money in this?"

"None of my pals own part of a business!" Buddy grinned. He shot a sidelong glance at Laurie. "If you're going to need a helper—"

"You can help after school and on weekends," Laurie said in her most quelling tone before excitement made her jump up and kiss Way on the cheek. "Oh, Way, that'll be grand! To have your own business!"

"*Our* business," corrected Way, taking her hand and Marilys's as he beamed at the boys. "I'll start huntin' bargains tomorrow but I won't quit my pumpin' job till I've delivered enough orders to let contractors and purchasing agents know I can hustle up what they need at a fair price."

"How'll you work your job and do that?" Marilys frowned.

He squeezed her hand reassuringly. "Sugar, until I can afford a big stock, I'll pretty much find my buyer before I put much money into something." When they all looked puzzled, he explained. "Let's say some major oil company wants to sell some used seamless pipe. I quote 'em a price and ask for a three-day option, or ten days, or whatever I need. If I find a buyer, I use my option, and the buyer gives me a check. I take out my profit and send the rest to the oil company. The buyer picks up his pipe, and everybody's happy."

"Looks like the company would just sell to the buyer to start with," said Everett.

"Too much trouble for a big outfit. I earn my profit by connecting the party that wants somethin' with the party that's got it. But sho', soon's as I can, I'll have a regular supply yard. I've already talked this over with Johnny. Wouldn't let him stake me like he wanted to, but I sure won't fuss at any business he sends my way."

A few days later, on a lead from Johnny, Way put together a deal for three hundred thousand feet of lapweld pipe. With the profit, he bought some tanks and a welding outfit, repaired the leaks, and swapped the tanks and some of the pooled cash for a load of seamless pipe. Within a few weeks of FDR's election, Way had done enough deals to rent a vacant lot. He'd wanted to make the sign read FIELD-KIRKENDALL SALVAGE but Laurie argued him out of that. "You can do a lot with your name, Way. The *Way* to save—the *Way* to good used equipment—the *Way* to better deals."

"Reckon so," he finally agreed. So the sign read:

*W*AY TO SAVE

*WA*Y TO BEST USED EQUIPMENT

WA*Y* TO BETTER DEALS

WAY *S*ALVAGE

The night the sign went up, Laurie was accompanying herself on the guitar as she sang in the dining room. Johnny and Crystal were at their usual corner table. Suddenly, Johnny looked startled, then joyous. Bringing Crystal's hands to his lips, he kissed them.

Laurie struck a wrong chord. What had Crystal told him? It wasn't that often, from all Laurie could see, that she said or did anything to make him glad. The woman was like a—a whirl-pool, an irresistible vortex that swallowed everything and wanted more. Laurie recovered herself enough to finish Jimmie Rodgers's "T for Texas." As she nodded and smiled her thanks at the applause, she sensed a presence.

Glancing up, she looked straight into eyes she thought tawny brown till the young man—boy, really, perhaps her own age—cocked his head so that better light revealed the green in his eyes.

"Are you Laurie?" he asked. "Laurie Field?"

"Yes." She felt spied on, taken unawares at a vulnerable moment. "Who in the world are you?"

The eagerness faded from his long, straight-planed face. When his flesh filled out to his bones, he'd make a strapping, handsome man. He already had a man's deep voice but something in his manner reminded her of Buddy. She wished she hadn't been so sharp.

"I'm Jim Halsell."

She stared. "You—you wrote my mother," he added.

"Mary Halsell?"

The eagerness was back. He nodded. "You met me in the camp outside Eden." He grinned. "You were Larry then."

Laurie rose, setting down the guitar, and warmly offered her hand. "I'm glad to see you again, Jim. Have you had supper?"

"No. I just got to town."

From the rumpled, gaunt look of him, she suspected he'd come on a freight and had missed a lot of meals. She remembered how that was. "I haven't eaten, either. Let's take that little table by the window and talk while we have a bite. The *chilies rellenos* are real good."

A rush of scarlet covered his freckles. "Sorry I can't treat you, but I—I don't have a dime."

"You don't need it. My meals are free when I'm working and I can have a guest now and then as long as I don't overdo it." She'd never tried it but if there was a question, she could settle up quietly.

To spare the waitresses, who were rushed as was usual on Friday nights, she placed their order in the kitchen, asking the cook to give Jim doubles, and went back to join him and cross the room to their table. Johnny watched, frowning. She gave him a brilliant smile.

"Who's your feller, Laurie?" called a black-haired Cajun driller she'd refused to date. "Better toss him back in the lake to grow a little!"

Jim stopped beside the driller, who was short but bull-chested, and renowned for stomping his opponents into the mud. "I reckon, sir, I'm growed enough to say that you better respect this lady."

The Cajun blinked coal-bright eyes. He started to scoot back his chair, then shrugged and grinned. "No offense, youngster. You bet I respect that lady. Just call me jealous."

To Laurie's surprise, Jim pulled out a chair for her and pushed it in before he took his own. Johnny did that for Crystal but most men didn't bother. "I want you to tell me everything you remember about my father," she said. "But first, how's your mother and sister and little Rob?"

"Rob's in second grade and just fine." Jim's mouth was straight but it curved tenderly as he spoke of his kid brother. "He's everybody's pet. Bernice—well, she's really why I'm here."

"How come?"

He studied his big hands. "Mom—she's—well, she's expecting a baby. She's having trouble, probably because she's older, so she had to quit her job. Her husband, he's a good man, I guess, and cares about her, but he can't see why a girl needs an education. He thinks Bernice ought to quit school and help Mom till she's up after the baby comes."

"And then?"

He shrugged. "He wants her to do housework for other folks or get some kind of job. Says she'll get married by the time she's eighteen so what's the use of wasting her time in school?"

"What does your mother say?"

"Oh, she wants Bernice to finish high school but she's not going to fight her husband about it, especially since Bernice isn't set on school herself."

"Buddy's the same way. I'm having to browbeat him to make him finish ninth grade." Laurie sighed. "I hope by then he'll have more sense. But how are you going to keep Bernice in school if she doesn't care and her stepfather wants her to quit?"

"*I* want her to stay in school," Jim said. "Before Dad finally died—it took a while and hurt bad—I promised him I'd see that Bernice and Rob got their educations." The angle of his jaw ridged tight. "A girl can't always count on a husband taking care of her. Look what happened to Mom and Dad. The way I see it, a girl needs to be able to make a living same as a man. Maybe more, since she may get left with kids to raise."

Jim might be young but he had a level head on his shoulders. It was too bad no one had cared as much about his schooling as he did about Bernice's and Rob's. The *chilies rellenos* came with refried beans and rice. Jim sailed into his with such gusto that Laurie suspected it was his first square meal since leaving home. She ate slowly in order not to finish before he demolished his double portions.

"The deal I worked out with Mom, her husband, and Bernice," said Jim when half the spicy food had disappeared, "is that I'll send enough money to make up for what Bernice could earn if she weren't in school. Figured the best way to do that was hit the oil fields. Mom didn't like me coming way out here, but she felt better when I said I'd look you up." He cast a shy glance from beneath sun-bleached lashes. "You know, we kind of feel like you're family, Laurie, on account of your daddy. He sure was good to us kids—to all of us."

Laurie's eyes stung. "I want to hear about him but I—I'm afraid I'll cry. And Buddy ought to hear, too. If you don't mind sleeping on the floor, you can come home with me tonight and stay till you get a job." She looked sideways toward Johnny. He was scowling at them. That sent a thrill of triumph through her. "I know a lot of drillers and I'm sure one of them can take you on. But we'll try first with that dark-haired man sitting back there with the blond woman."

Jim looked and whistled under his breath. "She sure is pretty."

"If you like that type."

"Who doesn't?" Grinning, Jim attacked his last *relleno.* "Your friend's really giving me the evil eye. I wouldn't bet on his hiring me."

"If he doesn't, we'll get you on someplace else." Laurie went to get their coffee and chunks of cherry cobbler, cutting Jim's extra big and mounding it with vanilla ice cream. As she set it in front of Jim, Johnny made his way to their table.

"Introduce me to your friend, Laurie."

It was an order, not a request. Laurie bristled but then remembered she wanted Johnny to give Jim a job. If Johnny took him on, he'd keep an eye out for him the way he did for Everett. The oil patch was a rough, dangerous place. It didn't hurt a bit to have someone experienced sort of look out for you when you first started.

"This is Jim Halsell," she said. When Johnny's frown deepened, she added, "He's the oldest of the family Daddy sort of

lived with out in California. I've told you about that." She
swallowed at the tight lump in her throat. "The Halsells *were*
Daddy's family there at the end, I guess." *He died for one of
them, bought a child with his life. I can't let that go for nothing,
can I? They have to amount to something.*

"Oh." Johnny looked a little sheepish but he scanned the
younger man closely as he put out his hand. Jim had risen. He
was taller than Johnny but beside him looked awkward, all
arms and legs. Johnny's every motion showed control, command of a body he'd learned to use to full advantage. "Glad to
meet you, Jim. I'm John Morrigan. What brings you out this
way?"

"Looking for a job in the oil field, Mr. Morrigan."

Johnny wasn't all that much older. He gave Jim a sharp look
and apparently decided the boy wasn't being a smart-aleck.
"Got experience?"

"No, sir, not working on a rig, but I've worked on roads, dug
irrigation ditches, driven trucks, and all such stuff as that. You
got something I can do?"

"I'll try you. If you're not scared of working with nitro."

"Johnny!" Laurie remonstrated.

"My last helper went in business for himself," Johnny said.
"If you're game, be at my office at seven tomorrow morning.
It's south down this street on the edge of the field."

Jim shook hands again. "I'll be there. Thanks, Mr. Morrigan! I'll do my darnedest to make you a good hand."

"You will or I can't keep you. Nitro's nothing to fool around
with." With a nod, Johnny went back to Crystal, who was
standing, arms crossed, tapping her foot.

"Looks like she's in a big hurry," Jim said.

"She likes to dance."

Jim's smile broadened appreciatively. "I'd sure like to dance
with her—except I don't know how and even if I did, I'd be
scared to ask."

Laurie made a noncommittal sound. Was Jim making com-
parisons between her and Crystal? If he was, did he see her,
Laurie, as immature and unformed as she found him beside
Morrigan? Jim slanted her a quizzical glance.

"Know something, Laurie? I saved up enough this summer to ask a girl I liked out for a movie and a malt. Her dad met me on the front porch. I didn't have notions past maybe kissing her good-night if she'd let me, but he made me so nervous I didn't even try that." He chuckled at the memory, then sobered. "That girl's daddy didn't look me over half as close as your Mr. Morrigan did. He some kind of kin?"

"No. I'll tell you about it later, Jim. Right now I have to play and sing for another hour or so. If you want to go to our place—"

"I want to hear you," he said with a look that balmed her feelings. She knew his gaze followed her admiringly as she went to the front of the room and picked up the guitar.

All right, he wasn't a man. But he wasn't an ordinary seventeen-year-old, either, any more than she was. She hoped from the bottom of her heart, as if her own pride and worth were at stake, that he could handle any task Johnny gave him and come back for more.

24

Jim stuck. Inside of a week, he was mixing "soup," filling torpedoes, and driving the explosives truck. He slept on the floor of the trailer till he got his first paycheck. When Marilys refused the board he tried to pay back, he bought her the biggest box of Whitman's chocolates and a huge basket of fruit and nuts. Johnny had found him some heavy laced boots and an old hat so after his board and room were paid, most of the rest of his check went to California to keep his sister in school.

Of course they invited him for Christmas dinner served mid-afternoon of the holiday, and had a green plaid shirt for him under the tree. After they sang carols and opened presents, Buddy asked, "Remember that tumbleweed we decorated in Black Spring? Boy, does that seem a long time ago!"

"Five years." Marilys's voice was soft and her hand slipped

into Way's. "It was the first happy Christmas I'd had since I was a girl but all of them since have been beautiful."

Way smiled at her and treasured her hand between both of his. "Before that, I'd plumb lost track of Christmas, Fourth of July, Thanksgiving—holidays don't matter when you're on the tramp."

"We always had a big tree on the farm," said Jim. "But we never could afford it out in California. Mom always found a little branch of something green, though, off an orange tree or bush. We'd sing carols, and she'd read us the Christmas story out of her New Testament. Then we'd pop corn and a couple of times, we could afford to make taffy. When Mom and Dad weren't flat broke, they'd buy each of us kids something we needed, socks, shoes, overalls, or whatever." He lowered his head. "We had a tree and presents after Mom got her job but it wasn't the same, not without Dad."

They all looked back to times after which nothing could ever be the same. This was Everett's first Christmas away from home. How could he not miss Rosalie and his brothers and sisters? For Marilys, Laurie thought, those days must have been before she met Dub and set off on that long road that had only ended when they found Way chained to the jail trees. Way could be remembering his childhood and those few years he'd had a wife and baby girl.

"We're all here together, and that's wonderful." Laurie smiled through a haze of tears, reached out to touch Jim's arm. "Some worlds end but if we hang on, another one begins."

He turned to her, hazel eyes brilliant. "That's right." He looked around at the others. "You've all helped me start this one."

Way drew Marilys to her feet and kissed her on the lips. He did that without any embarrassment. "Right now, folks," he said, "a rumblin' under my ribs allows it's time we started dinner!"

When they had feasted and the dishes were done, twilight was falling. Each Christmas, Laurie had continued to give a gift to her father and mother by helping someone in need. This year, she'd filled a Christmas card with five twenty-dollar bills saved from her earnings. In order to accumulate that much after investing in Way's salvage business, she'd forgone new clothes and skipped movies and hot-fudge sundaes. The envelope would go to the family of a roughneck who'd been crushed a few days ago.

"I'm going out for a little while," she said, pulling on her coat.

Jim rose immediately and helped her get her other arm into the sleeve. "It's nearly dark. I'll go with you."

It was part of this ritual to do it alone, in secret. "Thanks, Jim, but no one will bother me."

"Maybe not, but I'd feel better if—"

"It's nice of you, but please—I'd rather go alone." She smiled at him, tied on a scarf, pulled on mittens, and went out.

Cold nipped her face, chilled her legs in the nylons that had come on the market last year and were swiftly replacing silk stockings because they were cheaper and wore longer. She knew the roughneck's widow lived in a shack south of the railroad tracks close to a supply yard. Her husband's friends would surely have taken up a collection to help with the funeral and expenses till she got a job or went home to her folks, but with three small children, the woman could make good use of the money in the card.

The camp for oil workers, sprawling out from the older town, was just like Sludge Town in Black Springs except in these comparatively prosperous times, there were more trailers and newer trucks and cars. Just about every window showed a brightly lit Christmas tree, and a joyful medley of carols from phonographs or radios mixed with laughter. Laurie prayed that all these people would be alive and safe next year, and that the awful war would have ended, though it seemed to be spreading, getting worse. If America had to enter the fight—

She shuddered. Surely Buddy would escape since he was not quite thirteen, but Everett and Jim and most of the men she knew would be called up unless they asked for exemptions because they worked in the oil field and oil was vital. Johnny might even volunteer, no matter what Dub and Crystal said.

Cold to the heart in spite of her warm bundling, Laurie

paused at the shack. That tree must have been set up and ornamented with foil icicles, gilt ropes, and lights before the father died. Two little carrot-topped boys zoomed toy airplanes past each other. A dark-haired woman in a rocker held a girl child of perhaps three who had fallen asleep cuddling a new doll. The woman stared blindly till a whoop from one of her sons made her rouse and shush them.

Three young lives depending on her. It was a heavy load, but just as she'd held Christmas, the mother would have to keep going because of the children. She was pretty in spite of her hollow eyes. With luck, the children wouldn't grow up without a father. *Mama, Daddy*—Laurie thought, *this is for you.*

She tucked the envelope in the screen door, knocked, and ran. That was part of the gift, too, for the person not to know. Hidden by the night, she stopped to watch the woman open the door and find the envelope, whirled at a sound behind her.

Two shadows grappled. "It's all right, Laurie." That was Johnny's voice. "I was just seein' why this fella was tagging you."

"Mr. Morrigan!" Jim's voice thinned as if shocked back to boyhood. "Gol-lee! You like to scared me to death!" Jim gulped and swallowed. "Laurie wouldn't let me walk with her so I followed to make sure no one made her trouble."

"You did right," Johnny admitted, releasing the younger man. "Laurie, maybe I can guess why you didn't want someone along, but it's not real smart to be out alone after dark."

"But—"

"Don't argue, kid. No sober man would hurt you, but when a guy's drunk, there's just no tellin'." He linked his arm through hers. "Come on. I was headed for your place when I noticed a man keeping away from the streetlights and figured he was up to no good."

Forlornly, Jim said, "You're not mad at me, Laurie?"

She squeezed his hand and laughed. "Of course not. You're the one who almost got clobbered. Come on back and we'll make some fudge."

"Reckon I'd better not. My landlady said I could use her

phone tonight to phone Mom and the kids. I'd better call before it gets late."

He hadn't released her hand. He pressed it hard and suddenly, transferred from his other hand, there was something in her palm. "Thanks for a real nice Christmas, Laurie. Good night, sir."

"Mmmf," said Johnny, without much grace. "Better turn in early, Jim. I'll pick you up at four in the morning so we can shoot that well over by Enid."

"I'll be out front, Mr. Morrigan."

He moved away, vanishing in the night. " 'Mr!' " growled Johnny. "He makes me feel like I'm ninety!"

"He's just being respectful. Good grief, Johnny, why were you such a grouch? Isn't he making you a good helper?"

"He is or he wouldn't still be working for me. But anyone with one eye closed and the other half open can see that he's crazy about you."

"We're just the closest thing he has here for family." What right did Johnny have to fuss about her friends when he was always bringing that red-clawed platinum cat, Crystal, into the restaurant for Laurie to wait on? Voice rising, Laurie demanded, "Anyhow, if he *does* like me, what's wrong with that? He's a nice boy."

Johnny's laugh was more of a bark. "That's the point. He's a boy. You grew up too fast, Laurie." His voice roughened. She tripped on a hole in the sidewalk and he steadied her in immediate reflex. "You need a man grown up enough to be a kid with you sometimes but who can still take care of you."

"I can take care of myself."

"Sure you can. Along with any stray lamb who bleats around for sympathy!" His fingers tightened almost savagely on her wrist. "Damn it, Laurie, I want better than that for you!"

Startled at his intensity, she was at once gratified yet indignant at his concern. *I want a lot better than Crystal for you.* She couldn't say that. In the haughty tone she assumed with importunate men, she said, "Does that mean you don't want me to date anyone without running him by you for approval?"

Instead of squelching him, that brought a chuckle. "Not a

bad idea," he said with rueful humor. "No, to be honest, Way and Marilys can judge a man as well as I can—and I reckon you'd pay more attention to them than you will to me." He sighed and shoved back his hair. "What worries me about young Jim is that he comes and goes like one of the family. I'm scared first thing I know, he will be."

"He's just like a—"

"Brother," Johnny finished. "That may be how you feel, honey, but believe me, it's not what he's thinkin'. I like Jim. He's smart, keeps a cool head, and does more than he's asked. If he was five or six years older—"

"Huh! Then you'd say he was too old and worldly!"

Johnny stiffened. Then he laughed. "I probably would. Come right down to it, Laurie, I guess I'll never think anyone's good enough for you." His tone softened, warmed Laurie even in the chill wind. "Funny. We only knew each other a day but all those years, I kept remembering you—hoped your Daddy had found a good job and sent for you, wondered if you played that harmonica. I've met hundreds of people since then but you're the one who stayed in my mind."

"Maybe that's because you were in my mind." Laurie's mouth felt dry. This was probably as close as she could ever come to telling him how she felt. "I don't know what I'd have done without the harmonica and the songs you taught me. When I played, it made me feel close to you."

He folded her hand up inside his to completely protect it. "So you worked a charm on me without even knowing the Choctaw words?"

"I don't know. But I always prayed that you were well." It was very hard to speak. "I always prayed I'd see you again."

"Well, here I am. Big as life and twice as ornery." His laughing tone was a caress. "Proves the old saying, kid. 'Be careful what you wish for—you may get it.' "

I didn't wish for Crystal. But this closeness, this honesty, was more than she had hoped for. She'd be a fool not to be grateful for what she had of him. As they walked along, blanketed in the night, it was easy to pretend they were the only ones in the world.

Then he said, proudly, "Crystal, she's going to marry me."

Laurie never knew what she said, how she endured the hour Johnny spent at the trailer. From his jacket, he produced turquoise earrings for Marilys, a silver tie clasp for Way, tooled billfolds for Buddy and Everett, and for Laurie, a gold pin shaped like a guitar.

She thanked him and fetched his gifts from under the tree, a pullover of softest wool she had knitted with help from Marilys in setting in the arms and doing the neck and cuffs, gray-green to match his eyes. Way and the boys had bought him a special compass to fit in his truck. Marilys, undertaking the task of finding something for Crystal, had used their pooled money for a half-ounce of Crystal's favorite French perfume.

While Johnny had fruitcake and coffee, he gave the others his news. Way's jaw dropped. "Boy howdy! Never thought—"

Marilys broke in. "That's—exciting, Johnny. Are you getting married here?"

"Just stopping by a justice of the peace on our way to New Orleans. Dub's blowing us to a honeymoon there."

Laurie tried not to bad-mouth W.S. around Johnny but it got her goat when Johnny spoke with admiring affection of the man who'd kept them on the run for years, had almost destroyed Way, and even lately had tried to blackmail Marilys. It was a good thing Redwine seemed no more eager to encounter Laurie than she was to see him. Since he never ate at the hotel and was often gone for weeks at a time, she could almost forget what a threat he'd been. Almost. She didn't trust him, never would, but surely he'd learned some lessons and was clever enough not to try to dominate Johnny as he had his son and would have her if he'd had the chance.

"Dub says we've got to name our first boy after him," Johnny said and grinned. He looked so puffed up that Laurie wanted to jab him.

For once, she wished he would go, and was glad when he did. Escaping to her small room, she threw herself on the bed and wept stormily into her pillow, thankful that her sobs were muffled by the phonograph.

In the back of her mind, never quite acknowledged, hope

must have lurked that Crystal would tire of Johnny or he'd get fed up with her. This sealed it, though.

Head throbbing, Laurie went to the bathroom and cupped cold water to her swollen eyes. Back in her room, starting to hang up her coat, she remembered the small wrapped object Jim had slipped in her hand as he said good-night. She'd put it in her pocket. Now, taking it out, she untied the gold cord, unwrapped the tissue, and opened a little box engraved with the name of the town's finest jeweler.

Inside was a dainty gold filigree heart on a chain. No note but it said enough. She had done nothing to encourage Jim but a stab of guilt mixed with her annoyance, regret, and yes, the pleasurable sensation of knowing she was important to a young man as enterprising as Jim. He'll get over it, she told herself, but she revised the decision she'd made right after Johnny's shattering revelation.

She wouldn't begin accepting Jim's invitations to the movies. That wouldn't be fair. She never could love him. But she wasn't going to mourn after Johnny, either. She was going to start dating.

Johnny and Crystal were married on New Year's Day, 1941. They were on their honeymoon when Marilys kept stealing worried glances at Laurie as they walked to work one morning. "Honey," she said in a hesitant manner. "You didn't get in till after two this morning."

"We drove to Woodward to a dance."

"That's late hours when you have to work next morning."

"I can manage."

"Can you?" Marilys stepped in front of her, compelled her to stop. "Laurie, sweetheart, what are you doing? All this time you've never gone out with a man. Now, except for the evenings you play at the hotel, you're out every night till at least midnight."

"You and Way used to worry because I didn't date," retorted Laurie.

"This isn't dating. This is—" Marilys shook her head. Her deep blue eyes delved into Laurie's as she caught her hands.

"Dear, you started this right after Johnny said he was marrying Crystal. Well, he has. Running wild can't change that."

Flushing, Laurie started to break loose but the love and concern in Marilys's eyes melted her. Going into the older woman's arms, Laurie gave her a hug. "I haven't done anything wrong, darling! Haven't even kissed anyone but Matt Sherrod, and him only at the door."

"Way says that Sherrod has such a hot temper that he has trouble keeping a crew together in spite of his being a top-notch driller."

"I'm not his crew."

"He's got a name with women." Marilys still frowned. "Besides, he must be close to thirty."

"Well, that should tickle Johnny. He thinks Jim is lots too young."

"If you're doing this to make John Morrigan jealous—"

"Jealous? When he's got Crystal?"

Marilys gave up. "All right, honey. Just don't hurt yourself." She paused, then reached for Laurie's hands. "Don't get mad but—things do happen. If you—well, if you need any help, promise you'll tell me."

If I get pregnant, you mean, Laurie would have flashed back angrily except for knowing that when Marilys was a girl and needed rescue, there had been none. So, as gently as she could, Laurie said, "I promise. But please, Marilys, try not to worry." She grinned. "I hate beer, don't like the taste of anything stronger, and I choke when I try a cigarette."

"I'm glad you do," said Marilys, with feeling.

A tool pusher Laurie liked to dance with moved to Texas. One driller stopped asking for dates and she thought it was because she wouldn't kiss him, even on their fourth date. Jim seldom came around. When he did, he watched her with such misery that she tried to fend off guilt by getting angry. It wasn't her fault he had a crush on her. Why didn't he take out some cute fifteen-year-old and behave like the brother Laurie wished he were?

Without knowing quite how it happened, she was soon dating no one but Matt Sherrod. The driller was tall and rangy with eyes that were electrically blue in a thin, sun-browned face. His long, straight nose gave him an eagle look. They went to movies and respectable places where there was dance music. He never had more than two beers or one bourbon, always drove her straight home, always kissed her just once at the door.

That single kiss, though, was lasting longer. Matt was holding her closer, his mouth was hungry, and she felt his trembling, the sledging of his heart. One morning, when she brought Johnny's breakfast coffee, he scooted back his chair and eyed her sternly.

"Are you getting serious about Matt Sherrod?"

Good grief! If anxious parents were any worse than friends—

"Matt's fun," she said lightly.

"Is that all?"

She felt blood mount to her face. "I can't see that it's any of your business, Johnny Morrigan."

His jaw hardened and his eyes flashed green before he took a long swallow of coffee. When he spoke, his tone was even and controlled. "You know it's my business, Laurie. I care about you."

Then why, why, *didn't you wait for me? Why did you marry Crystal?* Laurie loved him in spite of that, through that, through her bitter hurt. She had to say honestly, "I like Matt, Johnny, but I don't know him very well. We don't talk much. But he doesn't—he hasn't—" She broke off, coloring even more hotly.

Johnny sighed. "Matt and I keep turning up at the same fields. When I heard he's made it clear around the oil patch that you're his girl, I dropped it in his ear real casuallike that I've known you since you were a kid, that you're sort of my little sister. Since you are, I think you'd better know something peculiar about Matt."

Laughter bubbled to Laurie's lips. Marilys, without going into details, had recently explained to her that there were men who preferred men and women who cared only for women. "You don't mean he's a fairy?"

Now Johnny reddened. "Not hardly," he said with a wry laugh. "Matt collects virgins." When Laurie stared at him,

Johnny went on doggedly, still crimson to the tips of his ears. "There's a name for guys like that. They can't seem to get worked up unless they're with a virgin. And once she's not, they lose interest."

Skepticism overcoming embarrassment—after all, Johnny had started this unseemly if fascinating conversation—Laurie asked, "How does a man know that? Matt's never asked me."

"He knows."

"I'm sure I don't see how." Other breakfasters came in. Going to pour them coffee, Laurie threw over her shoulder, "Thanks for the warning—I think! But I haven't seen any reason to worry."

That wasn't quite true. Those lengthening, ardent kisses; the hard length of his body molding her closer to him when once they'd kissed good-night at arm's length. She was intrigued with Matt, flattered at his gallantries, and the lightning-flash attraction that often flowed between them at the touch of hands or eyes made her feel desirable, a woman, not a child. But even if he were jealous, Johnny wouldn't lie to her. Maybe she had better cut down on the time she spent with Matt.

Matt had bought a lot of pipe and other supplies from Way. As the salvage business grew, Way was working almost full time at that as well as holding down his pumping job. Marilys and Laurie worried about him.

"Now you've got some stock laid in, we can get by on what Marilys and I are earning," Laurie argued.

"I don't aim to live off my womenfolk," Way growled.

"Shucks," laughed Marilys, kissing him. "We're aiming to live off you soon as you have the biggest salvage business in Oklahoma!"

"That's right," Laurie said, chuckling. "Think of the deals you could make if that was all you had to tend to!"

Way rubbed his chin. "Well—It would be handy if I could go off hunting for good buys and customers." He took his wife's hand and held it to his cheek. "You already keep the books, honey. Maybe it won't be too long till the business pays enough for you to work in it full time. Office manager. How does that sound?"

"Terrific!" The office was an ancient railroad car inhabited by a telephone, chair and table, and shelves holding small pieces of equipment. Way had given it a new coat of barn-red paint and Marilys had made curtains of harmonizing striped canvas.

"Remember, I've got a bunch of cousins we can hire as they graduate," Laurie said. "Not to mention Buddy."

"He's been good help after school and weekends," Way praised. "But Laurie, that brother of yours is headed for the oil field, at least for a while."

If the army didn't get him first. At the end of February, Way gave up his pumping job and plunged into the business with a zest that made him act more like he was having fun than working dawn to dusk and sometimes later.

Meanwhile, in that fearsome but distant war across the ocean, Britain's forces in North Africa wrested part of Ethiopia from the Italians. German troops overran Greece and Yugoslavia. The Lend-Lease Act of that March 1941, permitted all-out aid to Britain and other countries battling the Axis powers, Germany, Italy, and Japan. In June, Germany attacked the USSR along a front more than one thousand miles long, laid siege to Leningrad, and moved on Moscow. Hitler and his blitzkrieg seemed invincible, though at least he had given up on a quick invasion and conquest of England.

"Only a question of *when* we get into it, not *if,*" Way said. That summed up the general feeling.

The family took a big step that summer. "That nice old lady, Mrs. Barnes, who has dinner every Sunday in the hotel and lives by herself with her cats in that big house on Oak Street is going to live with her daughter in Dallas," said Marilys. "She can't take her cats. She told me if we'd take good care of the beasties, she'd sell us the house, mostly furnished, for a thousand down and fifty a month for a total of four thousand with no interest." She glanced from Way to Laurie, including Buddy and Everett in the sweep.

"Can we do it? Do we want to try? Even with separate rooms for each of you young folks, there's three rooms in one wing we could rent and more than cover the payments, water, gas, and electricity."

"Married feller offered us six hundred for this trailer," said Way. Marilys had surely already asked what he thought. "The salvage business isn't bringing us in money because I've been plowing the profits into more stock and we paid cash for that new truck."

"I've got eighty dollars saved," Marilys said. "I expect we could borrow the rest, using the truck and salvage business for security. But Laurie, you have money in the trailer, too. What do you say?"

"I say let's buy the house!"

A chance to have a real home with foundations laid on land that would belong to them? It was a dream Laurie had always cherished, never knowing when she would be able to let herself hope for it. To have it now seemed too good to be true. Laurie had often admired the gracious old house, built by the town's first doctor, with towered balconies and a broad veranda. She'd thought it a shame that it didn't get a coat of new white paint.

Surrounded by an ornamental wrought-iron fence, it set well back off the street, shaded by oaks and box elders. A neighbor's teenage son kept the grass mowed, but irises, daffodils, four-o'clocks, pansies, nasturtiums, zinnias, and marigolds had escaped their beds and borders, rioting as they pleased. There was a garage in back, a graceful wrought-iron gazebo, an overgrown vegetable garden, and that spring, apple and plum trees had bloomed in clouds of pink and white.

Controlling her excitement enough to be coherent, Laurie said, "I've saved almost two hundred dollars." As well as buying such of Buddy's clothes that he wouldn't pay for out of his paper route and summer earnings—Way insisted on paying him—Laurie insisted on paying half the groceries and utilities. She and Marilys never worked out the groceries precisely, each just paying for whatever they picked up, and Everett put in three dollars a week toward groceries and expenses. Laurie turned to Buddy. "Is it all right with you to put our share of the trailer in on the house?"

"Do I get my own room?" asked Buddy.

"Take your pick," invited Marilys.

"Then let's do it."

"You kiddos being underage," said Way, "I don't reckon your names can go on the deed just yet. But we'll get a lawyer to draw up a paper that'll show you as half-owners and our heirs." He winked at Marilys. " 'Course, my sweetie here is gonna outlive me so she'll need a lifetime estate."

"You're not getting off that easy," warned Marilys. "Why do you think I've weaned you down to two cups of coffee a day? You'll outlive me and marry some good-looking widow!" She punched his shoulder in mock outrage. He caught her hand.

"What I really hope is we can go out together or purty close to it," he said. "But for now, let's talk to Miz Barnes and buy us a home!"

The cats meowed accusingly or plaintively for a week after their mistress tearfully stroked them good-bye. "Cats get more attached to places than to people," Mrs. Barnes said, trying to comfort herself. "Even if my daughter wasn't allergic to cats, I imagine they'd run away. Maybe you can keep them inside till they kind of settle down."

Laurie smiled reassuringly into the misted blue eyes. "We'll do that, ma'am. They'll miss you, but we'll take good care of them. They're absolutely beautiful. How do you keep their coats so soft and shiny?"

"I brush and comb them every day." Mrs. Barnes glowed like a proud mother. "Winks won't keep still long so I have to do a little whenever she'll let me. And I put brewer's yeast in their food. Runcible gets hairballs sometimes so if he starts acting droopy, I give him lubricating medicine the vet prescribed and that takes care of it. Both cats are fixed. I can't abide the way most folks let their cats have poor little kittens that wind up starving or in the pound."

Both cats were black as ravens, except for a small white fluff on Runcible's front. He had a long, sinuous tail and golden eyes. Winks looked part Manx with a sleek, small head and lynxlike raised hindquarters. Her stub tail could twitch every bit as eloquently as Runcible's appendage. Since Runcible hissed at her attempted groomings, Winks's thwarted motherly instincts were lavished by her tiny rough tongue on any convenient human hand.

On her first night in her airy new room on the second floor, Laurie woke to a sudden pressure on the mattress. Something nestled at the back of her legs. There was a muffled thud and another body curled against her feet.

In her longing for a pet, she'd always wanted a dog, but soon she wouldn't have traded. Like the cat in Kipling's *Just So Stories,* Runcible and Winks walked by their wild lones, but when she was in the house or yard, they were usually *there,* observing. It was companionship that neither made demands nor accepted any.

Mrs. Barnes and her lawyer husband, dead ten years ago, had raised five children in the big house. After her daughters and son had collected the family antiques and sentimental treasures they wanted, the house still had enough furniture, not only for the Field-Kirkendall part, but once assorted bureaus, beds, chairs, and stands were cleaned of their shrouds of dust and brought down from the attic, for the three east wing bedrooms as well. Two drillers and a tool pusher were so eager to rent them that they helped move in the reclaimed furnishings. They would share the bathroom added on to the small side veranda where they had their own entrance, so the family would scarcely know they were there.

In the attic, Laurie found a graceful wicker bedstead and chest. She painted them ivory to go with the claw-footed gilt-trimmed dresser and what Marilys called an armoire. It was the first time she'd ever had a large private mirror, and now she had two, the one on the armoire almost full-length. Two big windows and a french door opened to the balcony. The age-yellowed net curtains shredded when she washed them. She made new ones of filmy heaven blue, and searched stores till she found the exact same shade in an oval rug to put by the bed with its freshly laundered dust ruffle under the bird quilt. The phonograph was in the big living room where Marilys could play it, too, but Laurie's books were in the shelf next to the bed, and Mama's cedar chest and New Testament were on the dresser.

Laurie thought it the most perfect room any girl could have, and the house the most wonderful house with its stairways, hidey-holes, and spaciousness.

"I can't really believe this place belongs to us," she confessed to Marilys, and added hastily, "or will, as soon as the rent pays it out."

"I can't believe it, either." Marilys returned Laurie's hug and smiled her dimpled smile. "I bet we'll believe it, though, by the time we get through scraping off the old paint and putting on some new! All those curved posts and casement windows and porches! And when we get through with the outside, I'd sure like to paper inside."

"We can paper a room at a time," Laurie said. "Stop for a while when we get tired. It'll be fun."

To her, and, she suspected, to Marilys and Way, it was a joy to work on their home, have a home to work on. If only Mama and Daddy could have had anything half as nice! That regret was the only one to taint Laurie's delight except for knowing that she'd never share this house—or any other—with Johnny. Could she have been with him, she'd gladly trade for a boom-town tent.

$$25$$

She was playing the guitar at the hotel one Friday night in August when Johnny came in, face begrimed, still in stained work clothes. Speaking under the applause, he said hoarsely, "Can you come over to the hospital, Laurie? Jim Halsell's hurt."

At the piano, Marilys had heard. Rising, she asked the question Laurie couldn't choke out. "What's wrong?"

"Gas forced a nitro charge back up the hole. I yelled that it was coming in time for everyone to run before the derrick blew up, but Jim's leg got pinned under a length of girder." Johnny wiped at his sweating forehead. "Jim'll live, but he may lose the leg."

"Go on, Laurie." Marilys gave her a gentle shove. "I'll play till closing time and then come by."

"Jim doesn't want us to call his mother," Johnny said, as he whipped the truck through alleys and side streets to get to the hospital faster. "Says he'll talk to her himself when he knows about the leg. He's one gutsy kid. I wish—" Johnny slapped the wheel as he pulled into the parking lot and stopped.

Laurie jumped out in the same instant. Johnny caught her arm. "Don't run. It won't make him feel better for you to rush in like he's dying."

"Did—did he ask for me?"

"He won't ask for anyone or anything. But Pete's sake, Laurie, anyone with half an eye can see he worships the ground you walk on."

"That's because of Daddy."

Johnny's long strides were almost noiseless on the tiled hall floor. "Nope." He steered her around a corner. "It's because of Laurie." He paused outside a half-shut door. "Right now you can help him more than anyone."

As they stepped in, a nurse was removing a hypodermic needle from Jim's arm. Clear fluid from a bottle suspended from a movable rack trickled through tubing to the inside joint of his arm where it was taped in place. Under the sheet, Jim's right leg seemed to be propped up on pillows.

"Dr. Mitchell's going to operate just as soon as he's through with a car-wreck emergency," the nurse said. "You can stay with Jim till then but don't let him talk much." She disappeared with a swish of starched white skirts.

"Jim?" Not knowing what to say, Laurie took his brown hand, was shocked. How cold it felt, how nerveless! She closed her other hand around it, hoping to warm the lax fingers.

His eyes opened. Dilated pupils almost blotted out the brownish-green of the irises. His hand tightened. "Laurie. Guess I must have tripped—Stupid. All this trouble—"

"You didn't trip, Jim." Johnny's voice was gruff. "The end of that damned girder got you."

323

Jim's pupils contracted slightly as they shifted to Johnny. "Am I going to lose my leg, Mr. Morrigan?"

Muscles tightened between Johnny's cheekbones and jaws. "Jim, the doc won't know for sure till he operates. He'll save it if he can, I promise that."

Jim's pale lips went even whiter. "If he can't, tell him not to worry about the bleeding. I'd sooner die."

"I never took you for a quitter, Jim."

"I'm not! But I sure won't be a burden on other folks the rest of my life." He groaned. "There's goin' to be the hospital bill and the doctor! I'm a month ahead on the money I send Mom and Bernice worked this summer stocking shelves in a grocery store, so maybe they can manage till I get back to work. But if I can't work—"

"You can work." Johnny took Jim's other hand, careful not to disturb the intravenous tube. "Hell's bells, kid, you'll have a job as long as I do!"

"Huh! What use would I be with one leg?"

"You can still mix soup. A truck can be fixed so you could drive. There's wells to check, leases to hunt, all kinds of stuff. You'd earn your check."

Jim's face took on a bit of color. "Yeah. Guess I could do a lot of things. But I like working in the field."

"Most likely you could. I've been thinkin' it'd be fun to unlimber my old spudder and try to make some shallow wells—sort of poor-boy 'em separate from the company, you know. Couple of men can do that, takin' their time, closin' down at night." Johnny wasn't making this up for Jim's benefit; he sounded wistful. "There's not the big rush and rustle there is on a rotary rig. Kind of restful."

"I sure would like that, Mr. Morrigan, even with two good legs!"

"Anyhow, you don't have to worry about a job, or the hospital and doc, either. I carry insurance on the men who work for me personal, like you do. Even pays your salary while you're laid up. When you talk to your mother, you can tell her those checks'll be along same as ever."

"That's true? You're not making it up?"

"You wouldn't call your boss a liar, would you?" Johnny growled. "And I wish you'd quit callin' him 'Mr. Morrigan.' I'm not all that much older than you!"

Jim's deep breath was almost a sigh. He smiled faintly. "Never meant it that way, sir."

"Sir?" exploded Johnny. "Now look here, kid—"

Three nurses came in. "If you and the young lady would step out, Mr. Morrigan," said the sweet-faced gray-haired one.

Laurie pressed Jim's hand to her face and kissed it. "We'll be waiting. We'll be praying."

They stood in the hall till Jim was wheeled up the corridor. A ragged breath escaped Johnny. "Let's get some coffee. There's a snack place next to the visitors' lounge."

Laurie took one look at his haggard face. Always lean, he'd gotten thinner. "You're going to have something to eat," Laurie ruled. "Let's sit where we can watch for Marilys. She'll be along pretty soon now." As they went downstairs, Laurie asked, "Do you really have that kind of insurance on Jim?" She couldn't imagine W. S. Redwine allowing it.

" 'Ask me no questions,' " quoted Johnny with a grin. Stopping by a pay phone outside the coffee shop, he opened the shop door and shooed her inside. "Order whatever sounds good. I'll be in soon as I call Crystal and wash up a little."

Marilys passed the window while Johnny was gone. Laurie beckoned her in and explained about Jim. "We'll just have to hope," said Marilys, pressing Laurie's hand. "Matt Sherrod stopped by to walk you home. He said he'd see you tomorrow night."

"We were going to see Humphrey Bogart in *The Maltese Falcon,*" Laurie said. "I'll have to phone his landlady and leave word that I can't go anywhere for a while. When I have time off, I'm coming to visit Jim."

"Way and I'll visit him, too," Marilys said. "Goodness, here comes Johnny. He looks like something the cat would be afraid to drag in!"

"Hi, pretty lady." Johnny brushed a kiss on Marilys's forehead before he slid into the booth beside Laurie. He seemed too exhausted to eat at first but after a few sips of the steaming

---

french onion soup Laurie had ordered, he devoured it all along with several rolls, slaw, and peach cobbler. When everything was cleared away except coffee, he settled back and grinned sheepishly. "I shouldn't feel better—but I do."

"Any man feels better after fresh peach cobbler," Marilys bantered.

Johnny glanced at his watch. "Wonder how long it'll be?"

"I'll go ask the floor nurse," Laurie had been too nauseated to eat and the coffee had upset her stomach.

On her third trip, the nurse looked up and smiled. "Your friend's in the recovery room. He should be back in his room in a half-hour or so."

"His leg?"

"The doctor will come in later and explain about that." At Laurie's anguished cry, the nurse said quickly, "The young man didn't lose the leg and probably won't, but he's going to have a severe limp. It's all right if you wait in his room and see him for a few minutes. Then he needs to sleep."

The breath Laurie gulped went so deep that she realized she must have been breathing from only the top of her lungs. "Thank you," she managed at last, blinking back relieved tears. "I'll go tell the others."

The three of them were waiting when Jim was wheeled in. He smiled at them groggily. "Still got my leg."

Johnny pressed his shoulder. "You've got a job, too. Nothing to worry about except getting well. Does your mother have a telephone?"

"No, but the neighbors do and won't mind getting her." Jim grasped Johnny's wrist. "I'll call her myself tomorrow." The hazel eyes traveled to Laurie. "Maybe you could talk to Mom, too, so she'll believe I'm all right."

Laurie nodded and touched his cheek. "I'll come in the morning as soon as visiting hours start. You go to sleep now and start getting well."

"Thanks for coming—for staying. All of you—"

"Hell of a thing if we didn't!" Johnny squeezed his hand. "Sleep tight, Jim. See you tomorrow."

"You've got work to do, sir," protested Jim.

"Don't you worry about that. Don't worry about anything. And quit calling me sir!"

Jim's grin was weakly impish. "Yes, sir, Mr. Morrigan." His eyelids drooped, fluttered, drooped again, fringing his cheek. The visitors went softly into the hall, where they hugged each other. Even Johnny had tears in his eyes.

Matt was waiting for Laurie when she got off work at eight o'clock the next evening. He startled her as she stepped outside, grinding a cigarette beneath his heel.

"Hi, baby."

"Hello, Matt. Didn't Mrs. Rogers give you my message?"

"No problem." He smiled down at her. "I'll drive you to the hospital and wait while you see young Halsell. We can still make the second show."

His tone was pleasant but determined. He slipped his hand beneath Laurie's elbow, guiding her toward his silver-gray Cadillac, which had obviously just been washed and waxed. Laurie stopped.

"I can't go to the movie, Matt. Jim doesn't have any family here. I'm going to stay with him till visiting hours are over."

"Isn't that overdoing it, baby doll?" His voice was still easy but in the shadows, light flickered in the depths of his eyes, so vibrantly blue in his tanned face. "It's not your fault the kid got hurt."

How to explain the linkage that ran back to Daddy's friendship with the Halsells and his grave beneath the eucalyptus? Laurie decided not to try. She'd given Matt no reason to believe he had first claim on her time.

"I don't feel guilty, Matt. I *want* to stay with Jim, cheer him up if I can."

Matt's face darkened. "Sounds to me like more than just friendly interest."

"It's not," flashed Laurie, angered. "But if it were, it wouldn't be any of your business."

He froze. She couldn't see his face now. He was a dark, looming presence, suddenly a stranger. "That's how you feel, Laurie? We've been going out three-four times a week for a couple of months and you think what you do is none of my concern?"

"I know that it's not up to you to tell me how long I can visit a friend who's not got many other people around."

Matt said in a flat tone, "I reckon John Morrigan's going to be there a lot."

Laurie knew she was blushing, hoped Matt couldn't see the telltale color. "Jim works for Johnny. Of course Johnny'll come to see him as much as he can."

She started on. Matt strode to the Cadillac, opened the door. "Hop in. I'll drop you at the hospital."

It would be rude to refuse. Besides, her feet hurt from a day of waiting tables. Relieved that Matt was being reasonable, she leaned back against the soft cushion. "I didn't mean to sound so grouchy, Matt."

"You're tired, baby. Look, stay with Halsell an hour, that's long enough. I'll wait and drive you home."

"Oh, I can't put you out like that! Anyway, I'm staying till the nurse throws me out or Jim goes to sleep."

"I'll wait."

He was there when she came down the steps a little after ten and got out to help her into the car. "So how's the kid?"

"His leg hurts but he can stand that since it proves he still has it. I read to him till he went to sleep."

"Was Morrigan there?"

"He came by earlier."

"Guess he wanted to get home to that well-built wife of his."

"No, he had to go out to a well."

"He doesn't *have* to do much of anything the way he's got Dub Redwine eating out of his hand." Matt slanted her a veiled glance. "Some folks wonder how come they're so thick."

Laurie jerked upright. "If you mean—"

Matt raised a disclaiming hand and laughed. "I never took Morrigan for that kind myself."

A motel light winked blue and red and they passed the roadhouse at the northern edge of town. "Matt, what are we doing way out here?" She wasn't really alarmed—Matt had always been a gentleman—but her voice rose a little. "I want to get home!"

"We need to have a talk."

"I'm tired. I have to go to work early in the morning."

He grimaced. "No, baby, you don't. You don't have to go to work ever again."

A chill shot down her spine. "Of course I do, Matt. Now please take me home. We can talk tomorrow."

They were out where the only lights were the ones that gleamed from the oil field. Matt swung the Cadillac off the highway onto a dirt road. "Matt—"

"Don't get excited, doll baby. I just want a quiet place to have our talk."

In spite of knowing Matt, the back of her neck prickled. Should she yank open the door and jump out? They weren't going very fast, couldn't, on this rutted track. But his legs were a lot longer than hers. He could easily run her down. Anyhow, she was being silly. Just because he wanted to talk where they wouldn't be interrupted—

He pulled off the road. The headlights shone on scrub willow and several big cottonwoods. They must be out by the creek that angled north of town. He switched off the lights, then the ignition. It was instantly so dark that his voice seemed disembodied as it came from the heavy August night.

"I was going to wait a while, sweetness, but hell, I've made up my mind and I'm sick of watching you wear yourself to a nub. You don't have to answer me tonight. You're young and you may want to talk it over with your folks." His hands found her shoulders, even in the blackness, brought her against him. His mouth closed on hers, hard, deliberate, bruising.

This was like no other kiss Laurie had experienced, the fleeting brush of Johnny's lips on her cheek, the smooth, clumsy, questioning or ardent ones claimed on the way home from a date, usually outside her door, or even those recent lingering good-nights of Matt Sherrod's.

He had never hurt her. He did now, holding her so tight against him that she felt crushed, unable to breathe. She couldn't escape his kiss but when she pushed at his chest, his lips gentled, moved warmly, coaxingly on hers, and though he still held her, his arms relaxed till they didn't feel like constricting steel bands.

Lifting his head just a little, he laughed shakily. "Good Lord, baby, you take my breath away! I thought no woman could do that anymore!" His fingers traced from temple to chin, paused on her throat. Laurie felt the pulse surge, beat weightedly, and though he was being nice, she felt as if a great cat rested its sheathed claws across her jugular.

"Matt—"

He kissed her lightly. Even in the dark she knew he was smiling. "I want to marry you, sweetness. I want to take care of you."

"Oh, Matt, no!" The cry was wrung from her in a passion of shock and regret. In her need to ease the pain of realizing that Johnny could never be hers, it hadn't occurred to her to scruple about whether she might hurt the men she dated, cause any of them to suffer as she did. Least of all had she expected Matt Sherrod to really care about her. She welcomed the bite of his fingers, a punishment she deserved.

"I—I'm sorry, Matt." What could she say to spare his pride? "You need a gorgeous lady who'll know how to do you proud, someone a whole lot smarter and nicer than I am."

His silence frightened her more than his first roughness. She tried to move away. His grip tautened. "If this is such a big surprise to you, Laurie, I can see you need time to think it over." His tone was barely louder than a whisper. "We could be engaged—six months, maybe a year. And if—well, if you're nervous about being with a man that way, I'll bet I can make even the first time good for you."

Confidence entered his voice. His arms went back around her. What was that Johnny had said? Matt preferred virgins? Johnny wouldn't lie. That braced Laurie. She hadn't ever hinted that she loved Matt, hadn't encouraged him beyond agreeing to go out with him. That had been a mistake but there was no use making it worse.

"I'm sorry, Matt. I can't marry you."

"Why the hell not?"

"I don't love you."

He sucked in his breath. "You could learn. Listen, baby—"

"I'm not a baby!" Anger warmed Laurie. She twisted from his hands. "I love somebody else. I'm sorry that I've hurt you, really sorry, but now I want you to take me home."

He didn't respond for a moment. "And not see you anymore?" His manner was so reasonable that relief washed through her. It was embarrassing, she *was* sorry, but after all, he was a tall, handsome driller who made good money. It wouldn't take him long to find consolation.

"It doesn't make sense to go on dating, Matt."

Again, he was silent. "Matt?"

He stirred as if rousing from a dream. "Since this is our last night, do me a favor. Come sit by the creek a while."

She wanted desperately to go home but since he was being decent, granting his wish seemed a small thing. He got his jacket out of the backseat. Their feet ground the thin crust of sand, sank ankle-deep. He didn't steady her, didn't touch her, till he tossed his jacket down.

He brought her against him, forcing her so close that she couldn't bring up her knee or free her arms and hands. He sought her mouth, brutally. His teeth cut her lips. With all her strength, she tried to wrench free, stamped as hard as she could on top of his instep. He swore and brought her down, pinioning her thighs and legs with one of his while he dragged her wrists above her head with one hand and opened her blouse with the other, shoved up her bra and sucked a nipple while he pulled up her skirt, drove his fingers over her belly and between her legs. Her writhing was useless, only made him laugh.

"This is what happens to a teaser, baby. I'm going to have that sweet little juicy cherry of yours. The more you fight, the more it's goin' to hurt."

Panicked blackness shrouded Laurie's mind. She heard her own voice crying, "Daddy! Daddy!" What use in shouting for him when he was dead? But she called him anyway from the depths of terror. "Daddy! Help me!"

The fingers probing at her body withered, stopped, slowly

withdrew. She could move her hands, her lower body was no longer trapped under Matt's. He sat up, breathing jerkily.

Dazed, terrified of precipitating another attack, Laurie tried to sit up without making a sound, buried her face against her knees and fought sobs that threatened to engulf her. She somehow knew that would infuriate him.

He got to his feet. "Let's go, little girl."

He didn't speak all the way home. There he parked, waiting for her to get out. Laurie opened the door and poised one foot on the drive before she asked what she had to know.

"Matt—why did you quit?"

He gave a raspy laugh. "I know your daddy's gone. You told me how he died. But when you yelled, I swear to God that someone—something—grabbed me." He shook his head, shot her a hard glance. "You were in luck, baby, but take it from me, you may not be next time. If you're so set on John Morrigan that you can't give other guys a chance, you better not go out with them."

"I—I'm sorry."

"You better be glad." He switched on the ignition. "Run along and cuddle with your teddy bear till you grow up."

The day Jim came home from the hospital to stay with the Kirkendall-Field family till he was better, she heard that Matt Sherrod had brought in the well he was drilling, paid off his crew, and left town.

26

Early Sunday morning, December 7, 1941, wave after wave of torpedo bombers, dive bombers, and Zero fighters attacked the immense quays of Battleship Row at Pearl Harbor. Torpedoes and bombs shredded the battleship *Arizona* and killed 1,103 sailors out of the crew of 1,400. In the less than two hours before the Japanese aircraft returned to their carriers, 2,397 Americans were killed and over 1,000 wounded.

"Our guys didn't have a chance!" Johnny had stopped to see Jim shortly after the news came on the radio. He shook his head in angry bewilderment. "It was seven fifty-eight when Admiral Bellinger broadcast the warning. Two minutes later, two battleships were sinking and hundreds of our boys were dead."

"Anyhow, twenty-nine of them damn planes didn't make it back," Way said with bitter satisfaction. "That chaplain on the *New Orleans* helped the other ammunition handlers feed the guns that fired back at them bombers and Zeros. Every time one got hit, he hollered, 'Praise the Lord and pass the ammunition!' "

"I'm glad you're just about ready to drive the truck and mix the nitro again," Johnny told Jim. "As soon as that recruiting office opens in the morning, I'm signing up."

Marilys said what Laurie didn't venture. "It'll take lots of oil to fight a war. You might do more good in the oil field."

"That's what Crystal says but there's no way I'll stay out of this."

"I'll have to." Jimmy directed a glare of hatred at his crutches. "When I throw these away, I'll still limp too bad to get in even the merchant marine."

"You'll take care of things here," said Johnny.

"I'm nineteen! If it wasn't for this darned leg, I'd be One-A."

"One of us needs to run the partnership, Jim."

"What partnership?"

Johnny grinned. "The one we're settin' up tomorrow to drill some shallow wells on those old farms I've bought up. The country's going to need all the oil we can find. I'm counting on you, Jim."

Joy lit the younger man's face, then dulled. "You don't need me. Mr. Redwine's your partner."

"Not on this deal. It's not the kind of thing he gets excited about. But I do have to see him soon as he gets back from Amarillo."

"I hope the war lasts long enough for me to go!" Buddy's

fifteen-year-old voice mounted and cracked. "I'll join the air corps and shoot down a bunch of those Zeros!"

"You won't get into pilot training if you don't finish high school," Laurie warned.

"Then maybe I won't be a pilot. I think if your folks sign for you, you can get in the service when you're seventeen."

"*I* won't sign for you!"

Buddy scrunched his nose at her and turned to Way. Redwine had dropped his rights to custody so, strictly speaking, Buddy didn't have a legal guardian, though Way or Marilys put their name on his report cards.

"You'll sign for me, won't you, Way?"

"Not unless your sis goes along with it, son."

Buddy groaned. "I'll sure be glad when she's not the boss of me anymore!"

"So will I!" shot back Laurie. Too upset about Johnny to try to outglare her brother, she gave him a brief scowl and whirled on Morrigan.

"What does Crystal say about your volunteering?" she demanded.

For a split instant, Johnny's eyes went bleak before he shrugged and grinned. "Guess I'll find out when she gets back from Amarillo. Dub can't seem to make a deal without her."

Critical occupation or no, Laurie would have felt the same way had she been a man. All those young sailors trapped on torpedoed ships, all those dead marines and soldiers—

Let us win, God. Let us win and help England and the Jews and Russians and all those other people Hitler's killing!

Next day, Monday, December 8, it took Congress only six-and-one-half minutes to declare war on Japan. Laurie listened to President Roosevelt's radio address with a heavy heart and the sense of doom she used to feel in her nightmares of the end of the world.

This could be the end. It wasn't just a few countries fighting halfway across the world, but involved all the major powers. American men didn't wait to be drafted but swamped recruiting offices. Laurie was waiting on Johnny's table that noon when he told W. S. Redwine and Crystal that he had volunteered for the marines and had passed up a chance to go to officer candidate school in order to get into combat faster. He'd report next week to Parris Island in South Carolina.

"What?" Crystal's face contorted. She slammed her cup down so hard that the china shattered and sent bits of porcelain flying while black coffee splashed and trickled to the floor. Crystal's green suit escaped. She ignored Laurie, who cleaned up the mess while Crystal ranted. "You're traipsing off to war without even asking me?"

"I told both you and Dub that I'd volunteer if we got into the mess."

"What about Dub?" snapped Crystal. "Some partner you are! He gives you a chance to amount to something and you—"

Redwine closed his hand over hers. Strange how that dark hair on the backs of his hands and fingers never seemed to bleach. "Take it easy, Crys. I know how Johnny feels."

She stared at him, jaw dropping. Johnny stared, too, but his dogged expression turned to relief. "Dub, you can't guess how glad I am to hear you say that."

"Maybe I can, son." Apart from threads of white in his straw-colored hair and widening jowls, Redwine didn't look any older to Laurie than when she'd first met him over six years ago, but she supposed he had reached his early fifties. A wistful grin showed his large square teeth. "If I was ten years younger and forty pounds skinnier, I'd try to sign up myself."

"Shucks, Dub," said Johnny awkwardly, "We've got to have oil to fight this war."

"That's what *I'm* telling *you!*" shrilled Crystal.

"Lay off, Crys," chided Redwine. He tightened his grip on her. "Johnny has to do what he thinks is right. I'm proud of him for that. So will you be when you calm down."

"Dub," said Johnny, "I can't tell you how much this means—your understanding and all. I'll make it up to you some way. Now if there's something we need to do about the partnership—"

"Don't worry about a thing." Redwine leaned across the table and settled his free hand on Johnny's shoulder. "I'll take care of things, son." There was a catch in his voice. "Least I can do. Crys won't lack for anything I can buy, beg, borrow, or steal."

Going for their food, Laurie missed the next part of the conversation. When she returned, Johnny was saying, "Jim Halsell can mix that soup just as well as I can but he can't shoot wells by himself. To keep him in a job, I'm lookin' for a partway retired driller who'd dig some holes with my old spudder on a couple of farms I've bought cheap. If I can't find a driller, though, Dub, I'll count on you to give Jim work he can do."

"Like I told you, son," said Redwine benignly, "don't worry about a thing."

On December 11, Germany and Italy declared war on the United States. The big white light that blazed over the White House driveway was turned off and the nation wondered when it would go on again—when lights all over the darkened world would shine—and what they would illuminate. It would not be the same world, never, ever again.

Johnny's train left in the afternoon before Laurie went back to work at the restaurant. At first she resolved not to see him off, stand on the platform with Redwine and Crystal as he disappeared, but as the time drew near, she had to seize that last glimpse of him.

After adding cumin, cilantro, and chilies to the beans stewing for Way, Everett, and Buddy—she and Marilys got their meals at the hotel—Laurie washed her hands and took off her apron. "I'm going down to the depot."

Marilys shot her a quick glance of sympathy. "Shall I go with you, dear?"

Laurie shook her head and forced a grin. "I'll probably lurk out of sight while Johnny kisses Crystal good-bye and then I'll go to the rest room and howl till I'm fit to come to work."

"If you want to take off tonight—"

"I'll do better working."

On the off chance that Johnny might see her while she stole her last look at him, Laurie brushed her hair till the waving mass of golden brown clung to her wrist and fingers. She tied it back with a velvet ribbon the tawny green of her eyes. Her hooded green cape covered her brown plaid pleated skirt and beige sweater. She had tried in vain to think of something to give Johnny, something small and special that would be a kind of charm to keep him safe. As she put down her brush, her eyes fell on her mother's little white New Testament. Afraid of wearing it out, she had bought another several years ago for the family's Sunday worship.

Apart from Johnny's harmonica, the Testament was her greatest treasure. Her mother's eyes had read every word, her fingers turned each page. Laurie picked up the small book, opened it. The purple satin bookmark and thin pages still gave out the faintest scent of lilacs. Again, Laurie smelled carefully folded flour-sack sheets and embroidered pillowcases redolent of handmade lilac sachets tucked among them. She had taken the sheets off her mother's bed that last sad time after Rachel Field's body was given over to the undertaker and the coffin.

Mama's Bible is buried with Daddy, Laurie thought. I can't give away her Testament. But if there were a power of love that lived beyond the body, if sometimes through some special grace the beloved dead could help the living—Laurie pressed the book to her heart. She had always felt that Mama sent them Johnny on that terrible day they left their home, their town, the world they had known, the selves they had been, that grave out on the dust-choked prairie. When, helpless in Matt Sherrod's hands, she had called on her father, she believed that he had heard, that in some incomprehensible way, he had intervened.

Mother, forgive me for not keeping this. You must know it's because your Testament means so much to me that I'm giving it to Johnny, that I ask you to help him if you can in the way you'd help me.

Laurie kissed the Testament, wiped her tears from the faded gilt lettering. She put it in an envelope that she could slip into Johnny's pocket if there was no moment to speak to him privately. On the envelope, she scrawled, "This is my mother's. It's to keep you safe, Johnny, and bring you back." On impulse, she slipped the harmonica into her cape and hurried down the stairs. Now that she had a talisman for Johnny, it would be awful to miss him.

A storm had howled through yesterday, leaving clear, frigid air that gave the lie to the brilliance of the sun. Laurie wished she'd worn slacks, which had become more common since women had started working in defense factories several years ago. Pulling the hood forward to protect her face as much as possible, she came in sight of the depot and the long train that would carry Johnny off.

He came out of the building with a duffel bag. No one was with him. Laurie gasped and then concluded that Crystal, who detested cold, was waiting inside till it would be time to wave final good-byes. But where was Redwine? Jim Halsell limped in sight then from the other direction. He shook Johnny's hand. They were talking softly and didn't notice Laurie till she stopped beside them.

". . . so if you run short of money before you make a well, just ask Dub," Johnny was saying. His gaze followed Jim's to Laurie and he caught both her hands, warming them in his. "Come to see me off, honey?"

Time and the southwest wind and sun had grooved lines deeper at his mouth and eyes but his face would always be to her the most handsome in the world. He answered the question she couldn't ask. "Crystal has a bad cold so I made her stay home. Dub hates good-byes. We had a steak dinner and good bourbon last night before he left to make some big deal in Fort Worth."

Even in the cold wind, Johnny's hands warmed Laurie to her sad heart. His smile, the glow in his gray eyes, melted the chill that made her bones feel like ice that would splinter if she moved. "Give me a kiss, Laurie, and I'll hop on the train. No use in you and Jim standing out here freezing."

"I have something for you." Laurie hated to slip her hand from his in order to get the envelope from her pocket. "Please keep it with you. It was my mother's—"

"Aw, Laurie! You can't give that away!"

"It's just a loan, John Morrigan!" she scolded. "I want it back when you come home." *And if you don't come back, noth-*

ing will matter. She thrust the little parcel into the pocket of his jacket, found a harmonica there. "Johnny! I brought the one you gave me! Let's play together."

"Sure. Let's do."

Turning their backs to the rising wind, they seemed to read each other's minds, one scarcely starting a tune when the other joined in. People catching the train or simply attracted by the music gathered around them as they rollicked through "Praise the Lord and Pass the Ammunition," written about the chaplain who had done just that at Pearl Harbor.

People stomped and clapped and shouted the names of other songs they wanted, but the conductor was yelling for passengers to board. Laurie met Johnny's eyes, raised his gift to her lips, and started the song he had taught her on the day one world ended and another began. *"So long, it's been good to know you, so long it's been good to know you—"*

Finishing in a crescendo, Johnny thrust his harmonica deep in his pocket and took her in his arms. She'd stolen her only real kiss from him. This time she'd only take whatever he gave. She closed her eyes as his lips touched her cheek, was starting to move back when his arms tightened. His mouth claimed hers. Not in a butterfly-big-brother kiss, or a cruel one, either, but sweet and warm and loving, that of a good friend.

Laurie couldn't stop herself. She closed her hands behind his neck, lifted her mouth to meet his more fully, let her lips part, soften, invite. His kiss changed. Swept with fire, she felt as if he drank her in, made her part of him.

He broke away. For a second, his face was grim and startled. Then he laughed huskily and touched her cheek. "So long, Laurie. I'm not much at writing but I'll scribble you a postcard now and then."

"Just let us know you're all right—" The tears she wanted to hold back till he was gone overflowed. She scrubbed at her face and tried to smile. "Sign your name on the card if that's all you can do."

He shook hands with Jim and boarded the train, swinging his duffle up first. "Never expected to ride in a passenger car," he shouted, grinning. He raised his hand in salute and vanished.

The seats by the windows were already filled. Laurie and Jim couldn't see him, but neither moved till the train belched and snorted, gave its lonesome wail, and started to chug along the track.

"Pretty tough that his wife wasn't here," said Jim.

"She's sick."

"Yeah." Jim sounded unconvinced. "Come on, Laurie, you're shivering! I'll walk you home."

"I'm going to work."

"Then I'll walk you there."

"Your leg—"

His young mouth twisted. "Looks worse than it is. You sounded good together on those harmonicas."

She'd remember that almost as much as Johnny's kiss. Every time she played those songs, she'd hear him. "Johnny gave me music the day we met." She spoke through the tears that scalded her throat. "He—he gave me a way to go on. And now he's done it again."

"That's what your Dad did for us."

She could cry then, accept Jim's shoulder, his comforting arms. The aching disbelief that Johnny was gone, heading into danger, was still there when she'd cried herself out, but it was some help to release her pent-up grief, to feel drained rather than explosive. She made good use of the clean bandanna Jim gave her, laughed shakily, and wiped the tears from his cheeks.

His eyes had never looked so blue. At a little over six feet, he had not fleshed out to match his frame but enduring his injury and convalescence had pared the last boyishness from his face. Jim, in fact, had never had much chance to be a boy. If she hadn't known Johnny—Well, someday there would be a girl who'd give Jim her whole heart. He'd always be Laurie's special almost-brother friend but she had to guard now against using him to assuage her grief.

"So men *do* cry," she teased gently. "Are you going out to one of those farms of Johnny's and get started on a well?"

"No."

She stared. "Whyever not? Didn't Johnny find you a driller?"

"Johnny was just making sure I had a job while he's gone. If

I'm really his partner, I'm not going to draw wages while he runs all the risk."

"What are you going to do?"

"You've heard of Soup MacNeal?"

"Sure." MacNeal, a small, quick-moving, red-haired man with merry dark eyes, operated out of Enid but he had eaten in the restaurant several times when passing through. "He's the best well shooter in Oklahoma outside of Johnny."

"I'm going to work for him. Mix the soup, drive the truck, help set the charges."

"But—"

"Vance Morrow, the driller Johnny located, draws royalties from several wells. He's willing to make some shallow holes for an interest in any oil he hits, but at least one helper has to be paid, and operating expenses. Soup will pay me enough to hire a roughneck and pay some toward expenses on top of what I have to send Mom for Bernice." His jaw hardened. "That way, I'll be a partner, not a mooch."

"Oh, Jim! Why be so hardheaded?"

He shrugged. "Haven't I heard you sing a song that goes, 'A man's a brother to a mule'?"

"Maybe you have." She added with honest respect, "You must be really good with nitro, Jim, for someone like Soup MacNeal to want you."

"I like it," he said with a slow grin. "Not everybody does."

How he could feel that way after his accident baffled Laurie but handling and controlling explosives must give him a justified sense of power. No one laughed at a well shooter even if he did limp. With a few more years' experience, Jim could fully partner Johnny in shooting wells, or start his own business. With pride honed fierce by his laming, Jim would probably do that.

"Come in for some coffee and pie?" she asked him at the door of the hotel.

"Thanks, but I've got to see Vance and make sure he's all set to go. I'm meeting Soup in El Reno tomorrow to shoot a well."

With a wave of desolation that took her by surprise, she asked, "Will you be moving to Enid?"

"Not for a while, anyhow. Soup wants to see how it works to have me over here. For jobs down this way, I can mix the nitro, load the truck, and get to the well, while all he has to do is jump in his truck and meet me."

"It's real exciting, Jim."

His laugh was rueful. "Scary, too, pulling this without Johnny's knowing about it. But with everything else he's got on his mind, I didn't want to give him an argument or act like I was ungrateful."

"Good luck, Jim. Come by and see us."

"You bet." He hesitated. "Laurie. If you need anything—if I can help—you'll tell me, won't you?"

They were linked by the man who had drowned outside Eden six years ago. Knowing Jim, she understood that he believed he owed a debt to her and Buddy. "Yes," she promised. "I'll tell you. Thanks for walking me to work. Thanks for being at the train."

That night, for the first time in years, she dreamed that as she watched the night sky, the moon turned red as blood and began to fall toward earth, swelling to blot out the stars. Dread stopped her breath. She woke to a scream breaking in her throat, lay there, heart sledging, as she came out of the terror.

"Laurie!" Way called from outside her door. "You all right, honey?"

"Yes. I—I just had a nightmare."

"Want Marilys to come stay with you a while?"

"Goodness, no." Jumping out of bed, Laurie opened the door and gave him a hug. "I'm fine now," she said with a sheepish laugh. "Sorry I woke you up."

But another world had ended.

27

No one had much heart for the holidays. There seemed to be no stopping the Japanese, who were overrunning the Pacific Islands. On December 23, American marines on Wake Island surrendered after a bloody fifteen-day siege. The family agreed to take the money they'd have spent on a special big dinner and each other's presents and send it to a group that provided food and clothing to English war orphans; Laurie added the money she'd saved for her annual gift to her parents.

There was still a nice dinner, with Jim invited, in midafternoon after Marilys and Laurie got home from work. The restaurant served a gala holiday dinner but would be closed the rest of the day. When the last crumb of apple pie had vanished, the family and Jim gathered around the dancing blaze in the big old fireplace and sang carols, Marilys accompanying with the guitar, Laurie playing the harmonica. When they paused for spiced cider and nuts, Laurie put on the records that had been Johnny's early Christmas present, Woody Guthrie singing Dust Bowl songs, hard-luck songs, church-house blues, most of them tunes Johnny had taught her that she had played all the way from Oklahoma to California and then through Arizona, New Mexico and Texas—Oklahoma, Arkansas, Louisiana, and back to Oklahoma.

On the fourteenth day of April in nineteen thirty-five . . . So long, it's been good to know you. . . . This was the song that they sang as they blowed. . . . You got to walk that lonesome valley, you got to walk it by yourself. . . . California water tastes like cherry wine. . . . Looks like I ain't ever gonna cease my wanderin'. . . . Ain't the banker or the planter, but it's me, O Lord, standin' in the need of a home. . . .

A long, lonesome road, but she and Buddy had been lucky. They had Marilys and Way and a home, this wonderful old house. If only this war would be over, if Johnny came home safe—Yet how could you pray that it would be others who died instead of the one you loved? Be with them all, she prayed. With everybody everywhere who's afraid or sick or sad or dying.

A child's prayer, a fool's prayer. Right now, thousands of American soldiers based in the Philippines were trapped on the Bataan Peninsula and Corregidor, a little island in Manila Bay. That very day, the British Crown Colony of Hong Kong had fallen to the Japanese.

Laurie shoved back the somber thoughts and drew comfort

343

from watching Marilys and Way sitting close together, cracking nuts and feeding the best ones to each other. Having his own business had given Way a new confidence, a prouder way of moving. It was hard to see in him the raddled hobo who had mooched food from Laurie and Buddy on the train.

As the business was to Way, the house was to Marilys. Only a few days before, as the women hung laundry on the line stretched where it got the most sun, Marilys warmed her chapped hands beneath her arms and gazed lovingly around the big yard. "I can't believe we really have a home, especially one this nice! Finding Way was all the luck I asked for, I wouldn't have the nerve to expect more. But isn't it wonderful to know this place is ours and we'll never have to move again?"

It was unlikely that Laurie would live out her days in the gracious old home, though knowing it was there would give her a sense of rootedness, of security.

"It *is* wonderful. After all those shacks and tents we've lived in, it's a pleasure to have furniture to dust and floors that look nice when you've finished mopping and waxing."

Sitting in front of the fire, Marilys and Way looked so blissful that Laurie wondered with a stab of pain if she would ever in the world sit by Johnny like that? To live with the one you loved, that seemed happiness and good fortune beyond what any mortal could expect. If he just came home safe, she'd never ask for anything else, but she couldn't help imagining.

That night when the blood-red moon swelled to fill the sky and fell slowly toward Laurie, when she woke with a scream lodged in her pulsing throat, she told herself as always, only a dream. Only a dream. She thought as she had learned to do of Johnny, conjured up his smile and voice and hands, listened to him singing. When she drifted into sleep again, the bad dream didn't come.

The New Year of 1942 brought desperate times for the Allies from the totally destroyed Dutch-British-Australian-American forces in the Java Sea to Norway, where Vidkun Quisling had been installed as the Nazis' puppet. On February 22, 1942, a Japanese submarine shelled an oil refinery near Santa Barbara,

California. The only damage was to a pumphouse roof, but that the mainland could be attacked at all sent a wave of panic through the whole country. While the seemingly invincible Japanese took Singapore and conquered Burma and the Netherlands East Indies, the U.S. government decided to move all Japanese—citizens of the United States, most of them born here—from the West Coast and Hawaii to relocation centers in the interior where they couldn't help hostile forces.

"Reckon the army's scared at the way Japanese soldiers don't surrender and them Zero pilots same as commit suicide to serve that emperor they think is some kind of sun-god." Way rubbed his scarred cheek. "They're takin' folks with as little as one-sixteenth Japanese blood and adopted kids raised by Cau-Cau—"

"Caucasians?" asked Laurie.

"Yeah. Sounds too much like that Nazi idea of being Aryan, whatever in the hell that is. Crazy, too. 'Cause just the way a drop of Negro blood makes a person black to some people, what they're admittin' is that a little tiny bit of Japanese blood is stronger than other kinds and stronger than being raised American."

Laurie wrote her congressmen, the War Department, and President Roosevelt. "You've done so much good for the country. Please don't let this awful thing happen. Except that we won't kill them, it's like Hitler's sending Jews to concentration camps." She never got an answer.

Allowed to bring only what they could carry, 110,000 Japanese-Americans reported to converted livestock stalls and stadiums where families were crowded into rooms furnished only with cots, blankets, and mattresses, separated from families in the next "apartments" only by thin partitions. These camps were surrounded by barbed wire and guard towers. Anyone who tried to leave would be shot.

"Most of them had to sell everything they owned," Marilys said with bitter shame. "Maybe there were a few spies out there and it was sure scary when that submarine shelled the refinery, but to do this to thousands of people—"

"There must be plenty of us who don't think it's right," Laurie said. "But what can we do about it?"

"Nothin' except write the government—and I guess unless everybody in the country did that, it wouldn't help. After the way our boys were snuck up on at Pearl Harbor and the way they're starvin' now over on Bataan, there's plenty of Americans hate all Japanese even if they're American, too."

"I suppose over in Germany right now," said Laurie slowly, "good ordinary people are talking this way about what's happening to the Jews. They hate it but they don't know what they can do."

"If they talk very loud, they'll wind up in a camp, too." Way grunted. "At least here we can still say we think our government's wrong—not that it helps those folks penned up behind bobwire on account of their ancestors."

Johnny had shipped out at the end of March. His APO was San Francisco, so it was sure his outfit was headed for the Pacific, where troops were so urgently needed. There was no way to get reinforcements to the besieged Americans on Bataan but he could go somewhere equally perilous. Laurie got a card that said: "Play that harmonica, honey. Take care, and write even when I don't."

Knowing that he was on his way to battle, that he could be killed or terribly maimed, plunged Laurie into agony. She worked and did her share around the house, but it was like moving in a trance. Then Way came home from the salvage yard one night looking so stricken that it jarred her back to reality.

"Dub's putting in a salvage and supply company right across the street from ours."

Laurie and Marilys stared. Way sank down in a chair as if his bones were broken. "Worked it slick. I never had the least notion."

"Are—are you sure?" Marilys whispered.

"Sure, I'm sure. Yesterday there was just that old overgrown field across from our place. By the time I got to work this morning, trucks were unloading every kind of pipe you can imagine along with tanks and pumps and generators—enough stuff to supply a whole durned oil boom."

"How do you know it's W.S.?" Laurie asked when her voice would work.

Way laughed mirthlessly. "On account of right on the side of the fancy new trailer that's plunked down close to the street, there's a great big sign."

"Oh." That was all Laurie could say.

Marilys poured Way some coffee and put in plenty of cream and sugar. "Sweetheart," she admonished, "you've been honest and gone to a lot of trouble to find what contractors needed at a fair price. Many's the night you've driven through a storm to deliver some piece of equipment a driller needed. The men that know you won't go flocking over to Dub's."

Way shook his head. "Sweetie, a contractor has to get the best price he can for his boss. If he don't and gets caught, it's his neck."

"Yes, but you don't tack on much profit." Marilys had often chided him about the need to charge more for his time. "No one can undersell you without losing money."

"Dub can lose money till he puts me out of business."

"But—"

Way raised a stilling hand. "It's there on his sign, sugar, folksy and bighearted as hell. 'Tell Dub the best price you can find on what you need. He guarantees the same product at ten percent less. Tell Dub what you've been offered for your used supplies and he'll pay you at least ten percent more.'" Way's body sagged. He had shaved that morning and his clothes had been clean then but some effect of shadow and posture suddenly, pitilessly, made him look like the tramp who'd hopped that boxcar seven years ago. "Reckon I was a fool not to guess Dub would try to wipe me out someday."

"He waited till Johnny shipped out," Marilys said bitterly.

A new fear clutched Laurie. Dub had acted so benevolent, so understanding, when Johnny volunteered. Suppose Redwine had decided to get even for what Laurie had been sure he'd view as a betrayal? What if he somehow robbed Johnny of his part in the company—all legal and correct, of course, so Johnny would have no remedy?

"I've let you down," Way groaned, clenching his fists. "Sunk all our money in it, Laurie's and Buddy's, too."

"You were trying to get ahead, make us a better living," Marilys comforted. "You were making a go of it, too. Who could suspect that Dub was just being patient all these years, waiting for his chance?"

"I should have seen through him," Way gritted. "The way he framed me for stealing, dogged me all over the country—"

"It's my fault," said Marilys.

Way stared. "That's crazy, sweetheart!"

"No. There's something I didn't tell you—thought it would just cause trouble. Dub tried to get me to take up with him again."

Way sprang to his feet. "Why, that—"

Marilys caught his arm. "He threatened to tell you—all the things I already had, back before we married. When he found out his blackmail wouldn't work, he never spoke to me again except when he had to."

"Can't blame him for wanting you back," said Way, "but that was a dirty way to go about it."

"He didn't want *me,*" Marilys said with a shake of her head. "He wanted to get at you. I was afraid if I told you, you'd get in a fight with him and he'd find some way to send you to jail. But his trying that proved that behind Johnny's back, he was the same old Dub." Marilys's lips quivered. "I should have let you know."

Way took Marilys in his arms and kissed her long and thoroughly. "I'd have done my best to flatten Dub's nose all the way to his cheekbones," he said with a chuckle, "but I doubt if we'd have picked up and left town what with everything going so good for us." He pondered for a moment. "No, honey, we none of us have enough poison in our systems to figure how a guy like Dub goes around just storing it up till he gets a chance to fang it into somebody."

"I'll bet there are some contractors who won't buy from Redwine," said Laurie, with sudden hope. "Matt Sherrod told me how W.S. cheated and double-crossed oil folks from one end of Texas to the other, and did the same in Oklahoma, till he partnered with Johnny. Johnny had so many friends that they let bygones be bygones, but I bet they remember."

Way brightened, then said dismally, "There may be a few outfits that wouldn't buy water from Dub in hell, but I doubt if there's enough to keep me in business."

"There's other towns," said Laurie, and stopped at the look in Marilys's eyes.

Give up the home they all loved, hit the road again, blown like tumbleweeds, with Redwine the evil wind that uprooted them, blew them over the plains? Slipping her arms around Marilys and Way, Laurie said, "Let's fight it out right here! If we can't stay in the salvage business, there must be something W.S. can't louse up for us!"

"I've still got my paintbrushes," Way said. "Won't pay as steady as my pumping job but I could journey around lookin' for jobs. And with the truck, I can always haul supplies."

Marilys's dark eyebrows drew together. "We just cashed a check from that farmer out by Woodward who bought some tanks and pipe."

"Sho'. He aimed to use the pipe and a couple of tanks to put in an irrigation system. The other tanks'll be silos."

"Just about every farmer left in both Panhandles must be planning to irrigate," Marilys pointed out. "That'll take a lot of pipe. And there must be all kinds of ways to use tanks."

The startled look on Way's face broadened to a grin. "Sweetie, you may have it! Puttin' in irrigation is probably somethin' many a farmer figgers on doing someday but he's busy and just doesn't get to it till a drouth hits. Bet I could drive around the back roads and drum up a bunch of orders, 'specially if I'll deliver." He rubbed his jaw. "But who's goin' to tend the salvage yard while I'm doin' that?"

"Buddy's there after school now," said Laurie. "And Marilys and I can work shifts so that one of us'll be at the yard most of the time."

Way hugged both women. "By grannies, you gals have the trick of makin' a good thing come out of bad. Dub may plow me under yet, but it won't be because I laid down and let him."

"He won't whip us," Laurie vowed. "One way or another, we'll manage. And when Johnny comes home—well, W.S. is sure going to have some explaining to do."

Next day, Laurie was minding the salvage-yard office, trying to ignore the big trucks unloading across the street while customers went around surveying accumulating rows of pipe and all manner of supplies. She hadn't had a customer all morning, not even a phone call, but maybe Way would get some orders. The crunch of footsteps made her glance up hopefully as Jim Halsell stepped inside.

"Marilys told me you were here," he said. "That lousy, sneaking Redwine!"

"He sure is!" Laurie hadn't seen Jim in weeks. He seemed to have grown another inch and his eyes blazed in his sunburned face like sun behind a thundercloud. "Is something else wrong, Jim? You look like someone just kicked you in the stomach."

"Might as well have." He sucked in a long breath. "You haven't heard, then."

"Heard what?"

"Redwine's cut Johnny out of the partnership—nice and legal—as of this morning. You know the spudder got dry holes on the first and second tries. Ev and Vance Morrow are about three hundred feet down on their third hole. When Ev went to town for supplies, he finds out their credit's shut off. He reckons it's a mistake and goes to the bank. Partnership's been issuing him a paycheck every two weeks." Jim swallowed hard. "The standing order's been cancelled."

"What?"

"The partnership doesn't have an account anymore."

Dazed, Laurie steadied herself against the wall. "But—but how—?"

"Ev went out and told Vance. Vance comes in with blood in his eye. He's an old-timer and knows how to get to the bottom of things."

"What's at the bottom?"

"Redwine." Jim balled his fists. "Seems like Johnny signed a power of attorney over to him so Redwine could do whatever looked like a good idea while Johnny was overseas. What looked like a good idea to Dub, I guess, was to plain rob Johnny."

She had been afraid Redwine might do something, but she hadn't thought of this. Cold to the heart, Laurie burst out, "Surely Redwine can't get away with doing this to someone who's gone to war!"

"Crystal might sue," Jim shrugged. "But a lawyer friend Vance talked to thinks Dub can prove most of the money was his anyway."

"But Johnny did the real work! He was always out in the field!"

"That may not cut any ice in court. What it looks like is Johnny's got those farms left, the old spudder, some drilling equipment, and his nitro truck."

Laurie checked a bitter laugh. "Well," she said after recovering some of her wits, "that beats nothing! Jim, we've got to manage so Johnny'll have a going business when he comes home—we've got to!"

Jim nodded. "You bet. But I'm already sinking what I can in the spudder holes." He paused. "I've got more good news. Ev's signed up for the marines. Leaves in ten days."

Laurie squelched the *Oh, no!* that sprang to her lips. Everett, working in a vital industry, could stay home but she could well understand that he wanted to fight. "Has he told his mother?"

"Said he'd go see her on his way to Parris Island, break the news then." Jim took a deep breath. "So what do we do about Johnny's affairs?"

"Let's see what Marilys and Way think. Can you come over tonight after I get off work?"

"Sure," said Jim. "But with Dub trying to wreck this salvage business, you folks are in no spot to help out."

"We'll think of something," Laurie said fiercely. A sudden hope struck her. Slowly, she said, "Maybe Crystal will make Dub pull in his horns. Jim, can you stay here while I go have a talk with her?"

Jim seemed to guess how much it would cost Laurie to plead with Johnny's wife. "Sure," he said gently. "But I wouldn't get my hopes up with that woman. She's got a cash register inside, not a heart."

"Well then, she shouldn't want her husband to go broke."

"She and Dub are mighty thick."

Laurie had no use for Crystal but she couldn't believe that she'd really let Redwine ruin Johnny. It was going to be hard, though, really hard, to beg. Laurie wouldn't have done it to save her own life. She straightened her shoulders. "I'll be back as soon as I can."

"Good luck," Jim said.

A sleek silver-green convertible Cadillac, one of the last cars made before manufactures were banned, was parked in the driveway. Crystal was dressed to go out, in spike heels, sheer nylons—no leg-paint or cotton hose for Crystal—and a clingy green dress that molded to her body.

"What do you want?" she asked ungraciously.

"Do you know?"

Crystal's lip curled. "Know what?"

"What Redwine's done to Johnny."

"Johnny broke the partnership when he went off and left Dub in the lurch."

"He went off to fight for our country—for you!"

Crystal shrugged. "He was a sap. He didn't have to go."

"You don't care that he's been cheated?"

Crystal shrugged. "The way I see it, he got exactly what he had coming."

"You're his wife!"

Crystal gave Laurie a pityingly superior look. "You're so crazy about Johnny Morrigan that you probably can't believe I only married him because Dub wanted me to."

"What?"

"It was the best way of controlling him." The woman's eyes glinted. "Or so we thought. Who could guess he'd throw away being Dub's heir?"

Staggered, Laurie put a hand against the doorframe. "But why—?"

Crystal's shoulders moved in a graceful shrug. "Dub wants a

son, as you should know better than anybody. He was careful with Johnny, never cracked the whip. But he wanted the whip to be there in case he needed it."

Sick realization knotted Laurie's insides. "There may be a name for you," she said carefully, "but I never learned it in all the hobo jungles, shack towns, and boxcars I've been in."

Crystal's eyes glittered and her mouth drew into a thin line. "Dub got me to marry Johnny. When Johnny started talking about getting into a war if it started, Dub asked me to try to get pregnant—that would hold Johnny, he thought."

"Did—did you?"

"I did." Crystal lit a cigarette. "But I learned for sure a week or so after Johnny volunteered. No use telling him then."

Laurie couldn't help it. She stared at Crystal's sinuous figure. "What happened?"

A blast of smoke stung her eyes. "I had an abortion."

"No! Johnny's baby—"

"It was in my belly. I wasn't about to waddle around and look ugly while that heel was God knows where." She brooded. "Maybe I was crazy not to tell Dub. He'd likely have paid me plenty to have the kid and let him play daddy. But when Johnny broke his news about joining the marines, Dub wrote him off and just waited till he was sent overseas to cut him out of the partnership."

"He won't get away with it."

"Oh, I expect he will." Crystal laughed. "And Dub's sort of put the skids on that junkyard of yours, hasn't he?"

"What did you get out of this?"

"None of your business, but it was plenty. I'm moving—you don't need to know where—and forgetting I ever married a loser like Morrigan."

Laurie drew herself up, surprised to discover that she'd be as tall as Crystal if the other woman weren't wearing three-inch heels. "I hope you get what you deserve for this."

"You ought to be grateful, stupid. If Morrigan comes home, you can have him." She laughed mockingly. "He'll certainly have grounds to divorce me for desertion."

She picked up her handbag and makeup case.

"What about Johnny's things?"

"Store them if you want to. It's nothing to do with me. I hope I never see this burg again."

"Are you going to write Johnny?"

"You'll do that, won't you, Miss Priss?" Crystal's laughter sounded like shattering glass. "As far as I'm concerned," she added viciously, "the marriage ended when he volunteered."

Unbelieving, Laurie stood there as heels stabbed the floor and sidewalk with a staccato beat. The Cadillac roared away. Crystal apparently got all the gas she wanted.

Moving in a trance, Laurie went through closets till she found Johnny's civilian clothes jammed in a dark corner with his oil-stained boots piled underneath and his old hat on the shelf. Pressing the hat to her face, she breathed in the smell of him. She would never have wanted this to happen but now it had, a sort of relief and hope mingled with her wrath. How could she write Johnny about this, though?

What could she say? How can you tell someone you love their world has ended? He didn't have many possessions. Laurie packed them all into two boxes, placed his guitar on top, and then phoned Jim to run over and pick up Johnny's things as soon as Marilys came to mind the office. It was time for Laurie to go to work. Leaving the door unlocked, she started for the hotel.

Jim picked Laurie up at the hotel and brought her home, where Everett, Way, Marilys, and Buddy were seated at the table with a jug of lemonade and bowl of oatmeal cookies.

"So that Crystal took off." Way shook his head. "A good thing if you ask me! But it's hard to believe even she'd let Dub skin Johnny while he's overseas."

"You can bet his lawyers have it all according to Hoyle," said Marilys. "How dirty can you get? This is worse than his putting in that big supply yard across from ours. At least Dub never pretended he was our friend."

"I rounded up six orders today," Way said proudly. "Dub may not put us out of business as easy as he figgered." His voice dropped regretfully. "We may keep our heads above water but

I don't see how we'll have the kind of money to keep Johnny's operation going."

He was right, of course, but hearing it made Laurie feel all gone in the pit of her stomach. "We've got to try!" With an effort, she steadied her voice. "If we keep the spudder digging, maybe we can make him a few decent wells—have something for him when he comes back."

"I'm already kicking in all I can," said Jim. "After all, Johnny made me his partner so that's only right." He looked straight at Laurie. "If Ev's leaving, though, and I could have his room, I could put what I'm paying my landlady into the drilling. And if you don't mind and could put another bed in the room, I know I can find plenty of decent guys who'd like to live in a nice place instead of a shack or tent."

Everett colored guiltily. "If I was goin' to be here, I'd work for board and a little spendin' money. But I'm leavin' next week."

"I could take over your job," Buddy suggested eagerly. "I'm almost big as you, Ev, and—"

"You're only fifteen and you're going to finish ninth grade next year," Laurie quelled him. "Besides, we need you at the salvage yard when you're not at school." She frowned. "If we didn't have this mortgage on the house to pay off—"

Buddy sighed, then said in a noble, self-sacrificing tone, "I could move up in the attic. Then you can rent my room."

Now why hadn't she thought of that? The attic was well insulated, had six dormer windows on each side plus one at each end, and though the walls slanted down at the sides, there was still plenty of room for living quarters. The floor was oak and would wax to a mellow glow.

"I can move up there, too," said Laurie quickly to prevent herself from clinging to her pretty "own" room that she loved so much. At Buddy's protesting yelp, she said scornfully, "For goodness' sake, don't carry on! There's space up there for a dozen people!"

"I'll wall my place off with those old bureaus and wardrobes and trunks." Buddy cheered up at the prospect. "Can I have one whole side of the attic?"

"Reckon an owner's got some say about what he wants," said Way, twinkling.

Buddy pressed his advantage with Laurie. "And you won't fuss at me to keep it cleaned up?"

"Not if you'll toss your sheets and clothes over the barricade once a week," Laurie conceded. "There are still some bedsteads, springs, and mattresses stored up there. Let's see, if we put two beds in the three rooms we'll empty on the second floor, that's six renters!"

"Charge at least a buck a night," urged Jim. "I pay that for a cubbyhole in a rundown old house where the plumbing never works and the sheets don't get changed till they're filthy."

Marilys and Laurie exchanged glances. Six oil-field workers would keep the bathroom tied up and dirty. Way read their minds. "It wouldn't be hard to turn part of the garage into an extra bathroom," he said. "Insulate the walls, lay some linoleum, maybe put in a shower so the fellas could wash off the worst dirt and oil before they got in the tub. Put in two sinks so a couple of them could shave or wash up at the same time."

"I'll help," said Jim. "And I can find you good renters who won't come in roaring drunk or mean."

Way whistled. "Boy howdy! Say we get seven dollars a week from six men, that's forty-two dollars!" He calculated in his head and whistled again. "That's a hundred and sixty-eight dollars for four weeks, say about a hundred and eighty-five dollars a month! That'll pay the mortgage and leave a nice chunk for Johnny's drilling and keeping the salvage yard going."

"Yes, but we need to put in the new bathroom and we're going to need a good wash machine to handle all those extra sheets and towels." Marilys puckered her forehead and then laughed as she clapped her hands. "Maybe what we need's a bigger mortgage."

Everyone stared at her. "We haven't missed a payment and we've whittled some off the principal, which brings our interest down," she explained. "I think the bank'd be happy to lend us enough to finance at least a couple more holes and give us a cushion for the salvage business. After all, they get this house if we don't pay."

Lose their home? Go back to a tent or trailer? The idea twisted Laurie's insides but she didn't hesitate. "If you and Way are willing, Marilys, I'm all for it. Buddy?"

"Sure." He slanted her a sarcastic look. "Maybe you won't kick so hard when I quit school next year if I go to work for what's sort of our own outfit till I'm old enough to get in the war."

"You better hope the war's over a long time before you can go," Laurie scolded. "And don't you start in on someone's signing for you when you're seventeen!"

He gave her a rebellious glare. She was used to his being taller than she, he had been for a year, but when she stopped to really look at him, she was amazed at how broad in the shoulders he was growing, how big and scarred his hands were. His brown hair waved like Daddy's and he had the same mouth, though his eyes were Mama's. When had he grown up? Laurie thought with a pang. Would they ever be close again the way they used to be out on the road? When he wasn't working, sleeping, or at school, he was usually with his friends.

Way said amiably, rising and stretching, "Marilys, we'll go to the bank tomorrow. And it already is tomorrow, so let's get to bed for what's left of the night!"

28

By the end of the week, the bathroom was ready and a washing machine with an electric wringer instead of a hand-turned one was positioned on the other side of the garage with lines strung inside for rainy days. Laurie and Buddy occupied opposite ends of the attic and had so much room in between them that it was more adventure than annoyance to share the huge expanse. Winks and Runcible followed Laurie and got their nocturnal exercise from chasing mice. Six sunburned young men roomed below but came and went by their own side entrance and were seldom in evidence except when they paid the rent. Jed and Bill Harris were brothers from Louisiana, lanky redheads with big grins. Lithe, quiet Quinn Sanders of Virginia was a driller, with dark eyes and curly hair. Towheaded Mark Steele and sandy-haired Jack Morris were roughnecks, even younger than Jim, away from their Kansas homes for the first time.

Dub's supply yard hogged customers but there were some Dub had cheated that would never buy from him. What with them and farmers, Way kept the yard going. Hauling supplies as far as he often did might cut his profit to nothing, but so long as he could pay bills and keep going, they all felt grateful.

"Dub'll get tired of losing money after a while," Way reasoned. "If he don't break us inside of six months, I bet he'll raise his prices to where I can come pretty close to matchin' them."

Marilys frowned. "I hope you're right, darling, but Dub can afford to lose a hundred times over what'd bankrupt us. Has Dub been around his new business?"

"Haven't seen him," shrugged Way.

"He'll come," predicted Marilys with a shiver. "When he finds out we're bucking him and that Johnny's outfit's drilling, he'll itch to know what went wrong with his nifty ideas to ruin us."

"Now, sugar—"

"I wish I could believe he'd leave us alone," said Marilys vehemently, "but I don't think he's done with us yet."

"Then we're not done with him, either," said Way, and hugged her, chuckling. Marilys smiled reluctantly but it was clear she was uneasy.

Meanwhile, of course, the war went on. The fate of the American Japanese still weighed on Laurie but not as much as fear for Johnny and grief for what was happening to vastly outnumbered American soldiers on Corregidor and Bataan who were running out of both food and ammunition. They surrendered on April 9 to an enemy that not only scorned them for not fighting to the death but lacked food for so many prisoners, men already weak from hunger, tainted water, and fighting in pestilential jungle.

Colonel James Doolittle raided Tokyo on April 18 with a squadron of B-52 bombers. These were launched from carriers but couldn't land on them so the returning squadron flew to a Chinese airfield. Tokyo wasn't much damaged but the raid lifted Allied spirits—which fell again as Corregidor surrendered on May 6 and survivors followed the captives of Bataan on the Death March to POW camps. Out of 76,000 prisoners, thousands were bayoneted, shot, or beheaded. Thousands more died of exhaustion, hunger, or dysentery. Oh God, if that happened to Johnny—

Laurie was glad to line up at the school May 14 to get her ration book. Getting by on a pound of sugar every two weeks wasn't much of a sacrifice but it made her feel she was helping a little. Since Way hauled supplies for the oil field, he was allotted enough gas for that vital work but apart from that, the family walked. The big Victory garden in back already had lettuce, radishes, and green onions with peas, green beans, tomatoes, cucumbers, corn, summer squash, yams, and collards coming on. They'd be able to can a cellar-full for winter besides supplying several neighbors who were too decrepit to garden.

Nylon, and of course, silk stockings were a thing of the past as were new trucks and cars. Laurie and Marilys turned in their nylons to hold gunpowder or be recycled into parachutes. Laurie went bare-legged that summer but Marilys used leg paint and grew expert at using eyebrow pencil to make a straight dark seam down the back.

"I detested cotton stockings when I was the only girl in school who wore them," Laurie told Marilys with a rueful chuckle. "This winter, though, they'll be in fashion for everybody."

To save fabric, skirts were shorter and narrower, and dresses had no ruffles or big collars. Men's trousers were cuffless and suits had no vests. High school kids, who were starting to be called teenagers, developed uniforms; outsized men's shirts dangled over girls' blue jeans rolled to the knee with football socks; boys wore shirttails out, jeans, and combat boots. With the manpower shortage, most of them had part-time jobs and spent their money on records, at soda fountains, or skating rinks. Though she was still nineteen, Laurie felt a generation removed from them.

The whole family put their galoshes in a nationwide rubber drive that began in June. Since rubber mostly came from countries occupied by the Japanese, there was a critical shortage of this essential material and no good substitute had been found. Kitchen fat was saved and turned in to make explosives. Boy Scouts collected saved newspapers. For a metal-scrap drive, the family contributed the handsome old wrought-iron fence that surrounded the yard, the gazebo with its benches, and the handrails of the steps, as well as all the tin they could scavenge.

Meanwhile, in early June, the radio and papers reported that an awesome Japanese fleet—8 carriers, 11 battleships, 22 cruisers, 65 destroyers, and 21 submarines—was approaching Midway Island where the Americans had only 3 carriers with 233 planes. All American battleships in the Pacific had been destroyed at Pearl Harbor or severely disabled. As Japanese bombers attacked the island, the Americans struck at the fleet. They lost the first assault. Thirty-five of forty-one torpedo bombers were shot down. But minutes later, thirty-seven dive bombers swooped down and sank three carriers within the hour.

Before the armada retreated it lost 1 cruiser, 4 carriers, and 330 aircraft. The Americans pursued, though they had lost 1 carrier and 150 airplanes. Lack of fuel forced them to give up the chase and the chance to deal a smashing blow.

"Glory be!" whooped Way as the news came in. "Maybe this means the Japs won't have it all their way in the Pacific anymore!"

Johnny was out there somewhere. Laurie hadn't heard from him in weeks but she sent a letter by V-mail nearly every day. Her sugar ration went to make candy and baked treats that could endure shipping and Pacific humidity. In these boxes, she sent cartoons, clippings, and little gifts she hoped would be useful or funny.

I suppose you've read in the *Stars and Stripes* that General Dwight D. Eisenhower's taken command of our forces in Europe. What do you think about the WAACS and WAVES? Isn't it something that after the way Japanese-Americans have been sent to camps, 10,000 Hawaiian Nisei volunteered for the all-Nisei combat unit that's being formed on the mainland? Maybe now the government will let up on trying to get the governor of Hawaii to deport Japanese citizens. I wish the president would close those awful camps but I guess people on both coasts are scared of someone's showing a light to guide in enemy aircraft. They have air raid warnings, shelters, blackouts, and all that kind of thing. Even here, the school kids have air raid drills. Buddy came home from school yesterday and said the principal's telling them to put big books like encyclopedias on their heads to protect them from falling debris and to put erasers in their mouths to lessen an explosion. I hope you have a lot of erasers, Johnny!

Her first real letter from Johnny smelled of mildew and cigarette smoke. "I'm writing this in the tent while the other guys shoot craps," ran the penciled scrawl. "I got five letters from you all at once—it was sure like Christmas, especially when I opened up those boxes of brownies and pralines. Don't use up all your rations on me, though, honey chile. We get candy bars and gum and I've sure eaten a lot worse chow than C rations. Our corporal, Tom Shelton, a cowboy from Texas, has a harmonica, too, and we get plenty of applause on account of we're the only show in camp." Some lines were marked out by the censor, sharply reminding Laurie that Johnny couldn't tell her where he was or anything about what was really going on. At least she knew that he'd had some of her letters and packages, that he was alive and well on the fifth day of June.

She sat down to begin her answer before she went to work. She never had told him about Crystal, or Dub, either. He'd have to know sometime, of course, but she couldn't find the words to tell him that his wife had deserted him and his partner-father-friend had robbed him and tried to put him out of business completely.

When Jim wasn't on a job for Soup MacNeal, he worked with Vance and Peavine Mitchell, the old roughneck who was helping on Johnny's land. Jim said the bailings were showing a little oil.

"They've got their hopes up," Laurie told Marilys. "But if they don't get a well this time, they're moving to another old farm of Johnny's."

"Well, I guess we can always mortgage the mortgage," Marilys joked, but it wasn't really funny. Drilling was costly. The last thing in the world Johnny would want would be for them to lose their home in the effort to have some producing wells going for him when he came home.

Laurie refused to even think about *if* he came, though she suspected he was in the Solomon Islands in the fierce fighting centering on Guadalcanal. Late in August of 1942, the papers and radio hailed a decisive naval victory over the Japanese, but the land battle raged on over a volcanic tropical island that neither side wanted but couldn't allow the other to hold.

The news trumpeted names most Americans had never heard of before. German troops met ferocious resistance at Stalingrad on the Volga River and General Rommel's famed Afrika Corps invaded Egypt.

On her twentieth birthday, Laurie *ooh*-ed and *aah*-ed over the cake that she knew must have taken all of the family's sugar ration for the week, but she hadn't heard from Johnny in weeks and had little heart for celebration. Everett had shipped out the first of October. That added to everybody's anxiety and Buddy's grumblings about staying in school while there was a war on.

Vance Morrow abandoned another dry hole, the one that had looked so promising. When the family promised to back him, he moved the spudder to Johnny's other farm and started making hole.

After the long stretch without hearing from Johnny, several letters came at once, all full of worry. His letters to Crystal were being returned, stamped with MOVED, NO FORWARDING ADDRESS.

362

I hate to think it but she must have left me. And you'd hate to say so, wouldn't you, kid? Tell me the truth, I can stand it better than not knowing. I can't blame her much if she did take off. I wasn't the kind of husband Crystal needed. She liked fun and excitement, dancing and parties. Looking back, I can't imagine why she married me. When I volunteered, I guess she figured I'd really let her down—and I must have, for this to happen. Dub never writes. Do you know if he's sick or something? Probably he's just out wheeling and dealing.

In her answer, compelled to it at last, Laurie said that Crystal had left town and Johnny's things were stored in the attic. Unable to bring herself to explain Redwine's treachery—after all, what could Johnny do about it except worry?—she wrote only that she hadn't seen W.S. since Johnny left. Crystal's desertion was more than enough for Johnny to handle now. The truth about Dub might make him as reckless as those kamikaze Japanese fighters on Guadalcanal who made suicidal attacks on the Americans, losing ten men for every one they killed.

Early in February, after seven months of hard-fought battle, the United States won its first big offensive victory as Japanese transports managed to evacuate their last starving troops from the island. The tide had finally turned in the Pacific.

The radio was turned up in the restaurant loud enough for everyone to hear the news. If Johnny's still all right and if that's where he is, Laurie thought, maybe he won't be in any more bad fighting. Maybe the Japanese will surrender. And Ev'rett, if he was at Guadalcanal—

She scarcely heard the phone ringing at the reception counter. Mrs. Marriott came to the door. "Laurie," she called softly. "It's Ev'rett's mama."

Laurie's heart sank. Her feet were so heavy she seemed to drag them. Mrs. Marriott pulled out a chair. "Sit down, honey. It's not good."

Sobbing, Rosalie read the telegram she'd just received. Ev'-rett had been killed in action. "He—he was only eighteen. He never even had a girlfriend, far as I know. He was my first baby—seems like just yesterday I looked at him for the first time. I held my wrist next to his skin and he was the same color, not red like all the other kids. I—I was so glad he had your Grandpa's eyes."

"Oh, Rosalie—"

"And a letter here from his chaplain says they can't recover his body. What does that mean? Was he blown up? If he was, how do they know it was him? But I don't want it to be any other boy, either!" Her voice broke.

"Rosalie, darling—"

"Why does any boy have to be shot and die? Why did I make him in my belly and carry him and birth him, love and rock and feed him, take care of him when he was sick, make him go to school—why did I do all that if this is what happens?"

"I don't know." Laurie moved back and forth with grief. "I don't know." She tried desperately to think of something to help, but it was Rosalie who knew. "The only thing that helps right now is to see and kiss and hug my kids—know they're alive and well."

"If I can get off work, I'll come for a few days," Laurie said.

"Can you, honey? I'd sure like that."

Ten days after Laurie got back to town, she got a letter from a San Francisco APO that was not in Johnny's writing. She read the name that wavered before her eyes: Lance Corporal Tom Shelton. Wasn't that Johnny's harmonica-playing cowboy friend from Texas?

She ripped it open, shook out the thin paper. An animal wail sounded. It tore from her throat again before she knew she was keening that primal, wounded cry. Marilys rushed out of the kitchen.

"What is it, honey?"

Laurie held out the letter.

I know Johnny thought the world of you, Miss Laurie. I wanted to let you know personal. Johnny didn't come back from our last fight. We hunted for him but with these jungles and swamps, we couldn't find him.

364

He's listed as Missing in Action. To be honest with you, he's likely dead, but there's a chance he's wounded and may turn up alive. I sure hope so.

He was the best buddy a guy could have. Saved my bacon a couple of times, volunteered for the toughest jobs. He always had a joke or a song except for a while there after he heard about his wife. I'll make sure his harmonica and stuff gets sent to you. If I get home, I'd like to come and see you—just to talk about him, you know. I can't believe he's gone.

"They—they haven't found his body," Laurie choked, clinging to Marilys, who walked her to the couch. "He may still be alive—"

"We'll pray that, sweetheart." Both of them knew that a wounded man wouldn't have much chance of surviving the jungle if he wasn't rescued and treated, but any hope was better than none.

Marilys gathered Laurie close and they wept in each other's arms.

Like a sleepwalker, Laurie got numbly through the days, working as usual, and when she was home, rolling bandages what time she wasn't doing house chores. It was only in playing Johnny's songs that she found solace.

Life went on, of course, a surface stretched above the dark gulf of her sorrowing. The USSR won back Stalingrad and began to push back the Germans. Rommel's seemingly invincible Afrika Corps had been stopped in Tunisia with a terrible loss of American soldiers under General George Patton.

As Way scanned the paper and photos of light American tanks failing to dent the heavier German tanks, he squinted at Laurie and said, "Remember that television thing CBS got started just before the war? They had to drop it till the war's over, but I'll bet in the next one—well, sure, honey, God forbid there is a next war—there'll be television photographers right along with the troops. Don't know whether that'll be good or bad."

"Newsreels are enough," said Laurie. It didn't seem right, from the comfort and safety of home, to watch men die or be wounded. Television might have to wait but Americans had built 150,000 planes in 1942, and were turning out a new ship every four days, enough to keep ahead of heavy losses to submarines. The country expected to make 800,000 tons of synthetic rubber next year and a new type of easily produced penicillin proved a boon to wounded soldiers. There might even be enough for civilians.

The Marriotts sponsored a weekly ration–stamp swap at the hotel where people gathered at pulled-together tables to trade stamps for butter, shortening, coffee, cheese, meat, and flour. Anyone willing to part with one of their ration of three pairs of leather shoes per year could reap a bounty in other stamps or take cash. There was a black market but no one Laurie knew used it. Most people gladly accepted rationing, just as they followed the motto: "Use it up, wear it out, make it do, or do without." It made them feel they were doing something to help even though it was so little compared to the hardships of the country's fighting men. With a gas ration of three gallons per week and a speed limit of thirty-five miles per hour, cars stayed in their garages most of the time.

Early in April, Jim hurried into the restaurant, skimming his crippled leg like he was skating, took Laurie's tray away from her, set it down, and gave her a hug and resounding kiss. "We made a well! A nice little forty-barrel-a-day one! Vance has it capped till the buyer hooks it up to the pipeline." Jim laughed with a joy she hadn't heard from him since his leg was maimed. "Ole Vance is already spudding in another hole that ought to hit the same formation. Is he tickled!"

"That—that's wonderful!" Laurie hugged Jim back though her happiness died as she remembered Johnny couldn't exult or share in the good luck. Still, there was a chance he was alive, that he'd come home. And even if he didn't, it was a triumph over Dub to have Johnny's little poorboy outfit hit oil.

"Let's celebrate!" Jim twirled her in a wide circle that made the nearest diners look up and grin. "Wish I could take you to that new Broadway show *Oklahoma!* that's such a hit, but there's two good shows on here."

"Oh, I can't—"

"Yes, you will!" Marilys, flanked by Mrs. Marriott, advanced upon her. "We can get along fine without you for one night. Go have some fun."

"But—"

"Take your pick," Jim commanded. *"Casablanca* with Ingrid Bergman and Humphrey Bogart or *Road to Morocco* with Bing Crosby and Dorothy Lamour."

Yielding, Laurie said, "Well—if we can go to *Woman of the Year* instead. I think Katharine Hepburn's just wonderful and I look up to Spencer Tracy because he's volunteered for the armed forces." Quite a few Hollywood stars had done that— Jimmy Stewart, Robert Stack, Cesar Romero, and Douglas Fairbanks, Jr. In spite of being forty-one, so had Clark Gable. His wife, Carole Lombard, had been killed in a January plane crash while on a war-bond drive. As far as Laurie was concerned, she didn't intend to ever go to the films of able-bodied actors like Crosby, Bogart, and Ronald Reagan who'd stayed home making money while others died.

It was fun to go out at night for something besides work, to be swept up in Hepburn and Tracy's sparring romance. It was the first time since that awful letter that Laurie had truly laughed and enjoyed herself, so much that she felt guilty as the lights came on and reality flooded back.

How could she laugh when Johnny was dead or gravely wounded? How could she forget that, even for a second? Gazing down at her, Jim took both her hands. "Laurie. Johnny's tough. He may crawl out of that jungle any day. And even if he can't, what would he tell you if he could? It sure wouldn't be to mourn and moan."

"I'm not moaning!"

"Not out loud." Jim caressed her cheek. "Johnny more than anybody knew that whatever happens folks need to laugh all they can, be happy as they can, and get on with whatever they have to do." He set his finger on her nose. "Make up your mind to this, Laurie. Every week or two, we're going to a show or out to dinner."

"Jim—"

He read the worry in her eyes and smoothed her brow with the ball of his thumb. "Listen good. I don't want to explain this every time I ask you out. I'll always have a special kind of love for you—and that's without considering what your father did for us. I wouldn't even try, though, to fill Johnny's place with you. If anybody can, he'll be a sight wiser and stronger and better than I am."

She started to protest. He grinned and drew her to her feet. "Don't feel bad about me, honey. I've got a bunch of girlfriends and I sure intend to have more." He moved Laurie toward the exit. "Meanwhile, lady, we're stepping out!"

Two days later, Laurie was tending the salvage-yard office when a car roared up. There was something vaguely familiar about the way the brakes shrieked. Going to the window, Laurie gasped.

W. S. Redwine. There was no way out except the door, which was now blocked by his broad figure. Battling to compose herself, she moved close to the phone. She hadn't seen him in months, not since he'd lied so smoothly, so shamelessly, to Johnny, told him not to worry, that everything would be taken care of.

"You contemptible—" she began and checked. "There's nothing bad enough to call you so I won't try!"

Those yellow eyes swelled and glowed. The square face was fleshier, the flat nose squeezed by ruddy cheeks. "Well, Larry-Laurie! If you're not plumb growed up and—"

"There's not a thing we can say to each other."

He laughed. "I can say plenty to you."

It was noonday but Laurie was getting scared. "Get out of here!"

"Not till we have a little talk."

"About how you've tried to break Way? Or how you cut Johnny out of the partnership? Doesn't that bother you the least bit now that Johnny's missing?"

"I figger he pulled out on me. If he'd of come home, maybe—"

"Maybe you'd have come up with some slick excuse and tried to wheedle him back to you."

Redwine shrugged. "Don't signify. More than anyone I ever knew, it's you who's stayed in my mind, Laurie. If you'd of listened to me, you'd be a big name now, big as the Andrews Sisters or that damned skinny little wop, Frank Sinatra."

Laurie shrugged. "I like to play for my friends. Folks I can see. I don't want to live out of suitcases and on the road."

"Wouldn't have to. You can make records. I've got a man at Decca all hot to listen to you." He gazed at Laurie in a manner that made her feel handled and dirty. "He'll meet us this evening in Oklahoma City."

"No, he won't. Do you think I'm crazy enough to have anything to do with you, W. S. Redwine?" She reached for the phone. He caught her wrist.

"Easy, doll baby! The police won't arrest a customer for coming into a business office. I'll put it to you straight. Come with me and you'll get famous and make a mint. What's more, I'll quit doggin' old Way."

"You must be out of your mind." She grabbed the hammer Way kept beneath the counter. It struck Redwine's wrist a glancing blow as he released her. He swore but she poised the hammer. "Get out! I wouldn't go a step with you to save my life!"

Redwine's square teeth showed in a snarl. "Once you traveled a long way with me, Larry-Laurie, and were mighty glad to do it." He turned and threw back over his shoulder, "Those days'll come again."

Shaking, sick at her stomach, Laurie went in the small bathroom and scrubbed with soap where he'd touched her. She couldn't tell anyone. Jim or Way would go after him and wind up in trouble. But what would happen, what was Redwine going to do? Way's salvage yard was staying afloat and there was one producing well on Johnny's land, but these gains, much as they'd cost, were tiny beside Redwine's resources, and they were so vulnerable that Laurie felt cold to the bone.

She couldn't sleep that night and was on edge all next day, but everything was normal. It was the following morning that Jim burst into the restaurant when Laurie was clearing away late breakfasters' dishes. "That crooked, conniving, low-life Redwine! He's leased the land next to Johnny's farm and he's drilling offset wells all along the boundary!" As Laurie stared in shock, Jim gulped and clamped his fists shut. "That skunk can suck up our oil before we even get that second hole down to pay sand."

Perfectly legal. Perfectly disastrous. Unless there was a fault or barrier to keep some of the oil in that formation from being pumped out of Redwine's wells, the partners' discovery would flow right out from under them, and with it the family's home, Way's business, and everything they owned.

"What—what can we do?" she choked.

"The only way to stop it is drill more wells faster on Johnny's side than Redwine's crews can drill on his. No way we can do that."

A wild hope thrilled through Laurie. "I've served a lot of meals to a lot of men and Johnny's worked with dozens. Maybe—"

"Maybe what?"

"Maybe we can get Redwine's drillers to quit. It's worth a try." Laurie started to clear the last tables but Mrs. Marriott, who had overheard, came over and untied Laurie's apron.

"You run along! I can handle things here. Next time Dub Redwine comes in here I'll tell him I don't serve sidewinders!" She gave Laurie a push. "Good luck, honey!"

The dirt road to the farm was clogged with trucks hauling machinery, drilling pipe, boilers, and all the parts it took to build derricks. As Jim maneuvered the truck close to the fence, crews worked up and down the boundary, at least a dozen different outfits, getting ready to build derricks. Over the boundary in Johnny's pasture, Morrigan No. 1 pumped away. A quarter mile east, the little spudder was valiantly making hole, though Vance Morrow had to know how hopeless it was.

Jim brought the truck into the middle of Redwine's swarming workers and leaned on the horn.

A driller came running up. "What in hell—" he began, saw Laurie, and checked, doffing his Stetson. "Beg pardon, ma'am, but what the devil are you barging in here for?"

He was a stranger but she had to hope. "Did you know Johnny Morrigan?"

"Sure I did. Shot a bunch of wells for me. Tackled me out of the way of a falling beam once." Other men were gathering. Laurie didn't know a soul and her hopes dimmed. Redwine had hired crews who didn't know the story behind what he was trying to do. The driller's blue eyes stared at her. "But what's Morrigan got to do with you bustin' in here?"

"Did you know he's missing in action? At Guadalcanal?"

The driller paled, shaking his head. Laurie pointed across the fence at the pumping well and the spudder. "That's Johnny's land across the fence—his first well pumping, his spudder digging another hole."

Jaw dropping, the driller said, "I didn't know that."

"And you probably didn't know that Dub Redwine waited till Johnny was overseas to take over Johnny's share of their partnership. Now Redwine's trying to make sure Johnny doesn't have anything left if he *does* come home—and he's missing in action, so that's possible."

"I sure pray he does," said the driller, and others murmured assent.

"Just where do you come into this, lady?" The blue-eyed driller scanned her narrowly. "Seems like I heard his wife ran off. You Johnny's sister?"

Jim tensed. Before he could make a sharp retort, Laurie got out of the truck. Standing in the prairie wind that blew back her hair and molded her dress against her body, she glanced at the faces—strangers, all of them, yet had not strangers been kind, most of them, all along the road?

"Johnny Morrigan happened by and helped us when our Model T was broken down seven years ago," she said clearly, loud enough for the men at the back to hear. "I've loved him ever since though I guess he doesn't know it. Anyway, when

Dub cut off credit to this operation of Johnny's, my folks and I—and Jim, here—pitched in to keep the outfit drilling. We took out a bigger mortgage on our house to do that—and if you don't believe me, you can go ask Mrs. Marriott at the hotel, or see the banker, or lawyer."

The driller watched her appreciatively. Slowly, his mouth curved in a grin. "I believe you, lady." Turning, he called to the men. "Fellas, I'm pulling my crew out of here."

"So'm I," growled a man built like a bulldog. "I knew John Morrigan and I'll have no part of robbin' him or his friends." Thrusting out a massive undershot jaw, he scowled around the circle. "What's more, I'll whup anybody who tries to stay!"

"No one's stayin', Brick," said a whippet-lean worker. "But if you want a fight, I'll be glad to oblige."

"Hold it, guys," called the first driller. "No need to tussle, Brick. It looks like everybody's ready to go. And let's make it our business to spread the word. No one's going to drill Dub Redwine's offset wells."

"If they try," rumbled Brick, "They'll sure wish they hadn't!"

The blue-eyed man took off his battered hat and ran his fingers through his hair. "I've got my own rotary drilling outfit. While we're here, men, why don't we make a well or two for Johnny? Prove that we're countin' on him to come safe home?"

Laurie glanced toward Jim, who said, "We can't pay you unless you bring in a well. If you do, we'll pay you shares."

"We'll drill two locations for Johnny. After that, if it looks like we've got a field and you want us, we'll work out something fair." He offered his hand. "I'm Bill Stafford."

Laurie and Jim shook hands and introduced themselves. They drove around to explain to Vance that he was going to have a rotary rig for a neighbor.

"Dadburn mud-eaters!" he grumbled. Old cable-tool men called rotary workers that. "Well, I reckon they're better on this side of the fence than the other. And I bet I bring in this well before they get their durned old skyscraper derrick set up!"

He did. And it only took the rotary men two weeks to make two more wells, Morrigan No. 3 and Morrigan No. 4, which both flowed eighty barrels a day. The partnership had a field. Vance kept using the spudder but he and Jim made a deal with Bill Stafford to drill up the farm on shares. It wasn't riches for anyone but the partnership could pay back the money the Kirkendalls and Fields had put into the drilling.

They needed it. Way had pretty well run out of farmers within a range where he could deliver without losing money. The contractors who detested Dub too much to buy from him weren't numerous enough to keep Way's business going, even with business from Bill Stafford and his friends. It was money from the roomers and what Marilys and Laurie earned that paid the bills and kept Way's office open.

His pride wouldn't let that go on much longer. If only Redwine would get tired of losing money in order to harass them! But Laurie shivered when she remembered how he'd tried to get her to go away with him.

Buddy finished ninth grade late that May as the United States battled the Japanese on the island of Attu in the Aleutians. When defeat was certain, many Japanese killed themselves by hari-kari, the traditional disembowelment, or with shots to the head. Fighting on the other side, Nisei of the 442nd Regiment and the 100th Battalion had been equally brave. There were no Nisei frontline desertions and the men were receiving so many Purple Hearts, Bronze Stars, Silver Stars, Distinguished Service Crosses, and Legions of Merit that they seemed likely to become the most decorated fighters in all American history—while their families lived behind barbed wire.

Hearing of Attu's fall on the radio, Buddy exploded. "The war's gonna be over before I get to fight!"

"I certainly hope so," Laurie said.

"That's because you're just a girl!" He flung out, banging the screen door.

Next morning when he didn't come downstairs, Laurie knocked at his door. No answer. "Buddy?"

When there was no response, she opened the door. There was a note on his pillow. "I'm going to tell recruiters I'm eighteen till one of them believes me. Don't worry, I'll be fine. I'll write when I'm so long gone you can't get hold of me. Laurie, I just have to do this, don't be mad. Don't be sorry."

She ran downstairs with the note. "Shall we call the police?" she asked Way, Jim, and Marilys. "Shall we try to get him back?"

"He'll never forgive you if you do," said Jim. "And he'll keep running off."

Way nodded. Laurie went into Marilys's outstretched arms. Buddy was on the road again, and this time she couldn't protect him.

29

Again, Laurie dreamed of the end of the world, of Buddy disappearing into a violent black storm, running to meet it, not heeding her cries, and this time Daddy couldn't save him. As she guiltily thought back over the last few years, it seemed to Laurie that she'd talked very little to her brother except to fuss at him about staying in school. She had been so busy working, so absorbed in her own concerns, that she hadn't paid proper attention to Buddy. He'd been well loved by Marilys and Way, of course, but all the same, Laurie was his only close blood-kin.

So she grieved for him, reproached herself, woke up sweating from the terrible dream, and really hadn't noticed that Way was looking drawn and worried till he came home one evening and announced his presence with a joyful whoop. Grabbing Marilys, he swung her in a spirited pirouette.

"I've worked a deal that ought to get the salvage yard back on its feet—pardon me, ma'am—it's pipes! Company that's going out of business called me this morning, wanted to sell a humongous inventory cheap. Ordinarily, my mouth would just have to water while I missed out on a big chance, but the last couple days it happens that I've had calls for the biggest part of the stuff!"

"Why, darling, that's—that's wonderful!" Marilys raised

herself on tiptoe to kiss him. "If you're getting that kind of offers and orders, it has to mean that contractors are learning they're better off dealing with you than with Dub."

"That's how I see it, sugar." He looked ten years younger and his eyes danced. "I always figgered if we held on long enough, things would break our way. Dub just naturally can't, not for very long, keep from pullin' scuzzy tricks and cheatin'."

"So will you tell your buyers you've made deals for them and then send on their money to the company after you take out your share?" Laurie asked.

"Can't do that this time," Way said. "The company wants its money all at once and I've got to deliver some of the supplies and a couple of the buyers said they'd pay me after they pick up their equipment."

Marilys frowned. "You mean you'll need to write a whopping big check before there's money in the bank to cover it?"

"Everybody does it," Way said. "I've told the company they'll have to hold the check for three-four days. The boss said fine, in fact he wouldn't cash it till I called to say it was okay to put it through."

"I guess I'm chickenhearted but I hate writing checks if the money's not there."

Way's face fell. "Aw, honey—"

Marilys said quickly, "You know a lot more about it than I do, dear. It certainly is great to have a breakthrough after all the aggravation! You go ahead with the deal just like you think you ought to."

Laurie was nervous about overdrafts, too, but she knew lots of business in the oil fields was conducted that way. A lease speculator, for example, seldom paid for a lease before selling it. Fortunes were made that way, though Laurie didn't have the gall or the nerve for it. When Way glanced at her for approval, she smiled and said, "I'm sure it'll work out fine."

Way left before dawn next morning to pick up a load of supplies from the company in Oklahoma City. He'd deliver them to a buyer at Ardmore, then had to return to the city and truck another order to Enid, so he wouldn't be home for several days.

After waving him off, Marilys and Laurie exchanged glances. Marilys sighed. "It's wonderful to see Way so excited and happy again—but I'll be glad when all those buyers' checks are deposited!"

Laurie nodded. The feeling of doom she'd had since Buddy ran off had deepened since Way took on this venture, and renewed her futile and continuous anxiety over Johnny. Sometimes, awful as it was, she almost wished she knew for sure he was dead if indeed he was, then would harshly rebuke herself.

There was hope. He *might* come home. It was wicked not to be grateful for that sliver of a chance.

When Way didn't return on the third day, the women began to worry. They sat up late waiting for him and went to bed heavy of heart and troubled. "I looked in the office today for the name of the Oklahoma City company," Marilys said as they climbed the stairs. "I couldn't find it, or anything that looked like the buyers' orders. Way must have taken all the papers with him."

"The truck may have broken down," Laurie offered.

"He could have phoned or asked someone else to," said Marilys. Her face crumpled and she reached out blindly. "Oh, Laurie, I'm scared!"

"Now, darling—"

"It—it's like the way he disappeared at Black Spring after Dub got him drunk," Marilys choked. "What—what if something went wrong with those deals? Something so bad he couldn't face us?"

Laurie's spine chilled but she said firmly, "There's nothing that bad. I can't believe Way would ever leave us again, no matter what."

"He might if he thought we'd be better off without him."

"Whatever's happened, he ought to know better than that." Thinking of Johnny, Laurie swallowed hard. "As long as people are alive, they can always start over." She held Marilys close, comforting the older woman who had so often consoled her. "Listen, dear. If Way doesn't come home by morning, we'll ask Jim to put out the word through the oil fields. Why, he could be picking up so many new orders that he's forgot what day it is!"

Marilys relaxed slightly. "That could be," she said with a wavering smile. "And after all, he never said exactly when he'd be back. I'm being silly."

"When he shows up, we'll give him strict orders to report in every day from now on," Laurie said in her briskest tone. The cats were rubbing against her legs. She scooped up Runcible and handed him to Marilys. "Here, you cuddle up with this critter tonight and get a good rest."

Kissing Marilys good-night, Laurie swept up a purring Winks and went up to the attic, which seemed vast and forlorn now that Buddy was gone. At least it was some comfort to have Johnny's things stored on top of some old trunks. She'd kept his hat where she could take it down and press it against her, breathe in his lingering odor of salty sweat and oil. She took the hat now and put it beside her pillow. *Oh Johnny, please be alive! Please come home!*

Holding Winks's soft, warm, resonating body against her, Laurie was grateful for another living presence. Even so, she left a small light burning so that if she had a nightmare, she might flash to reality faster on waking and not rouse Marilys with a scream.

When Laurie went down to breakfast, Way sat at the table with Marilys. Laurie's glad welcome trailed off as he turned and she saw his face.

Here was truly the derelict, the unshaven scrounging tramp of the freight cars. He even smelled the same, of male sweat, grime, and soured whiskey. But he had come home. Whatever else, he was here.

"Way!" She hurried to bend and kiss him but he caught her wrists and set her back.

"I'm too dirty to be in this house—"

"Hush that!" Marilys blazed. She pressed his hands to her face and kissed them. "There's nothing wrong with you a shower and scrub won't fix."

"I'm goin' to need a lot of 'em with my new job."

377

"New job?" the women chorused. Hope lit Marilys's eyes. "You didn't tell me—"

"I was fixin' to." He stared at the bowl of oatmeal in front of him. "Do I have to eat that?"

"Every bite," Marilys decreed. "It should stay down all right now you've had some toast."

"First, I'd better tell Laurie what a fool I've been."

"I'll tell her." Marilys filled his cup to the brim. "You drink and eat and get to feeling better, honey."

"You ought to slop me like a hog," said Way, rubbing reddened, bleary eyes.

"Eat!" He obeyed, grimacing. Marilys filled Laurie's cup and said bitterly, "What it amounts to is good old crooked Dub worked out a fancy scheme to snooker us."

"Dub?"

"None other, the mangy devil! He owned that company that was selling out. He controls the outfits that placed orders. So all he had to do was have the contractors renege on their deals, have the company try to cash a check for six thousand dollars we don't have—"

"And there I am, caught dead to rights in a felony." Way added with a groan, "Why I never suspicioned something like this when everything fell into place so nice—"

"I should have thought of Dub," Marilys cut in. "I know the lowdown swindler better than either of you do."

I'm not so sure about that, Laurie thought with a shudder, remembering Redwine's proposition. Maybe if she'd told Marilys about that, the other woman might have been on the watch for deceit from him. It wasn't necessary to ask what Way had done when he learned the truth.

"What's this about a job?" Marilys asked. "Won't the law—"

She broke off, flushing. Way patted her hand. "I'm not goin' to jail, darlin'. Dub had better notions."

"What?" cried Laurie and Marilys at the same time.

Shamefaced, Way still met their gazes. "The first buyer who backed out, I just thought, well, I could manage to pay the company with the money I'd get from the other orders even if

I wouldn't make a dime. But that big, second order—" He whistled. "Then I knew. And Dub must've given that contractor real good instructions—the fella said how sorry he was I'd brought lapweld pipe when he needed seamless, and he gave me a bottle and told me to get some sleep in a trailer there by the rig. Must've been another bottle, I can't remember. But when I was halfway sober again, durned if there wasn't old Dub."

Laurie remembered the rusty butcher knife Way used to carry. "You didn't fight him?"

"No, I managed to get up but I fell right back down. While I was throwin' up, he laughed and allowed as how he'd give me a chance to get out of the mess." Way's eyes fell. They could barely hear his next words. "He said if I beat him three hands out of five in stud poker, he'd tear up my check and let me keep the stuff besides."

"And if he won?" breathed Marilys. Laurie, paralyzed, couldn't say anything.

"He got our equity in the house, what's left of the salvage business, our truck—everything."

Dumbfounded, the women stared. Way's voice clogged with self-loathing. "I must've still been drunk to do it—I've got no excuse." He straightened slightly. "But it's all right. You won't lose the house, or the business, whatever it's worth."

"You won!" Marilys threw her arms around him but he shook his head while his big scarred hand smoothed her shining hair.

"I didn't, honey."

"But—"

"Dub won first, third, and last hands—kept it real interesting. And then we made our deal."

"What?"

"Dub won't send me to jail. He won't take anything away from us." Way managed a lopsided grin. "He's even given me a good, steady job cleanin' tanks."

"Cleaning tanks!" echoed Marilys. "Why, that's the dirtiest, most dangerous job in the oil patch!"

"It's dirty," Way admitted. "But it's not so dangerous if you're careful."

"What about that bunch of eight men who got killed in that tank-farm explosion last month?"

"They weren't regular tank cleaners. Just roughnecks." Way shook his head. "That big company they worked for decided to save money and use them in the tanks instead of paying a tank-cleaning contractor to do it right. They rigged up electric lights—never want to do that because the weentsiest spark'll set off a blast. And that's what happened. Those poor guys were inside the tanks when the sludge caught fire. I guess they yelled once."

At the women's expressions, he said quickly, "I've cleaned tanks before. You bet I'll use a battery spotlight and come out for fresh air when I need to."

"Your asthma!" Laurie protested. "Those fumes'll be awful for you!"

"It's a job."

Marilys caught his hand. "Dub's humiliating you!"

"I already did that."

"Please, darling—"

Way carried his wife's fingers to his lips. "Sweetheart, I got no choice. I work for Dub or he prosecutes and we lose everything. Damned if I'll do that to you and Laurie."

"Oh, Way!" Laurie got to her feet. "Maybe if I begged Redwine—"

"No." Way's voice was stern. Then he grinned. "Listen, gals, I'd a sight rather drown in bottom settlings than rot in the pen. And now I gotta have a bath and get some sleep. I start work this afternoon."

"Dub didn't waste any time," said Marilys.

"I guess he's wanted to break me ever since he saw you were likin' me back in Black Spring," Way said fatalistically. He knelt beside Marilys and put his arms around her. "We beat him anyway, honey. We've had some mighty good years and more love in a day than Dub's had in his life."

Marilys pressed his head to her breasts and held him with fierce protectiveness. "We've got each other. We'll get through this just like we have everything else."

"Sho'," said Way. But Laurie could see his eyes, and though

they were soft with love, they held the resignation of one who had not only faced death but accepted it. His next words confirmed her dread. "Whatever happens to me, you'll be all right, my ladies. Dub's signed legal, witnessed papers dropping any claims to our property provided I work for him a year."

"A year in the tanks!" Laurie gasped.

A death sentence for anyone with breathing problems. Way gazed at Laurie from his wife's embrace. "Kiddo," he said, using the old name. "I got us into this mess. There's no way I could've faced you if there wasn't this chance to square things up."

He meant—Dropping her eyes, Laurie knew what he meant. But she knew what she was going to do.

If a tank cleaner slipped and went down in the bottom settlings, he invariably drowned because he couldn't get to his feet again. Once he got the oily muck in his mouth and nose, it sealed them shut. If someone tried to help, they were usually dragged under, just as a terrified person drowning in water will try to get on top of a rescuer. But Way wasn't going into that dark slippery tank alone.

"I'll work at the hotel this morning," she told Marilys. There was no way they could keep the salvage yard going after Way sold off the supplies Redwine had duped him with, but that was something to worry about later. "I need to take the afternoon off."

Way climbed to his feet. "Don't you go pleadin' with Dub to let me off, girl. He'll plumb relish it but it won't do any good."

"I won't ask him for a thing." Laurie finished her coffee and hurried off to work.

She was home in time to dress in a shirt, jeans, and jacket of Buddy's. The tough, rubber-soled work boots he'd worn at the salvage yard fitted after she pulled on two pairs of heavy socks. For luck, she got Johnny's oil-crusted old hat from his stored belongings. She stuffed clean rags and a stout cord in her jacket pockets. There was a stained tarp in the back of the truck. She stowed away under that, glad that the weather was cool for early June.

Way wouldn't want her in the tank and his aboveground helper and whoever was in charge of the tank cleaning would have a fit, so she'd have to sneak into the tank somehow. Even if she managed it this afternoon, she didn't know how she could pull it off tomorrow, but right now she could only worry about today.

Way bumped along a dirt road for half an hour, then turned sharply onto an even worse track. Jounced around the back of the truck, Laurie felt like her bones and teeth were jarring loose. The smell of oil grew denser. The truck groaned up a slope and stopped.

"So here you are, Wayburn, right on time!" boomed Redwine. Laurie cowered under the tarp. It was silly but she somehow felt he could see through it. "That's your tank right over yonder. Your wooden rake and shovel and your broom and mop are already over there and the vents and hatch have been open about an hour to clear out the fumes."

"Real thoughtful of you, Dub."

"Oh, I don't want you passing out and dying on me. Not right away. When you clean out that eighty-thousand-barrel tank, there'll be another waiting. Why, I bet you can work off your year right here at this tank farm."

"See you're on a hill," said Way. "Before the inspectors got tougher about enforcing the law, I bet you ran your BS right down to that creek."

"Reckon I still could if I wanted," chuckled Redwine. "But with the war on, it pays to put the sludge through the refinery—get about eighty percent oil or wax out of it." He laughed from his great belly. "So you'll be helping the war effort at the same time you clean my tanks, Wayburn. Don't that inspire you?"

"I'll do it."

"You bet you will and I don't want any excuses about your damned asthma!"

"I came out to work, Dub, not listen to you." Laurie heard the crunch of shoes moving away.

Redwine's chortle swelled into a jovial bellow. "Enjoy yourself, Wayburn. I'm going over to the refinery for a little bit, but I'll be back to see how you're doing."

From beneath the tarp, Laurie caught a flash of black as Redwine drove off. Peering out, she saw rows of huge steel tanks with gently sloping domed roofs. The tanks were connected by steel walkways and a wide trench was dug around each one to contain any leak. At the end of the row, another tank was being cleaned. It looked like a car had hauled a big sludge-heaped board up to the opening in the side of the tank and held it there while a truck with a suction hose swooped the board clean.

Nothing like that was in progress at Way's tank, though. Laurie pushed her hair up under Johnny's hat—*Oh God, let him be alive!*—and jumped down from the truck. To any observer, she'd look like a worker. Way was pitching the wooden implements into the tank. Steel or iron tools could strike a fatal spark. Laurie moved up the slope. When she crawled through the opening, she was blinded. The smell of a thousand rotten eggs choked her. Her boot skidded in the sediment that reached to her knees. She caught the side of the opening to steady herself.

"So I'm goin' to get some help?" asked Way. "Welcome to the party. This durn stuff is glued to the bottom. How about hauling the rake through it so I can maybe scoop it up?"

"All right," Laurie muttered. Keeping her face averted, she took the rake that leaned against the tank wall. Moving as if her life depended on being careful—which it did—she scraped the tines into the thicker sludge at the bottom while Way dredged up spadefuls and tossed them out the hole.

The hole and the vents above let in some light but the vast steel container was as shadowy as it was inside a movie. They worked about ten minutes and then Way began to cough.

"Got—got to get out of here a minute!" he gasped.

Laurie's head was swimming and she felt nauseated. She didn't know whether she was being gassed or not, but she might as well follow Way and make it clear that she was going to work with him. Climbing out of the tank, she almost sprawled in its shade, where Way struggled for breath. That ominous wheezing had already begun.

How in the world could he get through a day of this, much less a year? He couldn't. He'd die. And Redwine would have killed him as surely as if he'd pulled a trigger. But what could she or Marilys do?

"Laurie!"

"Hush, Way."

Shock or comparatively untainted air seemed to have cleared his lungs. "Are you plumb, pure-dee crazy?"

"You're not going to work at this alone."

"Well, you're not working at it alone or any other way!"

"If you kick up a fuss, I'll go to Redwine. I—I never told anyone, but he tried to get me to—to go away with him." She stared at Way and measured out her words. "I'd rather slip in the tank—rather drown in the sludge—than go with him. But I will, so help me, if you won't let me work with you—and keep quiet about it to Marilys."

"Could be he'd rather watch me clean tanks than—" Way shuddered and gulped. "No, I guess he'd take you if you'd go. After what he did to Marilys, you might be better off dead."

"I'm not dying. Neither are you. Somehow, we'll make it through the year." Somehow, though she couldn't imagine a year of this.

Way's eyes flickered. "You bet we will! Now let's climb back inside that sucker before Dub comes toolin' back." He paused. "But you got to promise me this, Laurie. If I fall, if my head goes under the crud, don't try to help me. Once that stuff's in your mouth and nose, you're done for. Tank-cleaning contractors tell their boys that—if your buddy goes down, keep away. You can't save him and you'll just get drowned yourself."

"If I go down, will you leave me alone?"

"Now, Laurie—"

"Neither of us is going down," she said, and climbed through the hatch.

Men made their living this way, day in, day out, but Laurie couldn't understand how. It must be you got used to the fumes after a while. "Don't try to stay inside if you start feelin' dizzy,"

Way cautioned. "I've cleaned tanks where there was so much poison in the settlings that a man couldn't work for more than three or four minutes without comin' outside to breathe."

"Makes you appreciate good air," Laurie said. Her head throbbed and her insides twisted though she'd gone out of the tank five times in what, from the position of the sun, might have been an hour, though it seemed interminable.

Way, thank goodness, wasn't coughing so much, though she could hear his ragged breathing and feared that any moment it could tighten into that constricted laboring wheeze. Her neck and shoulders ached from scraping. The stuff was like solid tar. There was usually a certain amount of water in oil and it often contained particles of sand and clay. Under pressure, water emulsified with oil to form a mixture that was neither one. This emulsion, free water, and fine-ground minerals sank to the bottom of the storage tanks. Whatever you made the initials BS stand for, bottom settlings, basic sludge, or basic sediment, it was nasty stuff. Not all of it went to the bottom. Some flowed into the pipeline and it was usual for purchasers, before they paid for the oil, to deduct from 1 to 2 percent for BS and W, Basic Sediment and Water.

Way's coughing erupted. He doubled over, wracked by spasms. That frightful wheezing increased as he fought for air. "Get out of here!" Laurie called. "Way! Get to the hatch right now!"

Between fits, weaving, he made his way toward the opening. Struggling as he was for breath, the effect of the noxious fumes must have been multiplied. Laurie started toward him.

"Keep—keep away!" he choked, staggering.

Drenched with cold sweat, Laurie watched his lurching progress. If she tried to get close, it could upset him enough to make him fall; but if he started to go down, she'd reach for him, hang on to the rake dug into the muck, and try to drag him to the hatch.

It wasn't far. A few more steps and he could lean there, catch his breath. . . .

Redwine blocked the opening. "How's the air in there, Wayburn? From the looks of what you've shoveled out, you've been loafing outside more'n you've been working. Call that fair, good as I've been to you?"

"Get out of his way!" yelled Laurie. "Can't you see he's in trouble?"

Redwine leaned in, blinked, and stared. His bulk in the hatch made the tank even darker. She could scarcely see his face. He seemed to speak from a vast dark hulk that shut her off from air and light.

"Larry-Laurie! What in hell—" Shock changed to fury. "By God, are you in there with that lousy old bastard, that wino scrounger, that—"

"Get out of the way! Let him breathe!"

"You'd rather clean tanks with him than come with me!" raged Redwine. "You and that goddam Marilys! Well, you're not goin' to have a year, you sleazy tramp!" Redwine reared back and stuck a leg through the hatch. "I'm goin' to put you where you belong, you miserable, sniveling, whining son-of-a-bitch!"

Redwine heaved over the rim. One step brought him almost to Way, who was desperately trying to straighten up, to ward off Redwine's doubled fist.

Laurie brought up the rake. Instinctively bracing her feet, she pushed the rake against Redwine. Already off balance from his maddened haste, the thrust sent him skidding. He threw up his arms but there was nothing to catch. His feet went out from under him and he fell, head disappearing beneath the sludge.

The muck sucked and moved sluggishly from his struggles. Laurie took a step forward but Way shouted, "Leave him alone! Even if we got him out, there's no way to clear his mouth and nose before he suffocates. Get outside, honey!"

"You go first."

Coughing, gasping, Way lurched to the hole, leaned on the rim. He didn't look behind him. Neither did Laurie. The sounds stopped.

Awful, awful . . . When they managed to drag themselves outside, they lay on the ground a long time shaking, sick. But even in the horror, Laurie began to feel relief. Redwine couldn't hurt them now, not ever again! At last they dragged to their feet, got to their truck, and went down to the refinery office to tell what had happened.

Laurie trembled and leaned back against the seat for a while before she could drive them home. Way was still in the grip of his asthma attack, though it was easing.

"Yeah, honey." He touched her hand. They were both going to have a hard time getting clean, not only of the sludge, but the horror of Redwine going down.

"I—I guess I really killed him."

"He killed himself." Way's voice was grim. "If he'd got in range, I sure meant to take him with me."

The sun had never looked so bright, the sky so blue, the scattered cottonwoods so green. As they drove home, wind carried off much of the permeating stench, filled their lungs. How good it was to breathe! How good to be alive!

If only Johnny—

A few days later, Mrs. Marriott handed Laurie the phone. "Hello?" she said absently. Her mind was still on that afternoon in the tank. After questioning her and Way and the tank-cleaning crew that had seen Redwine climb through the hatch, the sheriff had called her use of the rake plain self-defense.

"Ain't nobody goin' to mourn after Dub Redwine," he said. "A wonder you got out alive, but I'm glad you did. If anyone deserved to drown in BS, it was him!"

The male voice coming over the phone startled her out of her preoccupation. "Laurie? Is that you, honey?"

That voice! She had never hoped to hear it again. Her ears were playing tricks. But she cried out anyway, "Johnny! Oh, Johnny, is it really you?"

"You bet it is."

"You—you're alive!"

He laughed and explained as she gripped the phone, still terrified that her wishes were tricking her, that she was imagining all this. He had crawled out of a swamp more dead than alive, badly wounded and with no identification. He was unconscious or delirious for weeks on the hospital ship and when he did begin to get better, it was a while before his memory returned. It came back as he was holding the New Testament, puzzling about who had given it to him, and Laurie's face rose up.

"Guess that's not too surprising." He laughed. It was the most beautiful sound she'd ever heard. "Honey, there's a line of guys waiting for this phone. I can't talk much longer. But I want you to know it was your face I saw before a battle, your face came to me when I thought of home. And it was your voice that sang to me while I was getting well."

The war was over for him. An explosion had deafened him in one ear and medics had dug out a lot of shrapnel, though bits were still lodged near his spine.

But he was alive, in San Francisco, and he was coming home!

Jim, Vance Morrow, Marilys, Way, and Laurie were all at the depot to watch his train pull in. They crowded forward, the others keeping Laurie in front, as the train appeared, whistled, started grinding to a halt.

Johnny, in his uniform, was the first person off. The other passengers must have held back to let him pass. He stood there, pale, thinner, but blessedly Johnny. Laurie couldn't move. She stood rooted to the spot. And then he called her name.

As if in a dream, she moved toward him. Would he kiss her like a friend, like a little sister? Then she was in his arms, finding her love, her home at the end of a long, long road. His mouth, hard and sweet on hers, told her all she needed to know.

People were shouting, cheering, and clapping. Laurie moved away so Johnny could kiss Marilys and shake hands with Jim and Way and Vance. When the greetings were over and his duffel bag was in the truck, Johnny said to Way, "It's so good to feel this ground under my feet again. Do you mind if we walk home?"

"Go right ahead," Way chuckled.

"There's so much to say," said Johnny as he took Laurie's arm. His eyes searched hers. "So much to ask. I don't know where to start."

"We've got time."

Time to tell him about Redwine's death and whatever he

needed to know about his partner's deceit and Crystal. Time to tell him his old farm was a producing oil field.

Time to share, to laugh and love and work and sing. She stopped in the street and kissed him. Time and the world were theirs now; with Johnny, no road could be too long.